The
Ryer
Avenue
Story

Also by Dorothy Uhnak

Policewoman
The Bait
The Witness
The Ledger
Law and Order
The Investigation
False Witness
Victims

The Ryer Avenue Story

DOROTHY UHNAK

St. Martin's Press   New York

Design by Guenet Abraham

Library of Congress Cataloging-in-Publication Data

Uhnak, Dorothy.
    The Ryer Avenue story / Dorothy Uhnak.
        p.   cm.
    ISBN 0-312-08888-4
    1. Bronx (New York, N.Y.)—Fiction.   I. Title.
    PS3571.H6R94   1993
813'.54—dc20   92-43655
                                                  CIP

First Edition: March 1993

10 9 8 7 6 5 4 3 2

In memory of my mother:
Josephine O'Brien Goldstein. She was short,
funny, and the smartest lady I've ever known.

For my father:
J. P. (Philip) Goldstein, who taught me, by
example, the dignity and honor of hard work.

For friends gone too soon:

Joan "O'Rourke" Alpert
Harold Smith
Tom Victor

And friends who cheer me on:

Nora Kelly-Polinsky, who has taught generations
of children to love reading and writing.
Dr. Irv and Blossom Handelsman
Kathie and Darren McGavin
Bob Markell
Hillary Handelsman
Dr. Dick Ward, who has shown me other worlds.
Doug Froeb, my designated "favorite uncle."

The Sunday Afternoon Irregulars—
especially Janet Culbertson

Special thanks for help and encouragement to
Hollis Alpert
Sam Vaughn
Len Leavitt

And, as always, to Tony and Tracy, my anchors,
my lifelines.

The
Ryer
Avenue
Story

PROLOGUE

On Saturday, December 28, 1935, at about 10:35 P.M., Walter Stachiew was murdered. His body, lying in the icy gutter where it had fallen on the dark winding hill along 181st Street between Valentine and Webster avenues in the Bronx, was a mess.

There were thick gouts of blood around his head, which had been battered with his own heavy coal shovel, with which he had sought to raise whiskey money by shoveling snow. Walter Stachiew was not a practical or serious man. He carried his inappropriate shovel more to show his good intentions than to perform a service.

When a police car heading up the hill toward the Forty-sixth Precinct came along, the patrolman saw Stanley Paycek whacking away at Stachiew, the shovel in both of his hands.

It later developed that the two men had spent some time together—as they generally did when one or the other had a couple of dollars, or any amount of loose change—in the neighborhood serious drinkers' bar. It was a place without a name, where you came not for companionship or sympathy or warmth but for the simple purpose of getting drunk. You could do this fast and cheap. No one stopped the headlong rush into oblivion as long as the money held out. When you were out of coin, you were out on the street. This was a simple and effective rule to which no one objected because what was the point? The owner was a huge man who made strange noises rather than speaking in words. He was understood completely. He made and enforced the rules. It was a desperation place and only the most desperate men frequented it.

The argument between the two lifelong friends that night was the usual incomprehensible bickering of two drunks who knew too much about each other and about the emptiness of life. It was bitter and loud and filled with threats. It was the boastful nonsense of two ineffectual men who lived their lives as bullies toward the weak, and of toadies toward those they perceived as having power over them.

All that was remembered was that Walter Stachiew left the bar first, after having jammed the handle of his shovel into Stanley Paycek's throat. Paycek, taken by surprise, couldn't catch his breath for a moment, but when he did, he bellowed in a clear and deadly voice: *I'm gonna kill that bastard for this. I'm gonna bash his skull in for him with his own goddamn shovel.*

The police investigating the case were not surprised that this information was passed on to them. The owner of the bar, articulate when he had to be, didn't want any trouble with the cops. He'd made it through Prohibition, he didn't need trouble now. And he had no loyalty whatsoever to the scum who drank in his establishment. They knew it and he knew it: you don't make no trouble for me.

Besides, the police were told by a somewhat dazed Paycek, still holding the death weapon as he stared at the corpse, "There. I done like I tole him I would do."

The trial was for murder in the first degree, since it was perceived as a calculated, premeditated crime. The story of this Christmastime killing dominated the *Bronx Home News* for a period of time. The *News* and the *Mirror* and the afternoon papers ran with it, then dropped it until the trial.

Stanley Paycek was convicted, without ever testifying, because he never was exactly sure of anything beyond the fact that he probably did bash in Walter's skull, so what else could he say? Because of his record as a man of violence, a drunkard, a brawler, a wife and child beater and now, finally, a murderer, the judge decided, after due consideration, that the Bronx would be well rid of this particular rat-bum, and so Stanley Paycek was sentenced to the electric chair.

On the night before his execution, the family of the convicted murderer visited him. First his wife alone, then five of his children, were allowed to join their parents for a somewhat hysterical prayer together, during which the father told them not to follow his bad example. Go to church, love God, and listen to their mother. *And pray for me. A lot.*

The oldest son, Willie, was permitted, at his earnest request and upon his mentioning that he was now to be the man of this large family, to have a few minutes alone with his father.

It was during this meeting that Willie, fourteen years old, told his father what really happened to Walter Stachiew on the night of December 28, 1935.

And who was involved.

And how someday, far in the future, he would tell the true story. When he knew how each person involved had turned out.

This is that story.

PART ONE

PART ONE

CHAPTER ONE

Sister Mary Frances was having a bad day. The class knew it the minute they entered the room. All the signals they had come to recognize were evident: the squinting, the constant shoving of the rimless eyeglasses up to the ridge of her small nose with a rough knuckle, the sudden stopping in the middle of a sentence, looking around for a culprit, for someone to blame for her pounding headache and obvious agitation.

She was a short, heavy woman who moved in a whirl of flying, floating black, the high stiff white wimple rising from invisible eyebrows high over her head, the starchy surplice advancing before her. Her target could be anyone. In Sister Mary Frances's class, good behavior was suspect. It was merely bad behavior hiding behind subterfuge. Oh, she knew these eighth-graders so well.

Teaching the eighth grade was just one of the many crosses Sister Mary Frances had to bear. Many years ago she had taught the third grade. It was her best time. The third-graders were the ideal students. They were over the first-grade tears and jitters and attacks of babyhood. They were ready to settle down and listen and learn, and she had reveled in teaching them. The reading and writing and arithmetic were all secondary to the real purpose of the education of these young souls. It had been her responsibility to initiate them into the mysteries of their true Mother, the Church, and from time to time, when some bolder parent complained that a child was nervous, sleepless, crying out in fear and terror of the pains of hell, Sister Mary Frances spoke with righteous authority.

"Would you rather they not know," she would ask the mother, "and be unaware of what eternity holds for the unrepentant sinner?"

The earlier you got them, the younger they understood. Let them be frightened and nervous and sleepless. Let them remember stories of the holy saints and their tortured martyrdom. The piercings and roastings and hackings were true historical events, suffered for and offered to Our Lord in perfect love. Let the little ones hear these true things now, let the history of the Holy Mother Church be impressed on them at this young age, when their minds were relatively pure and they had yet to be corrupted.

Twice in her tenure with the third grade, students were withdrawn and sent to public school. One little girl was a mess of tics and shrugs and movements and should have spent life in a straitjacket, as far as Sister Mary Frances was concerned. She felt she had acted properly, bundling the child into her coat and suspending her from a hook in the clothing closet. She only put the mittens in the girl's mouth when she began screaming. She was well out of the class. There was no room for one of those children who craved attention constantly. There had been more than forty other third-graders to deal with, and this bundle of nerves demanded too much time.

The other child would end up in the electric chair, no doubt about it. He had been more than an eight-year-old rogue. He was clearly and surely on the road to damnation with his cruel mischief, his laughter, and, above all, his filthy mouth. Sister Mary Frances did no more than was called for in the situation. She shoved half a cake of brown laundry soap into the vile mouth, forced the dirty words back down his throat, fought off his surprisingly strong hands (he actually struck out at her!). When she finally released him and headed him toward the door and the principal's office for more drastic punishment, the boy fell facedown on the floor. When she rolled him over, he was foaming at the mouth, which after all was natural, given the amount of soap he had bitten off. She grabbed him by his small shoulders and stood him up, but the minute she let go, the boy deliberately let himself fall backwards. He hit his head against the edge of a desk, knocked himself unconscious, and caused a terrible commotion in the class.

St. Simon Stock parish school was well rid of these two. There were plenty of others who were lost causes, and it seemed to Sister Mary Frances that a large number of them now present in this room should have been more harshly dealt with earlier on. Through the years, she had watched former third-graders enter her eighth-grade room. They knew her and she knew them and the class ran more smoothly for this mutual knowledge.

She set the class an assignment in reading, a geography lesson they had not expected. They would be tested on their reading within a half hour, and Sister Mary Frances sat at her desk, head tilted to one side, listening, watching, wary and suspicious. Did they think for one moment today was to be a special day? Last day before Christmas vacation, a day for acting up, for defying her. She had heard the low groan when she told them there would be no class party. The small boxes of hard candy provided for each of them would be distributed at the end of the day. Today was a workday, like any other. The soft moan that drifted toward her reverberated inside her head. She had her suspicions but she wasn't sure. Before the day was out, she would find which of these terrible thirteen- and fourteen-year-olds persisted in defying her.

She moved around the room, floating down the aisles, cracking a knuckle down on an unprepared head: a boy with his face practically making contact with his book. If he needed glasses, let him tell his mother or father, but do not sit like an old blind man, nose touching the printed word. She stood at the back of the room and surveyed her students.

It was in the very air around them. It permeated and spoiled and poisoned the atmosphere, this dangerous age of awakened physical changes. Some of the boys were still slender and smooth-cheeked, involved in childish mischief, but others . . . ah, the others, with their darkening voices, broadened shoulders, hair beginning to gleam over upper lips, and the girls, as restless now as the boys, perfectly aware of the physical changes taking over their bodies. Small breasts swelling, waists narrowing, hips widening, and she knew—*knew*—some of them sneaked lipstick when they were out of the class. She could see the evidence; lips that had been pale were mysteriously pinker, touched by cosmetic.

There was a nervous sexual energy surrounding all of them, and it was her job, her vocation, her determination to save them from the evil into which they were slipping. She did this with vigor and dedication.

There was no flirting, no whispering, no brushing of hands in *her* classroom. She filled them with enough stories of children gone wrong, struck by lightning or by mysterious disease: a childhood heart attack, the victim dead before arriving back in the state of grace that baptism had bestowed.

She glanced around the room, then focused on William Paycek. He was a thoroughly repulsive boy, with his greasy hair, his narrow, small, and bony body. He never looked clean because he never *was* clean and God alone knew the source of the terrible pimples and sores and bruises on his thin ferret face. He had little pebble eyes of no particular color that Sister Mary Frances could determine. No one liked him. The boys bullied him and the girls avoided him completely. He was devious and sly and a liar and a cheat. He came from a family of pigs, and the boy smelled of garbage. Polacks.

Dante D'Angelo was the biggest boy in the room: tall and heavyset, a dark complexion and nearly black eyes. He was turned out clean and fresh every day, which was a wonder to Sister Mary Frances, what with his mother having been so sick for so long before dying and his oldest sister going crazy and being carted off to an insane asylum somewhere. Probably one of the boy's aunts—the Italians seemed to have more aunts than other people—moved in and helped out. Well, that was good, Sister Mary Frances supposed. At least it was one thing in their favor: they took care of their own. She knew the boy helped out in his father's shoe-repair shop after school, and she checked his hands and nails carefully each day, but could find no evidence of the oil and black polish that had stained his father's hands permanently. He was not a particularly friendly boy, but the others seemed to look to him for leadership out in the schoolyard. Probably because he was bigger than the rest of them. Why else would they include the only Italian in all their games. He hadn't given her any particular trouble and, thought Sister, he'd better not.

Her eye kept going back to Megan Magee, the brightest girl ever in St. Simon Stock. She was a year younger than the rest. The child in Megan was still very much in evidence. She had the openness and innocence of a much younger girl, and Sister Mary Frances loved Megan in many ways. She realized that her first attraction to Megan was because of her startling resemblance to a girl named Margaret Forbes. The same dark red hair and orangey eyes, the same pale skin with collections of freckles over the small, slightly uptilted nose. The same dark red lips, turning up in the corners. The same dimples. The same competence as the girl approached any assignment, never freezing at the blackboard, ready to answer any question or complete any assignment.

The snow was beginning, just as it had been forecast.

Margaret Forbes was dead. This was a different girl altogether. As if anyone else could ever *be* Margaret Forbes. If only she could stop remembering the hurt, the pain, the awful sinfulness of loving that long-ago friend. She had to be very careful to remember that Megan was not Margaret. There was a different situation here. Not that Sister Mary Frances ever showed favoritism in any way. What she did with a child who moved her in some mysterious way—as did this girl—was to be twice as hard on that student. Demand much, expect little, but do not let her own weakness be evident, ever. She stood for another moment, turned and surveyed the class, deliberately avoiding even the slightest glimpse at Megan. She would ignore her completely for the rest of the afternoon. She would not think of Megan or Margaret again for the next twenty-four hours. With the help of the Lord she would banish all such thoughts, or at least keep them locked up so deep inside her brain that she would be free of memory and of remembered temptation.

Sister Mary Frances clenched her hands together tightly and turned for a quick moment to look out the window at the darkening day.

She was about to hand out the test papers when the door burst open and there stood Father Thomas Kelly. Sister Mary Frances would never, in her entire life, be able to accept with grace the presence of Thomas Kelly as assistant pastor at St. Simon Stock. She had been his teacher twice, first in third grade, then in eighth. To Sister Mary Frances, he would always be the overactive, smirking little boy who answered her back in third grade and mocked her in eighth. He stood there, as all heads turned, as her children grinned and answered his greeting in unison: Good afternoon, Father. Pushed aside their reading assignment, forgot about the importance of the impending test, played up to him and his boyish, smiling presence.

With his movie-star good looks, his calculated charm, he won them over as always. The girls beamed and blushed, more aware than ever of their own changing bodies. He joked with the boys as though he were one of them, an older brother, filled with their own excitement and turbulence.

The discipline in the room collapsed, as he knew it would. He strode to the front of the room, smiled, greeted her with that false, friendly, insinuating voice.

"Good afternoon, Sister." His voice went low and dangerous. "Any of these rogues giving you any trouble? If they are, just send them along to me."

"There is nothing in my classroom I can't handle, Father."

He reached over without warning and took the familiar sheets of test paper from her hands. The same boy, the same tormenting boy he'd always been.

"Aw, Sister, not a test today! It's Christmas vacation time." And then to the class, "Sister's present to all of you wonderful, good students is that there'll be no test."

They clapped and grinned back at him, observing only him, his wink to them, his conspiracy against her. They were on his side, he would always save them.

He turned to the table at the front of the room, spotted the candy boxes.

"Any leftovers?"

He approached the table and scooped up some boxes that he handed out to several girls, who immediately ripped open the boxes, extracted candy, and offered him some.

"Oh, boy, feed Father's sweet tooth. What do you girls care if I get a toothache?"

She stood, silent and tense, the headache pounding harder, and watched as he distributed the candy.

Finally, as though he had just remembered why he had come here in the first place, he told her, "Father Murphy is having me go around to tell all you teachers. School is over early today." He consulted his wristwatch. "In fifteen minutes, to be exact. The cleaning people are going to leave early, and Father wanted them to have enough time to straighten things out." And then to the class, "You be good now, do not give Sister any trouble, or I'll hear about it. Sister, you have any complaints about anyone, you let me know. Well, Merry Christmas, eighth-graders."

They called out to him in loud and boisterous voices and then he was gone and they were hers once more. She ordered them to close the candy boxes immediately. There was no eating in her classroom. They fell silent quickly, sat motionless, with folded hands as she demanded.

"I will wish you all a sacred Christmas. I hope you will be able to put aside your greed for games and new clothes and whatever else your parents see fit to gift you with, and take time to think about what the day means. Whose birthday it is. And how the mother was turned back into the cold. And where Our Lord was born and what his life was. And particularly, after you attend the joyous mass celebrating our Savior's birth, I want you to think ahead to the end of Our Lord's sojourn on earth. His Crucifixion. As you celebrate the Holy Child's birth, never, ever forget his death at the hands of his enemies, the Jews."

Her cold, hard eyes blinked rapidly through her smudged glasses and lingered helplessly on the face of Megan Magee. She turned abruptly and, without facing them, stood rigid as the school bell rang, announcing dismissal. No one in her room moved or made a sound. No one dared. Finally, when *she* decided, she turned back to her class and dismissed them for the two-week Christmas holiday. They gathered their coats quietly from the closet, marched out of the room silently.

Sister Mary Frances stood by the window and watched as they exploded noisily out onto the street, faces turned up to taste the heavily falling snow. She closed her eyes tightly and began to recite the rosary.

CHAPTER TWO

Willie Paycek hated more people than anyone else, anywhere in the world. His hatreds were cold, clinical, and for cause. He kept accounts deep within his brain and could, within a split second, bring a person to the front of his mind and run through the catalog relentlessly, without omitting a single injury. He made little distinction between damage done to him physically and damage done emotionally. It was all the same; he noted, he remembered, he would never relent in his determination to pay back.

And it was important that each one who did him damage knew that someday, without question, little Willie Paycek would finally take his revenge.

With one exception, he hated all of his teachers. They melded together into one large, indistinct form inside a tangle of black floating veils, foreheads obscured by hard white linen, pinched mean faces, pale eyes batting behind rimless glasses, mouths tight and dry. All spoke in the same accusatory voice, as though their very purpose in life was to catch out some child right smack in the middle of a sinful thought. They knew, these women, they could tell, they had been gifted with second sight that could pierce into the evil heart and brain of some luckless child. Usually the luckless child was Willie Paycek.

His very physical appearance caught their immediate disapproval. He was a narrow child with a gray complexion and thin hair that was always badly cut and always seemed unclean. His clothes never fit properly; they were either too-large hand-me-downs or his own, worn until his knobby wrists showed from the frayed cuffs of his shirts and his falling socks, sliding into his scuffed shoes, revealed the fish-white skin of his ankles.

He was always dirty, not with the healthy grime of childhood that came from vigorous, sweaty roughhousing, but with the fetid, stale uncleanness that came from lack of hygiene. His neck was a particular target of the sharp, inspecting fingers: neatly rounded nails dug in many times to make the point.

You see, class, this is what happens when you don't bathe regularly. William, you are a disgrace.

His hair was inspected regularly, but not by fingers. No, the nuns could not trust the possibility of finding that ultimate of horrors, lice, to fingertips. From first grade on, they carefully leaned over him, two pencils poking and prodding and separating his wispy hair in fruitless search of living prey. Their cold and musty presence overwhelmed him. Nuns had a peculiar odor, and he wondered whether it was something they had been born with or something given to them when they took their vows.

William knew that nuns were not born nuns. He knew they had been girls once, and that under all the floating black veils in which they hid were women's bodies.

William knew a lot of things the other kids never knew.

The only teacher he had ever loved was Sister Mary Catherine, who taught him in second grade. She was the youngest of all the sisters, and in her pale eyebrows and bright blue eyes, her pink complexion and full red lips, blond healthiness could be discerned. Her hands touched, they did not pinch or punch or jab. They did not form into rocklike fists that cracked into foreheads. They did not suddenly whack the back of an unsuspecting head, causing the face to crash onto the labored piece of writing, the ink to spill, catastrophe to grow because of a momentary lapse of attention.

She had once cupped her soft white hand under his chin and looked directly at him, which was difficult to do, he knew, because his left eye turned in toward his nose and no one seemed to know how to make eye contact with him. She had smiled at his drawing of the baby Jesus, had caught the meaning in the roll of the infant's eye toward his Mother, but too far inward.

Her hand on his chin was cool. Not cold, but cool. There was a difference. She had the most beautiful white teeth, even and small and clean, and she did not smell musty. She smelled, oh, he could not name the fragrance but it contained all about Sister Mary Catherine that he loved. A good smell, clean and fresh but with a hint, a wisp of her humanness, her realness. It was a fragrance he would remember from time to time all his life: something he could conjure up and think about on terrible nights.

She said to him words he would store away in the otherwise empty section of love deep inside himself.

"William," the soft girl inside the nun's disguise told him, "I think your baby Jesus is very beautiful. And I think he looks just like you."

It was a gift she had given him, and he cherished it all his life.

Such was his poverty.

He had new reasons to hate his father every day of his life. His father was "the Polack janitor." It was what he was, had always been, and would always be. Because his father was the janitor, they were all janitors. His mother was the janitor's wife; his brothers and sisters were the janitor's kids. He was the Polack janitor's oldest boy, a little rat. Looks just like his father.

He knew that to be a fact. He could look into his father's terrible face, lined and crusted, ragged, unshaven, the small eyes narrowed into tiny slits when he'd been drinking—and when wasn't he drinking—and he could see himself in the years ahead.

His mother had to mop the halls, lug the heavy metal garbage pails filled with shaken-down ashes from the furnace to the edge of the sidewalk, then later drag them back through the narrow alleyway to the basement. Willie had been pressed into janitor duty from the time he could remember. His main job now, at thirteen, was the daily collection of garbage from the tenants in the building.

At first he had helped his father, when his father was sober and tended to the collection, then helped his mother, then done most of it himself. He would stand in the opening, drag the heavy dumbwaiter to the top floor, ring the bells of the tenants on each side of the dumbwaiter. They would load their garbage, mostly in brown paper bags, onto the dumbwaiter, and then Willie would lower it down, hand over hand, and empty the garbage from the dumbwaiter into the metal containers. Then haul the dumbwaiter up again. People were not very considerate. Most were, he admitted that, but some were sloppy and put too much stuff on the shelf and garbage would come flying down, hitting him on the head or arms.

The top-floor people were okay; the fourth-floor people were careless, although Mrs. Commerford always yelled out—too late, of course—oops, sorry Willie, heads up.

Thanks a lot, fat slob Mrs. Commerford and your stinking lumps of vegetable scrapings and whatever else the hell came tumbling down. He had so much garbage land on him—on his arms, his head, his shoulders, his feet—that he had become accustomed to the stink. He no longer realized he smelled rancid a great deal of the time.

His father was a husky, short, but large-muscled, frightening man who bullied and abused all of them. He punched and kicked and twisted and stomped. Willie's mother was battered and bruised, her large, fleshy face discolored, her eyes vacant and staring through purple circles. It was bad when the father was sober, infinitely worse when he was drunk. Willie, as the eldest, was closest to hand, and the most sought-after target. He had learned to become invisible, to disappear, to melt and vaporize, to let some of the other kids take the brunt of their father's inexplicable fury and brutality. There were times, Willie knew, he had seen, when his father had done certain things to the girls. Not hitting, punching, pushing, shoving—something else. Touching, grabbing, pulling them against him until they cried out in terror, until their mother finally came and pulled them away, scolding the victim for some crime or other, but getting the child free. By doing this, she placed herself in jeopardy. Willie saw, he knew, he had begun to understand.

For as long as Willie could remember, Walter Stachiew had been involved in the life of the Paycek family. He was either a cousin of his father's or a boyhood friend from the old country who claimed the privilege of kinship.

In fact, he claimed far more than the privilege of kinship.

One day, when he was about five years old, Willie came upon Stachiew and his mother. They were locked in a tight embrace, his hands jammed on her body, her hands on his neck. The small, thin, frightened boy kicked and hammered his small fists against Stachiew, who pulled back, raging at first, then laughing. He lifted the frantic boy with one huge hand, held him high in the air, then tossed him against the wall.

Through his pain and panic, he heard his mother saying softly, no, no, don't hurt the child, Walter, don't hurt the child. There was an intimacy in her voice. Stachiew yanked the boy to his feet, leaned down, his breath sour with whiskey and passion and annoyance and spoke to the boy.

"Wha'sa madder, kid? You tink bad tings about me, huh? Or maybe you tink bad tings about your mudder, what kinda boy are you, tinks bad tings about his own mudder? Mudders are sacred, like Holy Mudder Mary, you not a good kid, little Willie, you a rotten little weasel, you got such bad toughts!"

He emphasized the major points of his speech with a shake or a poke, and the boy's body felt weightless, helpless, totally without value.

His mother, standing behind Stachiew, smiled, and whispered at him, "No, no, it's h'okay, all h'okay, he's just a small child, Walter, leave him alone."

"Ya, let him leave me alone," the giant said. Then, giving up the whole thing, he turned and lurched from the small basement apartment where the janitor's family lived, and went into the furnace room where he slept on a cot.

Willie's mother said nothing. She merely adjusted her clothing, brushed at herself, touched her hair with her thick red fingers, and went into the kitchen to cook.

Willie hated his mother, his father, and Walter Stachiew. He also hated most of his brothers and sisters, some of whom looked exactly like Walter and some of whom looked like Willie and his father.

His real everyday life—at home, on the street, and in school—was intolerable, and at times Willie fell into that most sinful state of mind: despair. Were it not for the other part of his life, the boy sometimes felt he would fade away, bit by bit become paler and smaller and finally invisible and nonexistent. And no one, not anyone, would realize it. Or care.

Willie Paycek had discovered another reality in the most unrealistic of worlds: the movies. He did not consider the movies he saw every Saturday morning of his young life the way most of the other kids did. He did not walk home pretending to be a cowboy or a gangster or a soldier, walking with an imitated strut or slouch, slapping reins against an imaginary horse, galloping along the sidewalks of the Bronx. He did not become the tall, handsome leading man, radiant with the magic absorbed during the matinee.

Instead, Willie Paycek left each movie show with a sense of wonder, curiosity, and determination that he discussed with no one. First, there was no one to discuss anything with, and second, he would not know how to put his feelings into words.

Willie, alone of all the kids in the audience, and probably alone among the adults, wondered about how the movies were made. He took the stories for exactly what they were: stories, written by people for other people, called actors, to bring to black-and-white life. What he wondered was who were all the unseen people involved. Who did what, who besides the actors caused these movies to come into being?

He made a practice of reading every single word in the credits either at the beginning of the picture or at the end. For everything, there seemed to be specific people involved: directors, producers, writers, makeup people, designers of clothes and sets, musicians and composers, location people, electricians, carpenters. They all came together and made a story that he sat and watched at the Avalon Theatre on Burnside Avenue in the Bronx.

The "Avvie" was the neighborhood cheap movie house: eleven cents before noon for kids, fifteen cents after that. They changed the program twice a week and you could follow the itinerary of the pictures from the first-run houses in Manhattan to the beautiful Loew's Paradise on the Grand Concourse, then to the Loew's Burnside for Loew's pictures, and from the RKO Fordham on Fordham Road, whose pictures then went right across the street to the Valentine, before hitting the Avvie. Even the cartoons interested him: not the action but the story, which was usually the same (somebody gets hit on the head, chased, blown up, run down by car or locomotive before being rescued and turning on his assailant), not even the animation, although he realized that animation was achieved through a painstaking series of drawings. What intrigued Willie was the overall putting together of the film, the realization that people somewhere were creating all of this—movies, cartoons, weekly serials—out of nothing.

Willie Paycek could not have said what all of this meant to him, why it intrigued him to the point of restless nervousness. He didn't really know what, if anything, there was in all of this for him, what promise, what direction for his life to take. All he knew was that when he entered the smelly, dirty, noisy, child-filled movie on a Saturday morning, everything else in his life no longer existed. This environment, that screen, that action, those stories, all those technicians and artists and actors were something that filled him with that rarest of emotions: hope. Somewhere in all of this was a promise he carried with him from one Saturday morning to the next.

It was the most important part of his life, and always would be.

It was not just at the movies that Willie Paycek learned, and filed away for future contemplation. Feeling always set apart from everyone else, discarded, nonexistent, gave the boy a freedom to watch, to learn, to puzzle over the behavior he saw all around him.

Who else noticed that the hands of Dominick D'Angelo, the shoemaker, lingered more than necessary when he helped a lady on with her repaired shoe, that his long, stained fingers slid unnecessarily over a well-turned ankle, that his eyes glittered, his tongue flicked over wet lips, his voice went lower, a hoarse quality deepening his innocent-seeming words:

There, now. Little lady, that good, huh? That feel better now on that pretty little foot, hey, should have only comfort, such a pretty lady.

And they ate it up. They beamed, they smiled, they let it happen.

They all, these ladies, these girls, seemed to wait for something, the way he was waiting for something.

At four-o'clock roll call in front of the Forty-sixth Precinct on Ryer Avenue, directly across from the building where the Payceks lived, the young mothers with their baby carriages, with their little kids, seemed to stand by, watching the blue-uniformed men as they lined up, important, listening, standing straight in two military lines, their faces serious, while the sergeant read out orders. Willie watched the women who watched the men. They glanced directly at the young, strong men, some bolder than others, until a glance was exchanged, some secret contact made, some understanding reached. To do what? To what end? To meet in some basement, some backroom, the way his mother did with Stachiew? Or what? Was it enough, the quick, easy flirting that the tough Irish-faced cops threw at these women, these young mothers?

Willie knew these were young women, despite the sometimes old look in their faces. He saw too much, he saw a certain tense desperation, a tightening of lips too soon, a drawn, unhappy look that was turned too often into blows on the arms and heads and backsides of young kids who most times didn't know what the hell they were getting whacked for this time.

Who were these young women, girls one day, flirting and holding hands with high school sweethearts, bragging, simpering, showing off, sporting small chip engagement rings, then having June weddings at St. Simon and big parties at home and then big bellies, little babies, kids running around yelling, getting chased by these girls, no longer girls, but women who watched, with bitter faces as their younger sisters came home from school, faces flushed from flirtations?

These were things that Willie Paycek, a rat-faced, cross-eyed, thin, pasty boy with a high shrill voice, noticed and wondered about.

There was also that other thing he had observed about Walter

Stachiew, and this one really bothered him. He couldn't figure it out, no way.

Walter Stachiew was a large man whose features, before they had become bloated and swollen, were handsome. His body was still muscular, despite the gut that hung over his low-slung belt. There were times, periodically, when he and Willie's father would dry out. They would get religion, for some reason or other, and they would both stay off the booze. Nothing helped Willie's father's appearance. He was an ugly, gross man, and his attempts at charm, politeness, helpfulness, were always greeted with contempt by the tenants: Just do your damn job, Paycek, and get the hell out of my apartment.

But Stachiew, during those times, actually had a charm, a manner that could win people over, that could make people care about him. What a fine young man he really was, off the drink. You could trust him to fix the window sash, tighten the valve so that the radiator stopped banging, at least for a while. He offered to do marketing for the elderly lady on the third floor, to walk the dog when Mr. Janowitz broke his leg. He could change into someone else.

But Willie always knew enough not to trust Stachiew. There was something else, something strange and confusing about Walter when he was sober.

It had to do with boys.

It had to do with how friendly and helpful Walter was with neighborhood boys. He would fix the wheel of a bike or wagon. He would help put together a great apple-crate skate racer. He could belt a Spalding with a broomstick (of which he had an endless supply). He could show quick moves while dribbling a basketball. Always with a hand on a shoulder, a squeeze for emphasis on an upper arm, a pressing against a young body as he helped a boy through a move. And the pat on the ass, the hand cupping around a buttock. Lingering, feeling, sliding around the body of some unsuspecting boy. Because what could a boy make of all this? It was something so strange and peculiar. The boy would know it was something wrong. Sinful. But was this sin his or Walter Stachiew's? And who could he ask, talk to, trust? It wasn't even something he could dump in the confessional. What could you say, this man put his hand on me, on my body and . . . and what? And I thought of bad things, bad things I can't even say because I don't know?

Stachiew never touched Willie, and Willie knew it was for two reasons. He only liked pretty, handsome, strong boys. And he knew that Willie was wise to him.

By Saturday, December 28, 1935, Walter Stachiew had been sober and charming and pleasant for roughly four weeks. He always sobered up for the holidays. It was a time when even the stingiest people became at least a little generous. If they didn't slip him a dollar, there was always a home-cooked plate of leftovers or a cake or some Christmas candy. So he planned his periods of sobriety. But the holidays were over, as far as his advantages were concerned.

Besides, someone gave him a bottle of cheap booze, and he began his drinking early in the day, taking the bottle to his cot in the furnace room so that he didn't have to share it with Willie's father.

Willie went into the storeroom to search for an old sled he remembered from last year, something that had been abandoned years ago by some people who moved away. It was how Willie got a lot of things: broken-down bikes, old roller skates. The sled wasn't bad, and the snow had been falling since before Christmas. It was cold out and slippery, and the night would be perfect for sledding.

He searched around behind large old trunks which tenants stored in the basement. Sometimes he pried them open but there was nothing but old clothes, rotting blankets, stuff people stored away rather than discarded.

He was way back in the corner, poking around, bored, tired from having shoveled most of the sidewalk. His father set him to work, promising to be right back. By the time he returned, the sidewalk was clear. Now his father was doing the easy part of the job, tossing ashes on the walk to keep it from icing up. He heard someone coming and automatically, instinctively, because Willie was a secret person who liked to spy on people, he crouched down, unseen. And watched.

It was Gene O'Brien, tall, slender, his pale face flushed from the cold, his white-blond hair shining with snow as he took off his wet woolen cap and slapped it against his long, slim leg. He looked around, then headed directly to the shelf where the O'Brien sled had been stacked away last year. Willie watched him, impatient to have the place to himself again. There were a few cartons he hadn't seen before and wanted to check out.

Gene reached up, and he pulled the sled down, turned, holding it against his chest.

The instant he saw Walter Stachiew standing in the doorway of the storeroom, Gene O'Brien froze. He had been taken by surprise. As he released his breath, there was a peculiar, troubling sound.

Stachiew caught it at once. Even before he spoke, the alcohol fumes began to fill the space between himself and the boy.

"Wha's a matter, you got scared? Huh? It's me, you know me, ol' Stach, huh?"

The boy realized how tightly he held the sled, how his tension seemed to amuse the drunken man. He inhaled quietly, eased the sled from his chest, rested it at his feet, balanced it, and put his wet wool cap on his damp head.

"You get that nice hair all wet, huh? What you been doin' out in the snow, making snowball fights, huh?"

The boy's voice was muffled. Obviously he was frightened but trying to control his fear.

"Yeah. Why don't ya come on out in the snow, Stach? We got a fort and everything."

"You got a fort and everything. Wha the fuck I wanna go out, you got a fort and everything?"

The use of the curse word hung in the air. It was not a word grown men used with boys. It was a dangerous, exciting word they daringly used among themselves, but here, now, with this man, it was something else. Something serious and threatening.

Stachiew steadied himself on the door frame. He laughed, low and hoarse and dirty.

"Hey. Look at you, you face turn bright red, like a little girl. I say 'fuck,' and you get all red." He blinked, leaned down closer to the boy, who instinctively took a step back. This insulted Stachiew.

"Hey, whatsa matter you? You know me, huh? What you pull back for, huh?"

Suddenly he reached up and yanked Gene's wet hat from his head, held it up high. The boy reached, then dropped his hands to the sled, which he held now, chest high. Defensively. Stachiew reached down and with a large, rough red hand, he tousled the silver blond hair.

"This is pretty hair you got, kid, pretty like a little girl's. Only little baby girls got hair like this."

He reached out his other hand, realized he was still holding the empty bottle. He tilted his face up, sucked on the bottle for whatever drops remained. As he did this, Eugene made a quick, graceful move to the side of the man, shoving the sled against his body as he tried to duck under his arms.

Stachiew dropped the bottle, which bounced against some cartons and then to the floor. He moved a few inches, so that the boy and his sled slammed into his body, dead weight, a sack of cement, an ungiving wall.

"What you think you do, huh, pretty, what you think, you gonna roughhouse with Stachiew, huh, I show you some nice roughhouse, you so pretty, such a pretty little boy."

Willie watched the struggle, fascinated. The air was charged not just with violence; there was something more to it. Something that both Stachiew and Eugene O'Brien were aware of. Something Willie had been expecting from the moment the huge drunk came into the room and confronted the handsome, silvery boy.

Stachiew kicked the door closed without looking behind him. The boy moved from side to side, breathing hard, the snow-reddened face pale now, the beads of moisture running down his cheeks a combination of melting snow and sweat.

Stachiew grabbed at the boy's face, cupped his hand under the fragile chin, leaned into the boy, squinted, nodded, licked his dry, cracked lips.

"You too beautiful for a boy, you too beautiful. Pretty, like a girl, huh? You a girl, huh?"

Stachiew was totally fixed on the boy, and Gene O'Brien kicked and punched and breathed in loud short gasps, falling back, trying to evade Stachiew.

Willie watched, amazed, fascinated. Excited.

Stachiew unzipped his dirty workpants and pulled out his penis, large, engorged. With one hand forced the boy's head down, with the other he manipulated himself.

"You do this now, you pretty boy, you do this, I make you feel good, let me see your pecker, let me see your pretty little body, you girl or boy, I wanna see, I . . ."

Suddenly Stachiew, reaching down, fondling and grabbing the boy, pulled back. His face, red and distorted, looked at first amazed, and then he smiled and laughed.

"Why, you little fucker, you little sonabitch, you like it don't you, you little fucker, you hard as a rock down there . . ."

Suddenly, Eugene O'Brien kicked his tormenter in the balls, and when Stachiew crumpled over in agony, he turned and kicked him again, and then he lifted his sled over his head and brought it down as hard as he could somewhere in the area of Stachiew's shoulders.

And then he ran out of the storeroom.

Willie Paycek remained hidden for a long time. He knew it wasn't safe to move until Stachiew was gone. He was prepared to sit, hidden, huddled, unseen and unsuspected. He didn't mind.

He had a lot to think about.

CHAPTER THREE

In the first week of summer, 1934, on a Tuesday morning at about 4:00 A.M. Angela D'Angelo went crazy. Neither the fact of her breakdown nor the form it took was surprising, really.

For almost eight months, until her mother's death—the day after her fortieth birthday in April—Angela had not only tended her mother but had taken care of the rest of the family. She cooked, cleaned and was responsible for her two younger brothers, her two younger sisters and her father, Dominick. She was eighteen years old and she gave up her senior year at St. Simon Stock High School without much discussion. It was her duty and she did it without complaint. She had help from her aunts who came on weekends from Bathgate Avenue, bringing baskets of cooked food and skilled hands to help with the washing and ironing, the cleaning and baking. They brought generations of advice and wisdom to offer the dying woman and her daughter.

No one noticed that Angela was becoming thin almost to the point of gauntness, that the resemblance between dying mother and tending daughter was extraordinary. They both had sunken blazing dark eyes, hollowed cheeks, tangled hair. There was a connection between them that seemed to make them interchangeable.

Her father didn't notice anything wrong with Angela. He worked twelve or fourteen hours a day. He knew she was a good girl who took care of her mother and her family. A good girl. Nor did the other children notice. Angela became, in effect, their mother. They followed her quiet instructions, changed from school clothes to play clothes, fetched items from the store, made their beds in the morning, picked up after themselves, set the table, cleared, helped out as always, showed homework assignments to her, reported—sometimes honestly, sometimes not—where they would be after school, whom they would be with and what they would be doing.

Dante was the oldest boy, and at thirteen he noticed things that he kept to himself. Disturbing things. He had come upon his sister staring down at the apparition who had once given light and center to their lives. Angela's hands twitched as his mother's hands twitched. Her lips moved silently and he could catch words only occasionally. The others assumed the two were praying, but Dante wasn't sure. There was a secret between the mother and daughter, and all else aside—the horror of the slow, day-by-day dying of this formerly robust, warm, hearty, noisy woman—there was something sinister and dark and frightening going on. There was no one he could tell. His father would only look frightened and stay longer hours at his shop. He could scarcely bear to look at his dying wife, and Dante didn't want to chase him farther away. He could not tell his aunts; they came, laden and busy and helpful and filled with noise and instructions and hugs and hard pinches and laughter and hearty good health, fussing with his mother, pretending, always pretending, that she would get better, that her life was not slipping away.

He could not tell his sixteen-year-old sister, Marie. The girl was too filled with herself. Her beautiful long black hair took up so much time, her clothes had to be pressed just so, she had no time to fuss with anything beyond herself. She kissed her mother twice a day, good morning, good night, and got on with her own life. The other children were too young. They accepted things, adjusted, escaped.

The secret between the dying woman and her daughter was a whispered revelation that became a litany between them. One day, when they were alone in the apartment, as Angela sponged her mother's forehead and eased her matted head against the clean pillowcase, smoothed covers over the concave skeletal body, her mother stiffened. Her dark eyes grew huge and protuberant, then glowed with the desperation of her message. She reached a hand toward her daughter, and for a moment the agony of the stomach cancer shuddered through her body. She let out a soft, sibilant hiss, fastened a remarkably strong hand on her daughter's thin arm, pulled her close.

With a dry tongue, her mother tried to moisten her lips, and in an aching, tormented voice, she told her daughter the terrible secret.

I am hanging on the Cross with Jesus.

It was the secret they shared between them, the secret agony that the doctor could not know about, nor the priest nor the aunts. It was between the two of them, and over and over, sometimes with the whispered words, sometimes just by the terrible, dartlike beam of light from her eyes, her mother told her what no one else knew.

Her mother was bearing, in addition to all other pain, the final agony of Jesus Christ on the Cross. It was a martyrdom she had been chosen to suffer and to share with her daughter.

After her mother's death, Angela talked with elderly Father Murphy about returning to school. It was left up in the air. She had not been much of a student. Her family needed her at home during this difficult time more than they needed her to achieve a general high school diploma. Later on, when the kids had all settled in to the loss of their mother, when they were older, when she wasn't needed so totally, a job could be found for Angela at the phone company or in a bank somewhere. She wasn't to worry about such things. She was to do what God needed her to do right now for the sake of her mother's memory and her family's need.

Life in the D'Angelo family seemed to stabilize. The aunts came less often. The children were good kids and helped out and reported in and did their homework. Dominick worked hard.

All was as before, with one exception. More and more often, as soon as the children left home for school, Angela left home for church. She stayed in church for hours, praying first at the foot of the statue of the Holy Mother and then at the base of the Crucifix that dominated the altar. She was home when the kids came home from school, served supper, cleaned up, supervised the evening routine of homework, baths, clean uniforms, and arbitrated the selection of the radio programs. Left a hot meal in the oven for her father. And then she returned to church.

Dante followed her, watched her. Worried. He spoke once to Father Kelly. He never would have approached the young priest, but he literally bumped into him as he was sneaking out of St. Simon's. He didn't want Angela to know he'd been spying on her, and he was moving backwards toward the staircase.

Father Kelly caught him in his open arms, laughed gently, turned the boy toward him, saw the troubled face, the hesitation. He walked along with Dante.

Dante was not at ease with Father Kelly. His fine light blue eyes always seemed ready to laugh, to turn something serious into something foolish. Also, there was that other thing. That *Irish* thing. Dante was an intruder here, in their church. All the sisters, all the kids, with few exceptions, were Irish. This was *their* place. But he had to talk to someone, and Father Kelly put an arm around his shoulder in a friendly, brotherly way and made it easy by beginning for him.

"It's about Angela, right? You're worrying about your sister."

Dante felt a quick relief. He wasn't alone now. Someone else knew there was something wrong going on.

They climbed the stone steps to the street level, and Father Kelly leaned against the iron piping and smiled.

"Give her a little time, Danny," he said softly, using the nickname no teacher ever used. "Your mother's death has been harder on Angela than on any of the rest of you. She's taken so much on herself, and she is, after all, only a young girl."

"Father," he said slowly, not sure, not willing to trust the priest, yet needing to tell someone, "she's gotten sort of . . . she's not like she used to be. She's . . . strange . . ."

The strong arm went around his shoulder again, the hard hand gave a reassuring squeeze, almost hurtful on his upper arm.

"She's been through her own ordeal, Danny. Look, you're a good kid and a good brother. I want you to know something. I've been a little worried about Angela too. I know how many hours she's been spending in church, and I'm keeping an eye on her. She's seeking solace, that's all. If it gets beyond that . . . Do you know the word *morbid*?"

Dante knew the word. He knew many words and he realized the priest was speaking to him as though he was an intelligent, responsible person, not a child.

"Well, sometimes when a person is overwhelmed with grief—and your sister has had an awful amount of responsibility on her— sometimes a person might become unrealistic about what she expects to find in church. It goes beyond looking for comfort and understanding and . . . Look, kid. I'll keep an eye on her, okay? She'll come out of it. Don't worry about it." He gave a playful sock to Dante's chin, a friendly, big-brother gesture of reassurance.

Dante was grateful, but he did not feel reassured.

On the night that Angela D'Angelo went crazy, nothing seemed different or special. Angela returned from church by nine o'clock, had dinner ready for her father, saw that the kids were all bedded down and quiet by ten, cleaned up, heard her father settle down in the bedroom with the boys. She sat with a cup of hot chocolate, which was her usual bedtime ritual. Sometime during the night, Angela D'Angelo slipped out of the apartment on the top floor, walked the two blocks up Ryer Avenue, went down the stone steps into the underground church.

At four o'clock that Tuesday morning, the shrieks of agony were so loud, intense, and frightening that even Father Murphy, with his fifty percent hearing loss, was brought awake and ran quickly after the younger priest, Father Kelly, into the church.

There at the altar, on her back, arms stretched into the crucifixion position, her ankles twisting together, her head jerking spasmodically from side to side, eyes rolled well up into their sockets, mouth wide open and emitting terrible screams, was Angela D'Angelo.

Blessed with less fortitude than her mother, from whom she had inherited the burden, she shrieked over and over again, "I am hanging on the Cross with Jesus."

The agony seemed so real, so precisely defined by her body, that the older priest almost expected to see blood flowing from wounds. By the time the ambulance from Fordham Hospital arrived, young Father Kelly had things well in hand. A puzzled, sleepy Dominick D'Angelo tried ineffectually to calm his daughter, caressing her clumsily with a roughened hand, then shrugging, falling back against the attendants who injected the girl with heavy sedation. He seemed to have forgotten his fair grasp of English. He turned from one to the other, demanding in his Sicilian dialect: What? What have you done to my daughter? What has happened to her? Where . . . where are you taking her?

His son, Dante, grasped his father's shoulders with a strength and maturity that surprised the man. This boy, this child, now saying to him the meaningless but soothing words: It will be all right, Papa. It will be all right.

Of course, neither father nor son believed anything would ever be all right again as they watched Angela, still in her religious ecstasy, being tied into a wraparound garment, arms pulled across her body, head lolling back heavily as she was carried, sacklike, from the interior of the church, up the stone steps, and into the ambulance. Shades were pulled, windows opened up in the apartment buildings across from the church. Father Kelly waved to the curious neighbors, go back to bed, it's under control, a sick girl, that's all. He faced the building, legs apart, chin up, glancing steadily as though memorizing who was still watching, nodding as they unwillingly did as he asked.

Father Kelly, his blue eyes bright with excitement and alarm, realized he was, in effect, in charge. The old priest was mumbling and shaking, nearly out of control. Father Kelly signaled to the boy. Dante, send your father home to the other children. You come along. And so the two younger men directed the two older men.

The priest and the boy rode with the possessed girl, each experiencing the situation in a different way. Dante took it as another disaster in his family. He felt isolated, totally alone in his awareness of what was happening. Father Kelly wondered what the meaning was, if there was any. Was this purely a religious ecstasy of the most profound kind, and if it was, why no stigmata? Or would that happen later? Or was this just a poor, exhausted, simple girl who should not have been allowed such intense access to the church, and was he at fault for not being more vigilant? The situation, in any event, provided more proof that old Father Murphy could no longer function. He was a shaken old man who should be put out to pasture. It would be a kindness. Father Kelly had worried the old man might suffer a heart attack or a stroke. He couldn't take this kind of pressure. A younger, stronger hand was needed in this perish.

Later, the aunts, of course, took the D'Angelo family over more than ever, and they made life as normal and warm and loving as they could. They were good women, solicitous and loving, tough and not given to crying, cheerful in the face of terrible events. This family would survive.

But Dante knew things were very serious for his family when the uncles got involved.

The uncles—the three Rucci brothers—were brothers of his dead mother. They lived mysterious lives. There was something tantalizing about the very fact that his father wanted nothing to do with them. They owned various enterprises: bakeries, restaurants, fruit, vegetable, and butcher shops, and, most amazing to Dante, they owned their own homes over near Bathgate Avenue. Small, neat, two-story brick buildings, one next to the other so that the cousins felt at home in any one of the buildings. They lived almost communally; only at holiday times, Easter or Christmas, did Dante and his family spend any time with his mother's relatives.

It had been his father's decision not to have much to do with the uncles. Dante could not understand this. They were loud, short, muscular men, quick to distribute dollar bills and hugs. Their friendly hard hands would rumple newly combed heads or tug playfully at long sausage curls resting on some little girl's shoulders. There was always the admonishment from his father: Do not take anything from your uncles.

But now they relied on these very men his father seemed to despise. It was the uncles his father had finally called to rescue Angela from the large, cold, terrifying city institution where she had been sent—where Dante and his father found her, sitting, unmoving, mouth open, eyes blank, in a thin hospital gown stained with food and other things they could not imagine. Within an hour of his father's visit, the uncles sent a special doctor to rescue the girl. Dante visited her after a few weeks, amazed at the beautiful resort-like place in the country, where his sister changed so completely. She had put on weight; the beauty of her face had returned; she smiled and talked with him. She told him about the courses she was taking, the teachers who came several times a week to teach her the mysteries of stenography. She showed him the small, neat typewriter on which she practiced every afternoon. She told him she had been promised a job, a real job, in the office of one of the uncles' businesses.

Dante studied her face for signs of the ghost, the terrified apparition, but what he saw was his beautiful sister, more mature and relaxed than he had ever known her.

They had never been close. Age and gender had kept them from being friends in the past. Each had been assigned a role. There were unwritten but definite rules. They never would talk about what had happened to her. That was past and over.

Dante had his own conflicts over his father's attitude toward the uncles. Dominick D'Angelo was not a jealous or envious man. He did not dream of wealth or property or acquisitions. He was willing to work long and hard hours to take care of his family. He had married their only sister and they had not resented him or the lesser life she had chosen for love of Dominick. They were always generous: they had, through the years, offered him opportunities to work with them. From what Dante could discern, they were good men, but he knew instinctively that he would never be able to ask his father what the problem was. It was impossible, ever, to speak with his father on a great number of things, including the night of his sister's breakdown. She was recovering from an illness. She was doing well. She would come home. She could go to work and get on with her life. It would not be discussed, there would be no point . . . *It had never happened.*

The uncles sent an old, distant cousin to take care of the D'Angelos. She was grandmotherly and a good cook and housekeeper and she smiled and spoke to them in a whispered, pleasant Sicilian dialect. She was loving and gentle and easygoing, and left it to Dante to enforce the discipline and rules of the household. His sister Marie, three years older, resented and challenged his authority and he spoke to her quietly, worked out deals and compromises and made her begin to realize her importance in the family. Dante learned that one of his uncles' cousins owned a women's clothing factory. Marie loved clothing more than anything in her life. Picking his time, carefully, he spoke to the uncle, and in return for doing some minor office work on Saturday morning she was allowed to pick and choose among the latest styles. The uncle would have given her whatever she wanted without any stipulation, but he listened carefully and with new respect to this nephew, at once so young and so wise. It was important that Marie learn the value of work, that she not just be handed things.

Angela came home for a few days before Christmas. It was a good time for the D'Angelo family. There was a constant family party. The uncles and aunts came to the apartment, and then they all went over to the houses on Bathgate Avenue. There was no time for anyone to feel uncomfortable or uneasy about the sister who went crazy. Besides, she was calm now, and smiling and beautiful and loving, and she was treated by the family as the cherished girl she had always been.

It was with a few of the neighborhood boys that Dante had some trouble. Some stupid boys who taunted him, with ugly imitations of his sister's terrible mad passion: arms flung wide, head rolled back, tongue lolling, voices screaming the words: I am hanging on the Cross with Jesus.

They were neighborhood boys, older than Dante, but not too much larger; he was a big boy for his age. They lived across the street from the D'Angelos. They were high school boys and they chanted at him on Christmas afternoon as he took the family dog for an airing.

Carefully releasing the dog at the curb, Dante crossed the street and confronted his tormentors. They failed to read the controlled passion of his approach.

"That is very unkind," he said softly. "I don't want to hear this kind of thing anymore."

They mocked him, his serious tone, his adult words, and danced around him, screaming the words again: I am hanging on the Cross with Jesus.

He moved so fast, so unexpectedly fast for such a large boy, and he moved against the largest, a boy four or five years older than himself. It was a rule he would follow all of his life: Go for the biggest. The rest will fall in line.

It was over quickly and decisively and the details, enlarged, embroidered, went around the neighborhood, as Dante knew they would.

He felt he had fulfilled all his immediate family obligations when he went sledding with some pals on the night of Saturday, December 28.

CHAPTER FOUR

Megan Magee cupped a small amount of cold water in her hands, sloshed it over her face, licked the chocolate pudding from the corners of her mouth, dried her hands and face quickly, and whirled toward the bathroom door.

"Whoa, now, jeez, dry your face, girl, or the water'll freeze solid. It's that cold outside."

He held her arm, glanced over his shoulder slyly, and leaned close to his daughter's shining face.

Frankie Magee took his daughter's damp hand, pressed a folded dollar bill into it, rolled the fingers into a fist, and winked.

"Not a word to Her Ladyship," he said.

"Oh, Pop, gee, thanks."

"Well, what the hell, it's two days to Christmas. You and that nut-head friend of yours, Patsy, goin' to the Loew's Paradise? Now that's class."

He studied the face so like his own, except for her light amber eyes; his were bright blue, but they were fringed with the same bright orange of her thick hair. The small snub nose, the wise grin of a mouth and the tough Magee chin. A don't-mess-with-me face, handsome in a man, striking in a girl. He'd only prodded to tease her; Megan kept her own counsel. If it had to do with a friend and she didn't care to reveal it, forget it. His wife—Megan's mother—called it secret-keeping, as though it were some dark and sinful deed.

Frankie Magee believed in confidence kept. Collecting and assimilating and sorting through years of information, scraps of knowledge, deals, plans, connections among the mighty and the lowly, was Frankie's stock in trade. He worked for "the party"—meaning, of course, the Democratic Party, as though there could be any other in the Bronx, the Little Flower's coalition notwithstanding. If the girl knew enough to keep things to herself, it was all to the good.

"Well, then, you cleared it with your mom, did you? And you did your share of the dishes?"

Megan and her younger sister, Elizabeth, took turns helping their mother with the setting, the clearing, the washing, the drying. It was a constant battle, a daily event: your turn, no it isn't, liar, cheater—Ma! But today Megan dried every dish, quickly and expertly, put everything in place, whipped the dish towel smooth, slung it over the towel bar to dry.

"Okay, Ma, can I go now?"

"Wash up, first—you've got pudding all over yourself, Megan. For heaven's sake, a girl of twelve, your little sister had better manners than you from day one."

It was no time to comment on her little sister. She could take care of perfect little nine-year-old Elizabeth any day of the week, any minute of the day. She was a short, fat, bloated, redheaded Magee, without the smart, knowing Magee expression. Her light eyes were so pretty. She was always smiling, always clenching her teeth so that the dimples showed in each cheek. She always pretended not to hear when people said, Oh, isn't she pretty, so darling, so cute. Little shit. Mama's darling little girl.

That was what her mother had thought Megan would be: darlin' little girl, first Magee girl in two generations. Four sons for Frankie and Ellen, the oldest all but grown, and then this little redheaded Megan, a replica of her daddy. But she fooled them. Megan knew that mistakes were made in high places. It was one of the first things she'd absorbed as a wiry, restless, active, pushing, shoving, jumping, running little girl, knocking other little girls over, grabbing their toys, belting them, ganging up on them with the little boys.

That Megan Magee should have been a boy. Wrong plumbing.

She knew what that meant. She'd seen her brothers peeing standing up. They all did that, all the boys, they unbuttoned and peed against a tree in the lots, or they pulled their things out and waved them at each other.

Well, the hell with wrong plumbing, she'd have to make the best of what she had—or didn't have. Aside from that, she could beat the boys at almost anything. She was fastest, toughest, bravest, would take a dare, give a challenge, and keep her mouth shut when it came to not talking. Megan watched the girls in school with cold contempt: Sister, I didn't take the crayon, Louise Donnelly took it and put it in my pencil box to get me in trouble.

The sisters at St. Simon Stock knew who they were dealing with when Megan Magee came into their grade. The same sisters had had all four Magee sons, and Megan was just the next redheaded Magee in line. They all, in turn, were delighted by sweet, simpering Elizabeth, who seemed to feel her role in life was to show everyone how terrifically wonderful it was to be the best Magee daughter, Mama's little girl.

Little shit. Megan flashed on a great idea. Tonight, when she came home from the Paradise. Oh, yeah, little miss, I'll get you then.

She collided roughly with Elizabeth coming up the stairs, spun her around, clamped a hand over her sister's open mouth.

"Yell and I'll kill you," she whispered, then gave her sister a shove and ran without stopping through the narrow hallway and out the door onto the cold street. She'd started to run toward 181st Street, when her father honked at her from behind the wheel of his black Chrysler.

"You headin' up to the Paradise, kiddo, I'll give ya a lift. On my way to Fordham Road myself."

She ran around the car and slid in next to her father, glancing back at the house. It was a two-story, single-family house of red brick, one of the three side by side, one of the best of the single-family houses down the hill toward 180th Street. Dr. Wolfe had his office on the first floor of the next house, and his family lived upstairs. The Sugarmans owned the third house, and no one ever saw them. They were Jews from Germany and kept to themselves.

The Magee's car was two years old, gleaming and polished, kept in the garage behind the house. Frankie Magee bought a new car every four years. Megan realized that the Magee's had a lot more than most of the people on the block. When she forgot, her mother pointed out to her how lucky she was, how she lived in such a lovely house and had a car and how the family went out to Breezy Point in Rockaway for two weeks every year and how lucky they were in times when so many others found it hard to make ends meet, what with unemployment.

That was one of the things her father did; he helped get jobs for people. Frankie Magee was the man to see to get a job for the boy whose wages were needed if the old man was out of work. To get transfers and appointments on the Civil Service list, to get assignments. Megan knew her father could do all kinds of things, do all kinds of favors for people, although she never understood the source of his power. Just that he had it.

"Now, nothing you see or hear within the four walls of this house goes any further, you understand?" Ah, Jesus, her mother always felt she had to say that, whenever Megan happened to walk into a room and there was her dad, talking in his quiet way, a hand on some worried woman's shoulder, a friendly jab to some working stiff, a "don't worry about a thing at all, now, Tommy" to the father of one of her classmates. And her father would say to her mother, "Now Ellen, that's Megan there, not a teller of tales, like some curly-headed little plump girl whose name I could mention but out of kindness will not."

God, she loved her dad.

Whatever it was he did.

"Let me out at the corner, please, Dad. I gotta call for Patsy."

"Go on and get her. I'll drive yez up to the Paradise."

"Naw, that's okay."

He never insisted on something she really didn't want to do. He pulled up in front of the five-story building just around the corner on 181st Street.

"Well, there you are, Megan. Remember, now," he called out the old joke, "if you can't be good, for God's sake don't get caught. And if you *do* get caught, don't give 'em your real name."

"I'll just tell them, 'clear it with Frankie Magee.'"

"You are a fresh one," he said, not the way her mother said it, but with a gladness that made her glad too.

The building where the Wagners lived was something of an anomaly on the corner of the Grand Concourse, which was, of course, where the Jews lived. The five-story building was owned by the Steiglers, who had been friends and neighbors of the Wagners when they were all young together in Hamburg, in Germany. Somehow Mr. Steigler had made a great deal of money, and while he and his wife no longer lived in the immaculate building with its spotless tiled hallway floors, freshly painted stucco halls, shiny brass nameplates and mailboxes, the tenants were not only of German background, but most belonged to the same Lutheran church down the Grand Concourse, a few blocks below the Jews' Reformed temple.

Megan usually took the five flights soundlessly, two stairs at a time, arriving with her heart beating just a bit faster, her breath regulated. It was a game; she and Patsy would race up noiselessly, then turn and catapult down the short staircases, landing with double thuds, and be out the front door by the time the neighbors would rush to the hallway. They would ignore the opening of front windows, faces calling to them, "Shame! What sort of girls! I know who you are, Patsy Wagner, I'll tell your mother."

Patsy would stop running, turn, plant her hands on her narrow hips, boldly face up toward the window, and shout back, "Tell my *father*, for all I care."

Megan was in awe of her daring. Confronting a neighbor, any grownup, was not something Megan could get away with. But Patsy's father, Arnold Wagner, was a small man, with tiny neat features and gifted hands, who never raised his voice and seemed intimidated by his own active children. His tailor shop was around the corner on 181st Street, between the kosher butcher shop and the Chinese laundry. He rarely seemed to have anything to say for himself. He sat all day long hunched over his sewing machine, or kneeling down at the feet of customers, with a bunch of pins in his mouth, turning up hems or cuffs, altering long coats for the neighborhood's younger sisters or brothers. Patsy said she and her brother, Carl, planned one day to sneak up behind their father when he had a mouthful of pins, and yell suddenly to see what would happen if he swallowed the whole works.

She never told Megan exactly how it come about, but Carl had finally moved out of his parents' home completely. It had happened in stages. In the beginning, before they made their fortune, the Steiglers had lived in the apartment next to the Wagners. They didn't have much luck with babies: two had been stillborn, one died while still in the hospital, and then they gave up. Little Carl, charming, funny, lively, with his thick mop of yellow curls and bright blue eyes, would come next door to play with Auntie and Uncle Steigler until it became natural for him to spend as much waking time with them as with his parents. When he was nearly three years old, and Patsy was born, the Steiglers moved some of his toys and clothes into their place to make things easier for Arnold and Rose. The new baby had the colic and Lord knew how tiring that was and what a lively rascal was little Carl.

By the time Carl was of school age, the Steiglers had somehow made a great deal of money, though Patsy didn't know much about it. They bought a mansion in some fancy place on Long Island and began by taking Carl for the summer, out near the shore, away from the heat. Arnold, Rose, and little Patsy came for weekends, for a few days when they could.

Carl would come home to his parents' four-room apartment, to the narrow room he shared with his sister, to the quiet of the kitchen table where the clacking of his father's false teeth drove him crazy, and his mother's whispering made it intolerable. He would stare at his father, hunched over his plate as though over his sewing machine, shoveling the food in with small quick bites, whiping his chin quickly with the paper napkin; and he would long to be back at the Big House, as they called the Steiglers' place. The Big House, with honest-to-God maids and caretakers and a chauffeur-gardener who all lived better than the Wagners.

It was agreed, by the time Carl was to start the seventh grade, that he would live full-time out at the Big House, would attend the wonderful prep school, which would prepare him for the best college, which in turn would ready him to take over Uncle's many business interests.

It was after he had been a student for nearly a year, when he was fourteen and his sister nearly twelve, that Carl Wagner began to teach his younger sister new games, which Patsy in turn described to Megan.

Back at the apartment for a brief holiday, Carl knew his parents had raced around, gathering all those things Carl favored. Patsy would be sent up to a special bakery on Fordham Road for a pound of the most expensive cookies, warned not to sneak any of them on the way home; she and Megan were adept at sliding the paper-thin cookies from the sides of the box, and would both swear they'd been short-weighted. Father would work carefully, late into the night, custom-tailoring the expensive trousers and jackets his son's school required, adding custom darts to the fine cotton shirts, hand-stitching button holes, securing buttons, everything the best for a boy who would arrive with an armload of clothes to be repaired. Steigler would laugh and tell Arnold Wagner not to bother, the boy was so rough-and-tumble on the playing fields, so popular and doing so well, the clothes would be replaced, don't bother patching. But it wasn't patching that Arnold Wagner did. It was *custom tailoring,* and he insisted on handling his son's clothing. It was a small concession. It made the little man feel good, so what the hell.

It was when they were alone in the apartment, just Carl and Patsy, that he would teach her things he said she had to know—secret, dark things she must never, *ever* reveal to anyone, on pain of death. His threats were backed up with samples of pain inflicted so quickly, so sharply, and invisibly that Patsy knew he meant what he said. He would double-lock the apartment door after first checking the hallway. Both parents were at the shop around the corner, his mother repairing and finishing off sewing projects for the neighborhood women, their father kneeling, always kneeling. To Carl and later to Patsy, the shame of the image was tinged with hatred and contempt.

Alone in their narrow room with the twin beds, Carl taught Patsy lessons. On your stomach, he would order her, flipping her over roughly, holding her down. Bite on the pillow because it hurts at first, and if you make a sound I will kill you and throw your body out the window.

And he taught her what he had learned at prep school. The boys practiced on each other, he said, so that they would be good at it with the girls. And what he was doing to her wasn't the *real* thing. It didn't count for anything. Christ, she was still a virgin, he just thought that as his little sister she had a right to know all the things boys did to girls.

Patsy confided to Megan that it hurt a lot at first, and then, after a while, it changed. It didn't exactly feel good, but she felt other feelings, in, you know, the other part of her body. Around the front.

Megan bit her lip, eyes unblinking, trying to visualize the mounting, the moving, the terribleness. It was a mortal sin, she knew that instinctively. Even hearing about it made Megan fearful, as though she personally had been involved in something so dirty she wouldn't know how to confess it. And *should* she confess this? Was it *her* sin? Just listening to this? The Protestants were lucky—they didn't believe in sin.

Megan felt confused, contaminated and excited by what Patsy told her. She knew boys had their thing—their dick, they called it, prick, and their balls. Girls weren't supposed to know the names. Though of course she knew. Girls with brothers knew. But Megan had brothers, and none of them ever so much as *showed* her. And Carl had put it in his sister's mouth. When Patsy told her that, Megan covered her own mouth, hunched forward as though to vomit, and then they both couldn't stop laughing. They fell down on the grass in Echo Park, just beyond their neighborhood, where they went to climb the monkey bars, play in pick up ball games, tease girls, challenge boys. They rolled around and laughed and punched each other, wrestled with each other, first one on top and then the other, like boys do, pinning each other down, arms and legs, fists flying, Patsy's mouth coming close to her ear, she whispered, "Want to know what it felt like?"

Megan filled with panic, fear, terror. She arched her body and flung Patsy off. Instead of following up, pursuing her for the rest of the fight,

Megan turned and ran away, shaking her head, running all the way back home, not even aware of Patsy's taunts, not wanting to see her face, hear her words. Afraid of something inside herself, some feeling, some warmth, something different that she dared not confront.

Megan jabbed twice, waited, then twice again on the Wagner button in the downstairs hallway. Immediately there was a response: one-one-two-three. I'm on my way down.

Megan listened and could hear each thud, right from the top floor down to the first, and she turned and jumped down the steps to the outside door before Patsy could get there.

Patsy Wagner was small-boned, athletic in a wire-tight way, her body always poised for action, ready to spin one way or the other, to leap, respond, dart, strike out. Her face was beautiful; in repose, which was rare, it had a distant look, as though the girl was dreaming. There was a delicacy to her cheekbones and jawline, a vulnerability about her light blue eyes. Her nose was small and straight, her lips full and turned up for quick laughter. But always there was a wariness and pent-up tension, a need to run, explode, attack before she needed to defend herself. She and Megan were constantly at war with each other. They argued over senseless differences, pushed, shoved, smacked; but when a target presented itself, they joined forces. They played perfect basketball, two parts of one singleminded entity, passing the ball back and forth, darting, twisting, skillfully jumping and making the shot. When just the two of them played, they argued constantly. When they teamed against boys, they felt invulnerable in their quickness and knowledge of each other.

They hit the cold street running, hunching into the wind, collars turned up, scarves flying. They both wore hand-me-down corduroy pants, outgrown by older brothers. They had both argued long and hard against their parents' protests: girls don't wear boys' pants. Well, Megan Magee and Patsy Wagner did.

Megan whirled around suddenly and yanked Patsy's woolen hat from her head and pointed at and taunted the mop of long yellow curls. The normally lank, straight hair had been curled and tortured into sausage curls.

"My damn mother," Patsy said, roughly grabbing back the hat, jamming the curls out of sight. "We gotta go out to the Big House tonight, for Christ's sake."

"I thought tomorrow, Christmas Eve."

"So did I, but my mother said tonight."

Megan felt the sudden loss. The next two days, okay, there was going to be so much family at the Magee's house, every damn cousin and aunt and uncle, all her older brothers and their wives and kids. But then, the whole long week, there'd be nobody.

"Race ya to the corner," Megan shouted, running before the challenge was issued. Patsy was faster, so Megan needed just the slight edge.

Patsy caught up quickly. The cold air hurt, the pain hitting the chest hard, but pain never stopped Patsy, and Megan couldn't give in.

"Race you all the way to Krum's," Patsy called back, dancing in front of Megan.

"Hey!" Megan waved her mittened hand. "Hold it. Look."

She dug the dollar bill out of her pocket, slipped it inside her mitten. "My father gave me an extra. What'll we buy?"

They jogged along together, making their plans. It was going to be a *great* day at the Loew's Paradise. They would create havoc, drive people crazy, send ushers running, the manager would bang his head against the wall, all the emergency doors would go flying open, the matron would be grabbing kids left and right.

At Krum's they waited impatiently, the excitement building. They bought half a pound of red pistachio nuts each, carried the small boxes in paper bags, stuffed inside their jackets. The Loew's Paradise was a movie palace with a high bright blue sky, with moving clouds revealing bright pinpoints of stars. Along the walls, reaching up to the high ceiling, were archways and grooves containing statues, God knew who they were supposed to be. Seen in the dark, they looked like Roman or Greek gods. The children's section was along the right-hand side of the large theater, down front, cordoned off by velvet ropes and patrolled by a large woman in a stiff white uniform. She marched up and down, crashed into the rows of seats, grabbing at squirming children, hustled them along or yanked them out, her large hand catching hold of collars or arms or necks.

She worked hard for her money, and she took her job seriously. When Megan and Patsy had tried the first time to sit in the adult section, she'd whirled around, found them with her flashlight, and ordered them out.

"I'm sixteen," Patsy had said indignantly. At the box office she'd claimed to be eleven to get the kid's admission price. The matron was not to be fooled.

The two girls waited, slumped down in their seats, watching the stupid cartoons and the Flash Gordon serial. Finally the main feature began—it was *Naughty Marietta*—and the kids began catcalling, the boys loudly kissing the air, the girls screaming, the smallest kids racing for the bathroom.

Megan and Patsy slid out of their seats, walked up the aisle against the wall, out into the main lobby. They walked through the vastness of the lobby, watched the huge goldfish swimming around in the large marble pool while smaller kids tossed bits of candy to them. With the timing of burglars, they raced silently up the thickly carpeted staircase to the balcony. They slipped into the darkness, watched for the usher, then slipped quietly along the half-empty row, slumped down in their seats, and began to work on their pistachio nuts. They ate the salty meat and dropped the shells in the paper bags. Staring at the screen, considering themselves invisible, not really following or caring about the movie— they only liked gangster movies or stories about French Foreign Legion—but intent on their shell collection, neither noticed the figure of a man as he sat next to Patsy. She felt his presence, glanced down at the pressure against her thigh. Her hand over her mouth, she poked Megan.

"Huh?" Megan leaned forward, looking across Patsy. "Oh, shit. Let's go."

Damn it, it happened every time. That's why they made you sit in the kids' section. What they ought to do was make these pervos sit in the pervo-section and then they could all sit with handkerchiefs on their laps and do their dirty stuff sitting next to each other.

"Wait. Megan, gimme your shells. C'mon, hand them over."

Patsy pulled back slightly, not allowing the man's contact. He, masturbating intently, didn't notice. Patsy leaned over and whispered to Megan, then, ready, ordered, "*Now.*"

Both girls stood up suddenly. Patsy far more daring than Megan, grabbed the handkerchief from the man and dumped the shells on his lap, and both girls stepped on his feet as hard as they could. Before he could react, they were gone, running lightly, soundlessly, invisibly against the darkened walls.

Megan knew she could never talk to anyone about what men did in dark, hidden places. Certainly not to her mother. It was one of those things that men did, but it made *her* feel dirty. If they stayed put in the children's section, they wouldn't have a pervo next to them. If they would just follow the rules, these things wouldn't happen. But it seemed to happen, no matter what or where. She and Patsy could take off to explore an unfamiliar vacant lot, or hike through Van Cortland Park or maybe duck down the subway station entrance at 182nd Street and cross through the tunnel to the other side of the Grand Concourse. So many times, there was a man. Was it something about herself, or about Patsy, some signal they gave off, some curiosity—did they really, maybe, *want* these men to do these things? Megan shuddered. She felt unable to laugh it off as Patsy could, to comment on what the man was doing. Did you see the size of that thing? Patsy could take action, call out from a safe distance like a player in a game. But it was a game that left Megan feeling uncomfortable, contaminated.

Back in the children's section, she glanced at Patsy, who sat on her lower spine, attention focused on the screen, munching nuts methodically. Didn't *anything* bother Protestants?

They waited until the show was over and the next audience had settled in for the third show of the day. The News of the World came on with loud, dramatic music, and Patsy poked her with a sharp, bony elbow.

They went quickly, quietly, back to the balcony level, stood unmoving, their eyes getting used to the darkness again. The ushers were busy flashing light along the carpeted stairs, helping couples into their seats.

The loges, the most expensive ten rows in the theater, were empty. The two girls crouched low, moved carefully to the center aisle, and waited. The coming attractions were over and the feature film began. They glanced around and chose their moment. A completely coordinated team, they flung their bagfuls of pistachio shells in wide, sweeping arcs and were halfway down the carpeted stairway before the first cries came from the orchestra.

An usher appeared, running, calling out, but they were on the street before anyone could touch them. They ran into a steadily falling snow as the evening turned darker and a feeling of exhilaration and joy filled them.

They pretended to be in great jeopardy. Squads of men, armed and ruthless, were pursuing them, but they were too fast, too smart, they could outwit, outrun, and, if it came to that, outfight anyone. They raced across the Grand Concourse, slick and wet, dodging oncoming cars as though they were part of the conspiracy against them.

Finally they stopped in the doorway of a bakery, letting the game wind down.

Megan stared at Patsy's face, flushed and wet. "Jeez, you got red pistachio stains all over your mouth."

Patsy's face froze, she jutted it a few inches from Megan. "Look in the mirror, clown, so do you."

They raced along the Concourse, scooped up snow from the fenders

of cars, scrubbed at their faces, then attacked each other. They reached
the triangle of benches wedged into a sliver of the Grand Concourse,
directly across the street from Patsy's apartment building. They walked
on the seats of the benches, empty of the old women and the young
mothers with little kids and the goody-goody girls who sat quietly on
summer days, reading or playing jacks in the warm weather.

Finally, perched on the back rest, feet on the seat slats, their day was
winding down.

"Got your tree up?" Megan asked.

"It took exactly ten minutes," Patsy said. "It's about two feet high
and Carl wouldn't even help put the stand on it. He said it was a waste
of time, since we weren't going to be here for Christmas. He said that
at the Big House, the tree is twelve feet tall and most of the ornaments
are antiques. Your tree up?"

Megan shrugged. "You know my father. Christmas Eve before we go
to midnight mass. He's been getting the lights all worked out and he's
got all the ornaments set out. So when will you be back?"

"I dunno. There's a lot of things to do out there. There's a skating
rink, and boy, I hope it snows hard. There's great hills. And they have
parties and stuff."

Patsy began to talk with animation, as though this were really what
she wanted to do: go out to the big mansion on Long Island and spend
the holidays with the Steiglers, who corrected her table manners and
grammar, who told her running in the house was not the proper thing,
who checked her hands and face as though she was three years old. But
not to worry. They'd work on her.

"They give you good presents?"

"Yeah. Probably a new bike this year. Hey, if they do, you can have
my old bike. It's only three years old. If you want it."

"Okay. So they gonna send their Cadillac and their chauffeur?"

"Just like in the movies." Patsy laughed. "You should see my mother
and father. They die every single minute from the time we get into the
big black car until they take us back here. They hardly say a damn thing
the whole time, they're scared shitless."

"So why do they go?"

Patsy frowned. "Damned if I know. I guess because they grew up
together. They were kids together."

Megan leaped up, landed with her face turned to catch the heavy
snow that was coating them like frosting.

"Well, Patsy, when I'm rich and famous, I'll send *my* car to pick you
up so you can come to *my* mansion and celebrate the holidays."

They began jabbing, poking, hopping, roughhousing. "Yeah, you do that, only I won't die waiting for you to become rich and famous. I'll marry some old fart and help him die and leave me millions and then *I'll* invite *you* and your poor husband and poor kids to come and see how the other half live."

There was a loud, shrill, jagged whistling noise. Patsy looked up and saw her brother Carl leaning out the open window of her apartment.

"Hey, get your ass up here, dummy. We're gonna leave in a few minutes. Move it."

Patsy waited until the window slammed closed, then softly she said, "Why don't you just die, shitface."

They walked together to the entrance of the apartment building.

"Well, have a good time with the rich people. Make sure you use the right forks and spoons. Don't drop anything in your lap. Don't put your elbows on the table, and don't spit in your soup."

"At least I won't have to wash the dishes."

"Hey, I got little cousins to do that."

"Well, I got *servants* to do that."

They played a quick game of touch-tag, gotcha–gotcha back, until Carl's shrill whistle blasted down at them again.

"Have a good Christmas."

"Yeah, you too."

CHAPTER FIVE

Miri O'Brien was thirty-five and pregnant with her fifth child when she learned that her father had died. Her sister Rhea, a year older than she, her one remaining contact with her family, came one night to tell her. He had been an old man, a great-grandfather who had buried four of his own children literally—and his daughter Miriam figuratively—as well as two of his three wives, and many other relatives.

Miri knew that in her father's eyes her life had been one continuous journey toward early death. As a sixth child, the fourth girl in a family that finally numbered eight girls and eight boys, Miriam fitted into the center of her family's life. Her chores were simple things, picking up clothes, dusting and tidying, helping prepare food. No one realized, or cared, that she was an excellent student, from the first day at kindergarten all through the eighth grade. She kept her abilities hidden. She knew that in her family, as in the families of all her relatives and neighbors in the crowded, noisy, busy Lower East Side, what a girl did in school counted for nothing. What was important was that she could sew carefully and quickly enough to get a job, and contribute her bit to the family's jar of money.

Because Rhea did the hard thing first, went to high school for two years, where she learned to type and take shorthand and bookkeeping, it was easier for Miriam to follow. But she wanted something different. She planned and calculated and waited and yes, prayed to the Almighty, He who was so powerful and terrible He could not be named, to give her the courage and the wisdom needed to tell her mother, who would then have to tell her father, that she wanted to be a nurse.

Miriam had all the information she needed, all the applications, the forms for teachers to fill out, the papers that would admit her. She had the qualifications, the dedication. All she needed was permission. And money for tuition. She had it all worked out. She would continue her baby-sitting jobs, her part-time evening job at Moise's market. She could get work at the hospital. They had plans for scholarships.

Her mother, always pregnant, her face a small worried oval, her hands forever busy with something, cooking or cleaning, polishing or sewing, washing, ironing, fussing, pulling a comb through thick hair, braiding, tying, dressing a child, smoothing, never just reaching out to pat, to touch, but always with a very specific adjustment, never any affection involved; her mother was one to be helped, not burdened. How could Miriam ask this thing? Her mother's face was always sorrowful, always ready to dissolve at some new disaster; she had lost two babies to pneumonia, she knew what tragedies could happen. Why must Miriam ask this thing, this special treatment? She was just a girl. Did Miriam think this was fair?

Miriam was her parents' first child born in the United States. She was an American.

It was not easy, but Miriam Greifinger finally attended and graduated from the Bellevue School of Nursing.

Tom and Miri met in the emergency room at Fordham Hospital one cold winter night. He had accompanied a jumper who seemed to have some life still in him.

Young Patrolman Tom O'Brien found it hard to look at the kid. What in God's name could he have been thinking, jumping from the roof of the six-story building where he lived with his family. He had ended up impaled on the iron gate that closed off the inner courtyard, and it had taken the rescue squad men nearly an hour to saw him free. They carried him to the ambulance with a spike protruding through his stomach. All during that time the kid was conscious, his family standing around saying a rosary, his mother deadly calm while his father became hysterical and passed out. This young nurse was the first to see him under a good light. She moved quickly, efficiently, her face showing nothing of alarm or horror. She glanced up at Tom, caught something in his face, and gestured him away.

"I have to stay with him," he said. He held up his notebook as though that explained his presence.

"You'll have time to get all that later," she told him firmly.

She moved aside as the team of doctors approached, and then stepped back as the parish priest arrived and gave the dying boy the last rites. She watched Tom O'Brien as he watched the boy die, and then he watched her.

He noticed that when the priest finished, everyone around the boy mouthed a prayer and crossed himself, except the nurse. She just bit her lip—her only show of emotion, although when she looked up finally, directly into Tom's eyes, he caught the caring.

There was something so clean and fine and strong about this young woman, a toughness and a womanliness that went beyond her age. She couldn't have been more than twenty-one or twenty-two.

She finished her share of the chores, then went to the staff room for a cup of coffee. Tom O'Brien, his heavy uniform coat thrown over a chair, his plaid flannel shirt sticky around his neck, stood up and nodded at her.

"Tough way to go," he said, indicating his notebook, which told the bare facts of a young man's death.

"Hard on his family. He's out of it. They've got to live with it."

She sounded angry, but he had a feeling she used anger as a shield. He had done that himself, many times, in many terrible situations.

They sat quietly, not saying much, comfortable in each other's company.

Tom O'Brien fell in love with Miriam Greifinger—who called herself Miri Grey—within two minutes of seeing her at the side of the dying jumper.

It took Miri Grey a little longer, but it was a quick and passionate courtship.

They faced the obvious problems of differing backgrounds without concern. Each was a strong individual. This was their own business and they would do what they could to minimize it. They lied to his family.

There was no need to lie to her family. Her father declared her dead. Her family mourned her lost life, sat shiva for their deceased daughter-sister, buried her in their hearts. Her mother died a year later in a terrible, unsuccessful pregnancy. Her father remarried after a year and continued expanding his line of descendants. He named one of his new daughters Miriam, after his dead daughter.

To the O'Briens, who either believed or did not believe, Miri Grey was presented as an orphan, totally without a family history. They had all been destroyed in a fire in upstate New York when Miri was an infant. She had no memory of them. She had been raised in a state orphanage without any particular religion, since her family records had been lost in the fire and no one knew much about them.

They were married by Father Murphy in his study, and while Miri Grey O'Brien agreed to raise her children as Catholics, she did not herself convert. She was a silent bystander who attended church on special days, but did not partake.

When she was pregnant with her first child, Miri asked Rhea to tell their father. This was to be, after all, his grandchild.

Rhea loved her sister but saw that nothing but the truth would finally allow Miri to be free of her past and get on with her future. She reported to Miri what their father had said:

"A dead woman can only give birth to an abomination."

All during her first pregnancy, Miri waited for something terrible to happen: a spontaneous abortion; a death in the womb; a breach, an abnormal child.

All of her first four pregnancies were substantially the same. Nausea the first two months; radiant good health until the last month; heartburn, discomfort, too much retention of fluid in the ninth month. Good, strong labor—two healthy sons and two healthy daughters.

Her fifth pregnancy, when she was thirty-five years old, was so easy she could hardly believe it. No morning sickness; no moods or craving or ankle swelling. Her labor was exactly on time. The contractions began strongly, went very quickly, and her fifth child, Eugene Sebastian O'Brien, was born without complications.

The only discomfort she felt was when the doctor came to her bedside instead of a nurse to give her the baby.

"What's wrong?"

The doctor shrugged. "With a war-horse like you, what could be wrong?"

"Don't patronize me," she said in her best nurse-in-charge voice. "What's the problem?"

"Maybe no problem. We're not sure."

He spoke quickly, quietly. The child seemed perfect. Seven pounds, three ounces, nineteen inches long, all toes and fingers in place, all the right equipment. Even a head of silvery blond hair some two inches long.

But there might be a problem with his eyes. Of course, that would be hard to determine in a newborn, but he felt she should be informed.

The abomination her father had predicted.

She lay back on her pillow, breathing in long, hard gasps as it flooded through her. Did she think, really, truly, in the center of her being, did she believe He who was too terrible to name would let her off that easily? Her father, who had studied these things every day of his life, knew things she could never know. And now would find out.

The infant in her arms was beautiful. His color was faintly pink, his features tiny and well defined, his eyes locked in sleep. She held him, studied him intently, and felt a chill run through her body, starting at the base of her neck, running down her spine, and turning into a sharp icicle in the pit of her stomach.

The locked eyes snapped open and stared. They were almost totally colorless. Two circles defined by a pencil-thin line, pinpoint pupils. Eyes of ice. Eyes that could stare holes through walls.

The child had been born with the eyes of her father.

"His eyes are all right," she told the doctor. "He isn't blind."

The doctor nodded. There was no way at this point to be sure, but if it comforted the mother, let her be so certain.

Of course, Miri was right.

She knew what she could never tell another living soul. *The child was possessed by a dybbuk.* The father who had condemned her for all time, who had died just before this pregnancy, had entered her womb and existed in the small body of this beautiful, special child.

When his baby brother, Charley, was born just thirteen months later, the silvery blond Eugene was not only toilet-trained, but had been completely weaned from the bottle. Within a month of his birth, he rejected his mother's breast, more content with a bottle, and within a few months he was happier with a cup. She noticed how he carefully pulled back from the admiring hands that reached out to stroke him, caress his shining head, play with the magical whitish hair. He avoided any unnecessary touch, and she felt his small, slender, yet strong body stiffen against anything more than necessary contact during his bath, at bedtime, anytime. Everyone commented on his maturity, his independence. He walked at nine months. He spoke hundreds of words and short sentences before his first birthday. He rarely cried. He was pleasant, easygoing. He seemed to accept the presence of a baby brother with relief; now he would not be the focus of attention.

As Miri watched him, the child watched her. There was a secret between them that could never be revealed. But she knew that he knew.

Though everyone, including her husband, Tom, was surprised that she became pregnant so soon after Eugene's birth—their other children were spaced at two- and three-year intervals—for Miri it was a deliberate pregnancy. She had decided that the dybbuk would not rob her of one last loving and loved child.

Eugene was five when he had his first epileptic attack. His mother was neither frightened nor surprised; after all, she had grown up watching her father suddenly waver, faint, his body arching in spasms, shaking, frothing, his eyes rolling upward until they disappeared. She calmly maintained the safety of the small, convulsing body. When those around her in the playground marveled at her calmness, she claimed it was her nursing background.

At home she merely exchanged a deep, long stare with those white eyes. Yes. I know you. What I don't know is what you want of me.

The child regarded his mother without expression.

Eugene was an excellent student. Teachers who remembered his older brothers and sisters were delighted by the boy. The less perceptive, less sophisticated teaching nuns were enchanted by his beauty and his manners. The wiser ones regarded him with something close to awe. It was as though a Presence were among the children at St. Simon Stock.

The parish priest, Father Murphy, noticed nothing special about Eugene O'Brien. A very pretty lad, a good boy, who worked hard and didn't cause the good sisters any problem.

His assistant, Father Kelly, knew that this academically gifted child was special. He was also lithe and lean, athletic and a team player. He was slow to anger, but when faced with a great deal of provocation, the silvery boy responded with his fists.

In Father Kelly's opinion, it was in religion that Eugene excelled. The practice, participation, and extraordinary understanding that Eugene showed was significant. The only complaint any teacher ever had about Eugene was his questioning nature. Of course, the good Sisters of Mercy had no answers to give: Faith is based on faith. Period.

By the time he was a sixth-grader, the boy had begun to receive special attention from Father Kelly. Not only was Gene the best altar boy any priest could pray for, but he was totally involved—his emotion, his understanding, and his soul—in the holy rituals.

It was a foregone conclusion, at least to Father Kelly, that Eugene would enter a seminary.

Miri was silent the night the boy told his parents of his vocation. She did not understand the word. Later, when they were alone, Tom tried to explain to her what a privilege it was for a child to become a priest. A nearly overwhelming gift from God.

"Maybe because I'm not a Catholic, Tommy. I don't know. I don't understand much of it."

"Well, maybe it's time you did," her husband said.

It was not enough that she had given all six of her children to his Church. They wanted her. Had always wanted her. The priest had come, through the years, to talk to her about her conversion. Told her what a wonderful gift it would be to her husband, to her children, to strengthen the family ties with the Church.

The nuns came and told her that when her husband and children died, they would be able to die within God's grace and would spend eternity in heaven. She could not enter heaven unless she converted.

In dealing with the priests, she had been polite and noncommittal. In dealing with the nuns, she was brusque and tough. After all, these were the same women who warned her that she had no right to work part-time at her nursing profession while she still had school-age children. By and large, she considered them stupid, ignorant, undereducated women whose childlike devotion to the parish priest was pathetic.

Miri told them flat-out to mind their own business.

Just as she had raced the two blocks from her apartment to the school when her firstborn son, Michael, came home at lunchtime with the hand-shaped bruise across his smooth pink cheek. Sister Margaret Veronica, the fourth-grade teacher, indignantly defended her right to control this boy, who was a scamp, a mischief-maker, a daydreamer. The smell of starch and dry age nearly choked Miri, and she spoke in a low and controlled but furious voice. "This is *my* son Michael, and if you have a problem with him, you call me or you call his father. *You* do *not* touch him." And then, in a whisper that made her words all the more terrible, Miri O'Brien said, "If you ever lay a hand on any of my children, Sister, I'll come up here and knock your head off!"

Obviously no one had ever said such a terrible thing to Sister Margaret Veronica, and she pulled back and gasped as though she had actually been struck.

Miri whirled away, not trusting herself, but turned back when the nun spoke.

"Oh, I know you, Mrs. O'Brien. I know all about you, and don't you think that I don't."

Miri never told her husband or anyone else about the encounter. But no nun ever again laid a hand on any of her kids.

Eugene wanted the seminary as much as the Church wanted him. Miri lay awake at night, wondering what it might mean. All his life, Eugene had seemed to be a spectator to his family's life: remote, unattached, sometimes seeming amused, sometimes disdainful. He was always polite, never fresh-mouthed or rough like the others. Never a problem, always the exemplary child. The epilepsy seemed under control. Through the years he'd had four grand-mal seizures and several petit-mal. As Eugene grew older, he was able to recognize a precipitating event or combination of events. He would immediately remove himself, if not physically then emotionally, from a danger point, as though he were the decisive arbiter of his own illness.

Between mother and son there were unspoken, unacknowledged understandings. His gaze, when turned toward her, was neither friendly nor hostile. Had she read meaning into those ice eyes that the boy did not intend? Was it all in her head? Was this nonsense, some craziness of her own, this belief in a dybbuk?

No.

She had been raised on the stories of her family. Dybbuks and golems and witches and ghosts and evil spirits were, indeed, loose in the world. The folk stories, the scary traditions, were not just to frighten naughty children, but to warn and inform.

They existed in different forms in the religion of her children. She looked over their religious textbooks at night, alone, unobserved. Their world was filled with martyrs who suffered in explicitly described horrible ways at the hands of demons. Her children faced Hell if they sinned against the edicts of their Church and their God. She wondered at the sad-eyed Jesus, stretched on the Cross, at the anguish of his mother as she knelt, watching. She worried at the terror to which they were exposed. If her own inner world was real, was not theirs?

When he finally left for the seminary, Miri admitted to herself that her feeling of loss was mixed with a feeling of relief, no longer to have the strange boy living in her home, not to feel her son's body stiffen away from her casual or accidental touch; not to have the presence of some knowing being whose merest glance could penetrate and pass judgment on her very being. He wrote home each week, short, polite, distant letters of inquiry. How was she? His father? His family? He reported on the weather: cold, snow coming early. On his schoolwork: with the help of Our Lord, he would survive. In his description of his daily routine, the regimented minutes of every hour of his waking life, ruled and directed, examined and scrutinized, there was never a hint of complaint. It was the life he had chosen, the way he wanted. The tests and tasks were, to Eugene, the necessary devices by which he must measure himself.

Miri handed on his letters to her husband, to the other children, without comment. She knitted warm sweaters, mufflers, socks. She wanted to prepare special foods for his visit home for the Christmas holidays. But she literally could not think of any special cake or dessert that Eugene favored. He had always approached food, no matter how prepared, as something necessary to good health.

Within hours of his homecoming, he was part of the holiday turmoil of his family. Returning married children, with their wives, husbands, children, cousins, aunts, uncles, filled Miri's hours. There was an exchange of visits back and forth across the street with one of her husband's sisters, Ellen, married to Frankie Magee. Some relatives from Pennsylvania had come to sleep over for a night or two.

The kids all seemed wild and uncontrollable, but the mothers saw to it that they behaved within allowable limits. They ate too much, played too roughly, broke new toys, compared their gifts with the gifts the others received, whined a little, complained a little, teased, joked, and got away with a few swear words during tussles.

Good kids.

All of them, cousins and young nephews and nieces, even his brothers and sisters, seemed to treat Eugene with the kind of deference they displayed toward adults. They vied for his approval, and worried they had been too rough or casual with their language in his presence.

Once Eugene turned and stared directly into Miri's eyes, and she gasped as though caught out at something shameful. His eyes seemed to impale her; then he shrugged boyishly, good-naturedly, including her in exasperation at all the commotion of children and grownups alike, as though she, as well as he, had no part in all of this. This *Christmas* celebration of excess in eating and playing and unguarded emotion.

She knew she thought too much about Eugene. He was just a boy.

But she knew other things, too.

Miri was relieved that the family had a good time, stayed for a few days, then all went home. She was glad to clean up, to gain control again of her home ground. And she was glad that it snowed steadily and that the night was crisp and clear, the snow clean and well packed, so that the boys would stay out playing and sledding and making forts and having snowball fights.

Most of all, she was glad that Eugene was as eager to go out with the rest of the kids as Charley was. He volunteered to dig around in the storeroom for an old family sled.

As he was going out into the cold night, Miri spoke to him sharply, as she would to any of her children. "You pull that hat down over your ears, Eugene, you don't want an ear infection!"

In an abandoned, boyish reaction, he pulled his woolen hat down over his face, clowned around for a few moments, then shoved it back up, revealing his wide forehead.

"You know what your trouble is, Ma?" he asked. "You worry too much."

They held it between them for a split second, then the boy winked and his mother waved him away.

It was a rare exchange between them.

CHAPTER SIX

Charley was the last-born O'Brien child, and the most difficult birth. He was a breach baby, and his mother labored nearly twenty-two hours before a cesarean was performed, producing a sturdy, round-faced boy with blond hair, brown eyes, and a loud, healthy yell.

This child of apple cheeks had an easy nature from the beginning, and everyone called him Charley-Dear. The first word he ever spoke was "dear," and the nickname stuck until he was of school age and let it be known that just plain "Charley" was it.

Charley seemed to love everyone who came into his world, but above all he adored his brother Eugene. The relationship was puzzling. Though a year younger, Charley acted instinctively as his brother's protector. It wasn't Eugene's fault that he was perfect, that he was a better-than-A student, an excellent athlete, a fine altar boy, a good friend. Charley sensed, without questioning, that Eugene's position in the family was that of the "special" child, much the way Stevie, the retarded kid in the Hoolihan family across the street, was a special case. The others looked out for him, made allowances for him, as they did for no other.

Eugene would join his brother and the other boys in a pickup game of stickball or basketball or handball or trading baseball cards, but he didn't have the *passion* for playing that Charley and the other kids had. When Charley played—at anything—his entire existence was subsumed in the activity. He played to win, and winning exhilarated him; losing made him feel angry, but always at himself. Charley knew that Eugene played competently, that he was a natural athlete, but he was only partly there, not totally engaged. Win or lose, it was all the same to Eugene: Just a game, Charley. Don't take it so hard. Don't make such a big deal of it.

Eugene rarely fought with his fists, and then only if attacked. He preferred to walk away, but if that didn't work he fought hard, fast, anxious to get the whole thing over with; when it was, he would extend his hand to his opponent. Charley liked a good fight, sock and smash and roll around until you exhausted each other, by which time the offense was usually forgotten by both combatants. Charley figured that Eugene probably prayed for the other kid. He never discussed this with his brother; it was just Charley's assumption.

There were a great number of things that Charley assumed but never discussed. Family things, neighborhood things.

He knew his mother's family was a secret never to be discussed. All dead, somewhere upstate, in some fire. Period. And he knew there were other darknesses in his father's family, which his parents talked about late at night when the kids were supposed to be sleeping.

That his father's sister, Ellen, married to Frankie Magee, his favorite cousin Megan's mother, didn't like Frankie's sister, the beautiful Aunt Catherine. Called her a whore, which Charley knew was a bad thing—he looked it up in the dictionary. Aunt Catherine lived with a man much older than she, and they weren't married; every now and then, Catherine would turn up on Ryer Avenue, move in with her brother's family for a few days or a few weeks, and then go back to "the old man"—whoever he was.

His cousin Megan loved Aunt Catherine, who was slim like a movie star, and had red hair that glistened, and wore lots of makeup and fancy clothes.

Sometimes Charley's mother would say nice things about Catherine, defending her against Ellen's complaints; but his father would take his sister's side, telling his wife to shut up and mind her own business. After all, what the hell kind of people did *she* come from? And Charley would wonder: What kind of people *did* she come from?

Charley's father was a police lieutenant and he was on the captain's list. Frankie Magee, his brother-in-law, looked out for Tom O'Brien, but Charley didn't understand how he could do that. Frankie was something his father called a "bag man," but that didn't make too much sense. As far as Charley knew, as much as Megan told him, Uncle Frankie worked for the "boss" at party headquarters in the Bronx, and he knew a lot of judges and district attorneys and lawyers and district leaders. Uncle Frankie somehow got jobs for people, and Charley knew how important that was.

Not everyone had a job, and there were people who had to take handouts in shame. The worst shellacking Charley ever got from his father came when he was one of a group of kids who made fun of Timmy O'Leary's clothes, taunting him, asking him if his holey sweater came from the Home Relief grab bag. It was one of the few times his mother didn't stop his father's strap, and after the beating she didn't comfort him but told him his cruelty was unacceptable. She told him about people having pride, feeling shame. Explained to him that Jim Ryan's father went out every day, dressed in his worker's clothes, looked all day long for an honest day's work, and returned home at the end of a workday, pretending he had a steady job. Everyone knew that. It was a neighborhood secret—there were plenty of men just like Tim O'Leary who, through no fault of their own, were unemployed. But they were entitled to their pride, and what Charley had done was heartless.

Charley cried half the night over his own cruelty, for he was by nature a kind, cheerful, and loving boy who would never intentionally hurt anyone. He liked people; he didn't call them kikes or guineas or Polacks or hunkies. He had friends all over the neighborhood, and he judged them only by what kind of guys they were.

Everyone said Charley O'Brien would grow up and become an animal doctor, a vet. From the time he was small, he brought home injured birds, bleeding cats, limping dogs. He once came home with a broken tooth and a bloody mouth for intervening when some guy down toward Valentine Avenue was whacking the hell out of a puppy. He got socked, but he grabbed the puppy and ran like hell. His father straightened that guy out. In his lieutenant's uniform, he spelled out the law. A grown man socking a kid of Tom O'Brien's gets off easy—with a broken nose (the result of his first punch) and some busted toes (the result of his size-thirteen right foot coming down hard and unexpectedly on the guy's feet). And anyone like that didn't deserve to have a puppy. The guy had a house filled with animals, all showing signs of abuse. Tom O'Brien and his friends took care of things. While the guy was in the emergency room at Fordham Hospital, telling the sad story of dropping a load of bricks on his feet and falling on his face from the pain, a truck pulled up to his house, and the dogs and puppies, cats and kittens, were loaded aboard and taken to a farm upstate.

"Charley," he told his son, "next time come to me first." Tom sounded stern, but he was proud of the kid. He stood up for what he felt strongest about. He wasn't afraid of confrontation. And the boy had the best heart of anyone Tom O'Brien knew. He just hoped the boy would toughen up enough so that the world out there wouldn't hurt him.

Maybe the kid would do well to become a veterinarian. There were enough cops in the O'Brien family: both older sons, nephews, cousins.

Tom O'Brien was proud of his kids, all of them—he would never admit it, because it wasn't something he consciously thought of or would probably even agree with—but Charley was his favorite child.

When Eugene went to the seminary, his younger brother missed his company in the room they shared. Though it was a strain at times to have a special brother, he loved Eugene and missed him and was glad that when he came home for Christmas vacation he wasn't changed. He was still Eugene, even, perhaps more so.

It seemed strange to Charley, the way his mother sometimes watched Eugene. She might seem the same to other people, but Charley felt her tension, her extra quietness around his brother, and she was not by nature a quiet woman. Maybe the fact that she wasn't a Catholic—he knew that much about her, but that was all—had something to do with it. Maybe she was puzzled by the prospect of having a son who was going to be a priest.

Charley wondered if his mother thought this was a scary thing. After all, priests were not like other people.

Charley wondered how it was going to be: his brother, Eugene, a priest. Well, he had always been someone apart, so he was probably born to the cloth. Charley couldn't imagine any other reason to want to become a priest. Not that he didn't respect them, and the sisters and the Church. It was just that Charley felt the Church and the school were all just one part of life. He knew there was a wide world outside and that one day, somehow, he would explore it. Like the adventurers in the *National Geographic* magazines that Megan hid away for him. The dirty pictures were exciting, but even though he'd never admit it, the stories about other parts of the world, whole different peoples living on the same planet, unknown and almost unknowable, excited Charley. Someday.

He was glad it had snowed on Christmas and for the next couple of days. If they hadn't had the snow, the sledding and the forts and the snowball fights, he and Eugene might have been uncomfortable with each other.

But the air was cold and clean and the guys were planning to charge down Snake Hill. They would slip away casually: not everyone was included, just the guys who could take care of themselves in case they encountered the tough guys from Webster Avenue who thought they owned Snake Hill. Charley hoped the Webster Avenue guys wouldn't show up. He just wanted the fun and excitement of that great, dangerous, twisting hill.

Of course, if the toughs *did* show up, Charley would have to hold his own. It was just that he really didn't love fighting, for real, and he hoped it wouldn't be necessary. He wondered what Eugene would do, if it came to a real fight. Bless them? Charley grimaced and shook his head. That wasn't fair. His brother would do whatever he had to do. Period.

CHAPTER SEVEN

When he was twelve years old, Ben Herskel decided he would no longer attend Hebrew school three days a week after school. Since he had no intention of being a Jew, he no longer wanted to waste valuable time that could be put to better use. He was a large, husky, quick, athletic boy with dark red hair, dark brown eyes, and smooth clear skin, and was seen to be utterly fearless in the presence of the goyim who followed the Jewish boys from the temple after classes. The others depended on Ben to protect them, to see them to safety. His real friends were the kids from St. Simon. He was their equal in running and wrestling and softball and stickball and Johnny-on-a-pony and ringo-levio, all the games the Jewish kids were afraid to play.

Fight back, he would tell them, shoving a yeshiva boy's reluctant shoulder; stand up to them. But their mothers had told them to be nice. To get along. To ignore. If they studied hard, one day they would be professional men.

On the day his sister Deborah came home in tears because of what her teacher had said to her, Ben made up his mind and told his parents. He did not want to be a Jew. He just wanted to be an American, like everyone else. He would not continue Hebrew school. What was the point? Even his father only went to *shul* on High Holy Days.

His father, Hymie, shrugged. Nothing ever seemed to anger him. So, I'm not a good Jew, he admitted. But I am a Jew, and so are you.

Dora and Hymie Herskel, the parents, were small people with pale faces, who looked alike. They were first cousins, but the resemblance was more than genetic. Each day, clad in identical long white aprons, rimless glasses sliding down snub noses, hair wispy and graying, they moved about the luncheonette–candy store with a rhythm perfected by years of seven-day weeks. While Dora put up the huge vat of coffee first thing in the morning, and buttered the rolls and bagels, wiped the marble countertop, filled the containers with the chopped egg and tuna salad she'd made the night before, checked the cream cheese, cleaned the jelly container, unwrapped the ham and baloney the goyim butcher's boy delivered, stacked the long loaves of rye and white, ready for the morning rush of policemen from the precinct house across the street, either going on the morning tour or off the midnight, Hymie did the physically heavy work. He hoisted the stacks of newspaper, broke the heavy string (which he carefully wrapped around his hand and saved), and spread the papers on the outside stand and weighted them down with small iron bars. He carried the cartons of milk and boxes of fresh Danish and doughnuts into the store. He moved things, arranged things, swiped at the floor with a dry mop, having washed it down the night before with clean, soapy water. He spritzed and polished the sliding glass doors of the penny-candy case, which were smudged by the grimy hands of the children who came and served themselves during the daytime. He checked the cookie cases on the counter, made sure everything shone that needed to.

There was a pattern throughout the day: first the morning rush, then a quiet time to catch up on the newspapers over a cup of coffee, talk with some older people who came to share some news, drink some tea, munch a bagel. The grocer next door came at ten o'clock exactly for his fast scrambled eggs, bacon, and coffee; his wife twenty minutes later.

By noon the Herskels were in constant, synchronized motion. The high school kids from St. Simon Stock came for lunch, to play the jukebox, to smoke a forbidden cigarette, to flirt, laugh, make noise. Dora took the orders, called them over her shoulder to Hymie, who spun back and forth from the counter to the griddle. Hamburgers sizzled, buns toasted, eggs fried, sandwiches were made by hands that moved in a blur of activity. Hot soup, simmering in a huge pot, was ladled, crackers in small packets balanced against the saucer, soup dripping over the sides of the bowl.

For Ben and his sister, the luncheonette was an extension of their home. At the end of a school day, their snack was set out in the last of the five booths. They went over their homework, discussed their day's events with their parents, who kept a quick and seemingly casual eye on the progress of their children. The apartment immediately behind the storeroom consisted of a kitchen large enough for the four of them to sit down to eat together, although this rarely happened; two bedrooms; and a bathroom. The only time they felt the need for more space was when, from time to time, some cousin or other distant relative, newly arrived in America, needed a place to stay, just for a while. They'd open a cot, they'd manage.

When he spent time with his goyim friends, Ben knew they accepted him because he was as tough as they were, because he was a fearless competitor. When they left the neighborhood, moved to a playground for some basketball, and other kids would jeer, "Hey, who's the yid?" Ben's friends would explain, "Hey, he's a Jew but he's okay."

Ben hated everything attached to being a Jew. Things he noticed about his parents left him breathless with rage. He watched as his father served "coffee and" to the endless stream of cops in the morning. They slurped and shoveled in doughnuts and Danish, sometimes paid, sometimes not. His father never asked for the money. Some guys from the precinct would come in at lunchtime, just before the rush of schoolkids, and hand Hymie a list: six sandwiches, a couple of egg creams, some Cokes. "And, Hymie, throw in a little extra, ya know? Some a' that potato salad Dora makes, and hey, for the captain, how's about next time you make some a'that chopped liver for the family, you make a little extra for him?" With a wink, a nod. A favor, Hymie.

As though his parents didn't have to pay money for every item in the store. Kids stole penny candy, every single day. Sometimes his mother stopped them, but always gently, as the kid filled the small brown paper bag with seven cents' worth of candy and handed Dora a nickel. You are on the honor system, his father told the kids, who were born thieves, who must have thought his parents were stupid immigrant morons. His mother would say softly, "Johnny, you didn't count so good today, ya gonna gimme two more pennies, or what do you wanna put back?"

"Kick 'em out," Ben would say. "Don't let 'em come back. They're goniffs, they steal from you."

His father would make a soft sound, a sigh, he would shrug. "Some big goniffs, they're gonna grow up and rob banks, they learned to steal from Hymie Herskel. They're children, they'll learn."

And the cops: "Well, they take from everybody, it's built into the job. They give a special look, late at night, that the lock is on the door, nothing bad is happening. Yes, it's their job, but so you give a little extra, you get a little extra. Goodwill, it's called goodwill."

But there was no goodwill involved in his sister's tears. Deborah was a tall, thin, gray-eyed girl of ten, an A student in the fifth grade. Miss Hewitt was her teacher. Ben knew Miss Hewitt. Miss Hewitt had never made *him* cry.

It was suppertime. The luncheonette was empty and the parents sat in the back booth, the children opposite. Deborah had waited all day and now she told them.

"She said, when I got up to recite the poetry, she said, in front of everyone, she said . . ."

The small mouth quivered, the tears flowed from the rapidly blinking eyes.

"So," Hymie said gently, "what did she say? What could a teacher say to the smartest girl in the class, that could make you feel so bad?"

Deborah looked up, and in a soft voice told her parents, "She said, 'It's a mystery to me, Deborah, how a smart girl like you still speaks with that old singsong Yiddish accent. Hasn't five years of American education changed that? What is it with *you people*, if you, my smartest girl, still . . .'"

She ran out of breath and gulped and shook her head. Dora motioned Ben out of his seat, came and sat beside her daughter, and put an arm around her.

"So, okay. So, not so terrible. Just words."

"But, Momma, she always says things like that. She asks the class, when Jewish holidays are coming, 'How many children are Americans? How many Jewish?'"

"So you are American and Jewish, both things," her father said. "So what's the big deal?"

Deborah sat, helpless to explain her pain.

Ben watched his parents, their softness, their absolute surrender.

"She's a rotten, miserable, hating woman, Miss Hewitt. She hates Jews, Papa."

"A lot of people hate Jews. So what else is new?"

"Papa, you should go to school and tell the principal. She shouldn't be allowed to talk to the children this way."

Dora looked up, alarmed. "No, no, Ben, you take things too seriously. This doesn't matter."

"This matters!"

"These are just words of an ignorant woman, Benny," his father said. "So next year Deborah will have Mrs. Roth, and this Mrs. Hewitt will be out of her life. *This doesn't matter.*"

It was at this point that Ben Herskel told his family that he did not intend to continue with Hebrew school. Did not intend to be bar mitzvahed. Did not consider himself a Jew.

In a hysterical outburst, he unleashed all the venom, all the anger, all the anguish and resentment, all the observed shameful behavior. He listed all the things he despised about the Jewish kids he went to school with, and how he perceived his parents and their friends.

"You never stand up," he said, tears streaming down his pale face. "You shrug, you tell us, 'Be nice, don't make trouble, be nice-nice-nice.' Look what it gets you. You let the goyim cops eat twice as much as they pay for; the Catholic kids steal the candy; the Polack janitor, that drunk, Stachiew, comes every morning, every single morning, you give him milk and cake and he takes two newspapers and he never pays and . . . and . . ."

Overwhelmed, Ben turned and rushed to the street. He collided with a customer, a neighbor with an old dog on a leash, who gasped, spun about, and nearly fell over her pet. Ben ran and never looked back.

From the corner of his eye, Ben could see his uncle, Nathan Goldstein, walking along the path in Echo Park leading to the playground. Ben bounced the small hard black rubber ball a few times, then smacked it against the high concrete wall.

"Uncle, ya wanna play a game?"

He turned, slammed the ball against the wall, expecting his uncle to take him on. It would be the other way around, of course. Nathan Goldstein was a superb athlete. Tall, thin, wiry, with smooth shoulder muscles and large strong hands, he was a neighborhood champion, beating not just men his own age, but the younger, faster, more aggressive kids on the way up.

Not only was he an athlete, Nathan was a fixer. He earned his living as a motion-picture projectionist, working the big Broadway houses. He knew everything there was to know about machinery; anything broken, a radio that didn't play, a toaster that didn't toast, a phonograph that sounded tinny, bring it to Nathan.

So now his parents sent Nathan to fix things up with Ben.

His uncle caught the ball, wrapped his hand around it tightly, and shook his head.

"Maybe another time we play ball, *kinder*. Tonight I think maybe we talk, you and me."

Ben shrugged. He jammed his hands deep into the pockets of his heavy corduroy pants, stared down at his sneakers.

"Nothing to talk about. I won't go back to Hebrew school. I don't believe in any of it. That's it."

"So. You aren't a Jew anymore and that's it?"

"Yeah, that's it."

Nathan's voice was soft and low-pitched. "Well, I got news for you, kiddo. Even here, in America, land of the free, a Jew is a Jew and you better find that out now."

"Why should you care? Why should my father care? You don't keep kosher. You don't go to the temple except on the High Holy Days. You're hypocrites about it. I'm honest about it."

"Well, to tell you the truth, according to the Orthodox, even the people who go to Conservative and Reform aren't Jews. So maybe you're right, you're not a Jew and neither am I."

"So?" he challenged his uncle.

His uncle reached out and wrapped his arm about the boy's shoulder, and they began to walk into the darkened park. It was nicely laid out, a grassy place with young trees, separate playgrounds for small children, benches for the mothers and grandmothers and old people, and a place for the older kids, for the rougher games.

"It's a mystery, Ben, about our people. About us being who we are. You're mad, your father tells me, because the yeshiva boys don't fight back. Because your father doesn't make a big thing with the policemen, with the Polack janitor who steals breakfast every day and the newspapers."

"*You* fight back, Uncle. I seen you one day, you knocked a guy's front teeth out, he called you sheeny."

"A big hero, I belted some jerk."

"Yeah, but he knew who you were. I get so crazy with the Jewish kids, they want to run, to get away, they . . . they're a bunch of cowards."

Nathan smiled. "You ever seen the mothers they gotta go home to? Who look them over, make sure they acted the right way, don't answer back, don't make a fuss, it don't matter. All that matters, you should get a good education. You should get a profession. That's what their life is all about, Benny. You don't know what they came from, the parents. So what they have here, so what, someone calls you a name. So what?''

The boy kicked out at a stone. He gritted his teeth in frustration. ''Uncle, *please*. We all hear stories about how terrible it was in the old country. But this is here, we're Americans.''

His uncle put his hands on Ben's shoulders, turned him so that they were face to face. ''We are *Jews in America*, Benny. Maybe someday it'll be different, but that's who we are. No different from the Italians, the Irish, the Polacks, any of the others. Not yet, Americans first. Maybe your children, but not you.''

''Uncle Nathan, when I grow up, I'll change my name the way the movie stars do, to an American name, and then I'll be a ballplayer or a fireman or a policeman or anything I want to be, because I will be just plain American.''

His uncle studied him in silence for such a long time that the boy felt uneasy. He had counted on his uncle, his modern, most Americanized uncle, a man who worked with his hands, who understood baseball and went to football games, who could take care of himself—this uncle would agree with him, tell him it was all nonsense.

There was something different about Uncle Nathan now, a look of pain and anger and anguish on his face. There seemed to be a battle going on. Something terrible was being decided.

Finally his uncle took him by the arm, led him to a bench, sat him down, stood over him for a minute, then sat beside him.

''Ben, I am going to tell you something I had hoped you would never have to know. That your *father* hoped you would never have to hear. He said the decision would be up to me, after I talked to you, to tell you these things or not. Well, I think you have to know. It is part of your life as well as mine and your father's and your mother's and your sister's and of all your people. But before I tell you, you must promise me, on your word of honor, that you will never discuss this with another living soul. Not with a best friend, not with your cousins. Not with your parents.''

For a split second, Ben was going to make a wisecrack. Say something smart, sharp. But the words caught in his mouth as he saw the look on his uncle's face. He had expected a song and dance, a soft-soap lecture, a bit of arm-twisting. He felt a shiver of fear run down his spine. He realized instinctively that he was about to hear something he didn't want to hear. But had to.

''I promise, Uncle. What? What, tell me.''

When I was a child, I heard the story of my father being conscripted into the Czar's army when he and his friends were between the ages of eight and twelve years old. Every few years, things became very bad with raids, attacks, beatings; and the worst was when they came down on the ghetto and rounded up the Jewish boys. Sometimes word came and the parents hid the children, or sent them away, alone, to relatives. Sometimes there was no warning, and the children by the hundreds across our section of the country were rounded up. My father survived. Many of his friends died. They were babies, little children.

My father became a rabbi and he taught at our little seder school. In those days, if a child did not learn, he wasn't stupid, he was bad, so they taught you Hebrew letters with a smack, with a pull of your hair, with screaming and poking and knocking, so you learned with tears, but you learned. Your father's father, your grandfather, was the village butcher, married to my father's sister, so we were all family. Cousins and in-laws, everyone related to everyone, we lived in shacks in a place we could not own. We could not go to regular school, we could only go to the town at special times, with special passes. The peasants came inside the ghetto to trade, to bring vegetables to sell, to get sewing done, letters written and read to them. We all lived so poor. All the time, cold, hungry, afraid, always afraid of the latest rumor, the latest story, the newest scare.

Yes, we were frightened people, kinder. *There were things to be frightened of. The peasants, soldiers, cossacks. They didn't come and take the children for the army anymore, but other things. Steal a girl, a woman, Terrible, terrible.*

So our fathers warned us: Stay close to home, take care of each other. And then a time came when the rumors began. Near the goyisher *holiday, always near Easter, when they crucify and resurrect their god. Always a bad time for the Jews, always stories; but this time there was something else. Trouble in the army barracks just outside of town. Some money the men were owed didn't come; stories went around. The peasants, who always wanted something for nothing, always said the Jews cheated them on a trade, the usual stuff, they started the story—the babies the Jews stole from Christians, babies murdered and cooked, who knows what their heads could think up. It was a bad time for everyone. A bad winter, crops failed. People were hungry. Blame the Jews. They had stolen the army's money.*

My father, who was a wise man and a good man, who had some medical training, helped the peasants when they needed advice about herbs and how to take care of a sick child, or even a sick horse, my father had friends among the peasants. There were times, when things got bad, the children in the ghetto could be sent away to the countryside, would be kept safe until the trouble ended.

The men heard stories. Drunken cossacks who were angry, wild, looking for blood. For Jews. My father sent a message to his peasant friends and they sent word back. It was not safe to send the children to the usual hiding places, to farms, to barns. They would be murdered along with everyone else.

So. The men tried to arm themselves with whatever weapons they could, but remember, these were shoemakers and rabbis, scholars and craftsmen. The children were to be hidden in a place in the woods, a kind of blind. We, all of us, were taken to this place and told to stay there, quiet, not a sound, until some grownup would come for us.

Because these things happened and then they were over and life went on for those who survived.

There were twenty-two children, all of us under thirteen. Thirteen, you were a man, so the bar mitzvah boys stayed to try to defend the women, the older people. Your father and I were eleven years old when the slaughter took place.

There was a silence now. His uncle turned his face away, rubbed at his eyes with a rough hand. The boy reached out, touched his uncle's arm, but the uncle roughly shook the boy away.

"These are terrible things that must be told. It is necessary for *you* to hear this, *kinder*, you who say you don't want to be a Jew anymore, like this is a terrible thing to be, so why bother? As though to be something else is better, easier."

Ben clenched his teeth against the chattering, which took him by surprise. This uncle, whom he loved and respected and tried to imitate, was a stranger to him. An angry, tense, dangerous stranger. He sat quietly, waiting, afraid to speak. What he wanted to do, with all his heart, was play handball with his uncle now, in the dark, the two of them laughing and falling over each other, making great impossible slashes at the hard black ball, measuring each other, matched, two of a kind.

What he wanted was for his uncle to stop speaking, to stop remembering. Because he knew what was about to be told was something he would never be able to forget, something that would now become part of his own history.

Your father was a quiet boy, but strong and tough. He was considered a good influence on me, because I was the kid always making jokes, getting whacked, breaking the rules, the troublemaker, and it was your father who would talk to me about it.

He was a smart boy; he thought about things he didn't tell anyone. He saw things, he understood things. There was something about the hiding place he didn't like. He went along, when the older boys led us, but before we got to the place in the woods, your father grabbed me by the arm, took hold of my little sister's hand. Your mother was a small girl, eight years old, crying. In the night, all the children were crying. They wanted their mothers. They didn't want to be in the woods hiding, even though we had practiced for "when the time comes."

And the time was here and the children hid in the place that had been prepared, but your father had seen something a day or two before. He had seen one of his father's customers, a peasant he traded with, a man he thought was a friend to the Jews, if any of them can be. He had seen the man in the woods, near the hideout, looking around, checking things. Your father came back and told the grownups, but they shrugged it off. What else could they do? Where else could they send the children?

Your father had found another place to hide. There was a huge oak tree, maybe hundreds of years old, who knows such things, at the edge of our section of the ghetto. For years, children had played in the tree. We were all good at climbing, at wriggling around, stretching out. There was hardly a kid who hadn't, when he was old enough, hid out in the heavy branches when he was going to get a licking, when he wanted to duck a job. Your father took my arm, told me to grab my sister. He didn't feel the blind in the woods was safe. He had a bad feeling, so we went with him. Your father and I climbed the tree, pulling and dragging your mother, this little girl, to a safe place. Your father tied a piece of rope around her body so she wouldn't fall, and then made her take off her coat and he tied it over her head.

He didn't want her to see whatever it was that was going to happen. He told her to bite down hard on her hand, her arm, her lips, anything, but not to make a sound. No matter what she heard.

It was a game we'd never played before, and we knew it was not a game.

So we watched, your father and I, we saw. They came like wild beasts, drunk and loud and without humanity, they came and destroyed and . . . Ben, you have no idea what a man is capable of. They were beasts, but they were men. It was as though they had waited a whole lifetime to do this terrible thing we had all heard about from the time our parents could tell us, what they knew, their parents knew. No one could believe, not really, you can't know, not really, God forbid you see. And we watched as they murdered and raped. They did terrible things. I cannot tell you in words, I do not want to leave you with the pictures I carry in my head, I cannot describe the sounds, the screams, the terror.

They killed everyone. No one was left alive who did not die within hours. And then they took whatever they wanted. There was nothing of value, but they took, and they burned the Holy Torah, and they burned the shacks we lived in, where we studied, where we worked, where we lived.

And then, when it was all over, your father saw the peasant, the man he had seen in the woods. He was speaking to one of the soldiers and the soldiers gave him a bag of sugar he had just looted and then they went into the woods and found the children.

The children were murdered, but first they were raped. Boys as well as girls. These are terrible things, things no one should ever hear or think about, but they happened and I must tell you.

We stayed up in the tree. When morning came, we could not believe the sun could shine, that it could be a spring day with a blue sky, that birds were singing. It wasn't possible that the world could go on, that God could permit such a day to be just like any other. At first we thought Dora, your mother, was dead, she was so silent. We took the coat off her head and . . . her face was so strange, a stranger's face, a frozen face, her eyes, wide open, looked blind. And there were bite marks all over her arms, bloody, little teeth-size cuts, and blood ran from her mouth and . . .

Your father went down first. He checked around, then he motioned for us to stay where we were. He went into the woods and he came back fast. We never asked and he never said, but we knew. We knew.

For days we hid out in the woods. We came back to our homes; we didn't look at the dead, we pretended they were invisible. We found some small amounts of food, some water, some clothing that hadn't been ripped or burned. We made packs for our backs and a whole week passed before we were ready.

Your father and I knew there were relatives, family, in Germany, in Berlin. That if we could get there somehow, there would be family to take care of us, to help us. The weather was good, thank God, it wasn't winter, but your father said we had to wait a few days. He was the leader, I don't know how that came about. There was something different about him. He said a thing, and it became the law for the three of us. So we waited.

Before daylight, Sunday morning, he said, we will begin our journey. But first, on Saturday night, he and I had a job to do.

They drank themselves into a rage on Saturday nights, those bastards, and they had no more Jews to rape and kill, so they went for the local peasant girls, only they gave them trinkets or bits of food, pieces of ham to the farmers for their daughters. They had music, singing, wild dancing, all night, all night, until nearly morning. All of them drunk, falling down, lying inside their barracks, on the floor, on the cots, the girls with them.

We, your father and I, had our plan. We had kerosene we had found in our village. Some things the soldiers overlooked, some things they just didn't get around to taking, so we took the kerosene and very late at night, almost morning—all you could hear was snoring and moaning, and night birds and animals who made low noises—we crept, your father and I, and we spilled the kerosene completely around the main barracks. Then we lit the circle into a fire *that burned everything, all of them. By the time they came to, by the time they realized what was happening, it was too late for them.*

The last thing we did was to take the empty kerosene containers and put them into the hands of two peasants, a farmer and his friend who had come to celebrate, to make music for the cossacks, lying dead drunk outside the barracks. By the time the soldiers who were supposed to be on guard woke up, it was all over. All they could do was turn on the peasants with the kerosene cans.

Your father wouldn't let us watch. It was time for us to leave. We left.

"So we made our way across the world, *kinder*. We found people who helped us, Jews who helped us. In Germany there were organizations of Jews who helped people from the east to get to America. We had the names of some distant cousins, aunts, uncles. Always there was a name. We walked, three children, we walked across the face of the world and came here and lived with relatives and we worked and your mother went to school. And we never talked about it."

His uncle stopped speaking finally, stood up, stretched, rotated his head, up, down, from side to side, as though trying to loosen a cramp. He took a deep breath and faced the boy.

"So? We were bar mitzvahed, your father and I, and so officially, we are what we are, what you are and your mother and sister and cousins, all of us, all over the world, *Jews*. For better or worse. So, you want to duck out of it? You're not tough enough to go along with it here, in this place, in this country?"

At the precise moment that Ben Herskel threw himself at his uncle, Nathan Goldstein opened his arms and caught the boy. It was hard to tell who was sobbing, who was grasping, who was shaking, both bodies moved together.

Finally the uncle disengaged, leaned down, kissed the boy on the forehead.

"So, you don't talk to your father about this, yes?"

"But I want him to know that I . . ."

"That you know he killed thirty soldiers and caused the death of two stupid peasants? He knows I was going to tell you this. But it is something you must not speak of with him or anyone. Remember, you promised."

"But why, Uncle? What he did was great. It was—"

His uncle stiffened. "What he did was part of the madness. Slaughter and burning and killing is not what we were put on earth to do. It is something that happened and that was done. So it is over, now you know about it. You make up your own mind now about bar mitzvah. Your father said it would be up to you."

After his bar mitzvah, Ben did not attend any synagogue. He was a Jew, and that was that.

He and his pals never discussed religion. They were Catholics, and, whatever their strange customs, beliefs, rituals, or obligations, it was none of his business. Nor was he even a little curious. He was comfortable in the company of the goyim; they accepted him for the large, muscular boy he was, with good, quick coordination, always a good competitor and a good winner, not too familiar with losing.

One of the advantages he enjoyed, as a Jewish kid, was that he could get all the Jewish holidays off from school and also shared in the traditional Christian school vacations for Christmas and Easter.

He had seen the O'Briens' Christmas tree: a ceiling-touching job, filled with strings of great colored lights in the shapes of elves and snowmen and Santa Clauses, stars and a few little cottages. He wasn't sure it made sense to chop down a tree and stick it in the middle of your living room, but the pine tree smelled good and looked good. He barely glanced at the Nativity scene displayed on a white cloth beneath the tree. That was them, not him.

Ben was automatically included in the street games and the school-yard games and he felt excited—and maybe just a very tiny bit afraid—of the adventure they had planned for this night, three days after Christmas.

It wasn't just the thrilling ride down twisting, darkened Snake Hill he looked forward to. It was also the possibility of running into real danger. An encounter with the Webster Avenue guys. They were different from the Ryer Avenue kids. Ben's pals were roughhousers. They would tussle and box and shove and push, but no one ever hurt anybody, at least not intentionally. The Webster Avenue guys were thugs. If they mixed it up with someone, the aim was to hurt, *really* hurt—to bruise, maim, cut, disable.

Ben spotted the O'Briens at the top of the 180th Street hill, but they didn't see him. They were pelting each other with handfuls of soft snow, clowning around. He threw himself belly-down on his sled and crashed into them, knocking them both down. They scuffled good-naturedly, everyone rolling around, getting snow down their backs, under their hats, jammed into laughing mouths.

Finally, red-faced, breathless, they called a truce and watched the smaller kids, attended by panting parents slipping down the big hill and hauling sleds back up the icy incline.

"How come you came so late?" Charley asked. "We've been here almost an hour."

Ben shook the snow out of his hat, brushed at his heavy woolen jacket. "I hadda go to the Feldmans'. My mother made a cake for them."

"For the Feldmans? They celebrate Christmas? Or is it your Jewish holiday . . . Chan–oo–kah . . . or something?"

Ben feinted a punch at Charley. "No, dopey. They're sitting *shiva*. For the old grandfather. He died yesterday."

Gene remembered the old man, a thin, pleasant, lean guy who liked to tousle his head when he was a little kid. "Ai, ai, such a beautiful little one."

"I didn't know that," Gene said, "that he died."

"Yeah, yesterday. They buried him this morning"

Charley looked horrified. "He died yesterday and they buried him this morning? Jeez. That's . . . that's pretty heartless. What was the big rush?"

Ben shrugged. Gene said quietly, "No, Charley, it's not. That's the Jewish custom. They don't believe in embalming dead people, so they bury them right away. Within twenty-four hours, right, Ben?"

"What the hell they teaching you at the seminary, Gene? How come you know all that?

"I'm interested in religious customs, Ben, that's all."

Charley said, "Hey, remember old man Dugan, when he died and they laid him out in the living room?"

Old man Dugan, a grouchy, mean-mouthed, cranky presence in the lives of the Dugan family, had left a sum of money and a note detailing how it should be spent at his wake—in the family living room, with all his friends invited over to toast him on his departure. It had turned into something of a brawl. The corpse had come close to toppling when one of his more enthusiastic old pals demanded that old man Dugan join in a round of drinking to his own demise. It had gotten pretty rowdy.

"Yeah, but at least people get a chance to get a last look at ya," Charley said. "I mean, remember when Dell's old man, the fireman, got killed at the warehouse fire? Jeez, they fixed him up at the undertaker's real nice. He looked just like he was sleeping. They did a really nice job on him, remember, Gene?"

"Charley, he looked like a painted doll. For three days his widow kept screaming at him to get up, that's how good he looked."

"I don't think I'd want people looking at me, laid out and with makeup on and stuff," Ben said. "Dead is dead. The Jews put you in a plain pine box, say a prayer over you, and you're on your way. Dust to dust. Hell, dead is dead, it's all the same."

Charley was puzzled. "And that's it? No wake, no nothing?"

"No, not exactly 'that's it,' Charley. The family sits *shiva* for seven days and family and friends come and bring food and pay their respects. Without the corpse in the next room, for Pete's sake."

"For seven days? Wow."

Patiently, Ben explained the process. "The family sit on wooden crates. And don't wear shoes, just slippers. And they cover all the mirrors, so the ghost of the dead person doesn't come back for a look at himself or something. And everybody brings them food and stuff, 'cause they're not allowed to cook. The real old-timers, the Orthodox, they tear their clothes. Just a small rip, so it can be fixed. To show how bad they feel."

"Hey, Benny, you know what the Irish say to the family at a wake? They say, 'Sorry for your troubles.' You know why they say that?" Charley didn't wait for an answer. With a broad grin he said, "Because nobody knows whether you hated or loved the bastard who died, but whichever, the whole wake and funeral and stuff is sure a lot of trouble!"

Charley roared with laughter while his brother jammed a handful of snow down his back. "Where do you pick up this folk wisdom, Charley-dear? I never heard any of that."

"Hey, they don't teach you everything at the seminary. Pop told me that a long time ago." He started to brush at his clothes and gloves. "So what do Jews do in the summertime? Ya know, when it's real hot and somebody dies?"

"Whatta ya mean, whatta they do in the summertime? The same thing. It's tradition, Charley, not seasonal."

Charley hunched his shoulders and shuddered. He tried shaking for a while, then shook his head. It was fairly easy to do on the cold, windy hill, but how long could you do it in an apartment, where the heat's on and you're sitting on a wooden box, or in the summer when it gets hot and humid?

"Jeez," he said, "the people must get awful tired."

Ben and Gene exchanged grins. "You wanna tell him, Gene, or should I? Or do you know?"

Gene nodded. He knew. "Charley, the mourners don't 'sit and

shiver.' They sit *shiva*. It's a ceremony to honor the dead. Charley, you dope, how could you think people could sit and *shiver?*"

Charley clowned around, shaking and jumping. "Well, I could, especially on a night like this. You think Danny's down by Snake Hill yet? We gonna go and see?"

They gathered their sleds, adjusted their collars and hats, pulled their gloves tighter, jostled against each other.

"Benny, when you die, I want you to know, I'm gonna stand around and *shiver* for ya, 'cause I'm a real pal."

Charley went into a crazy dance, rolling his eyes, shuddering. Ben reached out, grabbed Charley by the collar, and pulled him close.

"Hey, buddy. Forget it. I am *never* gonna die!"

They slammed into each other, cut each other off, knocked themselves off their sleds onto the icy hill, rolled and yelled and punched, bursting with energy and life and health.

They passed the ill-lit, dank saloon on the corner and walked along the darkened street lined with machine shops and garages. It was a light-industry, nonresidential sweep of hill, with hard-packed ice in the road. The boys put together a small block-walled barrier, an improvised fort, as they discussed who would check out the hill for possible problems.

They were all there, his pals, Charley and Gene O'Brien, Danny D'Angelo and even the jerk who had followed them uninvited, Willie Paycek, ready for whatever they could come upon. When Ben spotted Megan Magee, who thought she was hidden from sight behind some parked cars, he told her cousin Charley that he should chase the kid home. A girl, for God's sake, c'mon. Something happens, we got enough to worry about without worrying about little-girl Megan.

Charley spoke to her, returned to the boys, shrugged.

"She won't go. Danny, you go talk to her!"

The boys began to jeer and laugh and make rude noises. Everyone knew Megan Magee would follow Dante D'Angelo anywhere in the world.

Danny shook his head. "The kid's all right. Any trouble, I'll make sure she gets the hell outta here."

They stood around, shifting snowballs from gloved hand to gloved hand, sleds at the ready. Waiting for Danny as always, to take charge.

"Well, it would be stupid for all of us to go racing down Snake Hill and maybe run into an ambush. What we need is an advance man to sneak down the hill and scout it out for us. We got a volunteer?"

Everyone remained silent, but everyone did the same thing—stared at Willie Paycek, who was not one of them, who was tagging along with less acceptance than Megan Magee.

You wanna be one of us, you gotta pay your way.

Willie, thin, small, dressed in lightweight clothing, sneakers soaked and frozen, bare hands red with cold, nose running, red ears not covered by the small woolen hat jammed down his forehead, hopped from one foot to the other.

"Hell," he said, "I'm not scared a' goin' down Snake Hill to scout it out. Sure, shit, why not? I'm fast, I run inta any a' them Websters." He shoved his fists into his jacket pockets. "Can I take someone's sled, or what?"

No one offered him a sled, and Willie of course didn't own one.

"Well, what I'll do is, I'll work my way down and . . ."

"For Christ's sake, Willie, stop standing here tellin' us what you're gonna do and get going and do it," Ben said. His hands reached for the thin, bony shoulders, turning the boy around.

Charley O'Brien handed his old, short sled to Willie. "Keep away from the middle of the street," he said, "just in case."

"Hey, you want, I'll go." Megan danced among them. "I'll go right straight down the middle of the street—they don't scare *me*!"

Her two cousins grabbed her arms and held her back. She looked at Dante. "Whadda ya say, Danny? I'll do it."

Dante grinned. "Thank you very much, Megan. Okay, Willie, how about it?" Then, quietly, his eyes intent on the boy, "You're our scout, kid. Be careful, okay?"

Willie nodded. It was an important assignment, and he would come through for them. He was *their* scout.

CHAPTER EIGHT

They watched Willie Paycek disappear around the icy curve toward Webster Avenue. The kid moved like quicksilver, his weight seeming hardly enough to anchor the sled, to keep it from zipping right into the air. If the Webster Avenue gang was at the bottom of the hill waiting for anyone stupid enough to invade their territory, well, what the hell. It was only Willie. It was the price he had to pay to hang around where he wasn't wanted.

Danny didn't like or trust Willie any more than the others did. Willie was a rat and you couldn't turn your back on him. But Danny knew it wasn't really Willie's fault that he was the way he was. He'd keep an eye out, make sure the kid didn't get into real trouble.

Danny felt a heavy handful of wet snow slide down his back, inside his shirt, right next to his skin. He hunched forward, pretending to deal with it. Instead, he scooped up some clean white snow and, in an easy turn, shoved the loose snow into Ben Herskel's face.

Ben protested. "Hey, I didn't do it. But that's not a bad idea."

The snow fight was on. Charley made big, loose snowballs, handed them off to his brother. Eugene caught a basketball-sized clump of snow in the face, thrown by his cousin Megan.

They all turned on Megan, who ran behind Danny.

"C'mon, Danny. You and me against the three of them."

Eugene grabbed Megan's woolen hat, filled it with loose snow, and attempted to stuff it on her head.

"Hey," she taunted him, "what a way for a priest to act, jeez."

She was the first to break whatever reluctance the others had toward the seminarian, and they ganged up on him, knocking him into a bank of snow, hanging on to his flailing arms and legs, gasping, laughing, yelling as they tried to cover him with snow. They ended in a tangled mass of wet, cold, laughing kids, breathless, gasping. None of them was even aware that Willie had returned from his mission unscathed.

Willie looked around, approaching them with the urgency of someone who had successfully, willingly, risked his life for his friends. He stepped back slightly, having taken their attention. He didn't want to be involved in the roughhousing. He was too often a target.

Danny pulled himself up, turned, and yanked Megan to her feet. "Hey, here's our scout back. Well, kid, did anyone spot you?"

Danny placed a hand on the narrow shoulder, surprised at how bony it was, wondering how Willie could stand the cold, wearing just a cotton jacket over his thin sweater. The kid's feet must be numb in his wet sneakers. With a gesture unseen by Willie, Danny waved off the others, who were planning an ambush.

"Hey, all clear," Willie said out of the corner of his mouth. His eyes moved constantly, as though seeking danger. "Them bastards musta gone home."

Danny leaned closer. "Watch the language, Willie. We got Megan here. And Eugene."

Willie grimaced, shrugged. "Jeez, hey, okay. Sorry."

They stamped their feet, and brushed themselves off shaking the ice from sleeves and collars.

"You real sure, Willie?" Ben asked. "'Cause if we get down to the bottom of that hill and there's the Webster mob, *you* are the one we're gonna feed them."

Jew, Willie thought venomously. *All I gotta tell 'em is "Take the Jew."* "Hey," he said, "they're all with girls now. I seen 'em headin' for their candy store a block away. Them older guys, they'll stay with the girls." He pulled his mouth down and leered. *"Ya know."*

Ben jammed his hands in his back pockets. "Yeah, Willie, *I* know. But do you?"

Charley O'Brien put his wet, frozen, gloved hand over Megan's ears. "Hey, c'mon. No dirty talk. We got a little *girl* here."

Megan struggled, broke free, swung at her cousin, but it was all good-natured teasing. For almost a year, there had been a subtle but real change in the way the boys treated her. Boys her own age whom she could still beat at running or climbing seemed to hold back when it came to roughhouse. She sensed their new and growing strength and it frightened her, not for the sake of her well-being but for the message such changes conveyed. Patsy had said girls couldn't play with boys anymore after *you-know-what* begins to happen to you every month, because then boys only wanted *one thing* and if you wrestled with them, or jumped them, or had any kind of contact with them, they'd think you wanted *you-know-what* from them.

Megan didn't really know what, and as her regular boy pals became larger, in spurts of growth her own body didn't match, she tried harder, played rougher, moved faster. Some of the boys didn't hold back, and she was startled at times by their strength. When a more thoughtful boy held back the extra-hard punch, the more powerful tackle, she resented it. It was a dilemma. She didn't want to get hurt, but couldn't seem to keep up with them the way she always had. Not fair.

They were arranging the sleds, deciding who would go first, should they have a race or a jump-on-board or what. They quieted down, concentrating on the hill, which was steep, curving, and dangerous. It was quiet enough for them to hear Willie's sudden gasp.

"Oh, shit."

They turned toward Willie because his voice was filled with terror genuine enough to cause them all to freeze in position, then turn and focus on the lurching figure of Walter Stachiew.

Stachiew was a huge man, heavy with muscle, bulked with layers of booze-fat. He came toward them, head lowered, drunken footing uncertain on the icy street. He held his coal shovel midway down the iron-and-wood shaft, raised like a weapon before him. There was no doubt in anyone's mind that Walter Stachiew was drunk and on the edge of violence. They glanced at Dante, their natural leader, ready to take their cues from him.

"What you little bums doin' here, huh? Ya got no right bein' here in this place. This is *my* hill, ya sneakin' little bastards, I show ya!"

Danny backed off as Stachiew came toward them. His voice was low, reasonable.

"Okay, okay. No problem. We're leaving."

"Hey, you. How's your crazy guinea sister, huh? You crazy too?" Dante didn't respond, just waited and watched.

Stachiew reached out, caught Gene's shoulder. Then, recognizing the boy, he smiled. Suddenly, unexpectedly, his hand slid around to the back of Eugene's head and he forced his lips against the boy's, then, still holding him, pulled back.

"Yah, sweetheart, like I thought. You just like a girl."

Gene's advantage was surprise. No one expected what he did next. He hadn't planned it; he just reacted. He wrenched the heavy shovel from the filthy hand, pulled back, and swung at Stachiew, catching him full in the stomach.

Charley was right there, at his brother's side. The blow hadn't hurt Stachiew, just knocked the wind out of him. He shoved Charley aside and grabbed at Gene.

"Ya little faggot bastard! I'm gonna take ya head offa ya, then I'm gonna fuck what's left."

Charley had the shovel now, and he aimed at Stachiew's head, but hit his shoulder. It was a solid blow, but the drunken, enraged man didn't fall. He whirled around, swinging his long, strong arms, his fists hard balls. The boys moved back, tried to withdraw, but as long as Stachiew was attacking one of them no one would run away.

A kick of his heavily booted foot caught Danny just below the kneecap. He gasped with pain and went down, but a hand pulled him up. Danny grabbed the shovel. He swung. There was a great roaring howl, an animal's fury. Stachiew grabbed Megan by her hair and pulled.

He wrapped an arm around her neck, ignoring her kicking and punching, her attempts to bite, to get free. He held her close to him, breathing hard.

"Stay back, you bums, I kill this one." Stachiew shook his head. His laugh was harsh and hissing. "You all a buncha queers, you, pretty boy, this little girl, she wanna be a boy, ya know what, you, blondie, you give this girl your balls and she'll give you her—"

The blow came to the back of his head and he released Megan. She slipped to the icy gutter and felt herself caught and pulled toward her friends. Stachiew's hand went to the back of his head, then he turned.

Ben's second blow caught the man across the forehead and brought him down, but Stachiew grabbed at Ben's ankles and the boy fell beside him.

"Little kikey shit think ya gonna hit me and get away with it, I kill ya Jew shit, I fuck ya mudder and eat ya sister and—"

Ben felt the shovel behind him. He pulled back and hit Stachiew with a light, off-balance, glancing blow across the cheek. He stood up and felt his arms being held. He turned slowly and confronted Dante.

No one had ever seen Ben Herskel's face like this before. He seemed calm and controlled and deadly. He held on to the shovel and shrugged Danny back, but didn't turn back toward Stachiew, who was reviving, shaking himself, brushing blood from his face.

Ben reached out and grabbed Willie Paycek by the collar. He thrust the shovel into Willie's raw, wet, cold hands.

"Your turn," he said.

Willie looked around at the others. No one gave him any sign. Not Danny, to whom he appealed first, not the pretty priest-boy, who stared right through him, not the girl-boy, who wanted the shovel herself.

Herskel put his lips to Willie's red, numbed ear and said, "Your turn, Willie."

Stachiew, kneeling unsteadily, focused on the thin, reluctant boy. "You, ya little prick-sucker, I get you good, you wait till next time. I get you special good. You know, you know what I do to you—"

Willie Paycek raised the shovel over his head. The sound of the blow was terrible. He raised it again, saying, *"This is for all of us,"* but was knocked sideways when Danny pulled the shovel away.

"Lemme, lemme, lemme!" Willie struggled, but he wasn't strong enough.

"Gimme my shot," Megan said. She grabbed the shovel and landed a light blow on the fallen, unmoving man before Dante yanked the shovel away from her. He dropped the shovel next to the crumpled body.

"C'mon. Outta here, everybody, outta here. Meet up at the small lot. *Move!"*

He cautioned them, directed them. Go straight up 181st Street. Move fast, but stop and play, throw a couple of snowballs. Be seen. He and Megan detoured along Valentine Avenue. Danny pushed Megan onto her sled.

"Sit down. Make believe you're just a little girl going for a ride with her brother. Megan. Do what I tell you."

She sat, hunched, looking up at Danny. Whatever Danny said, whatever he said. When they reached the big hill at 180th Street, he pulled the sled over to the sidewalk and crouched next to her. A few younger kids, some with parents, whizzed down the hill. One last time. Just one more.

"Are you okay?"

She tilted her face up toward him. He was startled. Her face, in the glow of the street lamp, was beautiful. He'd never before noticed that Megan Magee had huge amber eyes, delicate features, upturned lips. Her red hair was wild around her face, and without thinking he reached down and tucked wet strands into her woolen hat.

"Megan, listen to me. Listen hard. You've been here all night, on the big hill, get that? You never went *near* Snake Hill. You've been here all night and now you're gonna go back up to Ryer Avenue and go home."

"Hey, c'mon, Danny, I'm just like the rest of the guys. I . . ."

Danny knew he was dealing with her pride. He stood up, took a slow and steadying breath, and his intuition guided him.

"Megan, I'm *counting* on you. I want you to do this *for me*. We're special friends, you and me, and I want a promise from you. No one, ever, no matter what, is gonna know you were there tonight. No matter what. Not even your pal Patsy."

She took a deep breath and stood up. Her focus on him was complete. She was trying to understand not only what had happened, but what commitment he was asking of her.

"You were never there. Promise me, Megan."

She brought her mittened hand to her mouth, pulled the mitten off with her teeth, and offered the hand to him. He took it with great solemnity.

"I promise you, Danny. No matter what."

"I believe you, Megan."

Gently, he touched her cheek; impulsively, he kissed her lightly on the lips.

"Remember, I trust you, Megan. Now go on home."

Softly, as she watched him head up the hill, Megan whispered, "I love you, Danny."

They waited for Danny where he had said, in the small lot. The ground had been chopped up by the little kids during the day. There were crisscrossing patterns from the blades of sleds; a couple of lopsided snowmen; an arsenal of snowballs abandoned behind a two-foot irregular wall of a snow fort.

Ben stood perfectly still, his hands deep in the pockets of his corduroy pants, his eyes moving first to Charley, who nodded, tossed a snowball

at him, as he sidestepped casually. He jutted his chin toward Gene, who
was leaning against the icy side of a thick old oak tree, and raised his
eyebrows. Charley shrugged. Gene was okay; don't worry about him.
Then he watched the little shit, Willie, as the kid danced around,
hopping from one foot to the other, tossing ice balls at imaginary
targets. The little bastard couldn't stand still. He slid on an icy patch,
went down, got up. It was all the same to Willie.

"Hey, look, there's Danny," Willie said, the words forced between
teeth clenched to stop the chattering. Willie moved toward the street,
but Ben put a large restraining hand against Willie's chest.

"Stay put."

Danny waved to them from across the street, made some hand
gestures. He stepped into his father's shoe-repair shop, spoke to the old
man, touched his shoulder, pointed to the wall clock. The old man
showed him, just this to finish, just this piece of sole to attach, then
quitting time. He reached up with a blackened hand, touched Danny's
face, smiled. Okay, okay, a few more minutes.

Danny joined them in the lot, turning once to wave to his father, but
the old man was intent on his work.

"Okay," Danny said quietly. They drew closer to him, and the boys
watched him intently, except Gene. Gene studied the melting snowball
that he rolled between his hands.

"We've all been sledding down the big hill. Then we went to the big
lot." He jerked his thumb over his shoulder toward the four-story-high
mountain of a lot on the opposite corner. "There's a fort the high
school guys built yesterday. We had a private war, just us. That's it,
okay?"

No one said anything. They all turned to Gene, who didn't look up.
Danny glanced at Charley, who shrugged.

"Gene?" his brother called.

Eugene O'Brien still didn't look up.

"Now, there's one thing. No matter what. *No matter what.*" Gene
looked up now. "About Megan. She wasn't with us tonight."

"Like hell," said Willie Paycek.

The four boys focused on Willie. He glanced around, and the glare
from Gene's pale eyes caught him. He shrugged, shuffled from one cold
foot to the other.

"Hey, yeah, sure, okay, okay."

"Danny?" Charley spoke softly, hesitantly. "Suppose somebody saw
us on Snake Hill?"

The tension froze them more than the cold. It was a question no one had wanted to ask or think about.

Danny shook his head slowly. "No one was on the hill but us and him. All the little factories and car shops were closed up tight. Nobody lives there, nobody hangs around there. There weren't any other drunks around, and—"

Gene asked, "Do you think he's dead, Danny?"

The other boys seemed to stop breathing. They focused completely on Danny, depending on him to make things all right.

"Drunks don't die that easy, Gene. C'mon, it was a dumb fight, but he attacked us, so we whacked him. He's sleeping it off."

Willie made a strange gurgling sound. He was laughing. "Hey, maybe he'll freeze to death and that'll be that."

Ben wrapped a large arm around Willie Paycek, lifting him off his feet. He leaned close and whispered, "Listen, jerk, you weren't with us tonight and you won't be with us any other night, ever, because none of us would be caught dead anywhere around you. Now you get lost, but . . ." He turned the boy around, confronting him face to face. "If anyone, anytime, anywhere, *ever*, asks any of us about anything that happened on Snake Hill, I'll know it was because of your rotten little mouth. And I'll take care of you. Got that?"

Willie's eyes rolled around, appealing to each of them, but no one moved or said a word. He reached up carefully and tugged at Ben's arm, which relaxed.

"Hey, shit, don't worry about me. Jeez, don't worry about me."

"I'm not worryin' about you, Willie. You don't worry me one little bit." Ben gave the boy a shove. "Get lost."

Willie backed away from them, shoved his hands in his pockets, hunched his shoulders, tried to keep from shaking.

"Hey, Danny, you tell 'em. I'm okay, right? Don't worry."

"Wait a minute, Willie," Danny said, speaking then to all of them. "We have to agree on this. No one, not anyone, says anything about this to anyone. I mean *nothing*, and I mean *not ever*."

He made eye contact with each of them. They all glanced toward Eugene, who had turned away.

"Gene?"

"Whatever is between my confessor and myself, Danny, goes no further and involves only me."

Danny put out his hand, nodded, and demanded a handshake from each of them. One after the other, they gave him the same promise Megan had given him earlier.

Willie Paycek shook Danny's hand last. It was a compact, a vow, an inclusion. He was one of them now, bound together by what had happened on Snake Hill.

Of all those who made the promise of silence that night, only Megan Magee kept her vow for the rest of her life.

CHAPTER NINE

When he heard the voices of the detectives in the hall outside the janitor's apartment, Willie Paycek wet the bed in terror. His brother Mischa, a nine-year-old with the mind of a dull child of three, but with a sunny nature, awoke in alarm. He thought he was responsible for the wetness all round him. He began to whimper and whine, automatically caressing the tiny penis which was his only claim to specialness. When he was born, the doctors and nurses gathered around the infant, studying him with amazement. The diminutive testicles were fully descended and normal size, but the penis sat like a minuscule bud, which, as the years passed, never flowered. Mischa knew nothing of the bitter, violent fights that took place over his paternity. When Stanley Paycek disclaimed a child with such a deformity, Walter Stachiew laughed insultingly and drew physical comparisons. The infant was examined, studied, and disowned by both men. One drunken night of speculation, when the child cried from exhaustion at the poking and probing and incomprehensible attention of the two huge men who hovered over him, one of them, deciding the kid to be the bastard of some unknown sonofabitch, grabbed the child by the ankles and swung him around. When Anna, the mother, rushed into the room, the child's head crashed into a wall, leaving a thin, bloody splash down to the floor.

The doctor accepted without comment that the eight-month-old infant had fallen from a table as the mother turned and reached for a diaper.

There was no way to determine whether Mischa's retardation dated from that night, or whether it was a genetic malfunction. Whatever caused his slow, plodding development, he was a quiet child who endured the taunts of both adults and children when his small pink bud was exposed and examined. He took delight in their laughter and could not understand why it was then wrong for him to undo his pants and show his treasure to others on the street. He had learned, through many whackings and shakings and smackings, that it was a terrible thing for him to do. All right for them to show—for his older brother Willie to charge other children a penny for a quick look—all right for his father and Uncle Walter to fondle and speculate on. But not all right for Mischa, for whatever reason. He accepted this as fact, and fondled his minuscule treasure secretly at night. But he held on in terror now as the wetness spread across the bed.

He reached out to touch Willie's face, to tell him how sorry he was.

Willie shoved his brother hard enough to bounce him onto the floor, then held a hand over the boy's mouth to muffle his cries.

"Shut you, you fuckin' freak, shut up!"

It occurred to Mischa that Willie wasn't all that interested in him. Even though his brother's rough hands held him hard, fingers digging into his cheeks, Willie just wanted him to be quiet so that he could hear what was going on in the other room. He held his breath and was silent so that Willie would know he would do whatever was wanted of him.

Willie sat absolutely still, listening. How could they know? Who had talked? Should he run? To where? There was no way to get out of the apartment past them. He heard them moving around outside in the courtyard, going into the coal room where Stachiew slept.

First the men's voices: cop voices. And then his mother's scream, over and over again in a rising and falling sound of anguish. The door to the small alcove that Willie shared with Mischa burst open and a detective, a big, red-faced mick, Healy or Heeny, stood over them.

"Hey, what ya doin' onna floor? C'mere kid." He gestured to Willie. "Come inside and stay with your mudder."

A strong hand pulled him to his feet. The detective wrinkled his nose, shook his head.

"Put on some clean clothes, kid. You the oldest?"

Willie nodded as he dug through a mound of dirty clothes on the floor, pulled out a pair of dry shorts. He turned his back as he dressed, shoved his bare feet into his shoes. The detective stared at Mischa, who sat bolt upright, his eyes bulging, his mouth open, his hand working frantically at his crotch.

"This kid all right, or what?"

Willie nodded. Yeah. Yeah, he's okay.

He began to think, to slow down. *Say the Jew did it, that's who, the big sonofabitch Jew kid,* Herskel, because Stachiew all the time stole rolls and bagels and milk from the front of his old man's luncheonette in the morning, before opening time. Yeah, that's why he did it. Benny, the big Jew kid.

The detective steered him across the hallway into the other half of the separated janitor's apartment. His mother stood in the middle of the kitchen in her stained house dress, her feet bare and swollen, her heavy arms thrown over her head, which had fallen back so that he couldn't see her face, just the tears and snot running off her chin as she howled. Two detectives stood watching her, and Willie saw the disgust in their faces.

His mother was a disgusting woman, fat, with lardlike arms and shoulders; the flesh on her face seemed to be melting down in heavy pouches. She smelled of garbage collections and cooking and her own intense female odors. She reached her rough, red, strong hands to her head, fingers raked and pulled at her wild graying hair. The detectives glanced at each other, eyebrows raised, and then at the collection of children. Willie's other younger brothers and sisters, four of them, all pale, thin, blue-eyed, blond children with faces vacant of fear or distress, silently watching their mother. They had seen this before. It usually took place after their father had beaten her up or stolen the house money for booze.

Finally the Irish detective said, "Calm your mother down, kid. We gotta take her to the precinct house."

Willie stared at the detective. We gotta take *her.* No one seemed interested in *him* except as someone to handle his mother. What the hell was goin' on?

"Ma, Ma, c'mon, willya, cut it out. What's goin' on anyway, wadda ya yellin'?" He switched to Polish and spoke softly. "Ma, talk to me in Polack, what's going on?"

His mother wiped her hand across her mouth, over her wet eyes and cheeks, then down the side of her dress. She blinked and leaned toward him, squinting, as though the tears had blinded her.

"Willie?" she said, "Willie?"

He whispered, to quiet her, to level her. "Yeah, Ma, Willie." He glanced at the detectives and repeated his instruction. "In *Polish*, Ma. What do they want? Them cops."

His mother's body shook with one great spasm that ended with a loud gust of wind. The detectives glanced at each other, grimaced, poked Willie.

"Tell ya mother to put some clothes on, kid. Some shoes. Hurry it up."

They were anxious to be out of there.

He led his mother inside to the bedroom she shared with his father, some of the kids, sometimes with Walter Stachiew.

She sat on the edge of the bed, put on the sweater he brought to her, slid her feet into the broken shoes, pulled the laces.

"Tell me what's goin' on. *Tell me, now.*"

She looked at him, surprised at his tone but responding to his demand—his masculine right to demand.

"Well, he killed him," she said softly, following his return to English. "He killed him. He said he would someday. They was gonna kill each other and now ya father killed him. Walter."

"Pa? Pa killed him? *Pa killed Walter?*"

She stared at her son and shrugged. "Who you tink he killed, Jesus Christ? The Jews, they already killed Jesus Christ. He killed *Walter*. Wit' a shovel, he hit him on the head and the cops seen him do it. They seen him do it and they took him to the precinct house."

"The cops seen him do it? *The cops seen him do it?*"

For the rest of the night, Willie Paycek felt as though he were standing outside of his own life and watching a movie. It was a surprising movie and he couldn't even begin to guess what scene would come next.

When his father saw his mother enter the detectives' office, he rose from the chair beside the cop's battered old desk, let out a terrible cry, then collapsed back into the chair. His mother responded immediately. Between them, their voices filled the room.

The mick detective put his hand on Willie's arm as though to hold him up. The boy's face was gray, his mouth twitched spasmodically, his small eyes blinked furiously. Although he was an ugly little punk, known to the detectives, as were most of the neighborhood kids, Heeny couldn't help feeling fleeting sympathy. The kid's body was trembling, but there was something peculiar about him as he turned from the sight of his hysterical parents to the momentarily solicitous detective. There was something sly, something sneaky and knowing, something about the kid that turned off any warmth or concern.

"Ya okay, kid?" Heeny asked, curious. The boy shrugged, a little surprised. Why wouldn't he be okay?—that was what Heeny read in the boy's attitude.

Jesus, what a life they must have been living in that janitor's back-alley apartment.

Willie listened casually to his mother as she spoke with animation and agitation to the detectives who fed her coffee and cake, who lit her cigarettes, who leaned forward politely, egging her on.

"Sooner or later they kill each other, one kills the other, who knows about these men? From children, they were like brothers, fighting, fighting. All the time, from the old country, always together, drinking. No good, them two, no good."

Then suddenly, reality would overtake her. It wasn't just another Saturday-night brawl, one or the other beaten and dragged roaring drunk into the courtyard, doors slamming and fists pounding, her room and bed and body invaded by one or the other. One was dead, the other in the next room.

"Walter is really dead?"

There was an endless procession of men in and out of the two rooms. Men from the district attorney's office, taking statements from his father, who sobbed and cried and beat himself in the head with clenched fists, banged his arms on the wall in sudden bursts of emotion.

"Walter, Walter, sonofabitch, look what you made me do, see, you made me do this, I kill you for what you made me do!"

They took down all his words, in notebooks and on clattering typewriters.

Reporters came from the morning newspapers and photographers flashed lights in his father's face, and aimed at his mother. Willie ducked away. He wanted no part of this. He was a spectator, a watcher through the night.

Finally his father came from the inner room, his hands shackled in front of him, a detective on either side. Willie knew his father's head was beginning to ache. He knew the first signs of a massive hangover. His father stopped in front of him, surprised. Although Willie had drifted close to him during the night, Stanley Paycek had been too self-involved to notice his oldest son.

"What you do here, you?" his father demanded his hands automatically rising.

Willie took a step back and watched as the detectives tightened their grip on his father's arms and moved him along to the waiting car. His father turned, looked over his shoulder, directly at his son.

No one caught the expression on Willie's face.

It was a look of deep and bitter and long-awaited triumph.

C H A P T E R   T E N

It ran through his mind, sometimes slowed down and sometimes speeded up. The focus was on himself; the others were shadowy spectators. He could smell the heavy, sweaty physicality of the man, the whiskey-beer aura that seemed to come from the pores of his face, glistening on the dirty stubble of his cheeks. He could see into the small, predatory eyes, narrowed and piercing, but he was not sure what was revealed. Each time he began at the beginning and remembered it to the very end, when he turned, his brother's hand on his arm, steering him away. Finally, Eugene realized that what he was doing was dangerous. He was distorting reality, and it was with reality that he had to deal.

Eugene knew that Charley was aware of him, rising in the predawn cold winter darkness. He had slid without a sound from the bed they shared, and dressed in silence, casting quick glances at his brother. His sleep-breathing was steady and deep, each exhalation ending with a soft sigh. His legs, sprawled out, never moved. One arm was thrown across his forehead; the other, along his side, was bent so that his hand rested lightly at his groin.

Dressed in clothes still damp from the night before, holding his shoes so that he could slip soundlessly from the apartment, Eugene hesitated. He studied his brother. Nothing gave him away, no slight modification of breath, no pucker of his slightly parted lips, no gentle movement of his hand against his sex. He stood at the foot of the bed and reached out gently, touching the uncovered foot with a slight pressure.

"It'll be all right, Charley," he said in a voice so soft it hardly left his mouth. "My confession is *mine*. It has nothing to do with anyone else."

He stood motionless for a few seconds, watching his brother, then silently left.

Father Kelly was not surprised that Eugene O'Brien was present at the six o'clock. He knew the dislocated feeling of a young seminarian home for his first visit. The boy was still on seminary time, and his presence in the darkness of St. Simon added a glow of youth and light.

Clearly, Eugene was upset about something. Father Kelly understood: the boy was back home. It was probably his first real struggle, the first real questioning of his calling. That was the purpose of the home visit. He smiled and nodded and, with a jerk of his head, invited the boy into the robing room.

Automatically, Eugene helped with the discarding of the priestly vestments, much to the relief of the dazed altar boys who had served the early mass as part of their rotation. No one volunteered for six o'clock, and they disappeared gratefully at Father Kelly's nod.

Father Kelly was not that far removed from the seminary. He remembered the first weeks, the first months, the doubts, the terrors, the astonishment of his own arrogance in thinking he had been called. It was something each of them went through. Some left and others, finding their own inner strength through a mystical intervention, continued on. He had never, for the slightly fleeting moment, thought Eugene O'Brien was anything but called.

Lighting his first cigarette of the day, pouring his first cup of coffee from the hot plate, Father Kelly gestured to a chair.

"You drink coffee, Gene?"

"No, thank you, Father."

The priest took a long, deep, satisfying drag from the cigarette, held the smoke against the back of his throat, then exhaled. He drank the coffee hot and black, felt the combination of nicotine and caffeine enter his bloodstream, clear and quicken his brain.

"Okay, then, Gene. You want to talk. Here I am. Let's talk."

The boy, who was normally pale, seemed faded to the whiteness of alabaster. His light eyes looked glazed and without focus. Even his lips seemed whitened by tension. The white hair, lank and shiny, added a glow, a nimbus. Gene touched his long, slender fingers absently across his lips, rubbed his sharp jawbone tentatively. He was having trouble, so Father Kelly helped him.

"It's hard, isn't it, son? To be there, with the whole force of the seminary, the rules and the structures imposed on every minute of your day. And then to come back to your family and friends and neighborhood. Everyone feels the same way, especially on their first trip home. Everyone."

"Father, I have a confession."

It didn't surprise the priest. Of course the boy had to make a confession: his doubts, his feeling of unworthiness, that he'd made a terrible mistake, that it had been pride which had made him claim a call.

"All right, Eugene." He started to rise. "Shall we go to the confessional?"

The boy shook his head.

"It isn't what you think. And I have to talk to you face to face. I need to see you when I tell you this."

Father Kelly nodded.

"Your choice. But it *is* a confession, right?"

"Yes, Father."

They went through the familiar rote, and the priest felt his curiosity rising. This tension, this emotionalism, seemed out of proportion to what he expected.

The young seminarian sat bolt upright, his spine not touching the back of his chair. He breathed in quick, short, sibilant breaths, like a runner. He glanced around the room for a moment, and then, with evident resolve, he looked directly into Father Tom Kelly's eyes and his gaze never wavered.

"Father, last night I killed a man."

There was a sudden stillness in the room, disturbed by a slowing down, a quieting, of Gene's breathing. Father Kelly blinked, felt a smile pull irrationally at his lips. This was not a boy given to jokes. Whatever Gene was talking about was deadly serious—at least to him.

The boy was so rigid that every part of him looked breakable. The only life blazed from his eyes.

"Eugene, what are you talking about? What man did you 'kill' last night? Take your time, boy, slowly now. Tell me."

And Eugene told about the encounter, carefully, discarding all the various versions he had played through the night, focusing on what had actually happened.

Father Kelly felt his hands begin to shake and his own breathing increase, the need for a full, deep breath aching in his chest. The boy spoke for no more than a few minutes, and then he waited, as cold and translucent as a cake of ice.

Father Kelly leaned forward, reached out, and touched the back of Eugene's hand as it rested along the arm of the chair. The hand was cold and felt as lifeless as wood.

"Gene, I want you to listen to me, all right? I want you to listen to me very, very carefully."

The boy nodded, but there was no way out. He had done what he had done. It was all over. *He* was all over, finished.

"Last night, shortly after eleven o'clock, I was summoned by one of the patrolmen from the precinct. He told me I was needed to administer last rites. To Walter Stachiew."

The boy jerked, his mouth fell open. It *was* murder then. The man *was* dead. It was all real, not some part of a terrible dream.

"Listen, Gene. I went with the policemen and administered provisional absolution. And standing there, beside the bloody mess that was once Walter Stachiew, was Stanley Paycek. He was yelling, for anyone to hear, about how he'd followed Stachiew from the tavern where they'd had a quarrel, and how he'd bashed his skull in with his own shovel. There were a bunch of witnesses from the tavern, standing around, all nodding. Paycek was obviously still drunk, but his drinking cohorts confirmed hearing his threats. He not only confessed, Eugene, but the most believable witnesses in the world will testify to what they saw."

"Who, father? What do you mean?"

"Two of the lads from the precinct were coming back to report on something they had checked out down on Bathgate Avenue. They were driving up the hill—you boys call it Snake Hill—and they *saw* Stanley Paycek. They saw him kill Walter Stachiew. They saw him bashing Stachiew's head in."

"They saw that?"

"They saw the murder, Eugene."

Reaching out swiftly as the boy fell forward in a dead faint, Father Kelly caught him in his arms, surprised that the slender body was so muscular. He eased him down to the floor, quickly elevated his feet on a stack of telephone directories, loosened the jacket and shirt from around Gene's neck. He brought the cup of bitter, cooled coffee under the boy's nose; the strong smell seemed to bring him around.

"Lie still for a minute, don't try to get up. A few deep breaths, son, lie still and let the blood get back to your brain."

He eased Eugene into a sitting position when the boy was ready, offered him the cup, and studied the change, the return to life of a face that had seemed cold dead.

Finally, seated across from the boy, the priest spoke quietly.

"This man, this Stachiew. He was a bad case. A drunk and a bully and a tyrant, as is Paycek. Two of a kind. They deserved each other." His eyes narrowed, and for the first time Eugene avoided his frank and questioning gaze. "Is there some other part of this whole thing, Gene? Some part you feel you are having trouble with?" When the boy nodded, the priest continued. "Would you feel better, would it be easier for you now for us to go into the confessional? All right, you go ahead. I'll join you in a minute."

In the dark, familiar safety of the confessional, Eugene O'Brien struggled with the terrifying reality of a sexuality he could not understand. He separated himself from his self-disgust and emotional embarrassment with a clean, cold, clinical description of the response of his body to the advances of a man he considered subhuman, brutal, and monstrous. He felt his soul in mortal peril because of the betrayal of his flesh. He felt himself to be two entities struggling for dominance. He knew the depths of his own intelligence, the passion of his religious feelings. But at times they became as vaporous as air, as insubstantial as words, without strength or power over the flesh. He wanted to punish, subdue, and mortify his body, which was beginning to betray all that was himself. He felt the terrible duality of his nature and the threat inherent to his eventual survival.

This the young priest could deal with. These were familiar, universal terrors and events. This was the eternal battle resolved by boys and young men through all of time by acts of personal defilement, by the ruining of young lives through indiscriminate and stupid couplings outside of marriage. The Church steered its tortured young men to early marriage and counseled its young seminarians to fall back on prayer, cold showers, exercise, determination, and seeking strength from God. It was all available. One had only to seek, wholeheartedly, honestly, accepting the pain, the difficulties.

"Do you truly want to be a priest, Eugene?"

The clear young voice coming through the carved grate that

separated them was strong and unquestioning. His vocation had been ordained in ways incomprehensible to either of them.

"There is nothing else I could ever be, Father."

The priest asked if there was anything else to confess: derelictions, shortcomings, evasions. He knew the boy's vanity caused him anguish, his very search for humility was a form of vanity. They had gone through this before. He knew Eugene had a lot to cope with, and that he was at the right place, with the Jesuits, to find his way.

Before he assigned penance, Father Kelly said, "I think, Eugene, you should return to the seminary. I think you should return as soon as possible."

"Yes, Father. Yes. I want to."

Leaving the church, on the way to the rectory, to his delayed breakfast, Father Kelly turned and regarded the boy as he knelt, earnestly praying his penance. He stood for a longer time than he realized, as if waiting for some message, some confirmation that what he had done was proper. What came over him was an absolute conviction that Eugene O'Brien was a specially called novitiate. There was a contained passion in the boy that could one day be channeled and focused and used for the greater glory of God.

That was the conviction with which Father Thomas Kelly was filled as he crossed himself, intoned a quick prayer, and left the dark, mysterious interior of St. Simon Stock for breakfast.

CHAPTER ELEVEN

Dante was surprised by how uninvolved he felt in the death of Walter Stachiew. He saw Ben and Charley horsing around with dirty snowballs, and Willie standing slightly away from them, all facing 181st Street, all waiting for him. To tell them how things were.

He crossed to the bench-lined triangle set into Anthony Avenue on one side, 181st on the other, and the Grand Concourse on the third. He kicked snow off the benches, then sat on the backrest, feet on the wooden slats. The others waited, watching him. He realized no one had yet spoken about what happened last night, after they had gone home.

Dante confronted it directly.

"Willie, your father do what they said?"

Willie Paycek straightened up, his chest pushed out, his head tilted up. He nodded and grinned. "Yeah, he done it. And right in front of the cops, the dumb shit."

Charley and Ben glanced first at each other, then at Dante.

"Exactly what did he *do*, Willie?"

"Ya know. Like what they said in the newspapers this morning. He's standing over Stach, and he's clobberin' him with the shovel, and he's yellin' his head off—'Die, ya fuck, I tole ya I was gonna kill ya.' And the cops jump outta their car and they see him, smashin' Stach's head in and he tells the cops, 'See that, I tole him, the dumb fuck, I was gonna do it and I done it.'"

Willie did a small dance step, a hop from one foot to the other, probably to keep his feet from freezing, but there was something jaunty, almost joyous in his attitude. He turned and looked at each of the boys, shrugged. So what? What the hell? Something about Ben Herskel brought his jigging to a halt.

Ben, so much taller and heavier than the others, hatless, his thick hair wild in the wind, maintained a distance, the mild disinterest of someone aware of an event but untouched by it. Outside of it. He stared at Willie as though at a curious, strange, unknown creature.

Willie took a deep breath and included Ben in the event. "Hey, Benny, you Jews get any kin'a confession or anything like that?"

Ben thrust his hands deeper into the pockets of his corduroy pants and didn't answer.

Willie turned to Dante.

"Hell, maybe this guy's gonna feel he gotta go and blab. And maybe he thinks he gotta start namin' names and stuff. I don't know about the Jews, ya know."

Ben remained silent and waited.

Dante said, "Willie, we're all going to just forget it. *We were never there.*" He looked around and they each nodded. Ben's cheek bulged as he played the tip of his tongue around in his mouth. He shrugged: Never where?

"Yeah, but how about O'Brien's brudder? Jeez, we got us a guy gonna be a priest and all."

Charley's hands came out of his jacket pocket. His fingers reddened with cold, stiff, grabbed at Willie's collar.

"My brother's got nothing to do with you. Or with any of this." He turned to Dante. "He's back in the seminary. He left this afternoon."

"Now, does anybody have anything—at all—to say? Willie, it's your father got arrested. You want to say anything? Because now is the time." Willie's grin and shrug were a little scary. "Okay, then that's it. It's over for us. Agreed?"

He put out his hand, and each boy placed his hand over the next. Ben quickly pulled his hand away and turned to Willie.

"Just one thing, Paycek. None of this means anything to me, as far as you're concerned. To me you were always a piece of shit, just like

Stachiew, just like your old man. So you just stay away from me. I don't know you, I don't want to know you."

He turned abruptly and walked toward his father's luncheonette.

Willie watched, his face twitching. "Fuckin' Jews, they're all alike," he said.

"Yeah?" Dante said, "why don't you go over and say that to Ben? Go on, Willie."

Willie kicked at a chunk of ice. He didn't need to see the look exchanged by the other two boys. He knew that nothing had changed for him. There had been no kinship, no special friendship forged that night.

"I gotta go. I got work to do," he said, and left them without looking back.

Danny and Charley walked to the Grand Concourse side of the triangle. They watched the cars splashing up and down the broad expanse of the Bronx's majestic main thoroughfare. Finally, Dante began.

"So, whadda you think, Charley?"

"Jeez, I don't know."

"I mean, how do you *feel* about what happened? About what we did?"

Charley shrugged, waiting. He needed Dante to say it first.

The dark-haired boy, his voice quiet and thoughtful, said, "You know what I find strangest of all in this? Not about Willie's father. I mean about—you know—that I don't feel anything. I mean, I just don't feel anything at all about it."

Charley exhaled a loud, breathy whistle. He felt a trickle of sweat, cold and clammy, running down his back, chilling him. "Jeez, Danny. That's the thing for me, too. I mean, what we did, I mean, aren't we supposed to feel bad or something?"

"*Guilty*, you mean?" He shrugged. "I don't know what we're *supposed* to feel. I just know what I *do* feel. Or what I *don't* feel. I just damn well *don't feel anything*."

Charley nodded, relieved. "I thought there was something maybe wrong with me. I mean, this bastard was some piece of work. This Stachiew. He's been foolin' around with kids for years. Hell, my oldest brother, John, when he came for a visit from Brooklyn last year, he seen Stach across the street and he asked me, 'That guy ever bother you?' I just said, 'Hey, whadda ya mean?' but John said, 'Just watch out for him, he's bad news.' So I guess everybody knew about him."

"He was a piece of garbage. And you know what? So is Willie's old man."

"So whadda you think?"

Danny slid down from the bench, planted his heavy boots on the wet snow, sat on the ice-covered bench. Charley stood in front of him.

Dante rubbed his full red lips with his leather-gloved thumb and spoke thoughtfully. "So what about Gene?"

"Gene went to Father Kelly yesterday morning. They talked. Father Kelly told him he went to the scene, after the cops called him, to give absolution and stuff to that bastard. And that Willie's father killed him. The cops saw it and all. So Gene went back to the seminary."

"You don't think Father Kelly would let him go back if . . . you know . . . if . . ."

Charley made a fist and swung playfully at Dante, catching him lightly on the shoulder.

"What do you think?"

"I think it was crazy. The whole thing. I feel like it never happened. Any of it. Us, I mean."

Charley frowned and kicked at a piece of ice, concentrating, buying time. Finally, "Danny, what about Megan?"

"What about Megan?"

Quickly, Charley reassured Danny. "Oh, God, she's more stand-up than anybody. I don't mean that. What I mean is—"

Danny spoke softly, intently. It was as though suddenly he had become completely grown up, his voice certain and decisive. Charley looked up, listening intently.

"There is no 'what about Megan?' in any of this. Megan was never on the hill. She didn't come sledding with us, we saw her when we came back up to Ryer Avenue and we watched her go home. Your cousin is not in this in any way. Okay?"

Slowly, Charley nodded. He exhaled, relieved that one part of this thing had been solved. "I'll talk to her and—"

"Taken care of," Dante told him. "I saw her this morning."

"And what about that little turd Willie?"

Dante shrugged. "I don't think we've anything to worry about there. He's made out really good. He got rid of two bastards, however it happened. So, Charley, we forget about it, right?"

"Can we do that?"

Dante reached down, scooped up a handful of snow, kneaded it, and tossed it out onto the Grand Concourse, then turned to Charlie. "I think we have to, don't you?"

"Yeah, I guess so."

"And I don't think we should talk about this again. Not ever. With anyone."

Charley nodded, then looked directly into Dante's black eyes. "Danny, do you think we killed that guy?"

Dante D'Angelo held his gaze steady, his face went blank, and he shrugged. "What guy?"

CHAPTER TWELVE

With his father in Sing Sing awaiting execution, Willie Paycek, for the first time in his life, was accorded a kind of respect by the tenants in his building.

He stood by his mother. He worked hard, taking on responsibilities and physical labor no one thought him capable of. From being the boy neighborhood kids were told to avoid, he became, through his uncomplaining industry, something of an example. He ran errands, fetched and carried, made deliveries from the various neighborhood stores.

From his point of view, Willie did what he had to do to survive and to get some time and some money.

His mother had always depended on men to tell her what to do, when and how to do it. Men had always supplied her with orders, commands, ridicule, and contempt. In this respect, Willie filled in very easily for both his father and Walter Stachiew.

It was at his insistence—although in truth she was really very glad to oblige—that the four blond kids, two boys and two girls, were placed in a Catholic Protectorate up in Nanuet, not very far from the prison where his father awaited execution. This left Willie, his mother, and little Mischa a privacy and serenity they had never before experienced.

"You don't bring no man in here no more," he told his mother in a thin but firm voice. "And you don't go sneakin' off to no bar or nothin' like that. And you gimme a good meal at night, you want I should stay here and help you with the work. See, if you don't do like I say, I'm gettin' outta here, and they'll throw you and the little freak into the streets. So you just do like I say and I'll help you with the work. You got all this?"

His mother mopped her sweaty red face and nodded. She started to say something: How could she just eliminate men from her life altogether? Willie was too young to understand, she was a woman. But her words caught in her mouth as her oldest son leaned back against the kitchen table and seemed to answer the protest she had never made.

"You try to cross me once, just once, Ma, and you are on the street."

She understood. All she had to do to survive was whatever Willie told her. Life would be easier, if somewhat empty, without the two men constantly having at her, quarreling, fighting, turning on her without warning. It *was* easier, actually, with both of them gone.

Still, she did miss the excitement, the sexuality, the feeling that came with being desired not just by one man but by both of them. Well, there was a long future. She would, for now, do what Willie wanted. She had never realized how much her son resembled his father.

If he thought that sharing a secret with the others would form a bond of friendship, he was wrong. He was still the outsider, but now he had no time to hang around. He had a life to take care of—his own.

Nothing much changed for Willie at school. Sister Mary Frances watched him with grim satisfaction. The fruit did not fall far from the tree.

Once she spotted some dereliction as Willie bent over a composition paper. She glided to his side, leaned in close, and whispered in her malicious voice, "You'll end up just like your father, William Paycek."

Instead of leaning even closer to his blotched paper, instead of hunching his shoulders in anticipation of her hard thump, the boy put his pen down slowly, deliberately, and pulled himself up straight in his seat. He raised his face to hers, and his expression contained such total and concentrated hatred that Sister drew back, intimidated.

His thin lips stretched over his small grayish teeth into a terrible grimace, and his voice was so low and controlled that it carried no farther than to her.

"Stay off my back, Sister."

She pulled away, glanced around. No one had heard their exchange, no one dared to look up from his work.

She faced the window and surreptitiously made a quick sign of the Cross. It seemed revealed to her that she was in the presence of pure evil.

To a large extent, Sister Mary Frances was right.

In the last week of October, 1936, Willie Paycek went to see Father Kelly. He needed a two-day excuse from school. He and his mother and brothers and sisters were going upstate to see his father for the last time.

Of course, Father Kelly and everybody else in school, in the neighborhood, in the Bronx and in the city, if not in the world, knew that his father was going to be executed for the murder of Walter Stachiew.

Father Kelly shook Willie's hand, squeezed his shoulder, asked him if he was gong to be all right.

"Me? I'm gonna be fine."

Father Kelly misread Willie's brusqueness for courage. He slipped him a couple of dollars. "Get your brothers and sisters some treat. Some hot dogs or candy or something."

Sure. Like hell.

The other kids didn't know how to act, so what they did was more or less ignore him. Just the way they always did.

Except for Dante D'Angelo. Mister Big Shot, taller than anybody else in the freshman high school class, going out for whatever teams he could, acing the exams as they came along. *Mister Everything Comes Easy to Me.*

"Hey, Willie."

Danny caught up with him. "You're going upstate tomorrow, huh?"

Willie craned his neck, spoke from the side of his mouth, the movie tough guy. "Yeah, up the river. To the big house. To see the old man get it."

Danny grinned. "Jimmy Cagney, right?"

"Yeah. Jimmy Cagney."

"Well, I just wanted to say . . . I . . . I'm sorry for your troubles. You know."

"*My* troubles? *Me?* I ain't got no troubles, Danny boy. Any troubles I got, I'm not gonna have no more, you read me?"

Danny's handsome dark face was motionless, the black eyes regarding Willie steadily. He reached out with a fist, and tapped Willie lightly on the side of his shoulder.

"Take care, Willie, okay?"

And then he walked back toward his friends, who were fooling around with the basketball until their star returned.

None of the others approached him. In fact, Willie had sensed an invisible barrier around himself. One cold night of being one of the guys, part of the crowd, in on something, meant nothing.

The damn pansy mick Eugene was back learning to be a priest; Charley O'Brien never had much to say for himself; his tomboy cousin would one day get herself in real trouble. And the Jew, well, what the hell, he might be a big guy and tough and strong, but what he was was a Jew, and sooner or later somebody would teach him what that meant.

Life hadn't changed for any of them. Not the way it had for Willie. And all the changes were for the good.

This was going to be an event to remember. Seeing the old man for the last time.

Willie had the last row of seats to himself. He had instructed his mother to sit toward the front with the four blond Protectorate kids and Mischa, who was excited to be riding in a bus. The nuns had turned them out like it was Easter Sunday, all decked out in navy jumpers for the girls and long navy pants for the boys, with crisp white blouses. His mother was dressed up too, in her one good dress, a large, flowing black crepe with big red roses all over.

"He likes this dress, ya fodder," she told Willie.

Sure. Sure. As if the old bastard ever noticed anything. Sure, Ma. Real nice, and the permanent wave she had had her friend give her looked terrific too. Tight curls all over her head, her sweaty face red, her eyes watering from the harsh chemicals.

"To look pretty for ya fodder," she'd told him when he sniffed the heavy air in disgust.

Mischa sat and stared in awe at his two blond brothers and two blond sisters. He hadn't the slightest idea who they were.

"He eats with his elbows on the table, Ma," the thinnest blond girl said. "Don't you have no manners?"

"*Any* manners," her sister, a year older, corrected her with a deep sigh.

The blond boys said nothing. They communicated with each other through signals: eye-blinks, raised brows, a slight movement of the hand, a shrug of the shoulders.

Christ, his family, all dressed up and nowhere to go except to an execution.

Not that the children would be allowed to watch, but they would get to visit the old man. The sisters had told them all about it. And then the next day would be the funeral, and he would be buried in a small Catholic cemetery not far from the prison. Because he'd repented, his oldest daughter said solemnly.

This one they could make into a nun, Willie thought. She had the right mouth for it, thin-lipped and tight. And she liked to watch the other kids, to poke them or jab at them or hiss at them, just loud enough for everyone around to hear when they weren't acting the way she felt they should.

Hell, for the year he hadn't seen them, he'd almost forgotten what they looked like. They were neater and cleaner and a little taller and heavier than they were before, but they were still cartoon figures with straw hair and round, empty, pale blue eyes. Willie kept them away from him. Stay away from me. Just that simple. Keep away from me. The girls sulked, the boys exchanged secrets without saying a word.

Willie stared out the window, watching the landscape change from towns to long stretches of empty land. He saw small houses, set high above the highway, and he wondered what kind of people lived there and walked around on the farms spread out everywhere. There was a kid standing by a mailbox, a big tin receptacle on a plank of wood by the road. He caught Willie's eye and waved to him. Willie kept his hands clasped on his lap. Dumb little bastard, that what you got to do all day, wave at strangers on a bus, who don't wish you nothing at all?

Maybe the little bastards, the Protectorate kids, would all get married off to kids like that one and live in the country and have kids of their own and wave to passing buses. It was about what they would be fit for.

He could hear his mother's voice, a droning, whining, unrelenting sound. There she was, sitting up there surrounded by those damned kids, giving hunks of herself away to total strangers.

She talked to the other women on the bus, also going to visit husbands, brothers, fathers, sons, all locked up in Sing Sing. His mother was the star of this trip, and all attention was on her. The women listened and watched, dazzled by their closeness to a major event. Her husband was going to fry tonight, and she and all these kids were going to collect him and bury him tomorrow.

Her starring role. Yeah, just like in a movie. That was how remote and uninvolved Willie felt. But if it *was* a movie, *his* movie, the focus would not be on that stupid, gross, obese, sweaty woman who literally couldn't keep her mouth shut or get control of herself.

Willie wasn't sure who would be the star. Not he himself—he

wanted no part of the action. He was the observer, cold, remote, unmoved. He wanted to control the scene, direct how it would be done, what each person would say, how each would react. His mother. He'd toss her out of the bus and let her wander around the empty land, hoping to find some stupid farmer she could stop and tell the story of her life to—tell about her husband and her lover and the murder.

How in the name of Christ had he come from such people?

At the prison, they were separated from the other visitors. After all, they were the condemned man's family. The kids were given bottles of Coca-Cola and baloney sandwiches and Yankee Doodles and a bag of penny candy. Whatever they couldn't finish, his mother devoured, waving off food that was offered to her. Too upset—no, no, how could she eat.

And then, in a burst of curiosity, with movie-learned wisdom, she asked what her husband had ordered for his last meal. The deputy warden looked surprised. He didn't know. Well, she could ask him herself. They would meet shortly. Would she like to see him alone first, or with the children? All up to her.

His mother looked stunned. Asked to make a decision, she began to cry.

"Bring him here with everyone," Willie instructed.

The guards were relieved that someone was taking charge of the situation. They knew immediately that the woman was going to be a real mess. The kids seemed well behaved. The oldest kid seemed very sharp, very controlled.

It was not like a Cagney-O'Brien-Bogart movie. There was a heaviness in the closed-in air, a pressurized condensation of smells rising from the floor, drifting from the walls and ceilings. As they passed through one set of sliding bars, Willie reached out, wrapped his hand around the smooth steel. The solidity of it fascinated him, the thickness, the rigidity. The guards marched along with them, two in front, one alongside his mother, holding her arm, a couple with the kids, trying to distract them, trying to pretend this was not the most incredibly awful place they would ever be in in their lives.

Willie absorbed all of it—the sounds, the smells, the totality of the place. Beginning and end of the world, all contained in concrete and steel. He had to relax consciously, to fight off the growing claustrophobia. If he showed anything, did anything, said anything, they wouldn't let him continue. They'd take him off to a room, along with the kids, and tell him to relax, no need to get so upset, kid, you just stay here, have another Coca-Cola, it'll all be over soon.

No. He wasn't going to blow this.

He'd waited too long for this day.

His mother pulled back. No, she didn't want to see her husband alone.

Her hands reached out, touching her children lightly. Without exception, each child pulled back far enough to avoid her seeking fingers. Willie shoved them all together.

"Okay. Bring him in to see all of us. That how you work it? We gonna be in a little room or something?"

The guards exchanged glances. The deputy warden nodded.

It was a small, green-painted room with a heavily grilled window, a long table, chairs, benches against one wall. The kids sat on the bench, under the window. Willie stood next to his mother, who leaned heavily, one hand on the table, one on his arm. She trembled so violently that Willie had to brace himself. If she fell, it would be against him.

Stanley Paycek was a stranger, aged and grayed by the months in prison. His thin, sallow cheeks were freshly shaved. He squinted through steel-rimmed spectacles. His scant, frazzled hair was combed wetly across his bald skull. The gray shirt was too large; it stood away from his wrinkled neck. His pants, prison gray, freshly laundered, were too short. His white socks showed. He stood absolutely still, then dropped the Bible he had been carrying.

Willie's mother gasped, pulled away from her son, picked up the Bible, kissed it fervently, and handed it back to her husband.

"Stanley," she said, not certain who this man was, but ready to react, impatient to react. "That's you?"

The small man nodded, lifted his hand to his wife's face, and touched her cheek.

"Yeah. This is me," he said. He seemed embarrassed by everything. The need for eyeglasses, the clean-shaven face, the obviously spruced-up picture he presented.

And then it began, exactly as Willie knew it would. His mother flung herself at her husband, nearly knocking him over. She screamed and roared. Her face became bloated and red and wet with tears and spittle.

Her husband held her as best he could. The guards provided backup. The woman was having a fit.

"It's okay, okay, okay," the condemned man chanted.

The children stood quietly, large eyes seeing, faces devoid of expression. They had seen, through all their lives, this kind of reaction from their mother. What was different was the lack of fury coming from their father. They had witnessed beatings, kickings, punchings. They had never before seen this man quietly holding their mother, trying to calm her down.

A cup of water was provided. The sobbing woman sat heavily on a chair, sipping and gasping and blinking at the thin apparition that was left of her husband, a man she had known all her life, through marriage, through children, and now at the verge of death.

"So," his father said finally, when things quieted down. He lifted both arms, still clutching the Bible. "Come, say good-bye to Papa." To the guards he said, "They are beautiful, aren't they?"

One after the other, the Protectorate kids offered a cheek, allowed him to touch a hand before pulling back and out of reach.

"And Mischa? Where is little Mischa, the youngest?"

"He's next door. In another room. He's too young," Willie said. His eyes locked on his father's eyes, hard to see beneath the smudged glasses. It was their first confrontation. The first acknowledgment that it was Willie who made decisions for this family now.

"But for the last time," his father said, his voice thin and uncertain. "To see his papa for the last time."

His mother began to scream and bang her head on the table. The guards looked alarmed. The woman was perfectly capable of causing injury to herself and anyone else.

"Ma," Willie said, his thin, strong hands biting into her fleshy arm. "Cut it out or the visit is over. Ma?"

She looked up, nodded heavily, swiped at her face with her arm. With a snap of his fingers, Willie demanded a handkerchief from one of the blond girls. His father dug out a huge prison-issue square of gray cloth.

He offered it to Willie.

"For Mama, okay?"

Willie smiled tightly and nodded.

Within minutes, his mother quieted down. The guards brought in coffee, slices of pound cake. His mother smiled, beamed, they were all so good to her. Her children ate more Yankee Doodles, the boys sucking the white creamy centers first, the girls glaring at them, correcting their manners. One of the guards brought Mischa into the room. Small, dazed, nose running, mouth stuffed with cookies, milk mustache. He seemed lost in all the activity, the pretty children, the uniformed men, his mother waving him forward, the thin man with eyeglasses leaning toward him, calling his name. Mischa dropped his cookie and leaned against a wall. His right hand went into his pants pocket, began to work frantically.

His mother lunged at him, screamed. "Dirty little animal, even in here you do this thing. Pig, pig, pig."

Willie moved faster than the guards could react. He had known what to expect. He scooped the hysterical, terrified child off his feet. He pressed Mischa hard against himself, felt the shuddering, the gasping, the choking. The guards escorted him out of the room. Willie thumped the child onto his feet, ran his hand roughly over Mischa's face.

"He'll be okay. F'Christ sake, I told you, leave this kid outta there." To the boy he said, "All over now, kid. Here, shove some more cake inta ya mouth. You're okay, ya got that?"

The huge, pale round eyes stared and the large head nodded, toppled forward like a flower on a too-thin stem. His hands reached for the cake. He let himself be lifted by one of the guards and gently placed on a chair.

"He okay, this kid? He gonna have a fit of some kind? Should we call for a doc, or what?"

"Just keep him outta there is all." He regarded his youngest brother, who looked back, grinning. "See? It's all the same to him. He don't remember nothin' that happened. He got no brains is what his trouble is. But keep him here, give him cake, he's happy."

The guards glanced at the child, then back at Willie. "Okay, I guess you know."

"Yeah," said Willie. "I know."

Finally it was time for the family to leave. The guards allowed husband and wife a moment alone. It was, of course, a mistake. She screamed hysterically, then went into a dead-weight faint, smacking her head on the edge of a chair. A nurse, standing by, revived her and Stanley was returned to his cell.

Willie waited until the family was resettled in the visiting room and arrangements were made to take them all to the boardinghouse where they would spend the night. A priest spoke with his mother. The kids, tired, expressionless, sat quietly.

Willie approached the older guard, the one with the nice face, the one who had been alarmed rather than repulsed by Mischa's behavior.

"Look," Willie said, gazing directly into the heavily lined face of the gray-haired guard. "I'm the oldest, ya know? I gotta take care a' alla them. I wanna say good-bye to my father alone. Man to man, because I'm gonna be head of this family now. Whadda ya say? I didn't get no chance to talk with him, my mother had to have all the time."

There was something so earnest and touching about the scrawny, gray-faced, cross-eyed boy that the guard could not resist. He knew there would be no hysterics, no fainting, no overemotional parting. He looked from Willie to the line of kids, to the heavy sobbing woman. It was little enough this kid asked for. It took a few minutes on the phone to arrange, and the guard took Willie through the heavy steel door with the barred grille, through a series of passageways, all enclosed by sliding steel doors, manned by other guards. Willie wanted to shrug off the heavy hand on his shoulder, but he knew the guard thought he was being kind.

Willie absorbed every inch of the atmosphere, with all of his senses. The very air *tasted* special. He would remember, forever, everything about this place. Nothing like in the movies; no movie had even come close. Prison movies should be shot in prison.

Finally they entered the last chamber. There was a row of cells to his left, a tile wall to his right. In each cell was a condemned prisoner, and they called to Willie as he walked past, ignoring but absorbing them.

"He's a good man, kid."

"Your pop's okay. He's gonna be tough."

His father was seated on the cot that was attached by bars to the steel wall. He was hunched over in prayer, lips moving. He looked up in surprise and wiped his face with the back of his hand.

"Willie. I'm glad you come. Mr. Watkins," he said to the guard in the obsequious, fawning voice he used when he sought favor with people superior to himself, "this is my oldest kid. My son. Thank you for bringing him here. You're a good man. God will bless you."

The guard let Willie into the cell, turning him around. "I gotta lock the door, kid, don't get nervous on me, okay?"

"Naw, naw, this is a good kid, Mr. Watkins," his father said. A good kid. He had never said anything like that to or about Willie in his life.

They were alone, father and son, locked in the death cell.

"Willie, ya wanna pray with me?"

"I don't wanna pray with you. Save that for the priest."

His father shrugged and patted a space beside him on the cot. "C'mon, you sit now with your fodder."

"No. I don't wanna sit. I want to stand here and look at you. I wanna watch your face."

His father finally caught the hardness in his son's voice. He squinted, noticed changes in his oldest son. The kid wasn't much bigger, he would always be a shrimp, but there was something tough about him that hadn't been there before. He stood up straighter, he didn't keep looking away. He looked directly at his father, who suddenly felt anxious.

"So, Willie, how ya doin'? Ya bein' a good boy for ya mudder, she gonna need you now."

"Fuck how I'm doin', old man."

His father's eyes became slightly frantic. This little bastard was a stranger, standing there, staring at him, his face looking like that. A slow, surging, familiar anger began to rise in Stanley Paycek with a hammering memory of who he was and who this punk kid was.

"Ya don't talk to me like that, you."

Willie smiled. Good. Finally his father had appeared from under the layers of religious convert, concerned father, worried husband. The bastard *was* here.

"I don't talk to you like that, huh? Well, I'm gonna talk to you, Pop, 'cause I got something to tell you. It's the last thing you'll ever hear from me, so you listen very hard, very good. You listen to what I'm gonna tell you, and every single word is the God's honest truth."

He snatched the missal from his father's hand.

"I swear it on your prayer book, old man. The truth."

Willie told his father about the death of Walter Stachiew. He described, blow by blow, exactly what had happened that cold winter night. Then he said what he was not sure of, could never be sure of, but he said the words softly and with controlled certainty.

"And *I'm* the one that finished him off, Pop. The others, they brought him down, but *I brained him*. What you done, you stupid sonofabitch, what you done was you picked up that shovel and beat on a dead man's head and then you told the cops you done it. You are one stupid crazy rotten old bastard and I wanted you to know. It's *me* puttin' you in that chair tonight. That's what I wanted you to know. When you feel that sizzle, *it's me put you there*."

Although he should have anticipated it, his father's attack surprised him. He was no match for this wiry, hard man, but the fury of the attack combined with the man's hysteria overwhelmed the boy. His father's strong hands went around Willie's throat. He managed one quick loud cry, a scream, combined with his father's howl of fury. The guard, for a split second in shock, fumbled with the lock, then was joined by two others as they rushed the cell. It took all their strength to pry Paycek's hands from his son's throat.

They half-carried, half-dragged the boy from the cell, patting him, massaging him, terrified of what had happened, of the possible consequences and their own responsibility.

One of the guards punched Stanley Paycek, hard, in the face, knocking him back onto his cot. They quickly locked him in, but he leaped up, came to the bars, hands locked in anger.

"I didn't do it," he screamed. "That little fucker, him, he done it, he killed Walter. Oh, my old friend, Walter, *he* killed you, not me. *He* should fry. Oh, God, they gonna kill me, they gonna kill me and he done it, that piece of shit, he done it, not me."

Those were the last words Willie Paycek ever heard from his father. The guards hurried him into their own private bathroom, washed the blood from the corner of his mouth, offered him a drink of water, a shot of whiskey, anything to get the kid's color back, to make sure he was okay.

Willie blotted his face on the rough paper towels, bunched them up, and dropped them neatly into the wastebasket. After all, he was the janitor's kid, he knew about being neat and tidy. He took a few deep breaths, as they told him to do; they shook his shoulders once or twice, rubbed his neck, and shrugged. He was okay.

He was more than okay. He was weightless, without solidity, without reality. He was an invisible presence causing things to happen. This was *his* scene; he was responsible for everything that had just happened and that was about to happen. It was all because of *him*. He would remember and try to recapture this moment for the rest of his life. It was a moment of absolute perfection.

· Later the guards cautiously discussed what had happened. After the body had been claimed by the hysterical woman, who was in care of a large, unhappy priest, and the small funeral entourage left the prison grounds, they looked at each other and it was unanimous. This kid, this Willie Paycek. Did you see the look on that kid's face? He was some cold piece of business.

It was their opinion that they'd see him back in their death-row territory someday.

They were wrong.

CHAPTER THIRTEEN

It was the beginning of her second week at Quinatree, the upstate New York CYO camp where Megan had spent the last four Julys of her life. She wished she could slow time down; it all went by so fast. She glanced at Kathleen O'Connor, still asleep in the next cot, the pillow held over her face with both of her tanned arms.

Kathleen was her chief rival. They were evenly matched, but this afternoon Megan was going to win the free-style swimming competition. Kathleen was faster at the start, but Megan had staying power.

Megan stretched, ignoring the achy feeling in her arms and legs. She must have been sleeping funny. She was all cramped.

She had tried to talk her mother and father into letting her stay for the whole summer. As a reward, she'd argued, for graduating number one among the girls and only one point off being top eighth-grader, and everyone knew Tommy Quinn was some sort of genius-freak. Her mother shook her head, wondering why Megan couldn't count her blessings instead of always wanting more. Her father had said, "What the hell. You want to be rewarded for doing what you're supposed to do, working your best at whatever it is? You think that's special or something?"

It was good to know she was finished with the eighth grade and crazy Sister Mary Frances. Megan couldn't figure her out. She was always watching Megan, leaning over her, insisting she could do better than ninety-six in an exam if she'd only try. Perfection, that was the goal. Megan, she said, you think all life will come easy to you, but I'm here to tell you, life isn't like that.

One minute Sister would praise her, the next find fault. Always staring at her, looking for something Megan didn't understand.

Patsy said it seemed to her like Sister Mary Frances had the hots for Megan. That, of course, was crazy. Not only was Sister a nun, but she was a woman. How could a woman have the hots for a girl?

Patsy told her the various ways between girls and girls. Her brother had explained it all to her.

Megan wondered what the hell went on at the Y camp where Patsy went. All those Protestants, not even caring that they'd all end up in hell. Or whatever. Maybe if they couldn't get into heaven, they couldn't even get into hell. Patsy never worried about these things.

Megan knew, even before Patsy had told her, that this would be the last good summer of her life. Patsy was a year older and she had begun changing, her body still thin but rounder, her waist narrower, her flat hips more in evidence. She was still flat-chested, but there was *something* different. And Patsy had started that damned bleeding thing.

Megan's sister-in-law, her oldest brother's wife, told her about menstruation and laughed when her first question was "Do boys get anything like that?" Her sister-in-law, twenty-three, with three children, said, "Don't worry about them. They have their own problems." Megan glanced at the explanatory pamphlet enclosed with the sample Kotex napkin, then ripped it up and tossed it in the garbage pail along with the napkin and the elastic band to hold it on. No. This was not for her. She wanted no part of it.

At thirteen, Megan was flat-chested, narrow-hipped, concave-bellied, with slim, strong arms and legs. Her hair was close-cropped for the summer and she thought she could probably be mistaken for a boy. She studied her face critically in her bedroom mirror. It was definitely a girl's face. A certain softness defined it, a fullness in her lips, a delicacy of her slightly tipped-up nose. She hated the damned red freckles that were spattered like paint all over her face and shoulders and arms and probably her back too. Maybe they would fade after she became a *real* girl. Megan had no idea what she would be like when the mystery happened to her.

She didn't want to become a different Megan. She wanted to play ball with the boys, to challenge anyone who bothered her to a test of strength, to make fun of the girls, to wrestle with Patsy, just to be herself. She didn't know what would be expected of her when she became a *real* girl. She didn't want to know.

With the exception of Kathleen O'Connor, none of the girls in her bunk was her kind of kid. All they talked about was boys and periods and bras. Endlessly they described boyfriends, real and imaginary: who was cute, who was fast, who they were in love with, who they wanted to date, to walk with, to talk with, to be seen with. And later, to marry. They had ideas about catching boys with good jobs. They would be the wives of important men. No one wanted to be anything herself. Just a girl who caught a rich boy.

Fuck that, Megan thought, venomously. How'd they like to hear her say the fuck-word? That'd make them scream and cover their ears, like they'd never heard it before, or seen it painted on a wall somewhere.

Megan wished, deep in her heart, that she could be spending her summer in a boys' camp where there would be real competition, hard and challenging. Boys were involved in doing things and building things and taking things apart and putting them back together again.

She knew that they did talk about girls. Patsy had told her the kinds of things boys said when they were alone. About girls who had developed into "real girls," and if you hung around with boys after that time, they'd give you a bad reputation whether you deserved it or not. You couldn't just be with them anymore. Not on the same old terms.

Boys, she knew from her own observation, were always rubbing, pulling, adjusting their privates. Getting together in the back of the big lot for peeing contests. A few times, when her police lieutenant uncle, Tom O'Brien, had given her a pair of tickets to the Saturday-afternoon hockey game at Madison Square Garden, she and Patsy had witnessed their obsession at first hand.

They were the only girls present in the free PAL section and they ignored the wise-cracks, catcalls and remarks from boys they didn't know. When they were pelted with popcorn, the two of them retaliated with pistachio nut shells, which traveled better and stung the target. Finally, in exasperation, a whole line of boys, maybe seven or eight of them, two rows above them, had, on signal, opened up their flies and pulled out their dicks and waved them at the girls. Megan had felt her face grow hot, her mouth go dry. Patsy had grabbed her arm, muttered a quick "Let's get outta here," but as they ran past the boys, Megan's eyes on the steps, Patsy had stopped, turned, made an obscene gesture at the taunting boys and shouted at the top of her lungs, "Ya all got shortchanged, ya jerks. I've seen better on puppy dogs!"

Megan couldn't talk about it afterwards, or explain to Patsy how she felt. Ashamed, guilty, dirty, as though she had done something to cause all of those boys to expose themselves. Why did they do things like that? What did they mean by it? What did they want from her and Patsy? Why couldn't they just be guys, and pals, why did they feel they constantly had to taunt and make fun of girls and try to make them feel awful.

"Screw 'em," Patsy said. "It's how they are because they got themselves their little pricks and they think they're special. Pricks and balls, big fuckeola deal."

Patsy said all boys and men were slightly nuts about their whole sex thing—always comparing size and shape. Patsy had told her about a hard-on: that was why the men in the movie seats next to them held what seemed like a club between their desperate hands.

"They play with it, see," Patsy explained. "Then, when it's hard, they shove it into you. You know where."

"Even boys get hard?"

"You better believe it."

There was no one with whom Megan could check this information. She kept it all to herself and was angry with herself for thinking about such things. She wondered if she should mention any of this at confession, but she couldn't figure what her sin was. Dirty thoughts? She felt she'd rather die than sit there in the booth, knowing Father Murphy or Father Kelly was hearing every word, thinking about what a filthy creature was saying these awful things. She took a chance that maybe God wouldn't consider it all her fault, should she get hit by that inevitable truck that waited around every corner to strike down the sinful, unconfessed Catholic child, doomed outside the state of grace to unbearable realms of torment.

Kathleen suddenly tossed the pillow from her face for a direct shot at Megan's head. Megan reached out, caught the pillow, raised it over her head to retaliate. Instead of directing the pillow, it slipped from Megan's hands, her knees buckled with a fierce cramping pain, she fell back onto her cot, her head hitting the steel frame. Her arms were at her sides, suddenly heavy with muscle spasms.

Kathleen thought it was a trick and she crept toward Megan, prepared for a counterattack.

But Megan didn't move. Her face was frozen into a look of astonishment, disbelief that her body had suddenly betrayed her. She couldn't move so much as a finger.

The last thing she saw before passing out completely was Kathleen's face, looming over her, the usually playful, wise expression changing into a look of sheer terror.

Megan knew with her last conscious thought that something terrible was happening to her.

Megan Magee was the first girl at Camp Quinatree to come down with polio. Within two weeks there were four more cases at her camp, and nine other cases at camps that shared the lake.

Throughout the state, camps, public lakes, and swimming pools closed down and people were advised to avoid crowds and public places. The summer of 1936 was the beginning of the worst infantile paralysis epidemic the country had ever known.

When it first happened, only her parents could see her and they couldn't stay very long or do much more than stand and look at her. Her mother would cry, a nurse would lead her away, her father would stand staring, looking very grim. Angry, Megan thought, as though somehow this was all her fault. Like it had been her fault all those times when she had broken something: her ankle, her shinbone, her right arm, left arm, two fingers. You're careless with yourself, he'd tell her. He was always proud that she played so hard at whatever the game, she knew that. But he also told her she paid too high a price. Learn to take care of yourself.

But this, of course, was different. Wasn't it?

Sister Mary Frances had come to see her one rainy Saturday, grim-faced, pale, her eyes two gray stones. She prayed by Megan's bedside until Frankie Magee, none too gently, moved her away.

Jesus, Sister, the kid isn't dead, you know.

That's my dad, Megan had thought, secretly watching the surprised nun pull back from her father's touch. She finished her prayer and stood motionless, staring, but didn't pray again. If there was anything at all to be grateful for, it was that this hadn't happened in the middle of the school term. She'd be back with Sister Mary-the-Nut-Frances.

Well, small favors.

Before she left, though, Sister Mary Frances came to her bedside, took Megan's hand, and pressed a holy medal into it. She leaned close, and in a don't-think-you-can-fool-me voice, she said to Megan, "God knows every single thing you've ever done and will do in your lifetime, Megan. There are rewards and there are punishments. Don't think you can ever get away with anything. Fortunately, there is God's grace. You must never forget that."

And then she added, "You must offer your pain and suffering to Our Lord. Constantly, no matter how bad it is."

That was something her mother had told her during the worst of it, in the beginning, when she was mad with the agony of muscles tightening, twisting, being wrapped in hot wet clothes, being manipulated and pulled and stretched.

"Offer your pain to Jesus," her mother had whispered as Megan grimaced with agony. "It mustn't be wasted, Megan. Dedicate your suffering to Jesus."

Finally, in a burst of anger and rationality, Megan had yelled at her mother, "What the hell will *He* do with it? If that's so great, fine, he can have the pain, all of it, every goddamn drop of it." She had thrown her head hard against her pillow and yelled at the ceiling. "Here, Jesus, damn it, take it all, take it all for yourself and leave me the hell alone!"

Her mother's hand had jerked Megan's face into position so that they made eye contact. Megan had never seen that look on her mother's face. It went beyond anger. It seemed the face of a stranger, hard, frozen, almost cruel.

"Don't you ever—*ever*—dare to speak like that again. Never, no matter what, as long as you live, Megan Magee. You remember what you said just now when the priest comes around to hear your confession, because you've just committed the worst sin of your life and I don't want to know you in this state."

It scared the hell out of Megan, and she asked to see a priest as soon as her parents left. The priest, a middle-aged, balding, paunchy, soft-spoken rector of the small Catholic church in the upstate community, listened quietly, calmed Megan down, nodded, and helped her wipe away the sin so that she could get through the rest of her day, at least, in a state of grace. Her penance was so light that Megan wondered if either the priest was a little stupid or maybe hadn't listened too carefully. It didn't really matter. He was a priest and he did give her absolution.

But she still couldn't understand the whole routine of offering up pain to Jesus. It seemed to Megan that he had enough of his own pain without everyone piling on more and more.

The first time she saw the brace, she felt her heart thump against her rib cage. Her breath caught in her throat. She didn't hear the words the doctor was saying, just the pleasant humming of his voice. He was explaining the brace to her; she knew that because he was pointing and handling different parts of it, showing her how to fasten and unfasten the various buckles.

"Okay, Megan, let's give it a try. It'll be a little strange at first. We'll get to the shoe later. Let's see this leg, kid."

He was a young doctor, about her oldest brother's age. He was tall and thin and had a beak of a nose, thin lips, small eyes beneath thick lenses. His long white hand flipped the cover off her lap and he knelt next to her wheelchair and reached for the withered, shapeless tube of a leg.

"Now watch, because this is something you'll do every morning and . . ."

Megan didn't think, she just acted. Her right hand shot out, caught the unprepared young physician squarely on the chin. Taken more by surprise than by force, he toppled backwards, flat onto his back. The brace flew from his hand, right at Megan. She caught it, raised it over her head and flung it, this time with great determination and force, across the room, narrowly missing a nurse who had just entered the room.

The doctor, his smooth face gone white, stood up carefully, shook his hands at his sides, flexed his shoulders, adjusted his body. He stood in front of Megan, whose breath came in short, hard gasps and he waited, silent for a moment, getting his own anger under control.

"Okay, champ. Do I take this to mean you do *not* want the brace?"

She glared, her lips tightly compressed.

"Well, then. So be it. But I would like to say that a simple 'I don't want it' would have sufficed." He started to leave the room, motioned to the nurse to take the brace and wait in the hall. He turned and faced Megan. "But lemme tell ya, kid. If you weren't in that chair and if you didn't have that leg, I'd knock the shit out of you for doing that to me."

He didn't wait for her reply, didn't see the startled expression, didn't realize she was impressed. It was the first time anyone had spoken to her as though she were still Megan, a pretty tough kid, not Megan-with-the-leg.

No one brought the brace to her again for a few days. It took them that long to realize that Megan Magee wasn't eating. She was hiding food in tissues and flushing it down the toilet. She was living on water, and her thin face began to look emaciated. That was when they sent for her father.

Frankie Magee never messed around. He went right to the point.

He held the brace in his right hand as he jerked her wheelchair around to face him.

"We gonna do this easy or the hard way? Let me know right now, because I haven't got time for games."

Megan felt the hot tears spill over, cutting down her cheeks. She smeared them away with the back of her hand.

"Daddy . . . I . . . hate that thing. I . . . ."

"You don't want it?" He leaned in close to her, his dark blue eyes narrowing. "Be sure now." She started to speak, but he held his hand up. "Listen to me first, then you tell me. If you don't want it, goddamn it, there are poor kids who'd be glad to get it. This was made for you, but it can be adjusted. So if you don't want it, fine. But then you tell me that you're willing to spend the rest of your life sitting on your skinny little ass in that goddamn wheelchair. And we'll take you home right now and your mom and your sister and your cousins and aunts will all take turns pushing you in that damn chair. They'll take you to the park and stick you under a tree and your little sister can teach you needlework and your mom can teach you how to knit and you can sit all day long and learn crafts.

"*Or* you can put this damn ugly heavy thing on and learn how to walk with it. It comes with a big heavy club-shoe, and then you can walk or hop or drag it along or any other damn thing. It's up to you, Megan. You gonna let your whole life revolve around that poor pathetic thing of a leg or just say the hell with it, and get on with being Megan. *Now*," he said fiercely, "Now you tell me what you want. Because that's exactly what you're gonna get."

She held her breath. She knew he meant it. Frankie always meant exactly what he said.

"Can you show me how to put it on?"

He dropped the brace in her lap. "That's what they got doctors and nurses for."

He left the room without another word, came back within minutes. Everything about him changed. He was calm and smiling, his voice warm and loving.

"See you Saturday, redhead. And, Megan, for the love of God, eat a little more. You're beginning to look like a ghost."

During the four months Megan spent at the rehabilitation hospital in Westchester, Patsy visited her once. Her brother, Carl, a college freshman, was on his way upstate to Colgate, driving his brand new convertible, and he gave his kid sister a break: Go ahead, visit with the cripple for a half hour, then I put you on the bus back home.

"I can only stay a half hour," were the first words her best friend said to her. They hadn't seen each other in more than two months, and both girls felt awkward and ill at ease.

Megan wasn't fully ambulatory yet, and the therapy was painful and intense. She sat up in her wheelchair, breathless at Patsy's visit. They treated each other like strangers.

Patsy told her about some girls at her Pennsylvania camp who had gotten polio. One of the younger girls had died; two others were in iron lungs.

"They got any iron lungs here? You been in one, or what?"

Megan told her, "Some kids, down the hall. They just lay there all day long and look into a little mirror. The iron lung, it's like a great big barrel. It makes awful noises, to help them breathe or something. It's pretty bad."

"Could we take a look? Could I push you down the hall to the room where they are?"

Megan caught a fierce gleaming excitement coming from Patsy. "No, we're not allowed." Aware that Patsy kept glancing at her leg, Megan pushed the cover aside, exposing the withered limb. "Go on, take a good look."

Patsy leaned forward, reached out, but stopped short of touching Megan's shrunken right leg. "Wow. How'd it get so skinny?"

"Atrophy. The muscles shrink. They stop working, so they shrink. Go ahead, take a close look, it's okay. It's not catching anymore."

Patsy got to her knees, ran her fingers lightly over Megan's useless leg. She looked up, her face puzzled. "Is it ever gonna be okay?"

Slowly, Megan shook her head. "No. Not like it was. But *I* will be okay."

Patsy ignored this. "Jeez, Megan. How does it *feel?* You know. To be . . . to be a cripple?"

Quietly, Megan said, "It feels *wonderful*, Patsy. Really great. It's terrific. Anything else you want to know?"

Patsy stood up and shrugged. "I just asked." She looked at her watch. "My brother is waiting outside. Ya oughta see his car. Red with a white canvas top. Brand new. But he already got scratches on it. What does he care? Papa Steigler buys darling Carl another one, it gets too beat up." She sat on the edge of the chair. "He said, Papa Steigler, that he'll get *me* my own car, my own brand-new car, when I graduate high school. Three years from now, can you beat that? And send me to college? Hell, I just want the car, the hell with college. I'll fake it, yeah, I wanna go and get educated some more. Like fun. Who the hell wants ta go to college?"

"*I* want to go to college," Megan said. It was the first time she'd ever said anything like that. She wasn't even sure she meant it.

"You do? What the hell for? I mean, you don't meet some guy by the time you're a high school senior . . . ummm . . ."

"Is that what you're hoping to do, Patsy, meet some guy in high school and get married and that's it?"

"Look, Megan, a lot of things are different for me this year. Papa Steigler got me into this dancing class on Long Island on Saturday afternoons, social dancing with some boys from prep schools. It's not as bad as it sounds. Some of them are real jerks, but some of them are pretty cute. And they take you for soda and stuff, after. Papa Steigler says . . ."

"Terrific. You Papa Steigler's little girl now? He gonna 'adopt' you, too? You gonna be Papa Steigler's girl-Carl?"

Patsy clenched her fists; her chin went up. It was the first familiar expression Megan had seen: combative Patsy.

"Nothing like that. Listen, I gotta put up with a lotta shit from everybody, okay? Always telling me how to do everything, how to eat and dress and sit like a lady and all that crap. But I figure, hell, I do what they want, I get what I want. I get plenty of clothes and books and money and stuff. What the hell? You think I turned into one of the dopey-girl types, all la-di-da, around the boys and act like a jackass? That what you think?"

"Christ, I hope not." Finally she was talking to Patsy, her pal. "But listen, if you do go to college, I mean if that's what it takes to get the car, what'll you take up?"

Patsy shrugged. "I dunno. Gym, maybe, you know, study to be a gym teacher. Boy, Megan, wouldn't that be something? I'd run the gym, have the whole place to myself sometimes, a pool and all, and I'd invite you over and we could . . ."

She stopped speaking abruptly, couldn't meet Megan's eyes.

"Hey, that's okay. Hell, I'm not gonna be stuck in this chair all the time. I got this brace and shoe and I practice every day. I'll get to move pretty fast after a while. Remember? 'Marvelous Megan'? I'll strike back, right, 'Peerless Patsy'?"

Patsy shrugged, not caught up in her friend's enthusiasm. "Dumb nicknames. Kid stuff."

"Come on, Patsy, lighten up, okay? Listen, I can still swim. Three times a week we have water therapy. Gee, in the water, it's just like it always was."

Patsy glanced at the shriveled leg. "Yeah, but it's *not* the same, is it?"

Megan glared at her friend. "Shit. Thank you very much, you jerk. I didn't realize it wasn't the same. Thanks for telling me. I appreciate it."

"Hey, don't get mad at *me*. It isn't *my* fault that you—"

"Right."

"Listen, I better get going." And then, remembering the gift she'd brought with her, she extended the Krum's candy box. "Jeez, I almost forgot. My mother bought this for you. Candy. Carl said we oughta just eat it ourselves, you'd never know the difference."

"What a guy, Carl. Tell you what, Patsy." She tossed the box back at her friend. "You and Carl eat it, okay?"

Patsy held the box of candy tight against her thin body. She met Megan's tough-guy, tight-lipped, teeth-grinding, don't-fuck-with-me expression, which usually preceded a punch or a shove.

Matching her belligerence, Patsy said, "Well, shit, you don't have to be nasty about it, Megan. I mean, I *didn't* have to give you the candy. And I *didn't* have to come and see you."

Impulsively picking up the challenge, Megan said, "Right. And you don't have to come again."

Patsy shrugged. "Fine. If that's how you feel about it, the hell with you."

They'd had arguments before, times when they avoided each other, but sooner or later they'd always get back together and neither of them would remember or care what the problem had been in the first place. This was different and they both knew it.

After a few weeks, Megan wrote to Patsy. She told her all that was happening: the new therapy, the ease with which she now could get around with her brace, the quick progress she was now making.

So many things happened during the day, so many small and large incidents, funny or stupid, provoking anger or amusement. Megan hadn't found any special friend at the rehab center. They were just a bunch of hurting kids, self-involved, damaged, angry or self-pitying and defeated. She *needed* to share so much stuff with Patsy. Hell, if she'd been home, they'd have been back to being good friends long ago. Their fights and make-ups had been going on for years, since she was six and Patsy was seven. She told Patsy that she missed her.

Dante came up to visit her every month or so, either hitching a ride with her father or by bus. He wrote her a long letter every two weeks, telling about his life among the geniuses at Regis, the Catholic honors high school he now attended. He sent along lists of books he was reading that he thought she might enjoy. He knew her father had given her a small portable radio and he listed programs she should listen to under the covers late at night that would scare the hell out of her.

The day she received Patsy's reply to her letter, Dante arrived for a pre-Christmas visit. He was loaded down with gifts her mother had sent—practical things, hand-knitted sweaters and mittens and hats; small packets of candy from her little sister; a book about baseball from her oldest brother; a stack of baseball cards from her cousin Charley; a missal from her cousin Eugene. Her parents would come up the day after Christmas, bringing more loot.

Dante scanned the empty room, dumped the packages on her bed, then found her sitting in the dayroom, facing the window. She barely nodded when he greeted her.

He pulled up a chair and touched her hand lightly with his fingertips. "Bad day, kiddo? Or are you mad at *me* for something?"

Megan shrugged.

"I got some good stuff for you. Couple of things from your family. And a great new game, from yours truly. We can play it together later." No response. Dante tapped her hand impatiently. "Okay, pal, what's the deal?" Again, she shrugged. He poked her shoulder playfully, put his fists up, ducked his head. "Okay, slugger, let's have it. You're mad at me because, mmmmm, because I'm so good looking and you're not? Because I got elected president of the student council? No. Couldn't be that, 'cause I *wasn't* elected. Narrowly defeated, but no dice. I give up." Finally his voice was serious. "What's going on, Megan? You hurting? This just a bad day, or what?"

Megan reached into the pocket of her shirt and pulled out a folded, crumpled letter. Wordlessly she handed it to him. She kept her face averted while he read it. It was from Patsy.

Dear Megan,

My life in high school is great. I thought it would be terrible to be in an all-girls school, but it isn't. When you were my only friend, you never really gave me a chance to make friends with other girls. We just hung around the boys.

Well, I've learned to make myself look good—the girls show each other make-up and hair styles and stuff—and I know some boys now—not the same way as when we were a couple of tomboys. You might be surprised to know I have gone on dates—real dates—to the Paradise and then to Krum's. For ice cream sundaes and stuff. If you hadn't got polio, I would still be on the outside just making fun of everyone. Well, it is much better being one of the in-crowd and I am very popular and having a lot of fun.

I feel sorry for you that you won't have the kind of life I'm having, with boys and dates and all. But I guess you'll just have to make the best of it. I can't imagine how you can stand it, but I know you are very brave.

Very truly yours,
Patricia Wagner

Dante whistled softly between his teeth, then carefully folded the letter and handed it back to Megan.

"Did you write back to her."

Megan nodded. "Ten pages long."

"But you didn't mail it, right?"

"Right."

"Good. Megan, look at me. C'mon, for Pete's sake, it's Danny you're talking to. I've seen tears before. You're entitled. She's a little piece of shit, isn't she?"

Megan shrugged.

"Okay. Tell me how you feel about Patsy."

In a soft, breaking voice, Megan said, "I miss her."

"The girl who wrote you this letter. You *miss* her?"

"No. Not *her*. I miss my pal, my buddy. I . . . you know what, Danny? When we were eight and nine years old, Patsy and I wrote a letter, a pact, like kids do, and then we stuck our fingers with pins and squeezed out the blood and signed the letter. An oath, you know? That we'd always be friends, forever, until we die."

"That was kid stuff, Megan. You're fourteen years old now."

"Well, I keep my word."

"Not everybody does. Besides, people change. Patsy's changed. Or maybe she's finally who she really is."

"I feel left behind."

"Then you gotta catch up, kiddo. You gotta catch up with *yourself.* You've done pretty damn good, from when they first brought you here to now. Christ, I thought you were gonna die, first time I saw you. Look at you now. You swim and exercise and get around like a bat outta hell. When you leave here, you'll be back at school, you'll get back into your *real* life and—"

"I don't have any friends, Danny."

"Well, thanks a whole helluva lot, pal."

"I didn't mean that. Just, well, you're a boy and now I'm growing up and . . . you know."

"You dumping me?"

"No. But *you* will. Dump *me*." There was a small silence. "Sooner or later."

"You think my middle name is Patsy? Listen, kiddo, get this straight. You're my friend, like Gene and Charley and Ben, and some new guys down at Regis. *I trust you.* You know that. And there aren't too many people in the world you can really trust. You're someone special, Megan. Listen, why the hell do you think I bother coming all the way up here to see you?"

Megan grinned slowly and shrugged. "Because I walk funny?"

He knew she'd be okay, at least for now. "Damn right. Funniest walker I know. Now get the hell up out of that chair and let's take a funny walk outside. I need the fresh air. And a good laugh. Then maybe I'll buy you a hot chocolate. If you walk funny enough to make me laugh, that is."

They spent the afternoon together, talking, arguing, comparing notes: her tutor wasn't too bad; his classes were very tough. They didn't seem to run out of things to say, and when he told her good-bye, he caught the hesitation, the holding back.

"Okay, slugger, what? C'mon, give, what do you want to say?"

"Friend to friend, right?" He nodded. "Well, I know Patsy's going out with boys and all. Okay, that's her, that's not me. But, Danny, I'm not sure if I'm *ever* gonna go out with boys and all that stuff. I mean . . ."

"Mean, what? What are you getting at?"

"Look. All I want is this. Just once. To say good-bye. Show me what it's like to kiss a boy good-bye."

"I wouldn't know. I never kissed a boy good-bye."

She turned her face up to him.

For the first time since that night on the hill when he pulled her on the sled away from where Walter Stachiew lay battered and bloody, Dante D'Angelo was struck by the delicacy of her beauty.

He leaned down and very gently kissed Megan on the lips. He held the kiss for longer than he had intended. He felt the warmth and stirring of something more than friendship. His hand touched her cheek lightly and he pulled back.

"Good-bye, Megan. See you next time."

"Good-bye, Danny. Thank you."

"Hey," he said, "what's a friend for?"

*   *   *

It was amazing how many people felt they had the right to tell
Megan Magee how to live when she returned from the rehab clinic to
continue her freshman year at St. Simon Stock High School. She had
kept up with the work for the last six months, so academically she was
prepared.

Her father told her just to be herself. Well, who the hell else could
she be? As if she had a choice. And Father Kelly told her to take things
slow and easy at first. *She* was to give the other kids a chance to get used
to her. Get used to her leg. Terrific.

Sister Mary Frances met her one day as Megan was on her way home
and told her that she should give thought to the possibility that God had
marked her as "one of His own special girls." Had Megan ever really
given serious thought to taking vows? Had she ever considered that
this deformity might be God's way of showing her just how special she
was in His eyes? Megan bit her tongue and shrugged. What could
she possibly say to this nuthead without getting into serious trouble,
since all of her immediate responses, bitten back quickly, were rough
wisecracks?

Her mother told her not to expect special privileges. She was still
responsible for making her bed and picking up her clothes and doing her
homework and taking her turn at the dishes. Thank you a whole lot,
Mom.

Her little sister, Elizabeth, offered to show her how to knit. Megan
told her what to do with the knitting needles and the wool and the
sweater instructions and warned what would happen to her if she told.

Even that warped little creep, Willie Paycek, thought he had the right
to approach her. She set him straight in a hurry. He was a rotten, mean
bastard and nothing would ever change that.

He followed her home one Saturday afternoon as she went up the hill
on Ryer Avenue after a double feature, two serials, and two cartoons at
the Avalon. All for seventeen cents.

She felt him behind her, before she actually saw him.

"Hey, Megan, you comin' from the Avvie too? Good pictures, huh?
You like the movies?"

"Yeah. Some of them." She could be civil to him, what the hell.

"That leg, it must be tough, huh?"

She didn't answer him.

"I mean, that sort of makes you different from what you used to be,
doesn't it? I mean, it sort of changes things for you, don't it?"

Megan stopped walking, turned, and glared at Willie. She was about two inches taller than her tormentor.

"Willie, go take a flying leap, okay?"

"Well, at least I *could* take a flying leap, right? I mean, you can't even walk so good anymore, never mind running and stuff."

Megan felt her fingers roll into tight fists. She was fourteen years old. Too old to flat-out belt someone. Probably.

"Willie, what's your problem? Whadda ya want?"

Willie Paycek shrugged. "Hell, I'm just trying to be *friendly*, Megan. You don't have your best friend, Patsy, anymore, do you, so maybe you and me could be friends."

"Get lost, Willie."

He smiled. It was a smile too old for a young boy's face. It was cruel and insinuating. "You lost your *girlfriend*, huh? That must be tough. I hear she likes *boys* now, in the *regular* way. The *normal* way. Like she and you used to like each other. You know—like *freaky girls*."

Megan froze. The boy's face was a mask, grinning, insinuating things she barely understood. "*Freaky girls?* I'll tell you who's a freak, Paycek. What kinda boy pulls his little brother's pants down and charges a penny to look because the poor kid hasn't got what he's supposed to have? You still doing that, Willie? And how about you, Willie? You got what you're supposed to have, you little creep?"

Willie ran his hand up and down his fly. "Wanna see, Megan? Wanna see what *you* got missin' . . . one of nature's mistakes, Megan. You're the freak here."

Her right fist lashed out so fast that Willie never even saw what knocked him to the ground. She stood over him, feet wide apart.

"Wanna see what I can do with my heavy club foot, Willie? I could crush you to nothing, you little prick."

She turned and walked away, trying, God, trying so hard not to rock from side to side, but she heard him wailing after her, over and over, Willie, the little bastard, "Cripple! Cripple! Cripple! Freak, freak, freak!

It took every ounce of resolve for her to keep going, not to turn back. Don't hear him; don't let him get to you.

But of course, everything Willie Paycek had said got to her and burned into her very being.

She saw Patsy around the neighborhood, sometimes with a group of girls, on their way up to Fordham Road to shop at Alexander's department store, or going to the movies or just walking around. Patsy always seemed to be smiling, laughing, having a great time. Megan saw her sometimes with a boy, holding hands, looking up at him like he was made of gold. Simpering, grinning, laughing at everything the guy said.

She was so jealous at times, she could hardly breathe. And she didn't know if she was jealous of the boy or of Patsy or of the life Patsy was living. She didn't know how to handle the intense pain of being left out.

Megan concentrated fiercely on her schoolwork. For all of her four years at St. Simon High, she was the top student. Not the top *girl*, the top *student*. She was two months shy of her seventeenth birthday when she graduated.

She had been accepted at Marymount, an expensive, top-line Catholic womens' college in Westchester. She would live in a dormitory during the week and come home on weekends. Her father told her how lucky she was, to be going on to college. The first one, boy or girl, in the Magee family.

The summer of her graduation from high school, her father got her a job working in John Daly's Real Estate and Insurance Company, up on Fordham Road. Twenty-two-fifty a week; after taxes, eighteen dollars and seventy-five cents. She opened a savings account at the Bronx Dollar Savings Bank. She deposited ten dollars a week toward clothing and other expenses at college. The rest of the money she could spend as she pleased.

Her father thought she was preparing to become a schoolteacher. Megan had no intention in the world of standing in front of a class of kids who would call her "cripple." Or to teach in a school for handicapped kids, as an example of what they could become if they really worked hard.

She knew she wanted to become something professional. She wanted to prepare herself to take care of herself for the rest of her life. No boy was knocking at her door to get married.

She had her boy friends. Not boyfriends. Just the guys from the neighborhood who, through the years, accepted her exactly as she was: still Megan, still able to sink a basket, smack a rubber ball with a sawed-off broomstick. Maybe she couldn't move smoothly, but she *could* move, and she never asked for favors. She was comfortable with the boys; she trusted them. There was no special girlfriend, since Patsy. She was cordial and polite but very careful to ignore any overtures from any girls; she could never trust a girl again. They were treacherous.

Her one friend, besides her cousin Charley O'Brien, was Danny

D'Angelo. He was the one person she trusted totally. He never treated her in any special way, never made her feel different, that he was being nice to "the cripple kid."

Sometimes he took her to the Paradise. Not a date, just a night at the movies, when neither of them had too much schoolwork. Danny was prelaw at Fordham.

He also never treated her like a girlfriend. Just a pal.

Megan wasn't sure how to handle that. She wanted it both ways. Wanted Danny to hold hands with her; to whisper to her in the movies; to look at her in a certain way. But still it was good to know that she could turn to him for advice, could confide in him when she needed to.

It was to Dante that she told her secret: she didn't want to go to Marymount. She'd had enough of Catholic school. She had her heart set on Hunter College, where all the smart Jewish girls went. There was no fooling around with the Hunter girls. They went for an education, not to put in time waiting for some boy to come along and take care of the rest of their lives.

"Well, I'd say you'll have to negotiate that one with your father, Megan. He respects you enough to listen to you, at least. But have your arguments ready and be prepared for his objections. You have to go one-on-one with him, and your dad's a really smart guy. You know, you're the first in your family to go to college, just like I am. Our parents are a bit awed by us; you have to be ready to tell him *why* you think Hunter would be better for you than Marymount."

She took a deep breath. This was the first time she had ever said this out loud. "Because they have a good premed and I want to be a doctor."

Danny whistled. "Wow."

"There's more." Megan hesitated. "This isn't something I just thought up. I've been thinking about it since I was in rehab."

Besides all the physical therapy, the painful daily workouts, twice a week Megan had a session with the staff psychiatrist, a fairly young woman with bright eyes, a soft voice, a reassuring manner. Megan had found out she could say anything at all. It was better than confession; she didn't have to do penance, just learn to understand some of the things that had been bothering her. She wanted to become a psychiatrist.

"I want to learn how to do what she does, Danny. How to make people feel . . . good. Not just sick people but, you know, people who need help."

"Then level with your dad. Let him know exactly how serious you are." Danny reached across the luncheonette table and helped himself to her bottle of Coke, took a long drink, then said thoughtfully, "Okay, I'm talking now as your attorney, right? You're my first client. Here's my advice. You offer Frankie Magee a quid pro quo. An exchange, something for something."

"Quid pro quo. Okay, what have I got to offer him?"

"He saves four years of tuition by your going to Hunter. He saves that money for medical school. You get your education, he gets a doctor in the family."

"You think I should tell him what kind of doctor I want to be?"

"I think you should do it one step at a time. It's pretty tough to get into medical school, you know. Ben Herskel was telling me he's got a cousin who's going to Scotland to go to medical school. He couldn't get into any American school because of the quota. Against Jews."

"Quota? Against Jews? Why? I don't get it."

"I guess because they're so damn smart. And ambitious. The medical colleges are afraid they'd have nothing but smart Jewish kids going to be doctors. I don't think it'll be easy for a girl to get into medical school, Megan."

She stiffened; chin up; tough guy. "I got the grades. I'll *get* the grades at Hunter. I can compete with anybody. Right?"

"Hey, I'm on your side, remember? Well, anyway, it'll be okay for you. You got the right rabbi."

"The right *rabbi*? What the hell does that mean? One minute you're saying Jews can't get in, and then you're talking about a rabbi. What rabbi?"

"In the political sense. A rabbi is someone with a lot of clout. Someone in a position to make deals, trades, a favor for a favor. Your dad is one of the strongest deal-makers in the Bronx. He's a power. Didn't you know that?"

"My dad?"

"Well, what do you think your father does for a living?"

She shrugged. It wasn't something she had really thought about. "He works for the Party. He does . . . I don't know. Whatever. He helps a lot of the neighborhood people get jobs and their kids get summer jobs and into good schools and stuff . . ."

She nodded. Yes, her father had influence in many areas.

"Quid pro quo, kiddo. That's your father's world. Favor for favor. He's a very powerful man. He's able to get kids into law school, med school. Hell, I might need him someday to help me get into Columbia Law School. They're not too thrilled with Italians."

"My dad, he can do that?"

"And a lot of other things."

Megan looked down, played with her straw, drawing it in and out of a puddle on the table. She lowered her voice.

"So let's say *you* want a favor from him. So what do you give him back?"

"What do you mean?"

She looked directly into Dante's eyes. "Do you tell him you've been a good friend to his kid? His little cripple daughter who hasn't got other friends, so maybe Frankie Magee owes you? Is that how it works?"

Dante froze. His face stiffened with anger; his eyes blazed. He looked away from her, ran his hand roughly over his face, shook his head. His controlled anger was frightening.

He leaned across the table. "You little jerk. You goddamn little jerk. Is that what you think? That I'm your friend because of what your father might be able to do for me? Is that all you know about friendship, Megan? Jesus. I'd like to knock you right off your seat. Damn you, Megan, don't you trust anyone? Don't you even realize what you just said to me?"

She hunched her shoulders and shook her head. "Danny. I . . . I just . . ."

He reached across the table and jerked her face up, forcing her to look at him. "You better learn what friendship is, kiddo. Do you really think . . . all these years . . . do you think . . ." He ran out of words, dropped his hands, shook his head.

He saw the long stream of tears down her cheeks, watched as she brushed her face roughly with the back of her hand.

"Danny, I'm sorry. Honest. I just said it . . . without thinking. I didn't really mean it."

"Megan," he said softly, "don't you trust me? Because I trust you more than anyone else I know. You should know that by now. We talk about things, you and I, and we confide in each other and . . . listen, I wouldn't care if your old man was a tap-dancing clown in the circus. That has *nothing* to do with us. You either believe that or you don't. I think you better tell me right now. Do you consider me your friend, or do you think I've been planning, all these years, to use you, to . . ."

She tried, weakly, for a joke. "A tap-dancing clown in the circus?"

He didn't smile. It was too serious. "I'm gonna tell you something, Megan, and you better remember it. I know Patsy hurt you a lot. But that was *her*. Not me. And not other people, either. You better take people one by one, starting with me. You got that?"

She nodded. Finally they slid out from the table and he followed her out of the luncheonette. She looked over her shoulder at him.

"So you wanna race me to the corner? I'll give you a head start."

He wrapped his arm around her neck, pulled her along, teasing. They were walking without looking, and they slammed into Patsy Wagner and her latest boyfriend. They were holding hands, giggling, flirting.

"Whoops, sorry," Dante said. They exchanged greetings cautiously, Patsy rubbing her hand up and down her escort's arm, glancing at him possessively.

Dante put his arm around Megan's shoulders, leaned over, and lightly kissed her on the lips.

"I guess I wasn't looking where I was going. When I'm around this girl . . . well, what can I tell ya?"

They watched the other couple enter Herskel's. Megan felt light and free and giddy. Not even the drag of her heavy brace held her down for the moment.

"Thank you, Danny," she whispered.

Frankie Magee did not make it easy for her. Megan knew that if she had been little Elizabeth with her fat yellow sausage curls and her round, damp blue eyes who had gotten polio, the whole world would have stopped in its orbit. Whatever little Lizzie wants, after all, the poor little kid.

No one, least of all her father, ever considered Megan a poor little anything. Usually this was the way she wanted it, but hell, sometimes it would be nice. Just to make things a little easier. But like hell he would do that.

The only times she ever confronted her father in his small office in the basement came when she'd done something wrong. She'd have to sit across the desk from him and explain herself, get caught up, under his tight probing questions, in her own lies. Why the hell should she feel so tense now, so defensive, so scared? Because Frankie Magee could be a very intimidating man.

"And when did you make all these major decisions about your life, may I ask? I thought it was all set and decided on. Marymount up in Tarrytown—and a finer school a fortunate young girl couldn't ask for. Prepares young girls to be good teachers. A teaching degree would serve you well all your life. Medical school? Jeez, Megan, how did you decide on that? I thought it was all set, you at Marymount."

"Daddy, you decided Marymount, you and Father Kelly. And I did talk to him about Hunter College. He agreed with me that even though it's a public school, it's one of the most highly rated, academically, in the country. And all girls, the same as Tarrytown, so all the students there are serious about their education. No fooling around and stuff. And there's no tuition—just the cost of books and labs and things. And I could pay for all that with what I earn this summer. And I could work after school, a few hours every week, until the work gets really intense . . ."

"You got this all figured out, have you? Do you realize you're the only kid in the family—and a girl at that—who ever planned on college? Let alone, God help us, *medical school*?"

"Daddy, Frankie junior always wanted to be a cop. And Patrick is happy working for the phone company. And Elizabeth is no great scholar and with her looks . . . and . . . well, she'll be married right out of high school, I can bet on it."

"We're here to talk about you, not your brothers and sister."

"Okay. Look, Dad, it would be a really good deal. See . . ."

"A *deal*? Is that what we're talking about? Well, then, we know what your end of it is, but what's my end, since you're talking about a deal?"

She was ready for him. She spoke about free tuition for four years. The money he'd save could be used for medical school. And then he'd have a doctor in the family. Free medical advice for life. And she'd be independent and self-supporting. A burden to no one.

Finally they came to a compromise. Not what she wanted, but better than she'd actually expected. She *could* go to Hunter. She *could* take all the science courses she needed for premed. *But* she had to agree to take all the teaching credits she'd need to qualify as a teacher. As a backup.

And she had to agree to one more condition. She had to get straight A's in all her premed courses. Nothing less, or the deal was off.

Megan leaned back. She studied the ceiling for a moment, then took a chance. "Okay, Dad. And what's *my* part of the deal? If I *do* get straight As, like you said, then what? Do I get to go to medical school? Is that the quid pro quo?"

Frankie Magee was stunned. His reaction was first anger, then astonishment; he burst out laughing, and smacked the top of his desk with his open palm. "Well, I'll be damned. The quid pro quo? Well, my God, girl, who's your mouthpiece, then? Sounds like you've been talking to your lawyer. I bet I can guess who, if I give it some thought."

"Well, you told me your requirement, Dad. And if I do meet it, will you see me through med school?"

"Well, the deal, as you put it, kiddo, is that then we shall see what we shall see."

Which, for Frankie, was as good as a yes.

"Okay, we got a deal."

She stood up, walked around his side of the desk, thrust her hand out at him. Frankie took her hand solemnly, shook it, then grabbed her in a bear hug, ruffling her unruly red hair.

"Jesus Christ, kiddo, you are some piece of work, you are. G'wan now, you've taken up enough of my time. I've got *important* business to take care of here."

He held the door open and watched, his heart breaking for her earnestness, her determination, as she hauled herself along, clumping the heavy steel-braced leg up the stairs rapidly.

Ah, jeez, Frankie Magee thought. That one was a winner all right. Damn shame she hadn't been born a boy. Even with the leg—hell, look at old FDR, that one would have gone right to the top. Top of the line, and he'd have been there supporting her progress all the way.

But she *was* a girl, and a crippled girl at that. Ah, well, let her have her ambitions. At least for now.

CHAPTER FOURTEEN

For all the years of her life, Megan heard so many different versions of what happened that day. It had happened so quickly, she wasn't sure what she really remembered.

President Franklin D. Roosevelt, campaigning for his unprecedented third term, was going to ride in an open car right down the middle of the Grand Concourse on his way to Fordham University. And La Guardia, the Little Flower, would be in the car, right next to the President. Her uncle, Captain Tom O'Brien, had arranged for all his family to have front-row seats in the reviewing stand built up in tiers across from Loew's Paradise. They could watch the whole July Fourth Parade right up close, but best of all they could snap pictures of old FDR himself.

The Grand Concourse was lined on both sides of the center lanes with cheering people, thrilled by the entourage headed up toward Fordham Road. They had all seen him in newsreels, heard him in his fireside chats, seen photographs of him. He was as familiar as any loved grandfather, and now he was about to appear, in the flesh, right in front of them. It would be a lifelong memory.

Megan felt a special thrill, because she knew her father had been on the planning committee, making arrangements for the police escort, the traffic clearance, the exact timing of an exact route. He'd been part of the team to arrange for the right welcoming committee, lining up the right power guys for the presidential handshake, the photographs, the quick interviews with the press guys, who weren't to flash their cameras at random—don't take the Chief by surprise.

Her father wouldn't be at the podium with FDR and the mayor and the president of Fordham University and all the pols who ran the Bronx. But he was the man behind the men, and Megan had learned how important Frankie Magee was.

The open car was preceded by ten motorcycle cops, all straight and military in their uniforms, riding two by two and perfectly coordinated. Then came a closed car; then, a ways behind, the black car carrying FDR and the Little Flower.

A wave of sound traveled along the Concourse, starting far down from the crowd that had already seen them, moving quickly to those still anticipating, then bursting with the cheers of those suddenly faced with the reality: Here was the man they had heard about all their lives. FDR, the President of the United States.

Megan stood away from the bleacher benches, clicked a few shots of the motorcycle cops, prepared her camera, ready for the best shot of her life. Standing next to her was a thin young woman, no more than a girl herself, clutching a crying baby against the left side of her body, her right hand trailing, resting lightly on the shoulder of a platinum blond girl of about five, who was holding the collar of a boy about three. As the entourage approached, the young woman was caught up in the excitement. It was really happening; behind the motorcycle cops was a closed car, and then . . .

The young mother raised her right hand to wave, enveloped by the cheers and excitement. The little girl released the hand of her small brother and stood on tiptoe, crying, "I wanna see too, I wanna see."

The small boy, lost in a forest of legs, surrounded by large, excited people who frightened the daylights out of him, pushed forward and ran, with short, clumsy steps, right into the path of the long black escort car.

No one noticed him except Megan, who dropped her camera and, with a sudden burst of energy and speed, flung her body headfirst at the small boy, knocking him clear.

The left front wheel of the heavy car rode over Megan's strong left leg, breaking the femur with a crisp cracking sound, then thumped over the heavy brace, bending it, snapping it, forcing a jagged edge into the polio-withered leg.

Megan remembered nothing of that moment, or the moments that followed.

She woke up in a clean-smelling, starchy bed in Fordham Hospital, dreamy and floating, surrounded by people.

She saw the faces in a quick blinking sequence, the way you riffled a thick wad of photos with your thumb to make them look like a movie:

Her father, a nurse, her mother, a doctor.

And then, the moment she *would* remember for the rest of her life.

He was a large man with strong shoulders; his big hands rested on a pair of canes. His face was so familiar, so known. An uncle, a grandfather, haggard but handsome, with a sad, tired, kind face. His eyes, behind those frameless eyeglasses, were steady and gray. His hand, relinquishing one cane, which someone caught immediately, lifted her hand, squeezed it hard.

"Young lady, you are the bravest girl I have ever seen in my life. And I've seen some brave ones. You keep up the good fight now, Megan Magee. You've made your family very proud. By golly, you've made *me* very proud. You're a strong, tough young girl. Now you just hold on there. You'll do, you certainly will."

He squeezed her hand again and nodded at her. He knew. He understood. There were flashes of light and flashes of pain and noise and then her father and mother and people taking more pictures and voices and then everyone moved away and it became quiet and she felt floaty again and dreamlike.

She dreamed—or did it really happen?—that her father stood beside her, leaning over, and kissed her forehead and said something he had never, ever said to her before in her entire life.

"Megan, I am so proud of you, kiddo. God, I'm proud of you, Red."

And she saw tears running down his face. Or so she seemed to remember.

There were pictures of Megan, not only in the New York papers, but throughout the country; and her family made a collection and started a scrapbook. Her father framed two editorials, one from the *Journal-American*—"Megan's Little, But Oh My!"—and one from the *Daily News*—"Never Underestimate the Power of a Girl Like Megan."

When the excitement finally died down, what she was left with was pain. Not the same kind of pain as the polio, although her brace had broken off and gotten embedded in her withered leg. She felt the pain of broken bones, something she'd been through before. The throbbing, pulling, screeching ache of helplessness. She couldn't even look forward to getting up in a few weeks, hopping around on crutches, knowing it was all temporary. What the hell could she hop on, her heavy, newly braced, healing, weak, shriveled little leg?

And then there was the prospect of Warm Springs, Georgia. At first it sounded great, exciting. A special guest, in a way, of old FDR. Away from home, no parents to bother her—a whole new world.

And she wouldn't miss out on her first year at college. Frankie Magee had worked it all out with Hunter College; all her freshman textbooks would be sent down to Warm Springs. There were professors from Emory University who monitored college students at Warm Springs.

Yeah, it would be tough, but she was the one who wanted college, right? Or did she want to chicken out?

She had gotten cold feet; she was scared. It was a long time to be away from home. She hadn't really been prepared for anything of this duration. Camp was a short-time deal. This was for nearly a year.

She had a couple of teary confrontations with her mother, who tried to convince her that Warm Springs would be wonderful for her.

"You just want to get rid of me, right? I'm too much trouble, right?" She prodded her mother, exasperated her, until her mother finally said, "Yes, damn it. Yes, it would be easier for me. But it would be *better* for you, and that's the main thing."

"Fine. Then I'll go," Megan said bitterly.

What she had expected to be the worst year of her life turned out to be one of the best.

It began with the trip by train to Warm Springs, in a special compartment, modified to make her as comfortable as possible; she rode supine, her head and shoulders propped up to face the windows. Best of all, her Aunt Catherine accompanied her on the two-day-and-two-night trip, and it was the longest, most private time they had ever spent together.

Among the things she had always loved about Catherine was that she was never patronizing, never spoke to her in a special grownup-to-kid voice, as though she were a simple-minded imbecile. Catherine was Catherine, and she treated Megan as though they were equals. And friends.

There was one topic that Catherine guarded, revealing only what she wanted to reveal; and she never apologized for omissions. That was about her life with Mr. Albert William Harlow. There were private parts of it that were no one's business but her own, but she did tell Megan about their travels and how they lived. They had been to Europe, to China, to South America—to wherever Pop (that's what she called him) had business interests, or just curiosity. They lived in the summers in Providence, Rhode Island, in a large house by the water; in the winters in Florida; at other times in a large apartment on Riverside Drive.

Megan knew the "old man" was a widower, much older than her aunt; he had grown sons he hardly ever saw. She knew her aunt seemed happy; she never felt she had to explain her situation to anyone. It was her life. Period.

Relaxed, lulled by the rhythm of the train, the sound of the rushing wind outside the windows—her pain alleviated at its worst by pills Catherine gave her sparingly—Megan finally, in the safety of this private world, was able to talk to her aunt about her own deepest worries.

"Do you think I should have been a boy?" she asked her aunt.

Catherine put down the bit of tatting she worked on from time to time, the little clicking ivory gadget that miraculously spun thread into lace. She dropped her work into her needlepoint bag and frowned. Considering.

"Well, I'm not sure. I think the question is, more, do you *wish* you'd been born a boy?"

Without hesitation, Megan answered, "Absolutely."

"Well, then. And why would you rather be a boy?"

"Aunt Catherine, did you ever know a boy who wanted to be a girl?"

Surprisingly, Catherine said, "Yes, as a matter of fact I do. One of Pop's sons. But that's another matter altogether, for another time. Let's talk about you. Why in the *world* would you want to be a boy?"

It was so obvious, how could she even ask? For all the advantages. Boys had everything, could do anything, be anything they wanted. It was even expected of them to be leaders, achievers, successful, ambitious. No one judged them on all their energy and dreams, telling them, "It's not *normal*; it's not *proper*; it's not the way to behave. You'd better wise up and change before people begin to talk."

And boys were better friends to each other; they trusted each other; they remained friends; they didn't turn on each other for someone else; they didn't rat on each other, betray or hurt each other.

"Well, now you're talking in some very broad terms. Generalizing. *Some* boys are pretty great. Some are not. Some are absolutely loyal and dependable, others not. But do you mean no girl can be any of those things you admire so much? What about you yourself?"

"Well, I *am* like a boy. I'm always being told that. *Be more like a girl.* Whatever the hell that's supposed to mean."

"I think it *should* mean whatever *you* want it to mean, Megan."

How could she explain? She had gotten her period last year—late, at fifteen, but there it was. And her body had changed. Her breasts, though small, were defined; her hips, though still narrow, had taken on definition compared to her slender waist. But nothing, really, had changed. No magical transition. She was *still* Megan, regardless of her changing body. In her head, in her very essence, she was still exactly who she had always been, the same Megan.

"Then *be* the Megan you are, sweetie. That's the best thing to be. Not whatever you think other people decide you should be. Be yourself, for your own reasons. For your own integrity."

She took a deep breath and tried to approach the really hard thing, what she had never articulated before, found hard to face, tried hard not to think about, though it was always there.

"Aunt Catherine, what if, I mean—there are such things as . . . you know. Queer girls. Girls who *should* have been boys. You know. *Freaky girls.*"

Very quietly, Catherine asked her, "Is that what you're worried about, Megan? That you might be that kind of girl?"

Megan shrugged and gnawed on her thumbnail.

"Well, then answer me this. Do you like boys?"

"Absolutely."

"Do you think, if you were a boy, you'd like girls? The way boys like girls? Do you understand my question?"

Megan wrinkled her nose. "Ugh. No way. I just like to be with boys. To be myself with them. I know they like me, and it makes me feel . . . like myself. I don't have to pretend to be someone else. But *me*, like girls the way boys do? Oh, Aunt Catherine, *no!*"

Catherine smiled. "Well, now let me ask you this. Is there one boy you like, in a *special* way? Different from how you like others?"

Megan grinned. "Dante. Danny D'Angelo." She felt her face become hot and flushed. "He kissed me once."

"And did you like it?"

"Yes. Oh, God, it made me feel . . . I don't know. It made me feel so good."

"You're okay, baby. Don't think about any of that stuff anymore.

You're absolutely okay. Just be the very Megan you are. Those who like it, fine. Those who don't, the hell with them.''

Her aunt told her things about men that Megan had never imagined, things that finally, in spite of her ambiguity and resentments, made her realize for the first time that she was glad to be a girl.

"They are afraid,'' Catherine said. "Almost all the time, they are afraid. They worry about not measuring up; they worry about their genitals. This seems to be one of the most overwhelming concerns. The size—constantly bragging, comparing, worrying, teasing, commenting, ridiculing each other, and hoping to God no one will say anything about their own particular 'family jewels,' the most precious and burdensome possession each man has. And I'll tell you this, sweetie. Maybe you're not old enough, but what the hell, you're smart enough to know this. A woman, during the sex act, can *always* fake it, pretend it was wonderful even if it was awful. But a man has to get an erection. God, no matter what, he has to 'get it up.' It's his measure of manhood.''

Megan knew the mechanics of sex. She'd been told, not very explicitly or accurately, but functionally. But nothing like this—this, which she could understand and wonder at. No one had told her things in the calm, matter-of-fact way her Aunt Catherine did.

"If they can't get hard, they blame the woman. Always, toots, the woman is to blame for their every sexual failure. And believe me, they have them. Their whole lives revolve around their sex, Megan; their sex organs rule them. And they are so threatened by women. They are scared to death of us. My God, what if a woman is actually smarter, more competent, can do things they can do, what only a 'real man' is supposed to do? They have to constantly put down a bright woman, a 'fresh-mouthed woman.' And if a girl is smart, and not smart enough to hide it, they compliment her in sexual terms: 'She's got balls.' And then they try to hurt her: 'She must be queer.' 'What kind of girl acts like that?' 'Who the hell does she think she is?'

"And the ultimate male put-down, their only way to deal with the threat when a smart woman beats them at their own game, confuses them, threatens them, is . . .'' Her aunt pulled her shoulders back, thrust out her chin, and in a low, gravelly voice, said, "What that dame needs is a good fuck!''

She put her hand over her mouth and rolled her eyes, shocked at her own audacity. "God, baby, don't ever tell *anyone* I said that!''

Megan was fascinated, totally in awe of her beautiful, golden-red-haired, wide-eyed, daring aunt, who laughed and giggled and took chances like a tough young girl.

"Aunt Catherine, how do you know so much?"

"Baby, I'll tell you a secret. *All* women come to know these things. Only they don't talk about them. We keep our mouths shut; we play the game. Let the men think they're so smart, so superior. But some of us—we don't play games. We live by our own rules, and we pay whatever price we have to pay." Then, sadly, she said, "You'll find out yourself, Megan. There are some great girls out there, and great boys, too, for you to be friends with."

Megan shook her head. "God, Aunt Catherine. It's so hard. To know how to be and all . . ."

"It is hard, Megan. Life is hard. Not just for girls, not just for women. For everybody. Here's my best shot for you, kiddo. You're so damn intelligent, gifted—pretty and brave and honest. You can laugh at yourself. If you feel yourself trying to be someone else, or what you think someone else wants you to be—then you'll know it's wrong for you. You be your own best self, and someday you'll meet a boy who will love you for every single thing about you that makes you Megan."

"But what if I don't?"

Catherine looked at her niece with such intensity that Megan held her breath.

"You *will*," she said.

Megan nodded. And then, taking a chance, she asked, "Did you, Aunt Catherine? Meet a man who loves you just for being exactly who you are?"

Her aunt chewed on her lower lip, then grinned and shrugged. "Now, that would be telling, wouldn't it? We're not talking about me just now. We're talking about people in general, and you in specific. Go to sleep now, Megan, I think I've filled your head with enough for one night." And then, in a soft and loving voice, she added, "Oh, you'll do, Megan Magee. Believe me, you'll do."

It was what the President of the United States had said, and now her wonderful Aunt Catherine said the same thing. And Megan believed her.

CHAPTER FIFTEEN

The ten months Megan Magee spent at Warm Springs had a profound effect on her life. At the rehab in New York State, she had often sensed from the staff feelings of indifference, obligation, sometimes resentment and sometimes outright cruelty in the face of the pain and suffering of the polio-stricken kids. Some of the staff—especially the volunteers—couldn't hack it. They mistook pity for empathy, and did more emotional harm than good.

At Warm Springs, the only cruelty was in the disease itself. There were more damaged kids gathered there than Megan could even begin to imagine. By comparison with some of the others, she realized that she was among the more fortunate. After all, her broken leg, though painful, did mend, did strengthen. She had the use of her arms, and eventually of both of her legs, the one weak and healing, the other encased in a newly fitted iron brace. Her swimming grew stronger; in the pool, she felt renewed and vitalized, always surprised anew when she got out of the water to realize her limitations. But she could get around; she was not one of the really *disabled*.

These were the patients imprisoned in the iron lungs: huge chambers encasing the entire body, with only the patient's head sticking out, lying forever staring up into a mirror positioned to show the victim a small portion of the world. The lung was like a monstrous living creature: it pulsated with a rhythm calculated to keep the damaged lungs functioning. It was the nearest thing to hell that Megan could imagine, to be so helpless and imprisoned.

The staff at Warm Springs felt privileged to be there. The proximity to "the little White House," FDR's retreat, caused a surge of excitement from time to time. *The Man is in residence, or is expected.* Once, while Megan was there, the President paid a visit to the patients. He hobbled awkwardly on his two canes, not needing to pretend to them that he was more ambulatory than he really was. He stopped off and visited Megan, who was so excited that she swept her books and papers and pencils off her desk in an effort to stand in the President's presence.

When an aide rushed to pick the items up, FDR brushed him away casually, seeing Megan's embarrassment.

"Well, this is Megan Magee from the Bronx, isn't it? I understand you've been doing fine, in your recovery and in your schoolwork. Getting along well in your first college semester, are you, Megan?"

She was dazzled by his politician's knowledge, overwhelmed by his interest. She knew—after all, she was Frankie Magee's daughter—that he'd been briefed, knew what to say to her; but she also knew he was kind enough to care. After all, here was the first man to be elected President three times, and here he was, asking how Megan Magee was coming along. He sat by her for a while, asking penetrating questions about her studies and what her professional goals were. He listened, commented carefully, spoke to her as though they were the same age. There was nothing patronizing or false about his interest, and Megan saw these moments as treasures she would store away forever.

Then he continued his rounds, having something cheerful and hopeful and kind to say to all of them, patients and staff alike.

Megan, in retrospect, remembered how tired he looked. The black rings extended under his eyes, down toward his cheeks. The tightness of his mouth revealed pain, tension. She wondered about his pain—was it with him all the time? He moved so slowly and heavily.

She didn't need the President's kind words to spur her on with her studies. Megan realized the time spent at Warm Springs, besides the hours given over to physical therapy, was a wonderful opportunity for her to get ahead of her own assignments. The professors from Emory were tough but fair; they demanded much of those students they felt could measure up, and Megan was one of their top students. They sent her grades on to Hunter, so that by next fall she would be easily admitted to the sophomore class.

When Megan arrived at Warm Springs, she was something of a celebrity—after all, how many polio-stricken girls, or boys for that matter, were nationally known heroes? Megan quickly played it down: "Hey, I didn't dive for the kid. Someone shoved me."

Both of her parents had taught her early on, don't make too much of yourself. When you finally goof up, the fall from grace won't be so bad.

Even with all her physical therapy and schoolwork, Megan had free time to be bored, to make herself a nuisance by following the staff around. She was practicing, she told them, for the day when she would join the medical profession.

One of the nurses, a crusty older woman, Miss Moore, decided to put Megan to work.

"I've got an iron-lung patient needs some company. She's just about your age, and sweetie, that's all you two have in common." She smiled at Megan, then nodded. "But I've got a hunch you two might hit it off."

Suzy Ginzburg was the only daughter of two successful avant-garde artists with studios in Greenwich Village and Paris. They lived all over the world, had traveled with Suzy to places Megan had never even heard of. As a result, Suzy, at seventeen the same age as Megan, was conversant in three or four languages; one of her proudest boasts was that she could use the slangy words for genitals, and what they could do, in every language—which she promptly offered to teach Megan.

It was hard for Megan to realize that there was a body encased in Suzy's massive iron lung. All that showed was a small, intense face: huge black eyes with thick, long lashes, heavy brows, a straight nose, a wide mouth that never stopped talking. There was so much life coming from this one small black-haired head that Megan felt exhausted trying to keep up. And the words had to be carefully coordinated with the rhythm of the machine that served as her lungs.

Suzy's voice seemed metallic, an accommodation to the pressure of the machine in which she lived, for the time being.

"I definitely will get out of this damn thing. Don't you believe otherwise, Megan Magee. God, what a pretty name. It goes with your face. A whole Irish thing—I love it. Jesus, a turned-up nose, red hair, what a great color. And those freckles, like spatters of paint. Great. Uh-oh. Did I insult you? I love freckles. They're so . . . clean and innocent."

"That's because you don't have any," Megan said. She didn't know what to make of Suzy. She'd never known anyone so outspoken.

As though she had read Megan's mind, Suzy said, "Listen, I always say exactly what's on my mind. That way you'll always know where we stand." She grinned bitterly. "In a manner of speaking. I heard about your saving that kid. Neat. Really neat. Listen, you can use that, one way or another, for the rest of your life. And it's legitimate."

"Use it? What do you mean?"

"Hell, your *father* would know. He's an ace politician, right?"

"What do you know about my father?"

"Hey, kid, I'm a New Yorker, right? My parents are New Yorkers. Of course, they're socialists. Does that scare you? You are a parochial school kid, right?"

Megan didn't know what to make of Suzy Ginzburg. She'd been prepared to be encouraging, warm, and supportive. She hadn't expected to be insulted and made fun of. Who the hell did she think Megan was?

When she complained to Nurse Moore, she responded with a smile. "You resent her for having spirit? For being as much like herself, before polio, as she can possibly be? Isn't that what you're trying to do? Let her be Suzy. There's a lot to this girl. She's plenty tough. Don't be so thin-skinned. Maybe you'll learn something from her."

Megan did. She learned that Suzy and her family and all their friends were free spirits who inhabited a world, just a subway ride away from the Bronx, that might have been a colony on Mars. Suzy was right there, taking part in a lifestyle that was amazing, if not confusing. There were no secrets, no lies, no baloney; everything was right out there in the open.

"My father had an affair with a model he was painting. She was a *mess*. When he dumped her, she told his fortune and predicted dire catastrophe. Hell, maybe she was right—look at me now."

"What about your mother?" Megan asked, wide-eyed.

"Oh, she's had her little things, too. I mean, so what? These two people are so crazy about each other. The outside stuff they've had—their little flings—don't mean anything; sometimes they just need to spice up their lives, that's all it adds up to. So tell me about yourself, Megan. You're seventeen. A virgin, of course."

Megan felt her face go hot. She wanted to walk away. Not hear this stuff. But then again she wanted to stay and hear more.

"Yes. A virgin. You say it like it's something terrible. Instead of . . . of . . ."

Suzy closed her eyes and quietly intoned, "Instead of a holy state of chastity, to be relinquished on your wedding night to the man who chose you for this honor." She grinned. "Bullshit. I had my first real sex when I was thirteen. He was fifteen and he'd been around, so he pretty much knew what he was doing. It wasn't sensational, and it hurt a lot, but all in all, for the first time it was, well, interesting. Of course, it got better as it went along. And then—"

Megan blurted out, "Hey, I'm not your confessor, okay?"

Suzy laughed, then became serious. "I'm sorry, Megan. This is just me, talking. See, your way of life is as strange to me as my way of life is to you. Wherever we go in the world, my family and I, we gravitate to our own kind. Artist communities, made up of painters and writers and sculptors and actors." Then, sadly, she added, "And dancers. Oh, yes, and dancers. We have our own standards and I guess we lose sight of the fact that the rest of the world doesn't live the way we do."

"You keep saying 'we.' Are you an artist too? Do you paint or what?"

Suzy bit down on her lower lip and closed her eyes. The only sound was from her artificial lung, working away noisily. Megan glanced in her mirror and saw two long streams of tears.

"I *was* a dancer. I was . . . pretty good. I was a junior member of a ballet company. One of the youngest ever. I've danced all over Europe since I was thirteen. Not prima—probably never would have made prima. I don't think I'd ever have been that good. Which was always hard to face. But I don't have to worry about that particular failure anymore, do I? I mean, what I have, at seventeen, are these memories. And now this really weird situation. Somewhere inside this huge iron tank, I assume, is what's left of my body. My God, do you know the sacrifices a dancer makes for the sake of her body? Do you know . . ." She bit her lip hard. "Whoa. I think Suzy has talked enough for one day, Megan. I am on the edge of self-pity, and that doesn't do me one bit of good. I'd like to just rest for now. Would you mind propping up that book for me on my reading ledge? I think I'll just read for a while, okay? See you tomorrow."

Megan visited Suzy Ginzburg every day for the next few months, and they became fast friends.

Suzy's parents came in a whirl of color and noise and laughter, bearing gifts of food and books and records and paintings that they shared with everyone in the room. Everything was for all of them. They were young and beautiful. Her father was handsome and lean, dressed in dungarees and a denim workshirt, like a laborer. Her mother wore a long, whirling skirt and a tight black top, and her hair reached down past her waist. It was thick and black and caught behind her neck with a beautiful silver clasp "made by a friend, a silversmith. Pretty, isn't it?"

They shared themselves with everyone—visited each kid encased in an iron lung. They drew sketches, caricatures of the kids and of the staff, turning them all into cartoon animal-faces, wise owls, fierce lions, sweet kittens, winsome puppies, but each recognizable. Then, using water-colors, they decorated each protruding face, added heavy eyebrows, long lashes, red cheeks, whiskers, and as a final touch, a third eye, in the center of each forehead—for good luck, to watch out for you while the rest of you is asleep.

They left a ward of dazzled and enchanted kids who refused to have their faces washed for two days.

Megan couldn't *imagine* what it would be like to have parents like that. Actually to live with them, be part of that life. Their excitement and loudness, their enthusiasm, was overwhelming.

Quietly, Suzie confided, "They're just scared, Megan. It's called whistling in the dark. Hell, I was their dancing girl. Imagine what it's like for them to see me like this. Well, the hell with it. Listen, Megan, baby, put on a Sinatra record for me, will ya? Bring over the phono, close to me. Something sad and lovesick and mellow. You know, music to masturbate by."

Megan reacted with shock. She couldn't hide anything. Her face registered it all.

"Suzy!"

Suzy grinned. "Relax, kid. Don't start imagining all kinds of nefarious activity going on deep inside my iron drum. Believe me, there is nothing, nada, that I can do. Damn it. What an opportunity it would be, don't you think? But I'm a girl who can't even breathe for myself right now. But someday. Right? C'mon, *right?*"

Megan laughed. "*Right*. You better believe it. Which Sinatra?"

"Oh, God, any one. Any one at all."

Megan played "All or Nothing at All" and watched Suzy's face relax. Watched the sadness disappear slowly; watched the dreamy way Suzy's eyes opened and closed. Watched her feel the music. Wondered if her body remembered what it felt like to move with music. Wondered how Suzy could stand it, to be inside that damn prison when her every instinct was for motion.

It was confusing. Suzy said the most unbelievably shocking, outra-geous things about sex, about life, about her body. But it was so different from the way Patsy Wagner talked about sex.

When Suzy talked, Megan felt a thrill of guilt for listening; but there was a difference when Suzy spoke. As though so many things were natural, normal, and, yes, some of it actually funny.

When she left Warm Springs, she felt sadness at leaving Suzy, but Suzy promised that she'd be back in New York "before you know it, kid. And then you'll come on down and see my part of town. You'll have a helluva good time, I promise. C'mon. Gimme a smile and a kiss and you get on home and knock 'em dead at Hunter."

Megan leaned down and kissed Suzy lightly on the tip of her nose and then on her forehead, the way her father used to kiss her when she was little.

Suzy lowered her voice and said, "I'll be back, Megan. I promise you, we'll get together in New York. And I promise you this, too, baby. I won't let anyone corrupt you."

They were the same age, but Suzy always made her feel like a little kid.

PART TWO

CHAPTER ONE

If the war changed the lives of most of the kids he graduated with from St. Simon, it seemed that nothing drastic or exciting would ever happen to Willie Paycek. After Pearl Harbor, he went to the Army recruiting booth on Fordham Road and the Grand Concourse, held his breath, and presented his draft card, with its 4-F designation, to the sergeant. This was different. There was really a war now, and the Army needed all the men it could get.

The sergeant looked at Willie and shook his head. A sorry-looking little guy with a punctured eardrum, missing the tip of the index finger on his left hand; deviated septum and ulcers. When Willie offered to get everything medically repaired—if the Army would help him out a little—the sergeant's compassion turned to scorn, and he laughed so hard the other young men in the room nervously turned just in time to see little Paycek leap at the muscular, tough-jawed sergeant and swing at his jaw. The sergeant sidestepped easily, lifted Willie by the back of his neck, and carried him to the door.

"Look, kid," he said softly into Willie's ear, "no hard feelings.

There'll be things for you to do. We can't all be soldiers. There'll be lotsa jobs you can fill in on."

It turned out that the sergeant was right. While he couldn't do the kind of war work his mother landed for herself out on Long Island— because it was essential when building airplane motors that one have an index finger on each hand—Willie quit his job as an usher in the fleabag Avalon third-run house, took a bath, got a haircut, put on fresh clothes and shined shoes, and presented himself to the manager of the Loew's Paradise.

His mother was making good money, living in a rooming house on the Island with a bunch of other working women. Willie took a three-room, fifth-floor apartment for Mischa and himself on Creston Avenue and 184th Street, right around the corner from the movie palace. Mischa would always be small and simpleminded, but he was always smiling. He loved any movies with singing and dancing. He tapped his feet madly through the apartment, convinced he was tap dancing. His mother agreed to send along enough money to pay an old lady, Mrs. Kelleher, on the first floor, to look after the kid. He really was a good companion to her; her own children and grandchildren lived in Chicago and she was lonely. At first she was a little put off by Mischa, but gradually she came to like him, and she could use the extra few bucks a week. Willie didn't give her all the money his mother sent, but held back some to help him with the rent.

Mr. Felnick, the manager of Loew's Paradise, glanced at Willie Paycek, dressed in his best, with a sinking sensation. He was the make-do wartime 4-F version, a direct opposite of the tall, slender, Irish-handsome, personable young men who had always represented the elegance of the Loew's Paradise. There was no uniform small enough for Willie, who claimed this was not a problem. He had a good neighborhood tailor. Mr. Wagner was indeed good with needle and thread and scissors, and in spite of Mr. Felnick's hope that hemming and not cutting would do the job, Willie showed up with a tailored, neatly pressed usher's uniform.

Mr. Felnick hoped the war would be over quickly and that all his wonderful tall young ushers would return.

Loew's Paradise became Willie Paycek's university, his magic place, his real world. He watched a movie over and over again, caught things he'd missed, picked up on moviemaking techniques. He felt envious that anyone could ever know enough to put so many things together, so many bits and pieces fusing finally into one smooth, finished movie. He carried scenes home in his mind, reworked them, tried different

angles, different arrangements, jotted down *his* ideas, then checked
them against what he saw on the screen.

He also began to revise his own memories, until reality and fantasy
became difficult to separate.

The night on Snake Hill turned, in his mind, into a great battle,
involving spontaneous brutality. Then he tried it another way—another
take—as a carefully staged, premeditated killing, designed with only one
end in mind: not the death of Stachiew but the eventual death of his
father.

The scene in his father's cell changed from a moment of terror into
a brave, heroic denunciation. The boy washing his hands of the evil
tormentor. Having his revenge as the brute turned coward groveled,
begged forgiveness. His was the ultimate patricide: killing both corrupt
fathers at one time.

One Saturday night, Willie had to fill in for old Mr. Reuben, the
ticket taker, who had developed a fever along with his hacking cough.
He scarcely looked up, just took each proffered ticket, tore it in half,
one piece into the tall glass receptacle, the other half back to the patron.
Just hands, feet, men's shoes, girl's shoes waiting off to the side.

"Willie." The deep voice was familiar. He looked directly from the
shining black shoes into the strong, handsome face of Dante D'Angelo.
He seemed to have grown a few inches, or maybe it was just the way
the naval uniform added to his stature. He was an ensign or something,
home maybe for the last time.

"Danny, hey, how ya doin'?"

He kept on tearing tickets automatically, handing stubs back to
outstretched hands. He wanted Dante to move on, to enter the theater.
To disappear with the tall, slim, gorgeous girl who waited by his side.
But Dante stood there, smiling, greeting so many people who knew
him, the neighbors out for the big Saturday night at the Paradise with
ice cream at Krum's later on.

The crowd thinned out; the rush was over. He looked Dante over
carefully. His own uniform—the short, custom-tailored red jacket, the
smart black pants with the red stripe along the outside seams, even the
stiffly starched white shirt and neat black bow tie—suddenly felt
uncomfortable. Willie felt like a clown standing next to Dante
D'Angelo, who was the real thing. With a real beautiful girl. They fit
together, both tall and movie-pretty. Making Willie feel short and ugly,
as though everything about him was wrong.

Dante introduced his girl—a blonde named Diana—and she smiled, showing beautiful straight white teeth, and told Dante she would meet him at the candy counter. She left them together.

Willie did what he always did when he was nervous and felt that awful feeling. He started to talk, too much, too fast, saying whatever popped into his head. Jesus, he *knew* he was doing it, but couldn't stop himself. It was Dante's fault; he should have just said hiya and kept going.

"Ya know, this job, it's nice and all, I mean, the Paradise, wow, it's the best. But I got plans, ya know, about the movie business. Now don't think I'm talking about acting, but you wouldn't believe all the other jobs, the really important jobs there are in making a movie. See, what I'm planning is . . . oh, this isn't my regular job, I'm filling in for old man Reuben . . ."

Dante grinned. "He still around, old man Reuben? He used to give the guys a hard time Saturday mornings when we'd all rush in and . . ."

Willie hadn't been one of the guys on those Saturday mornings. He'd never been one of the guys.

He found himself babbling about his plans, his ambitions. Told Dante about his mother working for the war effort; gave her credentials; talked and talked. Dante smiled and nodded. Politely.

"Well, you're looking good, Willie. It's great that you get to see all the movies at the Paradise. I'm sure you're learning a lot that'll come in handy someday."

Yeah. Sure. Great. Dante was standing there in his officer's uniform, in his navy blue dress uniform and Willie was dressed like some organ grinder's monkey. Suddenly he realized how ridiculous he was. Fuck you, Dante. Why'd you have to come here tonight and spoil everything? Maybe he'd get killed and come home in a box.

Dante turned when someone called his name. He shook hands with some old couple from Valentine Avenue; then some girls coming in late handed Willie their tickets—without even glancing at him. They kept staring at Dante; turned back, grinned at him. With his luck, the bastard, his ship would sink and he'd swim away from it. Like John Wayne.

The show was starting. Dante's girl stood at the doorway, shrugged politely, smiled.

Dante acknowledged her with a nod. Right with you.

"Say, listen, Willie. I was with my uncles, the Ruccis, Victor and Joseph, this morning, over on Bathgate Avenue. They got a meat and fruit and vegetable business. Do you have a driver's license?"

Willie tensed. Maybe something was coming his way. Those uncles over to Bathgate, they always had something going. Willie heard things; they were big money.

"I could get one, I know how to drive. Why?"

"Well, with the draft, my uncles are losing all their drivers. You work nights here? They need a coupla drivers early in the morning, going out to the markets at College Point, down to Fulton Street, for pickups and distribution. They pay good money and it isn't all that hard. They got handlers to load and unload. You interested?"

Willie's heart lurched. Was he interested?

"Well, I'll think about it." Don't do me no favors.

"Okay, I'll give my Uncle Joseph a call. He's the one to see. It's really good money, kid. Listen, I better get going. Really good to see you, Willie. You take care now."

Yeah. Take care now. Fuckin' guinea bastard. Take good care.

Joseph Rucci hired him within two minutes of his arrival. Don't worry, the license will be taken care of; Dante said you was a good boy, that's all I need to know.

CHAPTER TWO

Sergeant Charley O'Brien's cold was worse. His nose was raw and running, his throat scratchy, his ears clogged, and his eyes watery. But he'd seen Jacobs, a tall, rangy man with a mild manner, continue on duty and work his way through flu and a 104-degree temperature. It wasn't that Charley was trying to measure up to the old man—the captain was twenty-seven if he was a day—it was just that he didn't want to let Jacobs down. But it would be really stupid to die of pneumonia when the war in Germany was over.

It was a thirty-mile trip to the southeast, a cool day for April. The captain consulted his road map, gave directions, sat quietly. Very quietly. He was never what you'd call a great talker, but he had a dry sense of humor and a sharp wit. Sometimes it took Charley a little while to get the joke or decide if there *was* a joke. He wondered if maybe he was a little slow. Or if it was just that Jacobs was so damn smart. But then, if he was so damn smart, how come he pulled all the hazardous assignments—with Charley, of course, as his driver? They had been in too many precarious situations, with Jacobs, hunched over his note-book, calculating which army was where, trying to figure out who the fuck was shooting at them as they raced along unaccounted-for roads. British fire? German? American? It wouldn't matter, of course, if they got blown to hell, which side got them. But Charley sat tight, glancing from time to time at Jacobs as the captain consulted his maps and papers and made reports on the radio, telling the brass whether or not it was safe to send the troops along. Or to ask who, exactly, was shooting at their asses at the moment.

Abe Jacobs was probably the bravest man Charley had ever seen, and he had seen many heroes. Some cowards, too, along the way—but who knew how the hell you'd react in certain situations? What Charley did was to pattern himself on Jacobs. If Jacobs sat up straight, took a deep breath, and kept his eyes straight ahead, so did Charley. If Jacobs's voice went low and he jerked his head, said "Hit the dirt, Charley," they moved as though synchronized, leaping from the jeep, rolling into a ditch, hands over heads, waiting out whatever incoming seemed directed at them. Actually, Charley felt safe around Jacobs, as though he had some kind of magic powers. He was Charley's totem, his shield.

They had all heard about Ohrdruf, that it had been some kind of work camp, and all of the workers, prisoners, were dead. The locals had been recruited to deal with the dead.

The air was so heavy with the stench of death that it seemed solid. It permeated the area a good five miles from the camp, and as they drove closer the smell was cut with the sharpness of lime. All along the road, they passed Allied prisoner-of-war camps: hundreds of German soldiers standing behind quickly thrown-together enclosures of barbed wire nailed to wooden posts. As they drove closer to Ohrdruf, groups of German soldiers, arms in the air, shuffled under the guidance of a couple of GIs who looked exhausted with the work of rounding up the surrendering enemy.

The town itself seemed strangely untouched by war. The houses were neat; they even seemed freshly painted. Flowers bloomed brightly along clean brick walks. Curtains blew inward from gusts of spring air. The sparkling windows were evidence of good *hausfraus* hard at work.

Some civilians, neatly dressed—the men clean-shaven, the women well groomed—stood along the road, waving at them. Some people called out, clasping their hands together, to the officer and the sergeant as their jeep slowed down for a moment.

"What are they saying, Captain?"

"They're saying, 'Thank God for the Americans. No Russians, please God.'"

As they drove closer to the camp, there were no more welcoming, waving civilians. They encountered surrendering soldiers in groups and singly, a couple of buddies together, hands in the air, calling out listlessly.

"They want to surrender to us." Jacobs jerked his thumb over his shoulder, shouting to the Germans in their own language, telling them to continue straight through Ohrdruf. There were detention pens waiting. The soldiers nodded, heads bobbing, smiles. The enemy.

They came upon the trucks that were left behind, manned by no more than five or six GIs. Their assignment, right outside of the camp, was to collect the weapons being surrendered by the German army. They supervised the loading of the weapons, which were carefully handled by German soldiers who looked barely teenaged.

One of the two MPs approached as Charley brought the jeep to a halt. Jacobs identified himself and Charley. The MP escorted them on foot to the entrance of the camp, where they were immediately greeted by a short, stout German in what appeared to be a dinner suit, complete with crisp white shirt and black bow tie. He bowed several times, as though he was to be their host. Then he stood up straight, clicked his heels together, and saluted.

Jacobs ignored him. Charley nodded at the man, some petty town official, and followed Jacobs into the camp.

Inside the compound was a scene that brought to mind all that Charley had been taught about hell. Minus the fire.

He clenched his teeth and breathed in shallow gasps, trying hard not to swallow the taste of death and rot, which went deeper than anything he had ever experienced. It would permeate his clothing; it would adhere to his exposed face, his hair, his hands; it would be with him forever, this death smell.

The German functionary walked ahead and to one side, almost backwards, as he began explaining. Finally, Jacobs said something harsh and abrupt and the German dropped his head, took a few steps back, and stared at the ground.

The two Americans stood, transfixed, unable immediately to comprehend the horror. Bone-thin naked bodies with skulls that seemed too large to be supported by skinny necks lay stacked ten feet high. Charley could not associate the twisted feet, the frozen clutching hands, the glazed dead eyes with anything human.

"Who were they?" he asked Jacobs, trying to find some humanity in all this. All he could see and sense was debris, nothing human, something so obscene that it could not be real.

"*He says*"—Jacobs jerked his chin at the German—"they were

captive workers. Prisoners from the east. All civilians, many criminals, some crazy people. He says they probably died from disease. *He says there were no doctors or medicine, everything was for the army. He says they were very dirty and they spread the disease to each other. He says . . ."*

Jacobs's mouth closed tightly as he bit his back teeth together. Not looking at Charley, or at anything, he continued. "*He says*, this fat pig here, *he says* they tried to share food with these people, but they wouldn't accept it. They were very difficult people. Mostly Jews, *they wouldn't eat food that wasn't kosher.*"

Charley turned and stared at the man who had appointed himself their guide and their host.

The German shrugged, tried a smile: What could one do with such people?

A young American sergeant came up to Jacobs, saluted casually. "We've got a work crew of locals over here, Captain. They've been drafted for burial detail."

"How many corpses?"

"Hundreds. We got one group of thirty that got killed within the last forty-eight hours." Jacobs stared at the GI, who pantomimed shooting a machine gun. "They apparently were the only ones still alive before the pullout, so they shot them. The locals are digging their graves. We're having huge lime pits prepared—by them—for mass graves."

"Were there any guards left?"

"Oh, yeah. We got two live ones. Put in place by the SS last week. So they had nothing to do with any of this, right?"

"Right," said Jacobs.

They walked around, looking over the wooden barracks with neatly constructed, utilitarian bunks rising from floor to ceiling, each bunk built to accommodate eight people. Not more than a few inches away from each other, they lined both sides of the windowless room. The smell was unbearable: fetid human waste, the smell of indescribable agony.

Jacobs strode quickly through the barracks, seeming to see without actually looking, his eyes glancing quickly, his brain storing it all. They walked around the camp, watched the burial activities, watched the locals, all well dressed, well nourished, as they carefully dug with the shovels provided for them. They nodded at him, an officer, they ducked their heads in deference, mopped their sweating brows, adjusted the handkerchiefs tied over their faces. Women worked along with the men, their faces stony and unrevealing.

Jacobs had seen enough. He walked quickly back to the jeep, waited for Charley to take the wheel. He touched Charley's arm, handed him his sidearm.

"Hang on to this for me, kid, or the next German I see who wants to surrender is a dead man."

They traveled back to headquarters. Along the way, a very young, very blond, blue-eyed soldier approached the jeep, his hands in the air. He smiled, nodded, offered himself to them.

"Stop," Jacobs told Charley. He got down from the jeep, went to the boy soldier, spoke for a moment, then pointed back toward the camp. The boy's face crumpled, turned red, tears streamed down his bright pink cheeks. He reached out, clutched Jacobs's arm, pleading.

Charley stiffened, waited. Jacobs took the boy by the shoulders, spun him around, shoved him, then got back in the jeep and told Charley to get going. Fast.

"What'd you say to him, Captain?"

Staring straight ahead, Jacobs said quietly, "I told him he had to find the *Russians*. The Americans have their quota of Germans. I told him the *Russians* will cut off his arms and then his legs, after they all rape him, and then they will leave him in a ditch somewhere." He turned to Charley. "That's what I told him. Do you have any questions?"

"Absolutely none, sir."

"Then let's get the fuck out of here."

Ohrdorf was just the beginning, the first camp they saw. Jacobs was assigned to inspect and report on camps called Dachau, Bergen-Belsen, Buchenwald, Theresienstadt. And finally he was assigned to Auschwitz, where both his reportorial skills and his facility with German, Yiddish, Hebrew, and Polish would be of value to the U.S. Army.

Sergeant Charley O'Brien went with Jacobs, as his driver and assistant. After each assignment, after each tour, Jacobs told Charley the same thing: You don't have to come with me. It gets worse as we get further into this.

Jacobs, with his large, craggy, old-at-twenty-seven face, his narrowed eyes seeing right into Charley's heart, his voice soft and kind, told him, "It's all too much, Charley. I think maybe you should be reassigned. To headquarters. Maybe drive a general or two around for a while. Whadda ya say, kid?"

Charley straightened, swallowed hard, and shook his head. "I have to see it all," he said, not knowing why; God knew he'd seen enough.

At Auschwitz, there were huge Red Cross tents, trucks of medical supplies, Army barracks set up for command personnel. There were international relief personnel, trying to get histories on the survivors. Others were just trying to keep them alive.

"Don't feed anybody," a GI told Charley. "When we first got here, we gave anyone breathin' K rations and candy and milk, anything we had. Three hundred a week died. Jeez, they'd swallow down stuff, double over, and die. Man, you can't believe."

Charley had free time to sleep, eat, shower and shave, get a haircut. There was a small chapel in the compound and a young Catholic chaplain who heard confessions and offered mass on Sunday morning. Charley walked out into the blazing April sunlight, shaking his head to clear it. The contrast between the mass and the reality all around him was exhausting. He heard a man's voice, angry, tough, oh–my–God familiar.

There was a large, disheveled, hulking red-headed captain, his back to Charley, his legs planted far apart. He was yelling at a group of German soldiers who were lined up, enduring his anger, waiting for their lieutenant to straighten things out, officer to officer.

The German lieutenant stood very straight, stiff, military. "We are entitled to go to mass. It is all arranged, Herr Captain. Check with your commanding—"

"Turn on your heel, shithead, and get your men back into the compound. Right now."

It was Ben Herskel from Ryer Avenue, his hands on his hips, staring the German down. The officer said something to his men. They turned smartly and marched back to the compound.

Ben stood watching them, then turned and slammed into Charley O'Brien, who grabbed him in a bear hug.

"Whoa, take it easy, pal. I—" Ben pulled back and stared, looked away, then back. "No . . . Charley? Jesus Christ, Charley O'Brien?"

They stood, holding each other at arm's length. My God, Charley thought, he looks like a man of forty. We're twenty-three years old. They were studying each other as though looking in a mirror, each searching, each registering shock.

Ben punched him on the shoulder, the old guy-to-guy affection, but it was a forced playfulness. They walked along together, leaned against a parked jeep, lit up cigarettes, exchanged information—the official stuff, how they ended up here, what they were doing here. In this place.

"They needed officers who spoke German. I threw in Yiddish, Hebrew, Polish, so I can talk to the survivors as well as the Germans. Officer to officer. Rules of war, Charley. The Germans have become sticklers for rules of war."

Ben's face was hard and lined, his mouth a tight, thin line as he looked toward the camp. He breathed in the cigarette smoke as though it were oxygen.

"I've got good booze, Charley. The best. You come tonight. Then we'll talk, okay?"

Charley stared at the unfamiliar face, searched for Ben in the bitter man. "What'll we talk about, Benny?"

Ben grinned. "About innocent days, Charley, about old times, kiddo. About the Bronx and Ryer Avenue and old friends." And then their eyes locked. "We'll talk about this, Charley. You and me." He dropped his hands, grinned when Charley saluted him. He returned the salute, then feinted at Charley's chin with an affectionate touch. "Hey," he said. "You're with a good man, that Jacobs. A really good man. Tough guy underneath that sweet face. See ya tonight, kid."

Charley followed Jacobs from cot to cot in a section where the patients were kept who had the best chances of survival. Living skeletons with huge, shining eyes, the flesh barely covering the bones of their bodies, the skulls beneath their faces showing clearly. Jacobs stopped at each bed, reached out, took a hand, leaned over, said a few words. His hand caressed a withered cheek, brushed a shaven head. He spoke softly in Yiddish, leaning forward, bringing his ear close to catch whispered words. Carefully, as unobtrusively as possible, he lifted each left arm, turned and gave Charley the number to add to his clipboard, followed by a name.

"Rest, Solomon," he said. "The doctor said you had some soup. That's good. *Shalom*, Solomon."

Sometimes there was a reaction. But mostly the huge glass eyes just stared, warily, waiting.

They walked out into the afternoon sunshine of late April. The sky was blue, with soft, white clouds. Jacobs stared up, his mouth slightly open. He took off his glasses and cleaned them with his handkerchief, then looked at Charley.

"How you doing, kid?"

Charley stiffened. Anger overwhelmed him; his tightly held emotions began to unravel. "Why the hell do you keep asking me how I am? I'm okay. *Sir.* I'm as okay as anybody else. I'm as okay as you are. *Sir.* Okay? That answer your question?"

Jacobs nodded. His voice was as soft, as kind, as solicitous toward Charley as it had been toward the survivors. "I *need* you to be okay. Forgive me if I ask you. I'm not needling you, Charley, or worrying about you. I just think we all have to be very careful here. We have to take breaks. We have to . . . I don't know, take a walk, look at the sky, read a . . . a comic book, listen to music."

For the first time it occurred to Charley that Jacobs's control was just that—conscious control, to keep the center from exploding.

"For you, Captain, I'd recommend a game of basketball. With your height . . ."

"Actually, Charley, believe it or not, in college I was a swimmer. Water polo. But listen, thanks anyway, kid."

Charley told him about Benny Herskel. From home, from Ryer Avenue. Jacobs smiled. "Good, Charley. Good. Get drunk, get silly, talk dirty, be a kid again for a little while."

But they didn't get drunk, although he and Ben drank a great deal of Scotch. They didn't get silly or talk dirty. They didn't become kids again. They were both men, and they spoke carefully at first, testing each other, building on their memories and finally remembering that they had, in the past, trusted each other.

"Ya got the build and the connections, Charley. How come you didn't become an MP?"

"I looked at them, the MPs, when I was in basic. Jeez, I've seen mean-looking SOBs in my life, but these guys! Hell, they treated drunk GIs on weekend passes like they were punching bags. My family—the ones who were cops—always said you should see to it that drunks get home or find a place to sleep it off. You don't act like they're public enemy number one. I guess I didn't go for the spit and polish and rough stuff."

Ben smiled, leaned forward, and poured the last of the Scotch. "Funny how much it takes around here to get a buzz on. *Salud,* pal, bottoms up, plenty more around."

"I never knew you drank, Benny."

Herskel wiped his mouth with the back of his hand. "You mean 'Jews don't drink,' right? And Jews don't volunteer for the Army and Jews don't—"

Charley shook his head. "Jesus, that's not what I meant. Hell, Benny, you know me. Since we're five years old, you know me."

"Do you remember the first time you and I had a real knock-down, drag-out fistfight? I do. You went to St. Simon for your first day in first grade. I had been through kindergarten at P.S. 79, so first grade was no big deal for me. You came home and I asked you how you liked school. Do you remember what you said to me?"

Charley shook his head.

"You said, and I quote, 'The Jews killed Christ, and you're a Jew, Benny, so you're a Christ killer.'"

Charley shook his head. "Sister Mary Magdalene's introduction to religion. Yeah. I remember. You hit me right in the mouth. Jeez, we went at it. Yeah, I remember—and my mother came along with a bag of groceries and she grabbed us, two real thugs, and even then you didn't rat, when she asked you what was going on."

"That was me, super-Benny. Take care of myself, all by myself."

"When my mother got me upstairs, she shook the hell out of me. I told her what I learned in school, my first day, and she laid out the law to me. You know there was never any of that crap in my family."

Benny leaned back on his cot and regarded Charley with a strange expression. Amusement, sympathy, what? "I wouldn't think there would be. In your family."

"My mom was real tough about any kind of stuff like that about anybody."

"My family was too. Charley . . ." he stopped speaking, but even through the buzz, the haze that finally took control of his brain, Charley sensed that Benny had been about to say something. Something important.

"What, Benny? C'mon. What?"

Charley felt a cold shudder across his shoulders. He felt on the edge of something. Something about himself, his family, that he had known all along, without knowing. Some mystery he had avoided confronting. How could Benny have any answers when he himself didn't even know the questions?

Benny shook his head. "Another time, kid. Listen, Charley, there's something I always wanted to ask you. About that night. On Snake Hill."

For years, Charley had considered that dangerous territory. Dante had said we never talk about it, or think about it again. It happened; it's over. Period. But here—in this place, with the smell of death and anguish, with the still-unburied nightmare corpses and the barely living survivors, their eyes staring at things Charley hoped never to see—what had happened on Snake Hill, one snowy winter night when they were kids, seemed unimportant.

"What do you want to know? We were there, all of us. We all know what happened."

Benny leaned forward, hunched over, his elbows on his knees, feet wide apart. His eyes were bloodshot, his speech just slightly slurred, but the intensity never wavered.

"Your brother Gene is a priest. You guys all had to go to confession. What the hell did you say? What the hell did your priest say, that it was okay, it was all right for us to have battered that rotten bastard to death, who we all know deserved what he got? How did you handle it, Charley? I mean, I don't think you could lie to your confessor."

"Willie's father killed him. The cops saw him. He publicly confessed, and when Father Kelly showed up to give Stachiew last rites, Willie's old man confessed, right out in the open. Gene went to Father Kelly the next morning told him the truth. We *battered* the bastard. He was attacking us and we defended ourselves." Charley reached for the newly opened bottle of Scotch Benny had placed on the floor between his feet. He dumped a slug into his glass, swallowed it, caught his breath, shook his head.

"You been walking around all these years thinking *we* killed Stachiew?" he asked.

"Well, I didn't have the luxury of a priest telling me what I did was okay, and when Willie's old man fried, nobody told me, 'Hey, that was justice.'"

Charley's voice went cold and hard and sounded absolutely sober. "Do you think we killed him, that we're *murderers*?"

Benny smiled and shrugged. "Hey, who am I to argue with your priest? A long time ago, kid, a whole world ago. Like a dream, like a kid's story, like something in a comic book. Not important—the whole thing didn't mean fucking-A. How much Scotch do you think it'll take for me to pass out? I've been experimenting every night, but I can't seem to get to it. You, on the other hand, look like you're seeing double. Or I am. Jesus, Charley, there are two of you sitting there, looking at me. And both of you look worried. C'mon kid, forget it. Jesus, look around here and forget it. Come on, let me get you back to your quarters before those mean sonofabitch MPs come looking for you."

They walked to Charley's bunk, swaying, catching hold of each other, laughing, shushing each other. Ben helped Charley up the stairs, grasped him by the shoulders and spun him around. Charley was surprised that he was no more than an inch shorter than his childhood friend. Somehow, Benny always seemed larger than life.

"Wanna know what my assignment is tomorrow morning?" His hands tightened spasmodically on Charley's shoulder. He leaned forward, his face inches away. The fumes were so strong, Charley couldn't tell if they emanated from Benny or from himself. He squinted hard, tried to focus. Ben shook him, hard, and his voice changed. His words were clear and filled with controlled rage.

"Tomorrow, kid, I gotta march my Germans off to the local Catholic priest. They're gonna go to *confession*. So that on Sunday morning they can receive communion. *Do you read me? Communion.*"

He dropped his hands, and Charley couldn't think what to say. He was dizzy, he felt sick. He reached out for his friend, to soften the anguish, but Ben turned, waved away any response, and left.

What the hell *was* there to say?

God, I'm pissed, Charley admitted to himself. He didn't like the spinning sensation, the loss of control that forced him to move in slow, careful imitation of normality. That's what drunks do: move in exaggerated motions.

He pulled the hard flat pillow from under his head, put his chin up. Get the blood back to the brain. God, he felt floaty.

He started thinking about his parents. Or, rather, dreaming about them. He held his breath, ten years old, clenching his fists against the argument. He knew it was coming. When he came home from school, the two nuns swept past him, coldly dismissing him as though they'd never seen him before. He'd heard the door to the apartment slam shut, he could picture his mother's fury—tight lips, clenched jaw, narrowed angry eyes.

He went to the kitchen and she came in, poured him a glass of milk, handed him the Hershey syrup, told him not to make a mess. And change your clothes—don't forget to change your shoes, Charley.

His father was working a four-to-midnight shift, and Charley knew she was waiting, keeping her anger hot and explosive. His father came home and Charley covered his ears with his hands, sang softly to himself. To try to block it out. Of course, that never worked.

Sergeant Charles O'Brien shook his head from side to side, then sat up abruptly. He hadn't been *dreaming*. He'd been *remembering*. He hadn't thought about their argument, their continuing argument, for years. But now, his brain wide open, flooding, there it was. All the words he'd heard, through the years, late at night. It had started the way it always did.

His father, tired, gruff, sensing immediately what was coming. "Listen, I had a tough night, okay? A couple of crazies—"

His mother: "Speaking of a couple of crazies, Tom. They came again. This afternoon. Sister Holier-than-Thou and Sister Even-Holier. Tom, I'm telling you. Talk to Father Kelly. Tell him to keep them the hell away from me."

His father: "Miri, they are simple women. They think they're doing you a kindness. They are sincere in their belief that—"

"That when every member of my family dies, you'll all go straight to heaven and have a wonderful reunion, sponsored by Jesus and the Sacred Heart of his Holy Mother. And I won't be included in the party. Me, I'm bound for hell, because—"

"Look, Miri, I know you're upset. What the hell did you do, brood about this all day long? For Christ's sake, just forget it. They're ignorant women who mean well."

"They *don't* mean well. They are like vampires, smiling at the prospect of looking down from heaven at me, who could have been saved, but picked the devil instead. Listen, Tommy, I've had it with them. Let them keep their damned stupid medieval ideas to themselves. Not in *my* kitchen. *How dare they?*"

And now his father's voice changed. She had crossed the line. She never knew when to stop, his mother.

"You don't say another word about *my religion*. You can rant and rave all you want about these poor women, who've devoted their lives, by the way, to what they believe in. But don't you say a *word* about my religion."

"How *can* I say a word about 'your religion'? All my kids, I let you get them all baptized, I let you send them all to parochial school. I watched them and helped them with the catechism, and smiled at them when they made their first communion. My God . . . not even one of them—"

"Not even *one* of them? Is that what you wanted, all along? *To keep one of them?* To learn what? That when a daughter in the family marries a goy, a shit, a whatever, that daughter is *dead*? That the father rips his clothes and sits for seven days, mourning, then wipes his daughter from his family forever? You wanted one of them for that wonderful tradition?"

"Don't you dare. *Don't.* You want my opinion about what garbage they filled my children's head with? Saints to get pierced and burned and boiled alive—all for some wonderful 'someday,' 'somewhere,' when they die. If they die in a state of grace. Oh, Tommy, I know all about it."

How had he remembered all this? Where had it come from, all of a sudden?

Because every single day, from the first camp they entered, from the first emaciated dead faces to the frozen faces of still-breathing survivors, his mother's face floated, like a mask, over the dead and the near dead. His mother.

His mother, the orphan from upstate New York somewhere with no family, no history. Poor Miri.

Whose father rent his clothes and sat *shiva*. For his dead daughter, Charley's mother, who married the Irishman Tom O'Brien, who honored her promise to raise all of her kids as Catholics. And she did.

His mother, who became furious at Father Coughlin on the radio and declared, "Keep that lunatic out of my home." His mother, who shook each child in turn when he or she came home from the first grade with the incredible knowledge that the Jews killed Christ, and therefore they hated the Jews. Sister said.

His mother, who would have been sent to the camps, along with every member of her family, to starve and be abused and humiliated and tortured and gassed and burned.

His mother and every member of her mysterious family.

Charley O'Brien wished he was drunk. He was more sober than he'd ever been in his life, and every part of him ached and he didn't know what to do. He wished he could see her, talk to her, his mother. The Jew.

He and Ben Herskel hung around together every night when they had free time. But Charley didn't drink anymore, and no amount of Scotch seemed to affect Ben.

They talked about home, childhood friends, neighbors—who was where, what branch of the service, what theater of war. And finally, who of their friends and neighbors would be lying in those enormous, unreal, unhuman heaps of barely covered bones, with staring dead eyes.

They named neighbors. And then Ben stretched his arms over his head, then wrapped them around his knees.

"My family, of course. My mother and father and kid sister, my aunt and uncle and cousins."

Then he studied Charley, his face expressionless, and nodded as though Charley had asked him a question.

"Yes, pal. *You*. Your brothers and sisters. Even Eugene, the *priest*. It wouldn't matter."

As though he had always known, Charley said, "Because of my mother."

"Born of a Jewish mother, kid. To them, that makes you a Jew. If it had been the other way around, your father the Jew, it would have saved you. For a while, anyway."

"I don't get it."

Benny reached over and tousled Charley's cropped head. "Just a little bit of nasty Jewish thought, kid, that the Nazis adopted. Hey, when a baby is born, you *know* who the mother is. There's the kid right from her. Now, you can *assume* who the father is, but you don't *really* know, not the way you know the mother. Therefore, mother is a Jew, child is a Jew."

"The Catholics revere the mother . . ."

"Well, the Jews say a prayer every morning—the men do—'Thank God I was born a man, not a woman.' When did you find out about your mother? Did she sit down and tell each kid when you reached a certain age, or what? I always wondered."

Charley rubbed his face roughly, up and down, scratched his head. "How did you know that my mother was a Jew?" It was a peculiar thing to say, yet somehow it came easily to him, as though, yes, he'd always known this.

"Ah, Charley. You know our neighborhood is like a small town. Everybody up and down the block knows everybody's secrets and—"

"I didn't know, Ben."

"What?"

Charley shook his head.

"Charley? *You didn't know?* She didn't tell you? Then how . . ."

"Being there. Remembering things I'd heard all my life, when I was a kid. Hearing things late at night and then forgetting them, not asking about anything, not thinking about it. Then, last night, the words came back and somehow I wasn't surprised. It made sense, the nuns coming on to my mother, her getting so mad, throwing them out. Never letting them whack any of us kids around. Jeez, they are afraid of her. Benny, how did you know?"

"Charley, your mother was the daughter of an Orthodox rabbi. They were a big family, from Poland, living down on the lower East Side. He went through three wives, your grandfather; they all died giving birth. God, I think twelve or fourteen kids and—"

"My *grandfather?*" The very concept of an unknown grandfather, *a rabbi*, an old Jew with a beard. What did this have to do with him. Charley O'Brien?

"Your mother used to come in and have coffee with my mom at the end of a day, when your father worked late, and you kids were off to basketball or whatever. And one Friday afternoon my mother asked her if she'd like to come in the back, to the apartment, that she and my sister were going to light the sabbath candles, and your mother came, and she covered her head and her face, and she recited the prayer along with my mother and sister. And then she started to cry, and she and my mother hugged each other, and little by little she told my mother about herself, her family, the mourning ceremony that turned her into a dead daughter. I wasn't there, but . . . I guess the way you pick things up, little by little, I just knew about your mother. And that it was a very special, private thing and that I wasn't allowed to talk about it with anyone at all. Not even you kids. Especially you kids. I just grew up assuming you knew."

"It was never discussed. We never were allowed to ask my mother why she didn't take communion. She came to church, but just to bring us." Charley dropped his head into his hands and hunched forward. His voice was muffled, thick and painful. "Oh, Christ, oh, God Almighty. They'd have taken my mother . . . my mom, and turned her into one of those . . . and my brothers and sisters and me and . . . Oh, Christ, Benny. When you look at them, don't you see yourself, your family, your . . ."

Ben waited, wordless, as Charley sobbed into his hands. Finally, when Charley looked up and nodded to indicate he was okay, Benny said in a low, soft, firm voice, "That's why I'm taking care of as many of these bastards as I can. In my own way. What about you?"

CHAPTER THREE

There was an electric excitement sweeping the camp. Rumor followed rumor, and they were all true. *They* were coming to view the camp for themselves. Eisenhower had decided on the spur of the moment, with hardly a two-hour warning—he and Bradley, and oh-my-God Patton.

The colonel in charge of the officer-prisoner sector, old and haggard at thirty-three, with hollow cheeks and reddened eyes, gave the order. There was to be no spit and polish, no ceremony, that was the word. But at least, for Christ's sake, shave, tuck your shirttails in. A minimum honor guard. It was going to be a quick tour.

The Germans, the SS officers, heard the news almost as soon as the GIs did. They snapped into formation. In their tattered, dirty, incomplete uniforms, they stood stiffly at attention, waiting in perfect military formation, the smartness of their ranks somehow evident. They were after all, German officers, and they knew how to behave not only in victory but in defeat.

Some of the GIs ran to get their cameras, knowing they'd never get copies of the official photos. God, this was something they could tell their grandchildren about, if they ever got home and married that girl back there and had kids, and lived long enough.

The entourage arrived a few minutes before the announced time in a battered group of vehicles; dirty command cars, jeeps. The escorts arrived in a truck, battlefield-disheveled, but looking soldierly and proud.

Salutes were exchanged, quick; a minimum of army ritual. Charley watched as the colonel conferred with Eisenhower. God, it really was the general. The meeting was brief; the general was anxious to get on with it. A curt nod, and Eisenhower strode behind the colonel, flanked by Bradley and Patton.

As they passed the prisoner compound, the SS stood as rigid as picture-book soldiers. They saluted smartly, held the salute. Eisenhower never acknowledged their presence. Bradley glanced at them quickly, then looked straight ahead.

Patton, spit and polish, Christ, really wearing those pearl-handled sidearms, looked sharply to his right, snapped his hand up, nodded abruptly, and released the prisoners from their salute.

He, at least, knew how to act in the presence of the fallen enemy.

Without breaking stride or changing expression, Eisenhower viewed the barracks, then the stacked bodies, then the hospital quarters for those still barely alive, then the excavations readied for graves. He seemed unaffected by the death smells; the lime smells; the odors of unbelievable corruption.

He knew exactly what he wanted to see and spoke quickly, abruptly, to the colonel who escorted them to the warehouses where the Germans had carefully stored what they could use of the leftovers from the dead prisoners.

Great barrels of hair, carefully divided as to length and color, filled one room. A ledger itemized the amounts of hair collected each day.

There were cartons, their contents carefully itemized, containing dental gold, some still attached to the wrenched-out teeth of the dead, taken either before or after the gassing. There was a smaller amount of gold jewelry, a few rings and watches; God alone knew how these things had been concealed for so long. Small quantities of currency, bills and coins had been found hidden in naked bodies, alive or dead.

Everything was accounted for in individual ledgers, neatly itemized, a line for everything, an explanation. Spectacles, dentures, everything cataloged.

The last room was the worst. There were huge piles of shoes: tiny shoes with barely worn soles ranging from infant sizes to the shoes of children of four or five years old. The ledger was actually titled "Infant Shoes." The condition of the various sizes was neatly described. The younger the child, the better the condition of the shoe. After all, how much walking could a one-year-old have done? The smaller shoes were practically brand-new. Adult shoes were generally in poor condition.

The clothing, cataloged by size—men's, women's, children's, babies'— was mostly worthless. These Jews had long since been reduced to rags.

Finally the colonel handed General Eisenhower a piece of paper explaining the financial arrangements made between the commandant of Auschwitz and the I.G. Farben chemical company, whose plant had been built in proximity to the camp to take advantage of the continuing supply of slave labor. Prisoners who were reasonably able-bodied, whether male or female, who fit certain criteria of age, condition, or anticipated stamina, were not immediately killed. As long as they could meet the average life expectancy of nine months established by both the company and the commandant, they were sent to work at the plant.

Eisenhower read the accounting arrangements, and his expressionless face grew pale, but he said nothing.

Table of Profits (or Yield) per Prisoner in Concentration Camps (Established by SS)

Rental Accounting

Average income from rental of prisoner, per day	Reichsmark	6.00
Deduction for nourishment per day	RM	0.60
Average life expectancy 9 months:		
270 days by RM 5.30=	RM	1,431.00
Minus amortization on clothing	RM	0.10
Profits from rational utilization of corpse:		
1. Gold Teeth 3. Articles of value		
2. Clothing 4. Money		
Minus cost of cremation	RM	2.00
Average net profit	RM	200.00
Total profit after 9 months	RM	1,631.00

(This estimate does not include profits from sale of bone and ashes.)

Eisenhower handed the statement back to the colonel without a word. Bradley scanned it, shook his head.

Patton read it quickly. "Got to hand it to the bastards," he said, almost to himself. "They sure were efficient."

Apparently no one but the colonel heard him.

The generals left the camp after a brief exchange of salutes with the GIs. They barely stopped for official photographs, which would show a stiff, furious Eisenhower, a stunned Bradley, and an impressed Patton.

Their tour was so quickly accomplished it was almost as though it had never happened.

The SS captain dismissed his troops, but first he complimented his men on their behavior. The Americans had a great deal to learn about military conduct. They were the same barbarian mongrels they had always been.

Captain Benjamin Herskel's main assignment was the interrogation of the SS officer-prisoners, his reports to be evaluated in determining what was to be done with each officer. Almost from the first day, Ben knew that something special was going on. These men had been separated from the others who had run the camps. It was evident from their attitude and behavior that they were being treated, and expected to be treated, with special consideration.

At first Ben thought they were being interrogated and investigated prior to standing trial for war crimes. They had heard that many of the Nazis—from the top to however far down it was deemed prudent— would be held to answer for crimes against humanity. It was also evident, from the line of questioning with which he had been charged, that these prisoners were not going to stand trial.

They were to be neutralized to the point of being considered cooperating agents. Each of these men had, or claimed to have, information regarding the future plans of the Russian high command. They were specialists in biology, physics, research, scientists and mathematicians who had been assigned to work with Russian prisoner-specialists. They had vast amounts of information that would be of great value to the Americans. They were the new allies of the Americans. Their futures would be arranged quietly, secretly. They would be given new identities after they had cooperated to the fullest extent possible.

Their involvement with the camps, with the forced laborers and the gassed and cremated, was incidental. They had been recruited, assigned as a last measure when things had gone badly. Someone had to wind things up. Extermination was not their main function. It was only their last assignment, a matter of expediency. Their value to the Americans could not be overestimated. They knew of Russian plans that no one else had access to.

Yes, yes, they had supervised the last exterminations. But look at the survivors. When the SS had arrived, the camp was filled with these still-breathing corpses. Their orders had been—even though they knew the war was lost—to clear out the camps, to finish what had been started. The prisoners were disease-ridden, dangerous to whoever arrived at the camps.

In the long run, through the years, let's be honest, the world would come to understand and appreciate what the German Reich had accomplished—or tried to accomplish: a Jew-free Europe. That had been the unachieved goal, but they had come close.

None of these things was confided to Captain Ben Herskel. After all, he was a Jew. In fact, the highest-ranking SS prisoner, a major, had objected to his taking part in this business. He was a Jew, would he not be prejudiced? Would he really be the right person to take part in the interrogation and arrangements for the future of these officers?

The colonel quietly told the major that he was to order his men to cooperate with any and all American officers assigned to their interrogation. Was that clear?

It was.

Ben's SS informants were all captains and lieutenants, and in their relationship with him they forgot he was a Jew. His German was impeccable, and he seemed to be a good soldier.

"I've selected two," Ben told Charley. "This must be done carefully, and it must look like suicide. I'll need your help for the last, the captain who was responsible for giving the orders to kill as many survivors as possible, after he knew it was all over. He did it with great determination, deliberately, as his final gesture for what he believed in. That's the one I'll need your help with, Charley. These guys are going to get away with it, kid. With all of this. They are going to disappear, with new papers, new IDs. They're going to be slipped out of Germany, with the help of the Vatican, with the help of our government. They're going to have new lives in South America—money, businesses. They're going to live, Charley. What they've done here, all these dead people, all these damaged survivors are being traded off like they were worth nothing, for some information about the Russians, who've stopped being our allies and are now our enemies. Charley, I'd like to blow them all up, I'd like to . . ."

Charley O'Brien stayed calm, and his soft voice brought his friend under control.

"But we're gonna do something about it, as much as we can, without getting our heads in a noose, right? You tell me how I can help. I'm your man."

"We go back, don't we, Charley? God, things were so simple when we were kids."

Charley shook his head slowly. "Not really. Not if you think about it. Things were complicated at times. But, well, we're not kids now. We know how careful we have to be. Tell me what I can do, and you got it."

"Charley, you were raised in a police family. What's one of the first lessons an old-timer teaches a rookie cop?"

"Take care of yourself. Cover your ass. At all times."

"Charley, I need a throwaway. An officer's gun. By next week. Untraceable. And one bullet."

"By next week. Okay."

"I've got the cyanide for the first one. Charley, God, I'm glad you're here."

"Ryer Avenue boys, right?"

"Ryer Avenue boys."

The lieutenant had been a chemist working on the development of various drugs to reduce the shock effect of patients during surgery. He *had* to join the Nazi Party in the early thirties. He had no choice. They all had to. It had nothing to do with ideology. He'd ended up in the SS only because there was an elite unit for medical professionals. One had no idea what riffraff other areas of the party attracted. His work also involved devising medications and techniques to help victims of shock and massive battlefield wounds so as to get the wounded back on their feet as soon as possible.

There had been certain medical experiments at certain camps. He'd heard about that, though he had never taken part in any of these things. His work was mainly in the laboratory. His involvement with Russian prisoners was exclusively with captured scientists. They had been working on certain programs that the SS scientists had also been working on. Some of their experiments in nuclear physics really were old-hat to the Germans, but here and there some bits of information seemed worthwhile.

He looked forward to working with American physicists in the future. There were things he knew about Russian techniques. Well, all that would come later.

And his role here, in the last weeks of this camp?

An elegant shrug. He was, after all, a scientist. His orders were to wind things up as quickly as possible, to devise ways of speeding up the gassing and the disposal of the bodies. He actually did no more than observe. He was under orders.

His discussion today with his interrogator, Captain Benjamin Herskel, was to center on the numbers of those still living when he arrived at Auschwitz one month before Germany surrendered, and on what part he had played in the disposal of the slave laborers still working at I.G. Farben.

Ben had spoken to him several times, had taken the measure of the man who foresaw a golden future for himself working with his American colleagues. And how did he feel about the camps?

Terrible. They were a wartime expediency. No one, certainly not he or any of his colleagues, had any idea at the beginning that the concentration camps were anything more than a preliminary stop in a resettlement plan for the Jews and other undesirables.

But that, he felt sure, would all fall into the past. Life must move on. America must be ready for the real enemy of the world, the mutual enemy of all of Europe and all mankind: the Communists. What was done would be history, but the future could be shaped and controlled.

He settled into the hard wooden interview chair, and crossed his legs, anticipating the preliminary cup of coffee. The Americans had no idea what a cup of real coffee meant to those who had been deprived of this simple pleasure for so many years. It was an elixir of ecstasy, beyond description. Real coffee. American coffee.

After the corporal set out the cups on Ben's desk, he was dismissed. What was to be discussed was top secret, between the captain and the prisoner. The corporal was to stand guard outside the office in the interrogation barracks. No interruptions.

The coffee cups steamed. The fragrance was almost maddening.

The SS lieutenant, a medium-sized, slender man with a grayish complexion, poor eyesight not helped enough by outdated spectacles, a habit of licking his lips before speaking—an unprepossessing sight in baggy army fatigues—tried not to stare at the coffee cup. He tried to distract himself. His eyes tried to trace the contours of the desk, to estimate the measurements: height, length, width. God, hurry up and give me that coffee.

Captain Benjamin Herskel passed the palm of his hand over both cups, as though warming himself, then nodded. Go ahead, help yourself. He pushed one of the cups toward the prisoner.

Trying to maintain his dignity, trying not to make too much of it, the prisoner nodded, lifted the cup, took a small sip, and then, overcome by the fragrance and the teasing sip, took a large swallow.

And then he pitched forward, the cup falling from his hand, his face landing in the scalding puddle.

Ben walked around quickly, lifted the man's right hand and rubbed a tiny amount of cyanide under the thumbnail, knocked the chair over so that his loud voice added to the commotion. The corporal opened the door and saw the captain, standing over the prisoner.

"For Christ's sake, get a medic here."

"The bastard has taken cyanide," the Army surgeon said. He lifted the man's right hand and sniffed. "He must have had it concealed under his thumbnail."

Ben told his commanding officer that the prisoner had seemed somewhat more nervous than usual when he sat down. He had stared at the coffee, sighed, reached for it, sipped and said, "A wonderful last taste," then flicked his thumbnail against his teeth. He had pitched sideways, the cup flying from his hand. He was dead instantly.

The colonel was furious. What the fuck kind of security do you call this? He ordered a complete-inch-by-inch search of the prisoners' quarters, as well as a strip search of each of the protesting officers, their dignity be damned, their word of honor not worth shit. He then ordered the company barber to cut the SS officers' nails to the quick. The company dentist yanked and examined every crown in every mouth. There would not be a repetition of this under his command.

And there wasn't.

Ben waited nearly two weeks. Each prisoner was strip-searched before interrogation; but not after. Their barracks were scoured each morning. There was no cyanide to be found anywhere.

Captain Herskel palmed the small Walther PPK 9mm Kurz automatic pistol in his left trouser pocket as he studied SS Captain Rudolf von Zeeland. He was a tall, well-built man in his early thirties, the perfect German stereotype. Blond, blue-eyed, handsome, and arrogant.

Although it was obvious he wanted the offered cup of coffee, he shook his head and declined politely.

The captain, though a scientist, had been little more than an accountant when assigned to Auschwitz. It had been his responsibility to estimate, to the last pfennig, what the operation of the camp had cost the Third Reich and how the expenses, toward the end, could be reduced. His written recommendations included sending younger prisoners to work at Farben. Surely children could do some of the simpler tasks, and if they were in reasonably good health they would last longer, provided they were not exposed to the illnesses of the camp. Anyone showing the first signs of contagious disease should be eliminated at once. Also, children required less in the way of nutrition. A detailed accounting plan, in the captain's name, had been found among the half-destroyed records.

He denied none of this. But what he had of value to the Americans—or to the Russians, should they have captured him—was secret information relative to work being prepared for the future in the laboratories of I.G. Farben. A chemist by training, he had seen and memorized documents of great value, plans that could be implemented by either side for great advantage over future enemies.

His assignment was a matter of bookkeeping. He gave advice to those running the camp. He personally had never killed one single person. His work was theoretical; what was done with his calculations was none of his business. He fulfilled his orders and waited for his next instructions. His orders to leave Auschwitz never came, owing to some high-command foul-up. Things got very complicated and chaotic toward the end, but he should not be confused with those who actually ran these death camps, who actually murdered people. And remember, those who went to the ovens were the diseased and the disabled. Would America really want to undertake their medical care and rehabilitation? Think about it.

The children? His recommendations had provided for their well-being. Children were resourceful, and could survive. He had kept them from the ovens by recommending that they be put to work at jobs they could handle. He'd saved their lives. Think about it.

He spoke in a reasonable voice, with no attempt to persuade or influence. What he said was true, who could quarrel with this? The Americans were going to process him into their own system because he was of value, that was the way of the world. What he had done here was incidental to the information he could provide to American intelligence.

"All that you are required to do, Captain, is to record my civilian background and my wartime record and my proof that I was in fact in a position to gather the information I have volunteered to share with the Americans. It is not your position to judge me. You know nothing of the reality of the situation here, in these camps."

Ben Herskel leaned back in his chair. He clenched his teeth to control the emotions he felt. He must be very quiet, very calm, very persuasive. This bastard must believe him implicitly.

Without a word, Ben brought his chair to the floor with a thump. He stood up, dug in his pocket, and put the dark blue Walther PPK on his desk, close to the prisoner.

"This is for you, Captain."

The German smiled, looking questioningly at his interrogator. "So? The Walther is for me?"

"Listen very carefully, Captain. And *believe* every word I tell you. There is a plot against you personally, and I have proof of the reality of this plot. Among the survivors in the hospital are three men whose children were sent to the Farben works and whose corpses were returned for cremation. Eight-year-old boys. Also in this compound are two Russian scientists we have been rehabilitating. Men you 'questioned.' Men who have scores to settle with you."

"And this Luger you are giving to me for my protection? I don't understand?"

"Their plan, Captain, is to kidnap you. They have it well worked out. They will take you off into the woods. They will castrate you, stuff your genitals in your mouth, and force you to watch your own slow, systematic disembowelment. They say you have supervised such deaths yourself. Don't deny it, or speak about it. I really don't care. This is what they have told me."

"But surely your superiors have ordered extra security for me so that—"

"I am the only officer who knows of this plan. They don't just want your death, they want it to be a certain kind of death, Captain. And I should tell you their plan is to cut your corpse into pieces and return it to your barracks for your fellow officers to see."

He reached for the Walther, "There is one bullet, Captain." Ben carefully took the barrel of the gun and demonstrated, placing it in his mouth, and then removed it. "Your choice. A clean death or *they* get you. You can complain to anyone you want, Captain. I'll deny everything I've said here, and they'll never find anyone to back you up. But it *will* happen. Since we are both officers, I'm offering you a clean chance. An officer's death, although, God knows, you don't deserve it."

The German reached for the small automatic, weighed it in his hand. He pointed it at Ben. "And what if I put it to your head, Captain, and kill you."

Ben shrugged. "Then you will hang."

The captain slipped the pistol into the pocket of his baggy fatigue jumpsuit. He reached then for the cup of coffee, which was cold. He drank it down in quick gulps. "Is this where the cyanide was?"

Ben shrugged.

"You are very clever, Captain. But then, you Jews are all clever. For all the good it did you. I regret *nothing*, Captain. Nothing."

"Good. Then you won't regret your own death."

That night, at a little after midnight, there was the sound of a single shot in the SS officers' barracks. Captain Rudolf von Zeeland had put the barrel of a Walther PPK in his mouth and blown off the top of his head.

The entire security staff was replaced and appropriate entries made on their records.

CHAPTER FOUR

It had been made very clear to Megan Magee that had there not been a war, she would never have found a place at the Columbia School of Physicians and Surgeons. It was bad enough that they'd had to accept lesser students in order to fill the vacancies left by those students who had been drafted or who had volunteered.

The school was filled with 4-Fs, those who ordinarily wouldn't have been accepted—such as Megan, for God's sake, a girl—a polio-damaged girl, at that—and, fortunately, those able-bodied young men who had been smart enough to get a deferment.

Megan was the only woman student in the dissection room. She shared a corpse with Tim O'Connor, who, of the two of them, was the one to turn slightly green when they made their first cut. On the third day of dissection, when Megan approached her table, there was a medium-sized, gaily wrapped package with a gift card in her name. Carefully she glanced around the room, but everyone seemed too busy to look at her. She ripped off the gift wrapping, pried open the box, and studied the contents: a complete set of male genitalia, testicles and shrunken penis, tied with a pink ribbon. A note was attached: "You probably wanted this all your life. So here it is!"

Megan waited until after class, until the professor had left the students to clear off their various tables. She carried the gift box to the front of the room, cleared her throat to get everyone's attention. She held the box up and said, "Gentlemen, I'm sure every single one of you in this room is probably missing the items that were left on my desk by mistake. So, although it'll be difficult for the donor to claim this—after all, you don't have the balls, do you?—I'll leave this here for you 'gentlemen' to deal with."

She left the room and the matter was never referred to again.

In her second year in medical school, Megan Magee became pregnant. The tall, lanky, blandly handsome Tim O'Connor, whom she tutored through anatomy and supported during dissections, stared at her with horror that slowly gave way to calculation.

He had been a sweet, mild-mannered friend, admitting Megan's superior academic proficiency with far better grace than most of their colleagues. He had accepted her generosity with gratitude and honesty. If it hadn't been for Megan's noncompetitive kindness, he wouldn't have gotten through. Mean-spirited competition seemed the norm, and it occasionally became vicious. Megan was also a gifted teacher. She made the incomprehensible logical and clear.

One evening, exhausted by the long hours, the prodigious amounts of esoteric information she had helped him to absorb, touched by her continuing confidence in him, overcome by the glow of her pale freckled face, the golden amber warmth of her eyes, the tilt of her nose, the softness of her lips, the strong slenderness of her body, he made love to her.

Carefully he avoided contact with the steel-encased withered leg. Gently, recognizing her virginity, he performed with sweetness and consideration. Only once, deep into his passion, he whispered moistly into her ear, "Is it safe?"

Megan, who had not had any reason to calculate, to anticipate this event, ignored the question.

She was certain before the first-month morning sickness, and by the time she skipped her second period, she knew she had to tell Tim O'Connor.

Of course, *it was all her own fault*. Megan understood that. From earliest school days through their senior year at St. Simon, the girls had learned a liturgy of responsibility:

> *If you stand on a subway platform and there's a man across the way, turn your back on him. If you look at him, he will assume you are interested in whatever dirty thing he will be tempted—by you—to do. Because you are looking at him.*
>
> *If you go to a movie—never alone—always sit with a woman on either side of you or a man will think of you as fair game for his dirty acts. (She and Patsy had always attracted perverts; in the movies, in the parks. God, there must have been something about them, some signals coming from them; their fault; their sin.)*
>
> *If you walk alone on the street, keep your eyes straight ahead or slightly down. Otherwise, men will assume you have loose morals and will act accordingly toward you. Never, ever, even glance at a man alone in a car. You know why.*
>
> *If you wear perfume, it can drive even the mildest of men to terrible acts. Same with scented shampoo. Use Ivory soap. It does the job and you will be as clean as an innocent baby.*
>
> *Makeup implies a young girl wants to attract the wrong kind of attention.*
>
> *Smoking cigarettes, especially in a public place, advertises looseness and availability.*
>
> *Go only to dances sponsored by church organizations and chaperoned by Sisters. Go home only with other girls or parents. Don't go home with anyone's brother but your own. After all, they are males.*
>
> *If you wear immodest clothes—any form of slacks or shorts; in fact, anything more revealing than the large and shapeless school uniform—you are encouraging the lustfulness of men. (No one knew that Catholic girls in plaid skirts and knee socks excited certain types of men, probably former repressed Catholic schoolboys.)*

Megan had once asked Dante, her true friend, what boys were taught. He grinned, made a mock fist, and touched her chin. "We—all males—are wicked, lustful and disgusting, and need a lot of sports and cold showers. You females are out to corrupt us at every turn. I'll tell you, kid, it sure gave us ninth-graders something to think about. Especially in the late hours of the night. More solitary sins were committed on the nights of our lectures about sin—solitary and otherwise—than at any other time!"

And so Tim O'Connor was right to that extent. It was her fault that she was pregnant. Megan realized and accepted that. She never should have gone to his apartment. He was only a weak, lustful man and she had tempted him by her very presence. He was defenseless.

Tim O'Connor seemed to shrink and grow younger as she told him. She could see the scared little boy he had been, heard it in his first words, "Oh, my God, my father will kill me."

It was a stupid reaction, but Megan felt a wave of sympathy for his distress. She knew how hard he had worked, how difficult it was for him, the hope of his family. He was the only son among five children, and they had put it to him when he was just a kid. No fire department or police department, no priesthood for the only son. Because his early report cards were far better than his sisters', because his conduct was exemplary and he was willing to spend hours studying, memorizing at times without understanding, he had been marked out by his family. His father was a steamfitter, but way back, in the old country, in better times, the O'Connors had been scholars and doctors and lawyers. The O'Connors in America would see the glory of their family restored through their son.

Immediately, Tim caught himself and reached out for Megan. He was a good Catholic boy; he knew the rules. This was a good girl and they had sinned together. It was his responsibility as well as hers.

"Megan, it will be all right. We'll get married. My family will help me. Maybe your family—since you'll have to leave school—maybe they'll help with my tuition and all. Oh, Megan."

She reached up and touched his stricken face gently. He looked as grey as a cadaver—a man who has just seen his future unexpectedly, irrevocably destroyed.

"Timmy, it'll be okay. Thank you, but there's no way I can marry you."

She almost laughed at the childish relief, the unguarded expression of new hope.

"I meant it, Megan. I will marry you. If you want."

"Oh, Tim. No. I don't want." She hesitated, then said, "I'll have to do something about it."

He turned away, unwilling to face what she was suggesting, but Megan reached up and brought his face around to hers. For a silent moment there was no misunderstanding between the two medical students.

"Megan, I wouldn't know how to . . . *I couldn't.*"

"I wouldn't ask you, Tim."

The reality of what she was talking about filled him with new terror. "Megan, we'll get married. Look, other people have been in this situation. It'll work out."

"You don't get it, Tim. *I don't want to get married.* I want to be a doctor as much as—*more* than—anyone we know." She traced his frown lightly with her fingertips. "It'll be okay. Just don't ask me any questions. *Not ever.*"

"Megan, it would be a mortal sin. You couldn't—"

She pulled him toward her, kissed him lightly, tried not to be affected by his evident sense of relief that she was not going to involve him in anything.

"You're a terrific girl, Megan."

"You know me, stand-up Megan."

"I mean it." His large greenish eyes filled with tears and he tightened his grasp on her shoulders, shaking her slightly. "I wish . . . I just wish that . . ."

"Wish us both luck with our careers, Tim. It'll be okay." Than, as a parting gift, she told him, "You're a very nice guy, Timmy. Have a good life, okay?"

She telephoned Aunt Catherine, who agreed to see her immediately.

Catherine met her in the small private hallway that was shared by only one other tenant. Megan went from the elevator directly into her aunt's arms.

The old man was at his Providence, Rhode Island, mansion. His children were spending their mandatory few days with him, and Catherine had time to herself in the vastness of the Riverside Drive apartment.

Catherine led her through the servants' quarters and they settled over a pot of tea in the kitchen.

"Drink some tea first. We've got all the time in the world."

Avoiding Catherine's eyes, she blew steam from the cup, sipped, burned her mouth, put the cup down.

"Look up at me, Megan."

Catherine reached across the table and touched her cheek lightly.

"How far gone?" she asked.

It was one of the qualities Megan loved beyond all others. A practicality untouched by judgmental comment. Right to the heart of it.

Here and now: let's know the problem and figure out how to deal with it.

Within two days, late on a Saturday night, the abortion took place in one of the small bedrooms of the apartment.

The room had been arranged according to directions that were given during a quick phone call. A good light overhead and beside the bed; a twisted bedsheet; rubber sheeting; a pail. Soap; clean towels. Sanitary napkins.

There were two of them, and before Megan saw them, they had put out hands for money, which each in turn counted. Catherine never told her how much they charged.

They entered the bedroom without glancing at Megan, who sat, tensed, at the edge of the bed. They took off their dark, heavy suit jackets, glanced at her, and told her to stop looking at them.

They arranged her on the bed, her ankles separated and secured by the sheets and tied tightly and attached to the bedposts. Her knees were bent and wide apart. One of them jerked the rubber sheeting abruptly under her; he wanted it centered. One of them handed her a rolled-up towel and told her to use it to stifle any noise. He reached out and turned her head to one side.

"I told you not to look at us. Now if you make so much as one sound," he told her in a harsh, foreign voice, some unknown accent, more threatening by the mispronunciation of words, "even one sound, we will leave you. Immediately. In whatever stage of the procedure. Do you understand?"

Yes.

They gave her a shot of something that made her dizzy but did not blunt the pain of the long cold steel instrument that entered her body. She gasped, chewed on the towel, heard one of them say, "Not a sound! It's hard enough with the damn deformed leg." And then, to the other: "Pull it to the side, it's collapsing like a wet noodle, get it out of the way."

She felt the ripping, tearing, wrenching pain. It seemed to last forever, but it was probably over within minutes.

"There," one said. "Where's the pail?"

She heard a plopping sound; something being dropped into a pail half filled with water. "Where's the toilet?"

She heard her aunt speak quietly as she left the room, and then she felt the warmth of the sweaty face close to her. It was the one holding the pail.

"You're a medical student, huh? You wanna see the fetus?" He gave a deep hard laugh. "You wanna see, as part of your medical education? *A lovely red-headed little girl.*"

She heard Catherine's voice, furious, threatening. For a moment she blacked out, then came to, dizzy and weak. She felt the blood surging from her body, felt a towel jammed between her legs. They gave her abrupt directions. Gave her some pills. Told her to go to sleep. It was all over.

In the far distance, in some dream time, she heard the flushing, endless flushing, swirling and sucking, flushing.

When they were gone, Catherine came to her side, pressed a cool cloth against her face, lightly swabbed at her dry lips, stroked her hair. She opened her eyes.

"Listen to me, Megan. That was a filthy, vicious lie, my darling. It was just some bloody little glob. There was no baby, no little girl, nothing. Just a small piece of matter. I swear this to you."

Megan knew Catherine was telling the truth. It had been no more than six weeks. She knew about fetal development.

But she also knew that she would be forever haunted by the picture of a tiny baby girl, in her own image, being ripped from her body and flushed down the toilet.

CHAPTER FIVE

When he was discharged from the Navy, as a lieutenant commander, Dante took advantage of accelerated courses at Fordham University and finished his degree in one more year instead of two. Much to the chagrin of his Fordham professors, he chose Columbia Law School for his continuing education.

"I've been raised in the Catholic school system," he told his mentor, Monsignor McNulty. "I learned so many things in the Navy that I wasn't prepared for. It's time for me to continue my education outside the Church."

"And were you so ill prepared, Dante, by your Catholic education?"

He knew that no matter what he said, the slender, gray-haired, bright-eyed old Jesuit would find offense. He didn't want to engage in debates. The priest could beat him at semantics any day. It was decided. *Fini.*

The priest, who knew Dante thoroughly, shrugged. "Well, I have a favor to ask." He saw the wary frown and laughed softly. "Nothing life-changing, Dan. I'm asking one evening from your very busy life. We've received a request from Marymount to send a few of our very best graduates to attend their senior dance. Don't make a face at me. Consider this the last imposition of your Catholic education."

Of course, the women graduates were several years younger than the Fordham and St. John's invitees. The girls were untouched by war years. The boys showed their experience not by the ruptured-duck lapel pin, but by their attitudes. Some were blank and expressionless, others were braggarts, still others were amused and delighted by the glowing innocence of the Catholic girl graduates.

Dante was immediately attracted to a tall, slender girl. Her name was Lucia-Bianca Santini. Twenty-one years old, she had majored in foreign languages, and was proficient in French, Italian, and Spanish. She had made Phi Beta Kappa, and had a job lined up as an interpreter at the UN.

She was the most interesting girl Dante had ever met, tall and slender, with a face more handsome than beautiful: high cheekbones, a slightly pointed chin, and a straight nose in good proportion to the rest of her face. Her lips were full and deep pink, her color fair, in startling contrast to her black hair and dark eyes, which held his gaze steadily as they spoke.

They danced together once, and then both turned down other partners. She spoke in a low, slightly husky voice with none of the simpering nervousness of other girls he had known. None of the hidden pleading to be liked, to be considered special. None of the phony hiding of herself until she discovered what he might want her to be.

They talked about their education and their future plans. She thought it was a good idea for Dante to go to Columbia. Fordham was so provincial. She was genuinely interested in his service years, his time spent in Washington, D.C., in naval intelligence, and on active duty in the Pacific. Although he was reluctant to talk about his heroics, he found himself telling her, matter-of-factly, about the torpedoing of his PT boat, the long swim to a hostile island, dragging two wounded shipmates. His despair at realizing he had been hauling one dead and one dying man. His own injuries, his near capture, his time spent alone, in the Jap-occupied territory, living in a jungle, learning to survive. It was as though he were telling the experience of someone else. It had little to do with who he was, right now, in this hotel ballroom, with this incredible girl.

She neither gasped nor fluttered her eyes, or caught her breath. She studied him closely, and listened. They both felt that it was the foundation for their present and future.

Lucia-Bianca lived in a substantial eight-room house in the Pelham

Parkway section of the Bronx with her widowed father, Aldo Santini, a wine dealer. She introduced the two men on the night of the graduation dance, when Dante brought her home in a taxicab. Her father was a tall man, thin to the point of emaciation, with a startlingly concave face, a long nose, tight lips, and a small mustache and beard. His daughter had inherited his large dark eyes; his had the same liquid look, but could freeze under a quick blink. His hair also was black, but with threads of gray at the temple. He wasn't a handsome man—he was too thin—but there was a strange near-beauty about him. He was graceful in his movements; his hands were long and manicured; he glided when he walked; none of his gestures or movements were spontaneous. He was completely controlled, and if his daughter's intelligence was charming, his was fierce.

It was difficult for Dante to see her very often while he was at Columbia, but they did meet some evenings, when she finished working at the UN and he was finished at the law library. They went for walks, to movies, occasionally for an inexpensive meal. They talked *to* each other, not *at* each other; she was interesting and incisive and helpful to him at times when he needed to clarify the more obscure points of the law.

She was also unbelievably passionate. And a virgin.

They loved each other. They planned to be married. Her body against his, on the grass of a secluded section of a local park, was light and warm and yielding. They lost consciousness of themselves in the deep, incredible depths of their kisses. His hands roamed her slender but strong body—and then she would abruptly sit up, shake her head, adjust her clothing.

She would be a virgin bride. It was the way she was raised and educated. It was what she believed.

Dante suffered. He was not a teenager. He had been around. He had spent three years in the service. This was ridiculous; this was unhealthy.

He proposed and she accepted, and now, as courtesy and tradition demanded, he had to ask her father's permission.

Everything about Aldo Santini that had seemed understated now seemed to be intensified. The expensive dark suit added to the elegant gracefulness of the tall, slender body. His gestures were fluid and expressive. Have a seat, Dante. Here, would this not be more comfortable?

Dante fully expected the older man to seat himself behind the magnificently carved, glass-topped mahogany desk, to take a position of authority, to set the distance between them. Santini surprised him. He chose one of the two easy chairs that flanked the leather couch against the book-filled wall, waited politely for Dante to settle, then slid into place, his spine not touching the comfortably upholstered chair. His hands, fingers long and white, caressed the velvet pleasurably.

It was the first time Dante had really taken a close look at the man who would, he hoped, become his father-in-law. He was astonished by the resemblance between Aldo and his daughter. What was fragility in the daughter's pale, beautiful face was strength in the father's. It was a serene face, yet the serenity was contradicted by the intensity of the black eyes. As he offered Dante wine, a cigarette, only the hands moved; the eyes stayed on Dante, studying, watching, piercing.

Dante leaned back in his chair, but kept his hands still in his lap. He wanted a cigarette, but felt that smoking would betray his tension, which was intensified by the demeanor of the man facing him. There was something strange, mysterious, such a power of concentration directed at him, that he had to draw on a deep resolve not to do anything stupid. Get up and leave, for instance.

Aldo made a tent of his long fingers, rested the tips of his forefingers against his thin lips for a moment, then brought his hands back to the arms of the chair. It was difficult to see the smile, but his teeth flashed white against the blackness of his neatly trimmed beard, and his voice was soft and low and melodic.

"I understand your situation, Dante," he said quietly. "It is most difficult to be a young man, to talk to the father of the girl one wishes to marry."

Dante smiled, shrugged, tried to take a deep, relaxing breath without appearing to, then laughed. "Yes, Don Santini. It is most difficult."

He fell easily into the cadence of the man before him.

"Well, then, that is a given between us, so let us get on with this talk. My daughter tells me she loves you." The slender shoulders rose and fell, commenting on the love feelings of a young girl. Inconsequential. What does it mean, this adolescent claim, *I love him.* "And you have told me you love her and wish to take her for your wife."

"Yes. Oh, yes, sir. I love Lucia-Bianca. I want to marry her as soon as I graduate from Columbia in June. I have a job lined up at the Bronx DA's office. I will take care of her for the rest of her life. Make a home with her and have children with her and . . ."

Santini held up his right hand and made a soft, sympathetic sound, which stopped Dante cold. He hadn't realized how foolish, how childish, how boyish he sounded until the older man spoke, slowing him down the way one shushes an overeager child.

"Yes, yes, yes. All of those things. All of those things. Now there are some questions I would like to ask you, without your objection?" He smiled, "You see, I speak to you as one who will be an attorney."

"Anything, Don Santini, anything you ask me, I will answer."

Don Santini's eyes glinted. Of course you will answer me. What choice do you have? There was a contradiction between the softness of his voice and the hardness of his eyes.

The question was unexpected.

"Why did you go into the Navy instead of the Army? You would have achieved a commission in either service."

Carefully, Dante replied, "I thought about what my service might be. There was the very real possibility—and it did turn out this way with some of my friends—that I might be sent to fight at some time in Italy. Since my father and uncles still have family in Sicily, I didn't want to come face to face with cousins, to have to shoot at cousins." He shrugged. "As a naval officer, I served in Washington, D.C., for part of my time, and then in the Pacific."

Santini tapped his fingers against his lips and nodded. "And why did you decide against Fordham Law School and for Columbia Law School?"

And why do I have the feeling *you know* everything you are asking me?

"Because for all my life I have been educated in Catholic Schools. The Navy was the first time I'd ever been in a secular setting. I felt that my education, while good, was too protected, too limited, that it did not prepare me for a larger world."

Again, the slight smile, the nod.

"And for what are you preparing—in the larger world? What area of law do you wish to practice?"

"I'm not sure. As you know," he said, taking a chance on Santini's knowledge, "I'm working part-time in the Bronx DA's office. I've been promised a full-time position when I graduate. It will give me a year or two to decide where I might use my law degree."

"But not in criminal law, as a prosecutor or as legal aid." It was a statement rather than a question.

"Not as a career. But for experience for a year or two. Criminal law doesn't appeal to me as a career."

"Politics, perhaps?"

Dante stiffened. It was as though this man had probed into an area of his brain he had held closed off, even from himself. A secret, not faced fully, but tantalizing, darting elusively in and out of his consciousness.

"I thought it might be interesting to get involved in a political campaign, yes. To pick out a candidate and work for his election. On the local level."

"At first."

Dante nodded. "At first."

There was now a knowledge between them that Santini had brought out of Dante's subconscious and with which Dante now felt familiar.

"It is the way to proceed," Santini told him. "Carefully. Do the groundwork. See how things work. And build a network. You are a bright young man. And ambitious." Dante shrugged; it had never occurred to him that he was ambitious. "Oh, yes," Santini went on, "ambitious. It is a quality that only the successful have. Do not shrug it off. It is an essential ingredient. So. Now we come to some other matters."

Dante tensed. "Don Santini, I cannot right now support your daughter, as I am in school and I do help my family, but—"

Santini held up his right hand, sloughing off Dante's objection as unimportant, something that could be worked out. All of this with one casual gesture.

Dante watched the transition of the relaxed yet controlled man. Almost unobtrusively there was a stiffening, a drawing inward, the eyes narrowing, piercing, indicating a decision being measured and finally reached. The long hands locked across the dark fabric of the suit, clenched, then eased. Without actually leaning forward, Santini, by his voice, his body posture, his quiet air of intimacy, pulled Dante closer, riveted his attention.

"What I am going to do now, Dante, is to give you some information in deepest confidence. In total trust. You must understand first that I will expect two things from you." He paused, then slowly gave his conditions. "First, that no matter what happens in the future, whether you marry my daughter or not, what I say to you here and now will remain between the two of us. Eternally."

Dante's heart pounded. His mind raced. What in God's name was he to be told? Did he want some terrible secret from this intense man?

"Yes. Absolutely. You have my word."

There was a slight nod. The answer was only what Santini expected. "And the second condition. Listen carefully, please, and think before you give me an answer. In exchange for the trust I will place in you, you will give me the same fidelity of trust. In every man's life, even that of a young man, there is some fact, some deed, some event that he holds secret. You must confide that in me, as I confide in you."

Dante felt his jaw relax, his mouth open in surprise. Oh, my God, my God. Who is this man? He knows. *He knows.* The memory of that night, the shovel crashing down, the blood, the fallen body. Dante felt the icy wetness of that December night more than ten years ago down his spine, along the back of his neck.

Santini shrugged slightly, the elegant, indifferent gesture of a man who might be making a mistake. "It is up to you, Dante. Trust for trust."

Dante nodded. "You have my word. Trust for trust."

"So. Then I will tell you this thing that you should know, assuming you are to marry my daughter. You see her as a young, beautiful, bright girl, very protected in her home, in her schooling, among her friends. Innocent, carefully nurtured. As it should be with a cherished daughter. But more particularly with this girl, who has had tragedy in her life. You know she is motherless?"

"Yes. Lucia-Bianca told me—"

"Told you what?" The question was sharp and betrayed the expressionless face.

"That her mother died when she was a little girl."

"What else?"

"That she died in childbirth, along with her infant son."

"And how did she seem when she told you this?"

Dante thought the question made no sense. "Sad, I guess. I . . . it is a sad thing to lose one's mother."

"Yes. You too have lost your mother. But that was all she told you of the circumstances?"

"Just that she was a little girl, three years old, I think. That's all."

"And now I shall tell you the circumstances. And the reason I tell you this will become apparent. It is something the husband of my daughter must know."

Aldo Santini told his story. "My wife, Bianca, was a beautiful young woman, a northern Italian, fair of complexion, blue eyes. A carefully raised girl, cherished by her family and her friends. I married her in Rome and brought her here, where she knew literally no one. But it was not to be an immigrant's home. I was older than she, I had a good business, supplying altar wine to the Archdiocese of New York. I brought her here, to this house. It was what she was accustomed to. Within the first year of our marriage, Lucia-Bianca was born. A nursemaid, an elderly Italian woman, came from Bianca's family to take care of the child. My wife seemed lonely. I was, after all, at work all day, but I did not neglect her. I cherished my time with her. We had taken two trips back to her family by the time Lucia-Bianca was three years old. She went to church regularly, she became active in some church groups suitable for young women. But there was always this sadness. I felt always she was waiting to go back home. When Lucia-Bianca was three years old, my wife became pregnant, and we were told very early on to expect twins. She was a fragile woman, small-boned and tense. She had to spend a great deal of time in bed. She had many visitors, and to each of them she confided nothing of fear, anxiety, concern. Just a general sadness. The doctor said it was normal, to be expected.

"The delivery was terrible, an ordeal. Two boys. The first was robust, pink and healthy. The second born dead, strangled on the umbilical cord. Two of her sisters came from Italy for a few weeks, her nursemaid took care of the new child. She seemed disinterested. She ignored both the infant and Lucia-Bianca. The doctor said it would pass; some women were like that after giving birth, and the sadness was because of the loss of the one child."

He paused, considering the tips of his fingers as they tapped together before his face.

"Then, surprisingly, she insisted, one day, that she wanted to spend more time alone with the newborn child, my namesake, Aldo. The doctor felt this was healthy—finally, a show of interest. For a few days she fussed with the child, fed him, bathed him, sang to him. But still she kept Lucia-Bianca away. 'I must give myself to this small boy,' she said.

"And then, one day, when the nursemaid took Lucia-Bianca to the park, my wife was alone in the house with my infant son."

Santini's voice went very low, and Dante felt the small hairs on the back of his neck prickle. He leaned forward.

"The note she left said that she had known all along that this surviving child longed for his twin brother. That they had been conceived together and it was meant that they be together for all eternity. That it was a great crime to keep this child from his twin—it was a violence to the soul of each child. This was the note she left.

"It was my small daughter who found them. In the bathtub. My wife had dressed herself in her loveliest nightgown, filled the tub with warm water. She had slashed both of her wrists and her throat, as she lay in the water with the child to her breast."

Matter-of-factly he said, "My son died by drowning in his mother's blood."

The silence was so sudden that Dante stopped breathing as though fearful of missing something being said. The final shrug was all Santini had to offer. What else could one say?

"And . . . Lucia–Bianca . . ."

"Understood nothing. She saw them for no more than a few seconds. Whatever impression she might have had, God alone knows. The nursemaid was a cool-headed old woman. She grabbed the girl and rushed her to her own room, gave her a doll to hold, closed the door. By the time I arrived at my home, the infant was wrapped in his blanket, in his crib. The police came. It was all kept very quiet. I have a certain standing; these things can be kept within the four walls of one's home.

"My daughter was sent to Italy, to my parents, for nearly a year. It took me that long to . . . come to terms, one might say, to get on with my life. Well . . ."

Aldo Santini rubbed his bright eyes with his long, narrow fingers, leaned back slightly, then became stiff and straight again. His voice, so soft, so eerie, made his words all the more terrible.

"I will tell you this. I have *never* forgiven her for the death of my child. It may be my sin, at this point, but I rejoice in the knowledge that her soul writhes in the eternity of hell she deserves for her despicable crime. That is why no one—at any time—in this house is permitted to speak her name in my presence. I speak to you about her now, this one time, and then never again.

"And it may seem strange to you, but I will speak of her with others, on occasion, who know nothing about what she did. They will see me as a still-sorrowing, loving, devastated husband who was unable ever again to marry, because I had lost the perfection of my adored wife.

"She stole my posterity from me; I could not allow myself, ever, to trust another woman. Not with what had happened to my son. Of course, I love and cherish Lucia–Bianca in the special way a father loves a daughter. But there is a difference. With a son, there is a feeling of continuity. When the second son was born dead, I grieved, but was grateful to God for the first child, that he was healthy and strong and my wife finally seemed healthy. What could go wrong?

"I know, intellectually, that I should not blame her for what her madness did. But in my heart, for the rest of my life, dwells this anger, this hatred."

His eyes narrowed with the intensity of his need to communicate with Dante. "I tell you all this for a specific reason. My wife was a young, bright, protected girl. What happened was totally unexpected. Yet it did happen. It was not malice or exhaustion or neglect that caused her to do such a thing. It was a form of . . . madness. Something"—

he snapped his fingers—"broke inside her head. God knows, women have endured losing a child, losing parents, and do not do such a dreadful thing. So, you see, there was something wrong inside her head that made her act this way. If you are to be the husband of my daughter, you must know her heritage. This is my trust in you."

Dante didn't move. He was immobilized by the weight and force and reality of the confidence. He was numbed by the realization, but more, by its implications. Don Santini's revelation bespoke not only trust but obligation. Clearly, Dante was approved as a husband for Aldo Santini's only daughter.

"And now, Dante, for your part of our bargain." Santini settled back in his chair, unmoving, creating a sense of expectation and certainty.

He knows, Dante thought. Somehow, in some way, my God, he knows, and if I fail to tell him, I will lose her.

And so, quietly, unexpectedly, Dante D'Angelo, for the first time since that night in December of 1935, broke his vow.

He told Aldo Santini what had happened, what role he had played—everything but the names of the others. He told of the confession, trial, and execution of Stanley Paycek. And, during the telling, he had the absolute certainty that the story was already known, that what he was doing was confirming something.

"So." The older man nodded, then said, "And the other boys with you that night, who took part in the killing of this degenerate?"

Dante shook his head. "That was not part of our bargain."

For the first time, Santini smiled. It was with approval, as though another of his suppositions had been proven correct.

"Good. Excellent. Well, enough for one night, I think. Shall we share some wine? A toast, perhaps."

He stood up, went to the sideboard, and poured wine from a crystal decanter into crystal goblets. He held the wine up to the light.

"This is a special wine. Not the wine I provide for the churches. The priests should not sip such a miracle during mass. They might get carried away. It is miraculous, this wine. For special occasions."

This was indeed a special occasion. Dante waited for the older man to make the toast. It was simple, direct, and given in a positive, friendly voice.

"To the future. To good health to you, and to my daughter and to my future grandchildren. To a grandson. Accept my word of honor that I will help you in every way I can to achieve your goals. You will become my son when you marry my daughter."

"Salud."

Dante was making a commitment far more complicated than he had anticipated. He was handing over his entire life.

He wasn't quite sure how he felt about it.

Not even the official engagement, the giving of the small ring, the reading of the banns in Lucia-Bianca's parish church, changed her firm rule. She would be a virgin bride.

There was no way Dante could convince her of his pain, his frustration. Either let me make love to you totally, he pleaded, or we should not even touch each other until the wedding night in June, four months away.

Lucia-Bianca shook her head. She could not exist without the passion between them, the touching, the deep incredible kissing, the rubbing. Night after night, Dante walked from her house to the subway in an agony of denial. He had not the slightest idea that he was being followed, night after night, from his house to the subway, during the ride, and as he walked to Lucia-Bianca's house, then followed home. If he went from school directly to the house on Pelham Parkway, she assumed she had missed him, and went directly to the Pelham station and waited for him.

Maryanne Radsinski had, from the age of twelve, been called by the neighborhood boys "Maryanne the Cunt." Her parents were alcoholics who both held jobs, drunk or sober. Her mother cleaned apartments in the neighborhood. Her father was a mechanic and watchman in one of the garages on Webster Avenue. Maryanne discovered the fleshly delights by watching her parents, who were loud, passionate, boisterous, and hysterical in their lovemaking. She was their only daughter, and it was her job to cook for them and for her three brothers. She liked mothering her family. She also liked the idea of having fun for herself, and being popular with the neighborhood boys.

She confessed to the at-first-horrified parish priest, who was appalled at her casual stupidity and delight. She provided great happiness to the boys, she said. Was it a sin?

Finally, confused by her confessor's reaction, Maryanne skipped all that stuff and went to the usual sins. Name of the Lord in vain; cursed; answered back; lied. Both she and her confessor seemed content with this arrangement.

Maryanne became the legendary available cunt in the neighborhood.

High school boys barely mentioned their shots with her. Everyone aged fourteen and up had done it with Maryanne. What she couldn't understand was why none of the boys were nice to her.

Among the few neighborhood boys who never gave her the chance to share pleasure was Dante D'Angelo. He was the handsomest, nicest of them all. He would nod to her, smile sometimes, not in that mean way, just a casual smile and hello. She was madly in love with him for years, and all her daydreams revolved around what a lovely life they could have together. Someday.

After she finished eighth grade at the age of fifteen, Maryanne worked in the Woolworth's on Fordham Road, in the makeup section. She loved it. She also made a few extra dollars, now and then, when she felt like it, by doing some man one of her favors. It was after Dante came home from the Navy and was in law school that she made her plan.

She knew he was engaged, even before it became official. No guinea father allowed his daughter to go out with a guy that often without it was official.

She also assumed certain things about Dante: that he left his wonderful girl's house in an agony of frustration. Maryanne planned carefully. On the night she had chosen, she watched him leave the girl's house and head not for the subway but toward the neighborhood park. He looked sad, leaning forward, hands deep in his pockets. He stood inside the park, one foot resting on the seat of a bench. He turned when he heard someone behind him.

"What? Maryanne? Is that you?"

Instead of answering him, she stood close to him, ran her heavy, knowing hands along his chest, slid open his fly, and removed his quickly hardening penis. She hoisted up her skirt and inserted him. He didn't say a word as they slid down behind the bench, she on top, moving slowly over him, then helping him to turn over, to assume the man's position, to obtain the man's release.

It was her dream, but it was true, it was real, it was finally happening. She was giving pleasure to Dante D'Angelo, she was binding him to her for all time. He was her husband in her dream, and would be in fact.

She loved him so much.

''I was stupid. She was available,'' Dante told his uncles, Joseph and Victor Rucci.

They glanced at each other and then back at Dante. He was a handsome sonofabitch, with their dead sister's thick black hair and light brown eyes, and his father's square, determined chin. He was one of the lights of the family: Dante, getting a law degree, marrying a rich man's only daughter.

Joseph, the older of the two Rucci brothers, shrugged. He was short and thickset, his hands made for the butcher trade. "So everybody, once inna while, they give it to a whore. So what's the big deal here? Every kid in the neighborhood shoved it to this cow. So what's her story?"

Victor, the younger, with a shrewd face, the family's most successful businessman, sensed this was more than just an arm-twisting by a girl looking for some money. This was the scheme of a whore looking for a different kind of life. "So what she tells ya, tell me again, Dante."

Dante licked his lips. "That she hadn't let any man touch her for six months. That she wanted to be 'pure' for me, and that now she was carrying 'our child.' Jesus."

Joseph snorted and shrugged. "So who believes the whore, she ain't touched no man? Between us, we could come up with what, maybe fifteen, maybe twenny guys say they . . ."

His brother interrupted. "That's not the point, right, Danny? That's not the point."

"So what is the point?" his brother demanded. To him, this was a simple matter, easily handled.

"The point is, this whore could make trouble for Danny. She can open her mouth to this girl Danny's engaged to, his madonna with her father, right, Danny? She's a good girl, your Lucia-Bianca?"

"Yes. She's a good girl."

"Ah, nice," his older uncle said, kissing his fingertips and smiling. "That's the way a bride should be—good girl, clean, pure. A nice Italian girl, huh, Danny?"

"Yes," he said, miserably.

"So, what we gotta do is, we gotta have a talk, and make an arrangement with this whore, this Maryanne, who wants to marry you." Victor aimed a mock punch at his nephew's shoulder, tapped him twice. "You a good boy, Dante, you come to the family. You know we're here for you."

"You understand why I couldn't let my father know anything about this?"

"Your father, God bless him, would say you gotta honor a obligation to this woman. Your father, bless him, is one of the last innocent people in the world. A good man, your father. You done right to come here, Dante."

"Uncle Victor, I don't want you to . . . she's an ignorant, mean-minded girl, but I don't want anything . . ."

"Hey, you want I should make scrambled eggs but don't break no eggshells?" His voice was suddenly hard, but then he smiled. "Hey, we're none of us wiseguys in this family, kiddo. We're just blood. You'll see. We'll take care of it nice. You get back to your books, you study hard, you marry this good Italian girl, you have a good life, ya hear me?"

Dante embraced his uncles, one after the other. He pulled back, and he and Victor studied each other. Dante nodded. He knew it would be all right.

He was free of Maryanne the Cunt.

CHAPTER SIX

When the war was over and the heroes came home, Willie was the first usher to be let go. It was a legal matter; they had to reserve jobs for the homecoming vets. He told Mr. Felnick, yeah, he understood—*and how long do you think these heroes are gonna work in their little red jackets before they start school under this GI plan? Listen, don't call me, Mr. Felnick, I got better things to do with my life, too.*

They had everything, these returning bastards. Their jobs reserved; paid money by the good old U.S.A. for up to fifty-two weeks if they just wanted to loaf around; college tuition; extra points on civil service exams; low interest rates to buy a house. It was all for them and nothing for guys like Willie.

Except he still had his job with the Ruccis. Two of the drivers had been killed in the service, another was going to school, another came home with only one arm. At any rate, they'd have kept Willie on. He was a hard worker. He never complained about overtime; he didn't skim any more than anyone else, and he never ratted on anyone.

That was one of the lessons Willie had finally learned. You kept your mouth shut. You gathered all kinds of information, but you didn't pass it on. You added it to the storehouse of facts and feelings collected through the years. You put it all away, because in the future anything might be of great value. Finally he had learned to take care of himself—by keeping his mouth shut, even when he was nervous. Keep it all to yourself, Willie boy. Because someday.

The day came unexpectedly, without fanfare, three years after Willie Paycek had started working for the Rucci brothers. He had been told to come into the office; Mr. Joe wanted to see him about something.

Mother Superior wants to see you about something.

Father wants to see you about something.

Somebody wants to see you about something.

That always meant something terrible was going to happen to you, no matter what you had done or not done, said or not said. It was all the same. In a time of reckoning, everyone always had it in for Willie Paycek.

He stood in front of the battered desk, leaning against the door of the cubicle Mr. Joe called his office. His heart pounded so hard it hurt his chest. His mouth was dry and he had an urge to swallow, but when he tried he choked and coughed and had to cover it up. He knew every single emotion he felt was right out there. He was terrified, though he knew—or thought he knew—that he hadn't done anything wrong. Not recently. He didn't think.

Mr. Joe was a short man with a hulking torso who looked like a giant sitting behind his desk. His legs were disproportionately short, and he sat when he wanted to appear impressive.

He put one large dirt- and blood-caked hand over the mouthpiece as he spoke on the phone. His butcher apron was filthy with dark blood and other stains.

"Siddown, kid, siddown. Be witcha inna minute."

He listened intently, scowled, made a low growling noise deep in his throat as he searched through a messy collection of bills of lading, order forms, catalogs, government forms, and ledgers sprawled over the surface of the battered desk. He was very intent on his conversation and on what he was doing, snatching at scraps of paper, running a thick finger down a line of figures, shoving the paper aside, searching through ledgers, talking in his thick low voice, switching from English to Italian to some incomprehensible mutter.

He caught Willie glancing at the clock over his head: a big round Coca-Cola sign with small bottles for numbers.

"Be witcha inna minute, kid, siddown, g'wan, sit."

It didn't seem to Willie that Mr. Joe was mad at him. He was a guy who blew up, exploded, his arms and legs and fists going, striking out.

He had tantrums like a little kid, jumping up and down, battering his own face, howling, carried away. The first time Willie saw that routine, he almost wet his pants. Everyone else ignored it, just the way you would ignore a little kid until you just picked him up and smacked him. But no one ever smacked Mr. Joe, you just waited him out. When the tantrum was over, it was over, like a light being switched off. You acted as if it had never happened, and so did he. It was scary at first, but then became routine; Mr. Joe had a tantrum every couple of days.

His real anger, though, was a different matter. He became very quiet, very focused, very intent. His dark, unruly brows gathered over his thickly fringed black eyes; his pitted face froze; his thick mouth pulled back, the way a dog's lips pull back to show teeth. Mr. Joe's teeth were yellow and square and his voice became a growl. Mr. Joe's anger was a fearsome thing, and Willie had heard it was slow in coming and long in going and could be, literally, murderous.

Finally he shrugged at the phone, muttered something, and slammed the receiver into place. He chomped on his wet, unlit cigar. Willie froze when Mr. Joe got up, walked behind him, and closed the door of the small room.

"We gonna be private here, you and me, not disturbed by nobody, we gonna talk a little bit private, okay?"

Oh, Christ, Willie thought. He's gonna ask me how come the run over to Jersey with the black-market meat took so long. Did he know Willie had made a couple of stops, done a little business of his own, made a few bucks? Willie hated these runs; the guys at the other end scared the shit out of him. He was ready to confess, to throw himself on his knees, to beg forgiveness for his larceny, but he had learned to keep his mouth shut. And to wait.

"So what's this I hear, you love the movies, huh, kid?"

Willie stared and tried to swallow, without success. What was this, small talk, leading up to . . . what?

"Well, yeah. You know."

"What you wanna do with the movie pictures, huh? Ya wanna be the big movie star, like Clark Gable, huh?"

Mr. Joe laughed uproariously. Willie shrugged and smiled. They both knew this was ridiculous. So what the hell was this all about? Some kind of warm-up? To what?

Mr. Joe leaned forward on his thick arms and spoke seriously, his eyes studying Willie. "So you tell me, kid, what you wanna do with the movies?"

Willie hesitated. He had learned not to share his dreams. He had stopped giving things away, pieces of himself for someone to use to torment and ridicule him. He squinted to focus on the man behind the desk. He wasn't smiling; he wasn't teasing. He was flat-out serious.

"Why you askin' me this, Mr. Joe?"

"Good. You smart boy. You got smart workin' for me, kid. Yeah, I got the reason. I just gotta know first, how serious you are. You ever think about maybe going out there, to Hollywood, you know?"

He caught the sudden gleam of hope in the boy's eyes, the tightening along the jawline, the alertness. This was one hungry sonofabitch. Not a bad kid—he had something behind him, behind that scrawny body and thin face and those crossed eyes. The kid was a real mess, but he had something going on.

"Ya watch alla the movies, over and over. So watchawanna do, Willie, ya wanna own a movie theater one day, ya wanna be a projectionist? They got a tough union, ya know, but it can be cracked enough for a kid, maybe. What? What you want with the movie business?"

When the kid didn't answer, Mr. Joe leaned forward. "Ah, ya want more than that, huh? Ya got a look to ya, kid, and that's good. It's good to have a dream, but ya gotta go out and do somethin' about it, right? A dream don't mean nothin', ya don't follow through."

"I got follow-through, Mr. Joe. You know I work hard. So maybe one day . . ."

Mr. Joe smiled. "One day, one day. Ya gotta be in Hollywood, right, out there where they make the pictures. Ya wanna do that, kid, make pictures, huh? That what ya wanna do?"

"Yeah. But I gotta learn so much that I don't know . . ."

"So ya watch alla movies at the Paradise, all the other places, that's a good start. But there's lotsa ushers and they don't go nowhere, maybe become managers. That ain't for you. So tell me, Willie, ya wanna go out there? To Hollywood? To where they make the movies? There's all kindsa jobs out there, all kindsa things for a guy to do around a studio, but ya gotta start somewhere, see? But a guy at least is *in* the business and he can maybe do something, being right there, being on any kinda job, *right there*, ain't that right, kid?"

Willie went rigid, waiting for the big put-on. He struggled to keep his face blank; he didn't want to be caught out. He was too easy. All his life he'd been too easy. He was everyone's fall guy, the perfect sucker for a practical joke. The jerk who'd do anything, just to be liked, and no one liked him anyway. What he couldn't figure was, why the hell would Mr. Joe wanna play him for a sucker?

Joe Rucci knew how to read people. The boy was desperate. He had dangled a dream in the kid's face and he was too terrified to react. By his very stillness, he gave Joe his answer. He leaned back in his chair, locked his heavy hands across his thick stomach, and smiled.

"So how bad ya wanna go out to Hollywood, kid? With a job all set for ya? In a big studio? How bad?"

He wants me to kill somebody. That's it. He wants me to get rid of a body. To drive out to Jersey, to dump some stiff . . .

"What you thinkin', kid?"

Softly, Willie Paycek said, "If you want me to hit somebody, I'll hit somebody."

Joe let his head fall back and he laughed, a loud hoarse sound starting in his chest and roaring out through his mouth.

"Oh, Christ, kid, you the *last* guy I ask." He gasped, coughed. "You a little flyweight. I got guys got hands bigger'n you are. Ah, relax, Willie, relax. Nothin' like that, kid, but I like your style. You really want what you want. That's good. That's good." He leaned forward, his large hairy hands, fingers splayed over the various scraps and slips of paper on his battered desk.

Everything about the moment registered with Willie, was noted as though in a photograph and stored away to be looked at at a later time.

"Kid, you gonna get married."

Joe Rucci watched the girl as his brother's kid, Sonny, led her through the reeking plant. She glanced, without interest, at the slabs of meat hanging from hooks, at the bloody-aproned butchers hacking away, at the mounds of yellowish fat overflowing the large battered garbage pans arranged near the long, slippery cutting blocks.

Nothing. There was nothing there that could possibly attract a man. The thought had flashed through his mind before he saw her—what the hell, a quick one. Now he could only shake his head. That goddamn fuckup of a nephew. Ah, but what the hell. The kid was a man, and a man did what he did and that was that.

"Unca Joey," Sonny said, and jerked his head at the girl, then backed off, closing the door to Joe's cubicle.

"Yeah. C'mon in. Sit down."

The large, shapeless body overflowed the armless chair in front of his desk. Joe sat on the edge of his desk and studied the girl.

A large, pale, placid face—shit, a dumb pig face with small beady eyes, almost gray, a wide mouth smeared with bright pinkish lipstick, two round spots of color from dabbed-on rouge. Polack face, he thought. The girl worked in the five and dime. What the hell, she used all the latest stuff there. The strong, harsh dime-store perfume almost made his eyes water. It had to be really strong stuff, to cut through the stink of the surroundings.

"You Maryanne, right, from Webster Avenue?"

She moved about in the chair and turned her head to the side, looking at him with a smile.

Holy Christ. This big tub thought she was here for business.

Joe walked behind his desk, pulled out his chair, and slammed his fist on the desk. The girl jerked slightly. The smile disappeared.

"They call you Maryanne the Cunt, right? From the time you was in fifth grade, right? You pull down your bloomers for anybody asks you, that right?"

The girl tensed. He could see the small eyes calculating, trying to figure it all out. What he did not yet see was fear. It was time.

Joe walked over to the door, opened it, looked out, then slammed it with a force hard enough to rattle the ashtrays.

He came behind the chair and let his hands rest on her heavy, meaty shoulders. Fat—shit, layers and layers of it; he could hardly feel bone beneath flesh. He squeezed, hard, probing.

"You a hunka cow, that's what you are."

Under the pressure of his hands, finally, she spoke. Her voice was oddly thin for so large a girl. She turned, trying to look into his face.

"So whadda ya want?"

"Ya still sellin' it, cunt?"

The girl shook her head. He looked down on the dirty, thin, permanented, bleached hair. Joe dealt all day in slime and stink; he expected women to be clean and shiny. He removed his hands and wiped them down the sides of his heavy work pants.

"No. Ya made a mistake, Mr. Rucci. I don't do that no more. I got me a good job. At the Woolworth's on Fordham Road."

"Got yourself a boyfriend, have ya?"

The heavy shoulders rose and fell. She gripped her elbows with her heavy hands, hugging herself. She looked up coyly and smiled.

"Sorta."

It was enough. It was all Joe could take. He shook her by the heavy shoulders. Fuck it, for this piece of filth, that stupid kid. He heard her breath come in a gasp, a sob. He twisted her face around, his strong fingers pinching her cheek hard.

"You gonna get married, pig. You gonna get married and you gonna get the fuck outta New York. You gonna go all the way to California. Won't that be nice? Where the movie stars live. That's what's gonna happen to you."

Her first readable reaction was terror, then, as the words sank in, she began to smile. The smile broadened so that all her dirty, broken teeth showed. As the possibilities filled her, she reached up, her hand touching him, not trying to loosen his terrible grasp, just touching him.

"You mean it, Mr. Rucci? You mean it?"

Joe shoved her face away, pulled back from her touch. "Yeah." He studied her, curious at the way she processed the information. Or what she thought was the information. Her large body swelled, she took deep breaths, she leaned forward in her chair, almost fell off. Put her hand over her mouth, smearing the pink lipstick, the sweat now staining her dress, running down the front and sides of her body.

"Who you think you gonna marry?" Joe asked her softly.

"Him. *Dante.* I'll be real good to him. I'm changed because a' him. I never touched no nother man for six months, more, to get ready for him. Oh, Mr. Rucci, could I have the wedding in St. Simon before we go to live in California?"

Joseph Rucci smiled tightly and shook his head. He couldn't even maintain his anger. The girl was so fucking stupid.

"Ya can have the wedding before ya go to California. But not in St. Simon. We got a nice little church down here, all the guys go to mass in the morning, go to confession, a nice Italian priest, he does the whole thing. And then, Hollywood."

"Well . . ." She thought about it. She turned it over in her mind. She caught nothing from him. She picked up only the signals she wanted to catch. Everything was as she wanted it to be. "But can I get married in white, d'ya think? Ya know, every girl, alla her life, she thinks about her wedding day, ya know."

He had had enough. His voice went very low, the tone he used to hold someone's attention. At first she didn't even seem aware that he was talking. She was listening to herself, but she glanced at him, blinked, focused, and listened. As he spoke, Maryanne went even paler. Her damp skin gleamed with grayness. The rouged spots ran down her heavy cheeks. Her tongue licked at the smudged lips. Her eyes blinked frantically.

"Ya gonna marry a nice boy named Willie Paycek, and then ya gonna take a nice bus ride alla way out to California and you two'll get a nice little house out there and Willie will have a good union job and ya'll make a nice life for yourselves. Better than anything ya could ever hope for inna Bronx."

At first she shook her head. Her face tightened. She raised her chin, thought about it, what she had to bargain with. Dante.

"I'm not sure what Dante would say about . . ."

He crossed to her side of the desk so quickly she didn't have time to brace herself. He slammed his fist so hard into her jaw that she fell backwards, hit the floor. He kicked at her viciously, feeling the softness of her body. He leaned down, holding her by the hair, and told her the way it was.

"You gimme any trouble, you *ever* mention Dante's name again in your whole life, first you gonna get both legs busted, in three places, and then your arms, and then a couple other bones, and we gonna let ya lay around long enough to feel it. I got guys know how to break bones, and then they know how to strip off fat. Ya listenin' to me?"

"Yeah. Yeah."

"And then they'll just leave you in some garbage dump onna river and let you die, however long it takes. You gimme just one small reason. You get no second chances."

He stood back and watched her pull herself up, pat down her clothes, move her heavy arms, swipe at her face. She shrugged as though they had just had a slight misunderstanding.

"What the hell," she said in her small voice. "California should be fun, right?"

"You got it, girlie."

CHAPTER SEVEN

After he was mustered out of the Army with the rank of captain, Ben spent a few months taking special legal courses at Columbia. He had been approached by representatives of a Jewish relief organization and asked to participate in the prosecution of Nazi war criminals to be held at Nuremberg.

To his family and friends, Ben seemed a ghost of the hearty young man who had gone off to war. He had no time for anyone or anything but his studies and his preparations. He could not speak to anyone— certainly not to his family—about what he had seen and learned from the camps.

He spent a lot of time at meetings with people who were connected with Zionist organizations, people preparing for the creation of the state of Israel. He also spent a great deal of time in the privacy of the public library, writing down long drafts of information he had gathered as an interrogator. He passed this information on to undercover agents who wanted to keep track of those Nazis who had been allowed, by his own government, to escape with their deeds unpunished. He knew which of them had been relocated in various countries, which had actually been sent to the United States and were involved in scientific projects on behalf of the American government. He made use of the massive catalog of information he had prepared and brought home with him. Through his endeavors, some of these criminals would be found, if not now, at some later time; and they would be dealt with, if not officially, then unofficially.

It was with a sense of relief, of getting back to unfinished business, that Ben left the United States as a special employee of the government.

The Bronx had felt unreal to him, untouched as it was by the devastation of the war. There were small gold stars on flags in apartment windows; some of the neighborhood boys wouldn't be coming home. Others had returned with injuries that would either heal and allow them to get on with their lives, or remain and send their lives in new directions.

At home, in the Bronx, the war had been a private sorrow for those who lost a son, an inconvenience for those who had to adapt to rationing and blackouts. It had been a time when a great many unemployed people were put to work, at high salaries and long hours. Now, a whole generation of working-class young men were looking forward to a future unimaginable to their parents. There were low-cost mortgages available, amazing new suburban developments being planned. Sons were talking about moving away, having their own houses—being owners, not renters. People who had never even thought about college, some who hadn't even finished high school, were going back to school on the GI Bill. The government was taking good care of its veterans, and there was a feeling of relief, joy, and growth all around. But Ben Herskel felt like a stranger in the midst of all this activity, all this exuberance. His days at the camps had become the most important part of his life, and he could not explain to well-meaning friends his decision to accept employment back in Germany. It was inexplicable to anyone who hadn't been there.

Only Charley O'Brien, of all his friends, understood. He had witnessed. He had tried, along with Ben, to do *something*, however small, their own private attempt at justice.

Charley was coming to his own decisions; he would deal with what he had seen and learned in his own way. That was Charley's business. Dante was all set up in law school. He had been a hero, decorated and promoted and discharged with great honor and a great future. Dante was the smartest of them all, the most ambitious. He would go far. Even Megan had benefitted from the war. It would have been nearly impossible for her to get into medical school if all the ambitious bright young men had been home. Not that she didn't qualify; she certainly did. But it would have been different if there hadn't been a war.

And Eugene had been untouched by any of it. He had been at the Vatican the whole time, right in the midst of the Fascists, without having any real dealings or contacts with them. He wondered if Gene knew the role the Vatican had played in helping to transfer the war criminals to safety, to places where they would not only be unanswerable for their crimes, but would be guaranteed lives of safety and security and prosperity. He knew Gene could have had nothing to do with any of this, but he was a part of the church that had engineered and put into effect this ignominious "rescue."

It was a terrible, strange, almost irrational thing, but arriving back in Germany, Ben felt he had come home to do what he had been destined to do.

Ben Herskel served as an interpreter-interrogator for scores of witnesses who prepared to testify against the defendants at Nuremburg. He spent hour after hour comforting and coaxing, trying not to show any feeling beyond benign compassion. It was his job to help the international staff prepare the various cases against the defendants. He himself had seen the end product of the horror—the corpses and near dead at the extermination camps, and daily he himself had to speak with the survivors. It was more difficult than anything he had ever done.

He took their statements—accounts of the most extraordinary cruelties, perpetrated not on millions of anonymous people but on individuals— mothers and fathers, sons and daughters. When the survivors spoke of the roundups, they meant of themselves, their families, their neighbors. When they told of the transports, it was they who had been inside the cattle cars, had seen the weak and the old and the young die and lie untouched until the final destination. When they spoke of "the selection," they spoke graphically of families torn apart, of infants tossed, literally, to death in front of mothers, of husbands helplessly watching wives shoved to the death line while they, stronger, still of some value, were put into work lines. Ben Herskel knew that each was a human being with a past that reached back long before the Holocaust. Each had had a life before the Final Solution.

Yet the empty people he spoke with hour after hour, day after day, were themselves frightening in their very lack of emotion. Their voices were flat, their faces dull, their stories always the same. The Army psychologists counseled the interrogators, the translators, the international social and medical workers, to help them cope with the effects of this massive inquest. Still, some of the staff members eventually could not take any more. Hating their own weakness, their unfulfilled fury at the perpetrators, they found themselves unable to carry out the job they were assigned.

Ben Herskel hardened himself to the recitation of facts, which every day seemed more like a fiction concocted by sick minds. He stored emotion away for future use. He didn't need counseling. He asked the necessary questions, noted the necessary facts. He worked with organizations that tried to locate family members, that found few parents, few aunts, uncles, neighbors—who more often brought together the children who had been spared, the brothers and sisters. The meager joy was mingled with profound sadness.

At night, Ben wrote down the stories for his own diary. These had to be recorded beyond the courtroom, beyond the newspaper reports that listed only numbers—in much the same way the Germans had accounted for the concentration camp population. These lives were more than numbers; they had to be shown to be more than numbers. Ben took down the individual stories as told to him, and though the circumstances were numbing in repetition, it was his responsibility to present the survivors and to remember the dead as whole human beings.

When the complicated arrangements were finally completed and the trials began, Ben often visited the court. As he stared at the men in the dock, what he found difficult to accept was that these middle-aged men—with their prison-grayed faces, their stomach ailments, their coughs, their complaints about the light shining always in their cells, their requests for a different kind of soap or shaving cream—had been the same men who had planned and put into action the most savage crimes in history. They *looked* like schoolteachers, sales clerks, accountants, bakers, bus drivers. They looked just like everyone else, now, in their baggy clothing, as they sat, earphones on their heads, some nodding off, bored, impatient, some sitting erect, anger and indignation frozen on their faces. There were those who damned their judges and their victims. There were those who looked imploringly about the courtroom. *I am but a man; I had to do what I was told. I had no idea. I never really knew. I only followed orders.*

Ben had wanted the monsters to look like monsters, but they looked like men. After the trials, he felt no inclination to stay around for the executions. What difference did a certain number of hangings make? What did they change? Whom did they bring back? What lessons did they teach?

He couldn't face going home. There was no way Ben felt he could pick up his former life. He was aching and empty, he had unfinished business. When he was approached by an official of the American Jewish Relief Organization, working with survivors, he accepted employment without even asking about salary or working conditions.

His wasn't a job; it was a life. The refugee camps were overwhelmed with arrivals from Poland, where new, unpublicized pogroms had taken place against Jews liberated from the death camps. Except to provide food, clothing, and some sort of medical care, there was little the well-meaning organizations could offer the survivors. There was so much *need*: people died from disease and from the long years of maltreatment. And from despair.

Ben helped those with families in the United States. They could emigrate outside of any quota system. In some cases he even helped them to invent families, providing documents and forged papers. Not many asked to be returned to their original homelands. In their former ghettos or in their cosmopolitan cities, their friends and neighbors had either participated actively or watched complacently as they had been rounded up and deported. Their homes and businesses had been taken over; they were not wanted and their return would mean death.

Ben could not help noticing a young woman who seemed connected with no particular agency but was everywhere at once. Her name was Eva Fine, and she was exceptional.

For too many years, at the camps, during the trials and now, dealing with survivors, Ben had seen nothing but emaciated, death-faced women, lost and directionless, their youth and health stolen from them. Most of the organization women were older, stone-faced and stoic, trying to deal with the horror they encountered.

At twenty-three, Eva Fine was just a few years younger than he. She was tall and long-legged, with a look of glowing health. Her brown hair was thick and shot through with sun-bleached streaks. Her complexion was clear of makeup, shining with natural color. Her eyes were light brown and thick-lashed, and they looked directly at you when she spoke.

"Do you have the list of names I asked you for yesterday?" she asked Ben. It was almost a demand: Don't keep me waiting. She had requested the names of fifty of the strongest men between the ages of eighteen and thirty, who had no place in the world waiting for them. There were hundreds of thousands of such people, but she had been specific in her request. They must all be located within camps not more than five miles from headquarters. They must all be made available for her and her people to speak with as soon as possible.

She was evasive about what organization she represented and who "her people" were.

"Where do you intend to take these men?" he asked.

She seemed evasive, distrustful. "We are working on placement for them."

There was something disturbingly familiar about her demand for the best, the healthiest, the strongest. The word *selection* came to his mind and, in his exhaustion, to his mouth.

"Yes, I have a list. Of those *selected* who meet your qualifications."

Eva was quick; she caught the meaning and her face hardened. "*How dare you?* How dare you use that tone, that implication, with me!"

"Well, you have been very specific in your requirements. Exactly who are you, what is your organization? Where are you taking these people, and for what purpose?"

Without blinking, Eva Fine swung and smacked him across the face with the back of her hand. The attack was so unexpected, the blow so hard, that Ben was knocked to the ground. As he scrambled to his feet, she stood poised, ready.

He shook his head, held his hand up. "Whoa, slow down, lady. I think we better talk." And then, because she didn't change her stance, quickly, skillfully, Ben spun her around and held her against his body. Instead of stiffening, resisting, she went limp and he realized she was a trained fighter. He released her, pushing her away. "Okay, I give up. This is stupid, isn't it? I think we're on the same side. Look, I apologize, what I said was stupid. My choice of words—"

"Was *offensive*."

"Yes. Offensive. We are all very sensitive to certain words and implications. How about we talk, you and I? I can't just give you this list of people without having some idea where they are going."

"Do you really care?"

It was Ben's turn to get angry. He was being asked to identify himself, to justify his presence in this place of horror. Softly he said, "No. I don't care at all. I'm doing this for the hell of it. I'll probably write a book and make a million dollars and that's why I'm here. Okay? All right?"

Eva shook her head then held out her hand. "Now *I'm* sorry. And I apologize. We are, I think, both under terrific strain. Do you have a cigarette?"

They sat and smoked and studied each other. She liked the look of this large, healthy, handsome, redheaded American.

"I will assume you are here for very good reasons, so I will trust you. Some instinct tells me this will be safe. Yes?"

"Yes."

She was a third generation *sabra*, born and raised in Palestine on a kibbutz. She had enlisted in the Hagganah when she was seventeen, and had risen to the rank of captain. "Yes, the organization is illegal. Everything about Jews is illegal, according to the British mandate." She stubbed out her cigarette against a tree trunk. "But that will end. We will have our independence. We will have a Jewish state—Israel."

"Do you believe that will really happen?"

Her voice hardened. "Do you think it won't?"

"I don't know. I've never thought too much about Zionism."

"*Zionism?* You can call it that if you want. We are talking about the ultimate survival of our people. Who the hell wants us? Not your country. Not any European countries. We *must* have our own country. The United Nations is debating, debating. Do you know why? They are giving the Arab nations the time to organize a war to exterminate us as soon as Israel is declared. That will take care of the 'Jewish problem' once and for all. But it is not going to happen that way."

"Is that why you want the strong, healthy young men?"

She reached out, took his newly lighted cigarette, and sucked on it for a moment. "We have an underground system. We have way stations. We have friends, you'd be surprised. There are trucks and buses, but then they must travel on foot for many miles, to Yugoslavia, where boats will take them on the rest of the journey."

"To Palestine?"

"To Palestine, which will be Israel."

"But the British . . ."

"They intervene. They will use their mandate to the bitter end. They send those of us they capture to their concentration camps in Cyprus. A well-kept secret. But some get through—the toughest, the best. They are taken into the depths of our land. And they will be ready when the mandate ends. When Israel is declared an independent state. That will happen soon—within a year, it is predicted."

"And you are a kibbutznik? A farmer?"

"And a soldier. I am a captain and I lead my troops."

"Do you actually fight?"

"You mean, does a *woman* actually fight? My God, look around you. Who are half the victims, if not women and girls? In Palestine, we are *all* soldiers. We all do what we have to do. And you, Benjamin Herskel? What are you prepared to do? Are you going to return to the United States and become a doctor or a lawyer, or what? Will all of this just be a memory, war stories for you to tell the UJA—will you be a fund raiser for your people? You are, after all, an American, yes?"

Ben drew in a deep breath. He felt his spine stiffen and his heart pound. *"I am a Jew."*

"Yes? And what does that mean? Tell me."

"You know what it means. Look around you. You know what it means."

"Do you want to join up? With us? With Israel? Do you want to turn away from your home and make your home with us? This is a terrible commitment that we need. Is this what you want?"

Without a moment's hesitation, Ben answered, "Yes."

It was the direction he had sought since the first day he had seen the camps. He reached for Eva, and she responded immediately. Without another word between them, they lay down carefully, fumbled with clothing, and had a long, slow, surprisingly familiar and gratifying sexual encounter. Neither of them seemed surprised. It was something that was meant to be.

Eva caressed his damp face, kissed him gently. "Will you be ready to leave with this new group? In two days?"

"Yes."

A month later, on his second surreptitious landing on the beach at Caesarea, the British were waiting. Of the two hundred illegals aboard the small French ship, one hundred were captured and sent to Cyprus, seventy-five escaped into the night with their rescuers, and twenty-four were killed.

Ben Herskel was wounded, and subsequently lost his right leg below the knee.

But he survived to marry Eva Fine and to play an active role in the leadership of his adopted country, whose sovereignty was proclaimed by the UN one year after Ben's arrival.

CHAPTER EIGHT

Before he was mustered out at the end of 1945, Charley O'Brien had begun studying the precepts of Judaism. The Jewish chaplain, a twenty-five-year-old Reformed rabbi from San Francisco, told Charley to be very careful.

"It's your immediate reaction to what you've seen here, Charley. In one way, it's healthy, but in another it's a hysterical response. Go home, talk to your priest, talk to your mother. Talk to your brother. You have a lifelong religion already. Maybe what you really need is to fall back on your Catholicism in a different setting. This place"—he shrugged, opened his hands helplessly—"this place is hell. None of us can think straight here. Just don't rush into something that will be a lifelong decision."

Charley nodded and thanked the chaplain. He attended mass a few times, tried to talk to the Catholic chaplain, who advised him to go on an intensive religious retreat when he returned home. He also warned him about making a terrible mistake under the pressure of emotion.

Ben Herskel had changed his own life without the slightest hesitation, by staying in the Army to be promoted to major, eventually becoming

an interpreter during the Nuremburg trails. But even he cautioned
Charley to go slowly, to wait until he got home, away from this
place.

"Jesus," Charley said, "you Jews are a crazy bunch. If you said you
wanted to become a Catholic, you'd be baptized on the spot, given a
string of rosary beads, and pointed to the nearest church."

"One of the differences between us, kid. For someone to *opt* to be a
Jew—well, the first thing you think, 'This guy's crazy.'"

"But I *am* a Jew. From my mother's womb. Ben, I'm dead serious
about this. I feel a sense of obligation . . ."

"To do what? Replenish the world? Make up for the horrors?
Charley, do what you feel you must do, but do it for the right reasons,
okay?"

"You and I have *always* done what we felt we must, for the right
reasons, haven't we, kid?"

Ben sighed and smiled sadly. "We've done what we had to do,
Charley. Okay, that's all I'll say about it. I trust you to do what you feel
you gotta do. You take care, kid. Every now and then, say a prayer for
me. In whichever place you happen to be."

If Charley O'Brien thought his mother would be happy, or
touched, or gratified by his decision, he was badly mistaken. When he
left the Army and returned home, their confrontation was intense.

"It makes no sense, Charley. I've never practiced my religion, not
since the day I met your father. It was never important to me."

"It is important to me. And I need to know, Mom—why was this
kept a secret from all of us?"

His mother regarded him as a stranger. He had been a somewhat heavy boy, chunky, good-hearted, loving, with a quick smile,
a hug, a kiss. He had been the child who brought home the stray dogs,
the injured birds, who had fought off kids teasing cats or bullying
smaller children. He had been her last born, with brothers and sisters
already grown and out of the house. He was the only one close to
Eugene.

"Your father and I felt it was better for you not to know. You were
all baptized and raised to be good Catholics. It's what you are—all of
you. It was what I agreed to when your dad and I married."

"But we have another whole side to our family, Mom. I had

grandparents and uncles and aunts and cousins I never knew about. You said you were an orphan, without anyone."

"I *was* without anyone." His mother's face tightened. It was the angry, tense look he had seen when the nuns used to come to try to persuade her. "You want to know about my family, the Greifingers? All right. My father declared me dead when I married your father. I don't just mean 'we won't talk about her, we'll all forget about her.' I mean I was *mourned*; I had died and they grieved for me. They sat *shiva* for me. I wasn't the wayward daughter, I was the *dead* daughter. My father killed me. And my mother and sisters and brothers went along with it. Is that the family you want to know, Charley? What can any of them give you? You are the son of their dead sister. You and your brothers and sisters are impossibilities. You haven't the slightest idea . . ."

"I think I have a right to find out for myself. I think we had a right to know about our background."

His mother's voice was hard. "It wasn't *your* background. It was mine. It was none of your business, Charley! What good would any of this have done you?"

"But you still cared, Mom, didn't you? Ben told me about the Friday-night candles and—"

"Ben should have kept his mouth shut." As she hugged herself in pain, Charley noticed for the first time how old she had grown. The laugh lines around her eyes seemed as deep and painful as old cuts. The skin had crinkled on her cheeks; she had gotten thin through the war years, with three sons in the service and one in Rome, waiting for a terrible telegram. She had knitted hundreds of mittens and socks, scores of khaki and navy sweaters. She had sent as many food packages as the ration stamps allowed; cheated a little with black-market sugar for cookies for sons and for grandchildren come for a visit. She had comforted her daughter and daughters-in-law; she had waited and prayed and suffered.

She had resisted her priest son's attempts to convert her. Convert her *from* what, *to* what? And now, this steadiest of her kids, her solid, predictable, simple, and pleasant Charley, was crossing into areas of danger. Whatever his terrible knowledge was, what he had seen and smelled and heard and learned, she wanted him just to get on with his life, without making waves, without damaging anything she and his father had spent a lifetime building.

She closed her eyes tight and bit down hard at the inevitable question: Which of the kids knew the truth?

"I never discussed it with anyone. Except Eugene."

"When did you tell Gene?"

"When he asked me. After he became a priest, he asked why I never discussed religion, never participated in things at the church. He came right out and asked me, Charley. And I told him."

"And the others? You've never told any of them?"

"There was never a reason to, I guess. Through the years, they more or less knew, but it was never a matter for discussion."

"My God, Mom, you sound like it was a terrible secret, like you were guilty of something awful, as though . . .''

The tears spilled from his mother's eyes, which had become a washed-out gray, growing paler through the years. "Charley, it was all a long time ago. It was between your father and me. Why can't you just leave it alone?"

What other secrets were there? Was this the big-deal mystery that had hung over their childhood? Once he had overheard two of his older brothers discussing their mother's background. They made up wild stories: her father was a big-time gangster and she had run away from home with him; or her mother was an heiress forced to abandon her on the steps of an orphanage.

There had always been a pall over his family. Charley remembered sudden silences when the relatives all got together at holiday time— when someone, an aunt or an uncle or a cousin, told a joke, did a Yiddish accent, made fun of the Jews. Or when they talked about Father Coughlin's latest broadcast. On Good Friday, when the nuns told them in explicit detail about the Jews' role in the Crucifixion, his mother sat silent, her face unreadable, as they rushed home from grade school to relate what they had learned.

Once she had asked, "How does Sister Veronica know so much? Was she there?"

And Gene had never told him. It must have been one of the goals of Gene's life, to convert his Jewish mother.

"Mom, please. I don't want to upset you. I just wanted you to know I've started studying the Jewish religion and . . . I want to look up your—our—family. This is *my* life, Mother. You've had yours, now I'm gonna have mine."

His mother reached out, touched his cheek, felt the blond stubble. "You need a shave, Charley."

He caught his mother's hand, turned it over, and kissed the palm. "It's gonna be okay. I promise you."

His mother nodded and tried to smile.

"Hey, Ma, I bet I know what Gene said when you told him."
Charley raised his head. His eyes glazed over and his voice became
musical—a good imitation of his brother. He said, 'Why, Mother, our
Lord and Savior's mother was a Jew, too!'"

Finally his mother laughed. She slapped his face lightly, then hugged
him. "That is *exactly* what he said!"

CHAPTER NINE

Eugene had always been terrified by his own physical beauty. As a child he had heard himself described as an angel, silvery, golden, radiant, special, chosen. He tried to avoid seeing himself. When he brushed his pale, soft hair, he watched only the mirrored reflection of the hairbrush. Occasionally he looked into his own eyes, their pupils the color of ice water circled by a thin line of black, and he felt himself become mesmerized. He lost time; he lost himself for seconds, minutes, maybe longer, and as he grew older he accepted that this brief loss of himself happened from time to time. There was no one he could explain it to. He couldn't find the words to describe not only what happened, but his desperate guilt about it.

When he was a child, he had had several grand-mal seizures, but they had ceased by the time he reached his seventh birthday. The doctors said his prognosis was excellent. He had outgrown this form of epilepsy.

Through his early years, between the major seizures, there were a series of petit-mal episodes: the seconds-long removal of himself from reality, the wide-eyed motionless staring during which Eugene was no longer present in his immediate surroundings, but could not afterwards say where he had been.

In a less gifted child, such lapses would have been proof to the teaching sisters of wicked, deliberate inattention, and the child would have been shamed and castigated. But allowances were always made for Eugene; he was different. He was blessed.

He once spoke of it to his mother. Quietly, she reassured him. "It will pass. It's nothing dangerous. It's your brain's way of resting for a moment. You will outgrow it."

She said it with authority. She was, after all, a nurse.

His mother seemed relieved when he went to the seminary, but they never really discussed the decision. Whatever feelings she had about her son becoming a Jesuit priest, she kept to herself. To Eugene, his mother was a mystery. At home for a brief respite toward the end of his initial training, he asked his mother if, when he was ordained, she would allow him to baptize her and give her her first communion. She reacted oddly, her face hard, her voice strong.

"That will *never* happen, Eugene. Don't ever speak about that again. *Not ever.*"

She regarded him with the glare of a stranger, and at the same time with the deep intensity of one who held dark secrets about him. There were times when he wondered, as his mother looked deep into his eyes, who it was, besides him, that she was seeing, and why nothing of this could ever be spoken between the two of them.

After the seminary, Gene was selected to study at the North American College in Rome. For three years he studied with bright young men from seventeen states and the provinces of Canada. He learned not only fluent Italian, but Spanish and German. He learned enough accounting to qualify as a CPA, enough Church history to teach at the high school level or beyond, enough chemistry and mathematics to gain entry into medical school. A near-perfect student, upon graduation he expected to be sent, along with ninety-nine percent of the other students, back to the United States.

Instead, he was assigned to work in the General Administration Office at the Vatican. It was where all the business of the Church was centered: the running and coordination of expenses of those who labored within the one hundred acres of Vatican City. There were payrolls to prepare and supervise for the private police force and fire department; for carpenters and maintenance men; for the corps of Vatican lawyers, art appraisers, and specialists of all kinds. The Vatican ran its own pharmacy, post office, printing office; it supplied its own bricklayers and laborers, its own corps of workers to keep all the buildings and apartments and churches clean and shining and ready to receive visitors from all over the world. The most evident employees were the gorgeous Swiss Guards; unseen were the vast kitchens filled with chefs and workers, the garages filled with chauffeurs and mechanics, even priests on special assignment to the corps of international visitors, priests who spoke languages ranging from the common European ones to exotic African or Far Eastern tongues. The Vatican, aside from being the center of the Church International, was a nation unto itself, and had to be run as a business entity by the army of employees—all in the service, in their own assigned ways, of the greater glory of God.

Eugene's job, for the first year of his assignment to the General Administrative Office, was to oversee the budgets of the cardinals' staffs. How much was being spent on general household expenses: food, linens, cleaning bills, clothing, health care, entertainment. He had to keep account of gifts given by a small army of wealthy Italian noblemen, American Catholic business tycoons, potentates from small, wealthy nations with agendas of their own.

In his free time, Gene wandered the halls of the Vatican, studying the priceless paintings, the ornate treasure of furnishings. He attended private audiences with the Pope, gatherings of up to four hundred people admitted by special invitation. To be in the mere presence, to cherish for a lifetime the immediacy of the Pontiff, a small, hollow-cheeked man with deep black rings under his eyes, but splendid in his ceremonial garb—that was a privilege arranged for the wealthy and the powerful by a long series of favors for favors.

Sometimes the private audiences were smaller, for the maimed and the crippled, the faithful on the trail of miraculous cures, experiencing the one truly miraculous moment of a tormented life, an audience with Pope Pius XII.

Gene explored Rome, curious, disturbed, interested in the changing, dynamic political situation. The Fascists maintained law and order; the streets were clean, the country seemed to be running on new, successful schedules. The Duce didn't appear to his people as a comic figure; his posturing and posing made them hopeful and happy. There were parades, and workers were cheered. The government policy of encouraging the people to be fruitful and multiply was in line with Church doctrine. And the Church had made its peace, its deals, with the Fascists. It was not for Gene to question. This was Italy; he was an American.

Father Eugene O'Brien was considered a good worker—industrious, quick, careful, respectful, with something of a flair as a guide. He grew more and more knowledgeable about the Vatican, both its internal workings and its external trappings. He was asked to escort visiting groups of Americans or Britons, giving them a bright, informative lecture, pointing out the Sistine Chapel, head craning, marveling not just at the spectacle of creation, but at the stamina and moral strength of the men who did the painting.

He told them about the period in which the work was done, the number of workers, the hours involved, even the kind of paint that was used. He spoke not just with authority, but with a sense of delight and wonder. He was dazzled by the accomplishment, and so he dazzled his listeners.

Among the group one day was a middle-aged woman, an American widow more accustomed to private escorts than public tours. Special dinners and meetings were usually arranged for her, as they had been when her millionaire foodcanning husband from the Midwest was alive. Now, on her tenth or eleventh trip to the Vatican, having some time to spare before her luncheon appointment, she had wandered into this group and was taken by the beautiful young priest who spoke with such enthusiasm for his subject.

Mrs. Lyman Kelleher was, in keeping with her husband's established custom, a very generous donor to the Church's many causes. She had a large, affluent group of friends in Rome, who visited her in her villa some fifteen miles to the south, when she summered in Italy. She had friends among the nobility of Europe—former Russian nobility, princes without thrones, Italian aristocrats patiently waiting out the Fascist nonsense, but contributing, as a matter of convenience, to the government when asked.

Occasionally, she befriended a particular young priest. God knew, they needed so much, had so little of material value. God knew, they needed some time away from the tedium of their constricted lives at the Vatican. Especially someone like this young Irish-American priest, who she learned labored as a clerk in the General Administration Office, tucked away in some obscure basement. She also learned that he conducted many of the tours on his own free time, which showed a generous and giving nature. Surely he should be rewarded by some bit of luxury.

At the first dinner to which Eugene was invited, he was seated between a Russian countess who spoke German, and an Italian automobile heiress who wanted to practice her English.

Mrs. Kelleher watched carefully, discreetly, to see how her new find conducted himself. He turned politely, first to one side, then the other, speaking and listening to the German; then, speaking English, but breaking into Italian—"I need to practice my Italian far more than you need to practice your English, Signora."

The heiress smilingly protested, "But no, Father O'Brien, your Italian is wonderful. So very 'Rome'—so sophisticated."

Eugene became a favorite of a very wealthy, influential set, and his role at the Vatican was changed. He was assigned to Cardinal Rappolini, who had never had an American on his staff. But this American was different from the general run. He was brilliant with languages, amazing in his knowledge of the history and topography of the Vatican, quick-minded, articulate, and charming. Not to mention his almost angelic, physical presence.

Eugene was also loyal and tended to withdraw from the vicious infighting among the Vatican staff. Above all, he seemed to understand how things worked, the subleties needed to handle touchy situations. Loyalty came naturally to him. He was soon known as "Rappolini's man" and Eugene's growing contacts among the wealthy, titled, and important laity became more and more evident.

When Cardinal Rappolini confided to Gene his humiliation at not having his own personal automobile—at having to sign a request sheet, and accept whatever was supplied for him—Gene told Mrs. Kelleher, who replied, "A Cardinal like His Eminence Rappolini, not having his own automobile! Well, we can remedy that."

A week later, a Cadillac limousine was presented to the cardinal by a grateful Mrs. Kelleher, who cherished every opportunity to serve a prince of the Church.

Some of the young American seminarians began to turn to Eugene. They were not being given any of the better assignments; too many were being sent back to dead-end parishes in parts of the country without large Catholic populations. They had been prepared for advancement, but denied opportunities.

Gene put in a word here and there, among the elite who had befriended him, who felt honored to have the elegant Father Eugene at their table, at their side, at their villas. Other young priests, carefully selected, found themselves with mentors. Other cardinals found themselves with young American assistants.

Of course, not everyone was happy with Father O'Brien. Not that they could point to any particular arrogance or pomposity. But he did wield power to a degree unusual both for an American and for one so young of any nationality.

But Gene brought in more money in a mouth than many of his colleagues did in a year. Not just from the generous Americans, but from some of the others—among them a famous French auto racer who donated a generous share of his international winnings to the childrens' world hunger fund. Donations were made, in the name of dead ancestors, to favorite Church charities. Gene O'Brien was a money maker. And yet he kept nothing for himself. Any gifts given him, he turned back or converted into cash for donation to the Society for the Propagation of the Faith. The only gifts he kept—had to keep—were the beautiful, hand-tailored black suits Mrs. Kelleher insisted on giving him. If he was to sit at her table she said, he had to look as well tailored as the other guests; she was entitled to see him well turned out.

Eugene was shameless about collecting money. It pleased the giver to please him as much as it pleased the Church to receive. But to his confessor, Father Adams—an elderly Bostonian available to the Americans who preferred a countryman as their confessor—he brought a surprising set of troubles.

"This is not how I envisioned serving, Father," he said. "It's not what I studied for—to be a social butterfly."

"But you are serving as the Church wants you to serve, Eugene. You are doing what is asked and required of you."

It was difficult for Gene to get to the heart of what was bothering him. It had all come too easily; it seemed as though he had, step by step, in a calculated fashion, moved into the position in which he found himself.

"And why does that bother you, that you were prepared?"

"It seems somehow . . . arrogant."

"To be prepared to serve God's Church in any manner is not arrogant, Gene. It is expedient."

"But I don't think expediency is the same as true service. And, Father, the way things are in the world today, the war in Europe, with my own country getting closer to war, things are changing. I should be doing other things with my vocation."

Things were changing. The Vatican's wealthy friends could not travel to Europe anymore. The Europeans themselves were, by large, locked out. Italy was mobilized, at war. The Vatican was declared neutral territory through various agreements and accommodations with the government of Mussolini.

In December of 1941, when Eugene was twenty-three years old, the United States entered the war. He appealed to Cardinal Rappolini to send him home; he wanted to join his country's armed forces as a chaplain.

Rappolini replied, "It has been decided, Eugene. You will continue to serve at the Vatican. There are plenty of priests in your country to serve in the armed forces. This is where your Church needs you."

He kept up a sporadic correspondence with his family. For the first time in years, he felt homesick, and uninterested in the detailed administrative work to which the cardinal assigned him.

When the war ended, Cardinal Rappolini, eighty-six years old and out of favor, died. His staff was dispersed throughout the Vatican and the world.

Eugene O'Brien was sent home for a month's visit with his family and countrymen before taking on his new assignment as a pastor to a leper colony on an island off the eastern coast of Africa.

All his old friends and relatives were veterans now. They spoke of places around the world and unimaginable events that were no part of his life. They had been airmen and marines and sailors and pilots. He felt isolated and confused. Glancing through the *Daily News,* the *Mirror,* the *Journal-American*—all filled with stories about returning GIs he could not relate to—he felt like a foreigner in his own country.

For the first time he doubted his vocation. And he was out of uniform much as were the young returning servicemen. But he didn't have a small, gold-colored "ruptured duck" to wear on his lapel to show what he had been doing during the war.

He heard his mother in the kitchen, returning from shopping.

"Can I help you, Mom?"

At first she shook her head. She was quick and efficient and had her own way of doing things, but then she glanced at him and nodded and he handed her canned goods that she placed precisely in her well-regulated larder.

"Are you hungry, Gene? You look so thin. Shall I make you some lunch? A boiled-ham sandwich. It's so funny, shopping without ration stamps."

"Just coffee will be fine, Mom. I'm not hungry."

She stopped putting things away, turned and studied her son. He looked so much older. There was a weariness in him, an uncertainty she had never seen. He had always seemed so *directed*. Now, wearing an open-necked collar under a bright red sweater, as he had when he was a young boy, he seemed ill at ease.

"Gene, where is this place they are sending you? This island? Have you had shots?"

He told her he had been assigned to a leper colony. Not to worry, he would get all the necessary shots. He had been doing some reading about the disease; yes, it was terrible, without a cure. His job would be to offer spiritual comfort to the dying.

"And how do you feel about that, Gene? It's such a change from your years at the Vatican."

He shrugged. He didn't know how he felt.

"You know, Gene, maybe you should spend some time in your own country. Your uncle Frank has some influence; he could—"

"No. It wouldn't make any difference. I mean . . . I'm just a bit disoriented, I think."

"Maybe you need to be home." She watched him closely, saw him draw back from her touch, self-contained, even in his uncertainty.

"My home is wherever the Church sends me. I'm a priest, and that's the way it is. You know, I think I am hungry, Mom. I'll take you up on that offer of a ham sandwich."

He gave her that much; aware of her stricken look when he backed away from her, knowing she wanted to do things for him, to help him somehow, he allowed her to give him food. It always made a mother feel good to feed her child.

A few days later, it seemed crazy, but here he was, talking with his kid cousin. Little Megan, interning at Bellevue, preparing to become a shrink, of all things. This little tomboy girl, all grown up, but still a kid in her gestures, shrugs, and grins.

She sat with him in her family living room, describing her training, her patients—without revealing anything confidential.

"We have our code, too, Gene, like priests. Only we don't hear confessions to offer absolution. We try to offer explanations and understanding, to get the patient to understand himself."

"Is that enough? Understanding?"

"Hey, it isn't easy. It's hard to dig into your deepest emotions. My job is to lead the way, be a guide, help people to see what's *really* bothering them, and why, and what to do about it."

For her part, Megan studied her cousin. God, beautiful Eugene, with his pale hair and fine features. So tall and lean and graceful. And so troubled.

"So, cousin, what's going on? What's bothering you?"

"Me? Hey, nothing. I just wanted to visit with you. To find out what's going on with *you*. Not to talk about *me*."

"I'm fine. I'm doing exactly what I want to do with my life. Not many people can say that. All these guys coming home, they've got lots of problems, lots of pressures. I'm doing some work at the Veterans Administration Hospital, counseling husbands and wives. It's a whole new world for me."

She shifted in her chair, leaned her chin on her hand, and studied him. "You having unreal expectations, Gene? You having doubts? It wouldn't be unheard of, you know."

He didn't protest immediately. He seemed to be thinking, to be making a decision. Finally he said, "Not really. It's just that it was such an adjustment at first. Those years in Rome. And then I'd gotten used to a certain . . . lifestyle. Settled in, I guess."

"Hey, I heard you had it pretty good. 'Luxe all the way." When he looked surprised, she shrugged and grinned. "Hey, you know. Tabs are kept. Frankie Magee has his sources. He knows."

She got serious, went right to what she saw as his problem. "And now, wow, what a change. Sending you to a medical mission in the middle of God knows where. A leper colony, for God's sake. That's got to be scary." She hesitated. "You up to it, or what?"

"It's what I've been assigned to do. I'm just not sure what I'm going to bring to the people there. I've been . . . spoiled. Protected. I've been living a very privileged life, by any standards. All the fellas, the guys I grew up with, they've gone to war, they've had experiences I can't even imagine, while I—"

"You've done what the Church told you to do. You did your job, right? Like all the others. They had no more say in where they ended up than you did. Gene, is it your calling? Are you having doubts? Maybe you should take some time, a leave, try to get your bearings."

Little tag-along Megan, sitting on the couch, leaning forward, watching him so earnestly, her eyebrows drawn into a frown, looking directly into his eyes. Concerned. Trying to be helpful. Caring.

"Hey, I'm your cousin, not your patient, right?"

"Right. But you can talk to me as a cousin, as a friend. Talking helps. Hell, I do it all the time. Helps me when I get screwed up."

"I have some . . . stresses. Some things to resolve. I will go on a retreat before my assignment. I've arranged it already. I guess it's a matter of getting my priorities in order. I think, in all these years, I haven't yet even *begun* to serve my priesthood. Now I've been assigned to get right down to the very basics of my religious calling. Yes, I find it . . . intimidating. Threatening. I don't know if, after all, I will be equal to it. It is . . . scary."

Megan leaned back, stretched her arms over her head, then relaxed. "I think, Gene, you will be equal to any job you decide to do. You always have been, you always will be. I think . . . whoa, let me skip the shrink talk. As your cousin—I hope as your friend—I think you'll be absolutely equal, and more, to the job. Whatever it turns out to be. It's up to you to decide for yourself."

When they stood up, he leaned down and kissed her on the forehead.

"Little Megan. God, a doctor. I think you're going to be absolutely terrific, kid."

Megan hugged him, then pulled back. "I think you will be, too, Gene." And then, softly, gently, she added, "*Be happy, Gene.* You're entitled. Just try to be happy, okay?"

What had been intended as a banishment, a time for contemplation of the uses and abuses of power, turned out to be the most valuable time in Eugene O'Brien's life as a priest.

The heat and humidity bothered him, and he began to discard his spotless, pressed and starched clerical garb, even though the services of the youngest nursing nun had been offered to keep his clothing immaculate. He wore the lightweight khaki slacks and shirts favored by the colony's doctor, an elderly, bearded Frenchman with rough manners who rarely spoke to anyone about anything.

The colony was run by a nursing order of French nuns who ranged in age from their early twenties to their late sixties. They were, without exception, cheerful women who went about the most repulsive of physical chores without a flicker of emotion. He noticed that they touched and stroked and bathed and groomed their patients almost as though they were young girls playing with favorite dolls.

His days took on a boring sameness. He said mass at daybreak, attended by the nuns and a few of the ambulatory patients. He gave communion, never really looking at the decaying bodies who sought closeness to God.

It was the youngest nun, Sister Veronica, a pale, slender girl with pink lips and greenish eyes, who taught him more than he had learned through all the years of his academic accomplishments and all his political years at the Vatican.

He made rounds with the doctor one rainy morning, standing back slightly, avoiding any physical contact, as the young nun, kneeling at the bedside of a woman whose face was ravaged, talked to the doctor. This patient, she knew, would not last until the end of the day.

As she spoke, she supported the dying patient with one arm and fed her with the other. When she glanced up at Gene, she smiled.

"Father," she said lightly, "this woman will be in Paradise tonight. Isn't that *wonderful?* Isn't that *incredible?* Will you bless her, Father, and pray with her? It would give her such joy."

He nodded, bowed his head, made the sign of the Cross, and prayed as the doctor continued on his rounds. He kept his eyes closed and was surprised at the sudden light touch on his clenched hands.

"Father," the girl whispered in her soft French-English, "would you touch her? She is in a state of holiness, and it would be a gift." And then she added, "Not to her. To you."

Of all the things ever said to him, of all the prayers and convoluted arguments and rationalizations and sophistry, nothing like this had ever been said to him. He reached out, his hand cold in the hot, humid tent, leaned forward, and, with the tips of his fingers, traced the sign of the Cross on the corrugated forehead of a woman with no lips or nose.

The black eyes opened and shone into his with a purity that took his breath away. Her life was gathered in that still-functioning sense of sight, though what she saw, Eugene could not imagine. There was a joy in the depths of those dark eyes, not of gratitude for his touch, but of sharing the secret miracle she was confronting. He left the bedside shaken, and spent several hours alone, in his small wooden cabin, on his knees, praying without words, for words had deserted him.

It was the first *true* religious experience of his life. The feeling he had lived with since childhood, that he had been predestined to serve the Church, had all been framed by words. There had never been one moment, not one flashing second of true religious insight or fervor. Not even at the moment of his ordination, not even at the serving of the body and blood of Christ for the first time. Never, until the moment when his fingertips touched the forehead of the dying leper.

From then on he made rounds several times a day. He held the children, gently massaged their ruined feet and stubs of fingers and decaying noses. He whispered softly into their ears and they turned to him, glowing with a love he had never wanted before and received now as a benediction.

For the first time in his life, Eugene was looked on as a priest, a messenger of God and a voice of consolation. These souls did not see the superficial beauty that had damned him all his life. They saw what he was beginning to feel: the beauty from within that came from loving and caring and giving without recompense.

That wasn't true, of course, because Gene received a gift of serenity and peace and understanding and acceptance he had never known before. His touch became automatic; his embraces were part of his being, and his love grew as he shared it.

At night he studied the medical textbooks the doctor shared with him. He visited the lab, such as it was, that the medical nuns attempted to keep going.

He petitioned Rome for money for medical supplies, for textbooks for the children. He thought about the glamour and excesses of his time in Rome, and about the funding of the Church and the distribution of its wealth, as he looked around at the poverty in which the colony struggled to survive. The rich spiritual lives of these people were shamed by their physical, material dearth.

When supplies failed to arrive, or arrived in insufficient quantities or ruined condition, Gene prayed to be free of the anger and vindictiveness he felt toward his own Church. He remembered the luxury of his own life at the Vatican; the splendor with which he had been surrounded. He calculated how many lives could be made easier by the selling of one painting, one carpet, one set of brilliant crystal goblets.

But in the evenings or in the early mornings, when he was alone, contemplative, Eugene felt an overwhelming exaltation. In this place of death and the dying, his religious message was brought to him by the very people he had been sent to comfort and counsel. They brought the true reality of pure belief in the message of Christ Arisen.

Without sophisticated questioning, Eugene *felt,* accepted, and glowed with the purity of the faith all around him.

He came to terms with a Church that had often puzzled, exasperated, angered, humiliated, and deserted him in his spiritual quest. It was as though the *meaning* of his Church, in its purest form, had finally entered into him.

And then the powers shifted at the Vatican, and it was decided that the gifts of Father Eugene Sebastian O'Brien were being wasted in the small, unimportant leper colony. His time should be spent now, in the service of his Church, among the living, not the dying.

After six years of an almost miraculous, holy existence, Eugene was recalled to Rome, where he was promoted to monsignor and assigned to the Society for the Propagation of the Faith, operating out of Los Angeles, California.

CHAPTER TEN

Willie Paycek loved everything about Hollywood. It was as though his four days and nights on a bus were only a prelude to his own dream. He was in a land where he had the freedom to be anyone he wanted to be. Farm-girl waitresses with platinum hair and long legs and spectacular breasts would be movie stars, once their "transition period" was over. Handsome boys with southern accents who pumped gas were just making stay-alive money "until they connected with a studio." They were all stars-in-waiting, and they never had time to look at their counterparts, who had been around for five, six, ten, even fifteen years, and were still waiting. They were too concerned with the ever-younger, ever-fresher, ever-more-beautiful, boys and girls getting off the buses to join their ranks.

Willie loved watching them. Damn, there wasn't an ugly waiter or busboy or usher in Hollywood, male or female, who wasn't motion-picture-pretty. Any one of them could slide in front of the camera and replace any of those big stars. It was a matter of chance, and deep in every young heart, at least in the beginning, was the absolute conviction that the magic would happen. *They* would be singled out and *they* would talk one day to all the movie fan magazines and columns about what lousy countermen, short-order cooks, cocktail waitresses, bartenders, or cabdrivers they had been. None of them bothered to learn a marketable skill, beyond some girls who were passable typists and file clerks. God, no one wanted to get lost in a regular-hours, salaried job where you might be considered competent and be expected to stay with the company.

There was only one real business, the fantasy business, and anyone with even marginal skills, besides singing or dancing or acting, tried to work his or her way into the mailroom or the commissary. It was an "in" to be a messenger.

Every industry office employee under the age of forty talked about go-sees, call-backs, maybes, look-goods. And about friends who "knew someone." And about unfairness, about talentless nothings—*who did they know to get what they got?*

What Willie noticed, after he settled in as a studio driver, after he really began to look around him, was that everyone, top to bottom, was worried about the next assignment.

He came to Los Angeles gifted with a job that paid well. Within a week of arriving, he and Maryanne settled into a small furnished bungalow in a colony of fifteen identical houses set around a long, narrow swimming pool surrounded by a rough concrete sidewalk. The water in the pool was dirty, the beach chairs were broken, and there was a vague sewery smell, but it was an honest-to-God swimming pool, and Maryanne grabbed her Brownie camera and used a whole roll of film taking shots of the pool, the bungalow, the tall, skinny palm trees.

His first purchase, on the advice and with the help of his new boss, Gus Russo, was a shiny 1940 Plymouth. It was Willie's first car ever, and it had, as advertised, been owned by a pair of elderly people who had bought it for their son in the Navy as a surprise for his twenty-first birthday. The kid used it for a month and then was shipped out. In 1941 he was killed at Pearl Harbor and the car had never been used, because neither of the elderly parents had the heart to touch it. Willie paid fifty dollars for the five-year-old, brand-new car.

Willie Paycek was a good kid; that was the word on him. He had done some favors for someone in the East, so—no questions asked or answered—he was presented with his Teamsters card and paid his dues and kept in good standing.

Assignments were a matter of who knew whom or what. Since Willie Paycek came recommended, he was carefully watched the first few weeks. He drove heavy, midsized, and lightweight trucks, carrying scenery to location shoots; he assisted the technicians in loading valuable equipment for delivery from place to place. No matter what the cargo, Paycek was interested, alert, bright; he showed interest not only in the cargo, but in the technicians responsible for its use. He was hungry to learn, and, facing long layovers and wait-outs, the technicians, knowing he was a teamster, and no threat to their jobs, shared their expertise with the funny-looking, bright little guy from the Bronx.

Willie was fascinated by the young extras on the set who had left their homes, places like Iowa and Arkansas, and found their way out here, searching for the dream. He watched the kids who counted themselves lucky to get one or two days' shooting as "background." Bright-faced youngsters, smiling their hearts out, trying to hide sweaty underarms, dying when some third assistant director screamed. "Who the fuck put that curly redheaded boy in the middle of that crowd?"

Hollywood had its own rules and those who would succeed were by nature not only ambitious, determined, and driven; they were also the best at *lying*. It was essential not just to make up your life, but really to *believe* your own creation. Willie watched and studied the most successful up-and-comers. All the middle-aged Jewish producers became more American than the flag, with their thin blond gentile wives and their blue-eyed children sent off to private schools after having been raised by Irish or English nannies. Their tailoring was impeccable, and why not? They were the sons of sweatshop tailors, and they knew how to get their money's worth. Willie knew from the product they put on the market what their perception of America was: shiny-faced lovers who locked eyes, but blinked quickly so that there could be no possible hint of lustful follow-up. Eventually, he was assigned to drive studio limousines.

Willie knew the moviemakers themselves were lusty men. He delivered their girls to hidden locations, skinny, gorgeous young things who smelled so good he wanted to suck their skin. Mysterious girls, filling the car, from the deep well of the back seat all the way to his open glass chamber, with the fragrance of sex.

From time to time, Willie was approached by an assistant director for a favor. A between-us-no-questions-asked assignment, which paid over and above overtime. Discretion was the main thing; the word on this skinny, funny-looking kid was pretty good.

He drove a long black studio limo up into the Hollywood Hills, waited outside the door, patiently turning his head as a studio star was carefully loaded into the backseat. He was handed a slip of paper: some sanitorium out toward Vegas. *Don't talk to the guy, don't open the glass window, just drive straight there; people will be waiting to take him off your hands. You don't even have to go inside. In fact, none of this ever happened, so you don't even have to forget it.*

Willie began to keep notes in a small five-and-dime spiral notebook. Whom he picked up and where; their condition—drunk, drugged, unconscious, loudly carrying on (in which case there was often an escort to quiet things down, to maybe shoot the guy up en route, or hand him a bottle); the destination. He came to recognize studio people, semi-big shots who always seemed able to maintain a nonspecific assignment with a good-sized office, a large, pretty staff, not too many working hours. Sometimes the passenger was a woman: a face known, revered by the public—the storybook wife, the girl back home, the loving daughter. Howling filthy words, tears smearing her makeup. Always, his face was implacable, unconcerned, as he drove her to a well-established Hollywood abortionist. His job was to drive the car from one location to the other. To return the limo to the studio, check in, leave. Period.

Drug deaths were turned into unfortunate, terrible, witnessed and documented car accidents. He had driven a corpse, leaning upright against stone-faced executives on either side, to a remote location where a prop car waited, skid marks to be provided by experts. He had watched the famous face placed inside the accident car, had taken part in the faking of an honorable death for a dishonorable man.

To his surprise, one star, a tall, blond, handsome sonofabitch he had admired through the years on the screen of the Avalon, asked for him as a driver. He was sober, just returning from a month's stay at a dry-out clinic. The star, healthy and easygoing, a good-guy cowboy, sat up front with Willie and thanked him. He knew Willie had helped save his life and certainly his reputation. Discretion was hard to come by out here.

The star confessed that he felt awkward here in never-never land. He was genuinely a small-town boy, a Midwestern soda jerk with few acting pretensions. He was the right type in the right place at the right time, and the camera caught something he didn't even know he had, in a small, one-line part. He was catapulted into a starring role in a major western, where he was required to do little more than appear. His presence dominated every scene; his lines were kept to a minimum, since he had a poor memory and a somewhat light voice.

His hours were filled with acting lessons, with voice lessons. It was discovered he had a pleasant singing voice—untrained and natural. They trained the naturalness out of it and starred him in a musical for which they finally hired a stronger, more professional voice to overdub all his numbers. He was, in effect, a mannequin.

"I watched you shooting today," Willie confided. "Don't put yourself down. I think the problem is that director don't know shit from Shinola."

It was Willie's first directing job—unofficial, off the books, secretive, and intuitively excellent. Day after day, the young star grew in confidence as he absorbed Willie's advice on the ride to the set in the morning and home afterwards. Soon he was inviting his driver over after work, which led to more lessons in how to move, to pause, to hesitate, to speak a line quickly, to get deeper meaning out of a scene.

The director of the film didn't really care enough to object. The handsome schmuck wants to try something new, what the hell. People came to look at him, not to listen to him. The guy was box-office no matter what—even if he was turning into a real actor.

At a large party held in the incredibly lush Beverly Hills mansion of a Hollywood lawyer, the actor confided in a few of his colleagues. This guy Willie Paycek, my driver, this guy is a gem. He has a gift for direction. Someone should give him a chance.

One of his drinking companions, a huge, dark-skinned Arab, listened politely, snapped his fingers at one of his aides, who dutifully wrote down Willie's name and phone number. He looked at two of his companions, who nodded approval. They chatted up the star for a few more minutes, then put their untouched drinks on a silver tray on a small, silver-topped table.

"So perhaps we have found our director, yes? An unknown, desperate to make movies."

His partner shrugged. "Why do we even need a director? That to me makes no sense. These sort of things . . . they take on their own momentum. Who needs a director?"

The heavy man stared coldly and said softly, "Because all of these damned movies are the same. We should make one special movie, one classic, one perfect example of the art."

They were talking about a snuff movie.

CHAPTER ELEVEN

After one brief conference in a deli, over a less-than-wonderful pastrami-on-rye and iced tea, they hired Willie Paycek. They would provide the location, the scenery, the lighting and the cameras. They would allow him to write a script, since he felt this was important. They agreed not to question his decisions and to allow him to rehearse, since those were his terms. They would provide the male stud. The older, heavier, black-browed businessman would play a crucial role.

It was left to Willie to provide the girl.

He remembered when he was a kid, on his way to the Loew's Burnside, off the Grand Concourse, down Burnside Avenue; on certain days of the week there was a long, milling line of black women standing outside of Woolworth's. Waiting. Some had small children. Some were girls in their early teens. They all carried brown paper bags with their working clothes. He had watched as neighborhood white women would look them over, talk to one or two, make a selection, and lead the chosen woman along. For twenty-five cents an hour, a cleaning woman had been hired.

Willie, sensing a possibility, carefully screened the line one day when he was about fourteen years old. He was short and thin, hunched forward, pimply, his eyes crossed and devious. There was one beautiful girl, more girl than woman. She had light skin and pale eyes and she was tall and bone-thin. She stood with her legs apart, hands on her hips, head up, not making eye contact with any of the white women. She seemed to intimidate them; no one approached her.

Except Willie. He slouched over to her. In one respect, he felt sorry for her. Hell, she had to earn a living, same as anyone else. He fingered three quarters in his pocket: they had been hard-earned and would see him through a week of movie-hopping. But she seemed worth it.

When she realized the dirty little riffraff white boy was speaking to her, she leaned forward, glared into his face.

"What you want, boy? What you after?"

"You", he said, looking directly at her for one split second. His hand slid into his pocket, he showed her his three quarters.

The girl roared in a loud voice, calling attention to the boy and his offer. The other women laughed, some of them nearly falling down with the release of tension, the amusement, the anger, the furious insult. They laughed at the trashy white boy. The girl smacked his hand, and his quarters went flying.

He had a choice. He could turn and run from the line of mocking black women, or he could creep around and find his quarters.

Willie shut out their voices, their taunts, their filthy remarks, and reclaimed his quarters. Then he stood up and stared at the girl, memorizing her face. Remembered the moment and how she had made him feel. To him, his request had not been insulting or demeaning. He had wanted to buy some portion of her time, for himself.

The whole scene was projected again in his mind now, years later, the moment he spotted the slender, light-skinned black woman as she turned away from an extra call. He watched as she sighed heavily and left the lot without speaking to anyone.

Willie followed the girl from a safe distance. There were certain required qualifications for his star. Looks were one, and she qualified. After two days of watching her, Willie was convinced that she met the rest. She lived alone; she never seemed to talk to anyone: she answered only open calls, and was never selected; she seemed to be totally disconnected. On her own.

She would not be missed by anyone.

On the third day, Willie approached her as she turned away from yet another rejection. He bought her a cup of coffee at a diner a few blocks from the studio. She was out here alone from Detroit; her mother was dead, her father had split. She'd had hard times; anything she found out here would be better than what she'd left. No, she'd never connected. There was no film footage on her of any kind. She was registered as an extra under her "professional" name, Kitty Jones. Her real name was Serena Johnson, but no one knew that. She'd earned a few bucks, enough to pay for her furnished room and a meal or two a day. Never mind how. None of his business. Unless he was offering her something. He wasn't a pimp, was he, because she worked alone. Didn't see any reason for sharing her hard-earned cash, such as it was.

As she spoke, he watched her carefully, recalling and then releasing the memory of his humiliation in the Bronx. No, this was another girl altogether. He explained the movie. It was a skin flick, but with a difference; it was a love story. It would be shot in a very luxurious location.

As he went on, Willie explained even more to Serena; the film was going to *appear* to be a snuff movie. Some very big money was behind it. A very expensive set, beautiful costumes, all done with great style.

The trick was, of course, that no one was going to get killed. But it was going to be done so realistically that anyone seeing it would be fooled. What he showed her now was a plane ticket, in her name, to New York City. He admitted he knew a great deal about her.

"See, you'll have to leave L.A. You're supposed to be dead. We can't have you turning up in casting calls and maybe getting on film. This is a really big deal. One thousand bucks for a coupla hours work, then, right from location, a limo takes you to the airport, you're on your way to the Big Apple, and there's a contact who will meet you. Guarantee you work, maybe in Europe, but definitely in New York. In a big-time nightclub, sell some cigarettes, then a little singing, a little dancing. You'll be able to afford to decide what you want. Now, this is it, *right now*, I gotta know. Yes or no. If it's yes, we go *right now* out to the location for fitting and for rehearsal. We get it done right away. You got any problems with that?"

She sat motionless as she turned inside to her own thoughts. What the hell was this guy up to? On the other hand, he showed her the ticket, with her name on it. He explained he'd been watching her, selecting her. He opened a brand-new red leather wallet, stuffed with hundred-dollar bills. Her new wallet. There would be a new suitcase for her, with some clothes. She could shop for more in New York.

She thought about the dirty, musty room with the landlady who smelled of her six cats and who made Serena pay for her own forty-watt

bulb replacement and still yelled at her for using too much electricity.
And about the landlady's lecherous old shit of a husband, who breathed
on her in a whiskery, dirty way every chance he got. She thought about
her narrow bed with the stinking mattress and the unclean sheets and
the smelly pillow. She thought about the few ragtag dresses she had
hanging on hooks in the room, absorbing the awful smells; her meager
supply of underwear; her stockings with rips she couldn't mend or hide.

"You mean *right now?* We go and do it *right now?*"

"After I make a phone call. For the limo to pick us up."

They waited a few blocks away, on a dark streetcorner, and sure
enough, a large black limo slid up to the curb. Willie opened the door
for her, and she slipped inside and sank back against the luxurious softness
of new-smelling upholstery.

She was on her way.

The set was in a large room, separated from the main part of a
huge house, in the Hollywood Hills. It was soundproof, carpeted,
isolated, and beautiful.

The scene of the action was the inside of a luxurious tent, furnished
with magnificent silk pillows, carpets, lamps, and low tables laden with
fruits and candies. The lighting man left after briefing Willie, who
would be his own cameraman. He put the cast through their paces. It
was not to be a rip-the-clothes-off, jump on, grunt and groan, fall-back-
and-be-discovered epic.

But there was very little dialogue, since Willie didn't trust either of
his two main actors.

"This is a love story," he told them. "She is a slave in the caliph's
harem, and you, Ali, have fallen in love with her. Genuinely in love
with her. You are to look at her and feel your heart breaking; she is a
captive, and you are a captive. Your love could lead to your deaths,
both of you. But at this point you don't care."

He led them through several rehearsals, until he got some response.
They were to make eye contact; they were not to think of the sex act,
but of each other. They loved each other to the point of recklessness. If
the cost of their love was death, then it would be better to die together
than to go on this way, both slaves of a hated caliph. They were to take
each other's clothes off carefully, as lovers. No ripping and tearing.
Gently, sensuously, each discovering the other, each loving the other.
No sense of speed—slowly, tenderly. They were to touch each other

tentatively, kiss lightly, then with more passion, their hands moving over each other with lovers' discoveries.

He rehearsed them carefully, stopping them before the sex act had been accomplished.

"Save it, Ken," he told his stud, a large blond actor who had a barely double-digit IQ but a magnificent body. They faked the intercourse, and then the caliph entered. He wore flowing robes and ballooning pants, with a silk turban and soft slippers. His anger was quiet, rather than histrionic. He was genuinely sorry for what he had to do. He had, in his way, truly loved the girl. He was hurt because of her betrayal, and heartbroken because she must die.

The blond slave was taken away, and the caliph removed his billowing trousers and simulated inserting himself into the girl. Then he rolled off her, snapped his fingers. An aide brought in the head of the blond stud. It was a good papier-mâché likeness, and the caliph's guard, displaying a bloodied scepter, carried it by the yellow hair, the neck dripping bloody liquid.

The caliph sighed, stood up, and removed a prop dagger from under his shirt. He pulled the slave girl to her feet and simulated stabbing her in the jugular. The blade of the knife retracted, the girl gasped, grabbed her throat, and slumped in his arms (her blood would be supplied for shooting). The caliph gently placed her on the carpet at his feet, knelt for a moment, and sobbed.

"I really loved you," he whispered to the dead girl.

He dropped his head, kissed her dead lips, collapsed over her body. End of rehearsal.

"It must be played as a genuine love story," Willie told his cast for the final time. "That is the difference here. It is a tragedy. The two slaves love each other and are willing to die for their love. The caliph loves the girl, too, and sacrifices her because she has betrayed him and he has no choice, but it is awful for him, too."

They all sat quietly, waiting. Willie had the girl and her lover sit together. They were to touch each other, tenderly, wordlessly, while they waited for the take.

Finally the shooting began. The two young lovers moved carefully, slowly, lovingly, just as he had instructed. They looked into each other's eyes, they connected with each other first spiritually and then, finally, sexually, in an act so surprisingly tender that Willie could hardly believe it.

The caliph entered, and the scene moved on.

After the caliph raped his slave-love, the guard entered the tent. He was carrying the head of the male slave. It was a *real* head, the porn actor's last appearance on the screen or anywhere else.

The girl, at first not quite taking in what she was seeing, stared and then blinked and gasped. She started to rise, but the strong arm of the caliph prevented her. She started to scream, but he blocked her lips with a deep kiss. He plunged his dagger into her throat, and pulled back as the spouting blood covered the girl's naked body and splashed on his face and shoulders. He put his bloodied hands over his face and sobbed. He looked up, his expression anguished, his voice rasping.

"I really loved her. I truly loved her. Why did she betray me? Oh, why?"

The picture ended with a long, loving shot of the dead slave, her body still positioned for love, her arms flung out. And then Willie focused on her face. The pale green eyes were open, staring in total comprehension, her mouth twisted in horror.

It was the most artistic, realistic snuff movie ever made, and it became a classic on the circuit.

Willie Paycek was paid twenty thousand dollars for this movie, which would be the only work in his oeuvre not to bear his name.

CHAPTER TWELVE

On his wedding day, Dante D'Angelo felt as though his life belonged to someone else. It was all too much for a boy from Ryer Avenue.

His father, Dominick D'Angelo, had arrived in New York City at the turn of the century, a frightened immigrant, fourteen years old, wearing the clothes his widowed mother had made for him before he left Sicily. He had the address of an uncle, five American dollars, and promises he had made to a mother he would never see again.

He would be an honorable man, always. He would give his word only when he knew he could keep it. He would work hard, every day of his life. He would take no charity, for the bread of charity was made of dust. He would pray for his mother and brothers and sisters. He would send home a picture when he found a wife.

He would never dishonor any woman, just as he would not permit anyone to dishonor his sisters. He would raise his children to be good Catholics and honorable people.

He lived near starvation, working at any job that required a strong back. He was not a large man, but he could lift and carry. He never cheated on his hours. He never claimed one penny he had not earned. For seven years he saved every single dollar he could toward his own business. He was a good shoemaker. Although in this country there were shoe stores filled with shoes of all kinds, they were not made to last. Although his shop was called Dominick D'Angelo, Shoemaker, he was really a shoe repairer. He knew which children were hard on the tips and on the heels, so he reinforced those places with small steel crescents that tapped and clattered and delighted the kids and pleased the parents. After all, shoes were expensive and should last longer than from the store to the home.

On Sundays, after church, after tidying the small apartment at the back of his shop on 181st Street, he walked in the spring air all the way to Fordham Road and then cut down to Bathgate Avenue. Here were the fresh fruit and vegetable stands, the kosher live-chicken markets (the Jews were careful to get the cleanest poultry and meat). Although he rarely bought anything but vegetables and fruit, Dom D'Angelo liked to wander about, just looking. There were any number of clothing shops, discount places where you could buy a slightly off-size coat or pair of pants, an off-color shirt, or socks or underwear that hadn't been cut exactly right.

Mothers dragged cranky children in and out of the shops, holding clothes against their bodies, wrapping a sock around a child's fist for size.

The men waited outside the shops, smoking, talking about jobs, politics, word from home. Dom edged closer to the men who spoke Italian, listened to their accents, until he felt comfortable. Sounds of home.

He rarely spoke to anyone. He was too shy.

But each week he went to the stand in front of the Rucci Family Vegetable and Fruit Company and bought exactly the same thing. Three red apples, two yellow apples, two oranges, three bananas.

The girl who served him, a plump, bright-eyed girl of fifteen named Angela Rucci, smiled at him, held up her hand, said, "Don't tell me, let me guess." She filled a brown paper bag with his order, and Dom D'Angelo walked home to 181st Street in a daze. She was aware of him. She remembered him from week to week. She had noticed him.

Her family did not approve of him. He had one small shoe-repair shop, period. He had no family here; what kind of life could he offer their youngest sister? Angela was an orphan living with her married brothers, part of a large, growing, affluent family who actually owned not just their shop, but a two-story clapboard house farther down the street. And they were preparing to buy two more houses, so that they would always be close together, as families should be.

What he had, this twenty-year-old boy, strong in the shoulders, with black hair, clear skin, and good features, was his love. He would never bring dishonor to this girl. He treasured her. He rented a four-room apartment on Ryer Avenue, where they could make a home for themselves and for the children they would have.

When it was clear that Angela would have no other for her husband, when she threatened to starve or even mutilate herself—"I'll shave my head. I'll be so ugly you will have to hide me away forever!"—there was nothing to do but give permission. And offer this boy a place in the family business, so that one day, he too would be able to live in a two-story house of his own on Bathgate Avenue.

They hadn't realized that Dom D'Angelo, though quiet and respectful, had a will of his own. He worked for himself. He would never live in a house he could not afford. He would take care of his wife and their children without any help, thank you.

At times, the Rucci brothers gathered in the crowded living room of one home or another, while the women and girls worked in the kitchen, filling the house with marvelous hints of what was to come for Sunday dinner. They spoke of things that Dom did not understand—of midnight runs, or trucks that "lost their way" in New Jersey; of meat that had to be saved or it would rot in the road when the driver had disappeared. They spoke of bargain prices for refrigerators, radios, clocks. They bragged about the newest appliance the wives had: a washing machine with a strong, rubber-coated wringer, to save red hands the hard task of squeezing water from soaking clothing.

Whenever they offered Dom D'Angelo any of their treasures, he turned them down. He would shop at Macy's for what his family needed. And if he couldn't afford these things, they would do without.

The Ruccis felt sorry for their youngest sister, but what could they say? Within nine months she was rounded with her first child; then, later, beautiful with her second; then, still later, glowing with her third. She visited her family and invited them to her home, and she seemed happier than any woman they had ever seen. They always felt they could make sure Angela and her kids were okay, without the stiff-necked Dom knowing anything about it. Who could explain why one person loved another?

The Rucci boys were raised in the family business; some graduated from high school, some went on to college. Others ran the meat markets and various other enterprises. They married, had children, moved to the suburbs.

None had the golden future that awaited Dom's oldest son, Dante.

He had a law degree, a job in the Bronx district attorney's office, a madonna of a bride who was not only beautiful but a college graduate who spoke many languages. She was an only child with a rich father—a wine merchant, who supplied the Church with altar wine, who knew the score and dealt in real estate from time to time.

When Lucia-Bianca told Dante that the ceremony would be held in St. Patrick's Cathedral, he thought she was kidding.

"Not at the main altar, of course. There are alcoves, lovely, beautiful. An old friend of my father, from his boyhood in Palermo, is an assistant to the cardinal, a monsignor. He'll marry us. We have approval from my parish priest. It's all been arranged. Dante, don't look like that. It's for my *father*."

Her father, of course, told Dante. "It is for my *daughter*. She is my only child. I would do whatever in this world I could for her happiness."

The wedding dinner-dance reception was held at the Waldorf-Astoria. Dante's maternal family—uncles, aunts, cousins—was awestruck by the cathedral, impressed by the Waldorf, dazzled by the bride. The bride's relatives came from Italy; quiet, well-dressed, handsome businessmen and their wives. They even approved of the handsome bridegroom. It was his family they disdained.

Dante didn't worry about his aunts and uncles and cousins. They were happy, relaxed; they were themselves, accustomed to rising to an occasion on their own terms. Take them or leave them, here they were, the Ruccis.

He worried mostly about his father, stiff and uncomfortable in the new dark blue suit, his neck irritated by the starched collar held tight by the good silk tie. The tall, thin man had carefully combed the remaining strands of black-gray hair across his small skull, rubbed his hand over his chin several times to be sure the quickly growing dark beard wasn't evident, making him look like a bum. Dante knew his father was overwhelmed by the entire event: the cathedral, where the cardinal himself says mass and gives the homily. The Waldorf-Astoria, where once, long ago, he had washed pots and pans for fifteen cents an hour. Now he was a guest at the table of honor. What if he should spill things, forget how to eat properly, what if . . . ?

Dante wrapped his arms around his father, kissed his cheek, and gently chided him, "Papa, if it weren't for you, for the kind of man you are,

I would be nothing. I would have married some girl right from high school, made a poor life for us, never have gone to law school. It was you who told all of us about working hard, setting goals."

The older man shrugged, studied his nails to make sure they were clean. "I'm still a shoemaker, Dante. This family you are marrying into, they are . . . in the old country, they would be the *padrones*."

"This isn't the old country, Papa. The only *padrones* here are people who work, who earn. My sister's husband, the son of a laborer, owns his own construction business. He employs fifty people. My kid brother is studying to become an engineer. In the old country, we'd all be field laborers. You brought us this chance, Pop. Your courage." He hugged his father again, pulled back and looked directly into his eyes. "I am proud to be the son of my father. I only hope I will give you back pride in me."

Dom D'Angelo wiped a tear from his eye, nodded, whispered. He would try to have a good time. After all, it was his son's wedding day.

The surprise, to Dante, was his father-in-law, the austere, bone-thin, bearded, sinister-seeming man he had never seen smile. He sat next to Dom and they drank wine together, and whispered, and finally laughed together. Dante kept a quick eye out: Was this guy patronizing his father? Finally, Aldo gestured Dante away from his friends.

"We have much in common, your father and I. We were just comparing. Two old widowers, we have confided to each other why we have never remarried. Who could ever compare to the mother of our children? Your father blushes, but his marriage to your mother was truly Romeo and Juliet. As was my marriage to Lucia-Bianca's mother. Two old widowers with our memories."

Santini held a steady gaze with Dante, who nodded slightly, accepting the lie.

"Ah, but what good memories," Dante's father said, smiling. "My Angela was plump, not in the thin way of these American girls. She ate like a woman should eat, with"—he snapped his fingers—"with *gusto*, yes?"

Dante had never seen or heard his father like this before. He was totally at ease, sharing memories with this man that he had never shared with his children.

When it came time for the father of the bride to dance with his daughter, and the mother of the groom with her son, Dante's sister Angela, beautiful in her third pregnancy, did the honors for him. And then Dom D'Angelo, whose children had never seen him dance, took his new daughter-in-law in his arms and glided gracefully around the floor in a waltz. No one else danced; they all watched, spellbound. The old man, out of his shoe shop, out of his apron, his face clean, his body straight, was beautiful. He danced Lucia-Bianca over to her new husband and, with a courtly bow, presented her.

"*Bella*, beautiful girl, my son. You be good to her, she is your treasure."

It was the happiest moment of Dante's life.

His best man, Charley O'Brien, uncomfortable, like Dante's cousins, in the rented usher's suits, took him aside.

"God, you got it all, Danny. She's gorgeous. Listen, I have to duck out early. I'm on duty at midnight. All the best, kid."

Dante punched him playfully.

Aldo had reserved a fine room for the young couple at the Plaza Hotel, so that they could slip away from the party and not feel self-conscious. They had reservations to fly to Bermuda the next morning for four days. It was all the time Dante could arrange. And then they would move into a neat brick two-bedroom home on Pelham Parkway, on which Aldo held the mortgage. They would pay a moderate rent, the money going toward purchase of the home, if that was what they eventually wanted.

That night Lucia-Bianca came out of the dressing room, glowing in heavy satin lounging pajamas. Neither of them had eaten a thing all day, and room service provided an assortment of hot and cold food and a bottle of Dom Perignon that had been preordered by the bride's father.

Dante could not take his eyes off his bride. He had seen her in glimpses throughout the day, surrounded by others. She had been hugged and danced with and fussed over, swallowed up by the love and attention of others. His first sight of her in her wedding dress was a complete blur: there, underneath this magnificence, was his wonderful girl, but he couldn't really see her.

Now, her dark hair casually finger-combed, freed from the bridal headpiece, her tall body outlined by the wonderfully clinging heavy pink satin, her breasts erect, small, neat, her hips touching the flowing material, her thighs and calves appearing and disappearing as she moved, her bare feet with their neat, pink-polished toenails—all of her—he devoured with his eyes.

"Just let me look," he said, ignoring the food.

She lifted her head, waited for him to meet her eyes.

"First some champagne," she said softly. "You pour."

She nibbled on shrimps and little hot sandwiches, and sipped the wine. She fed him bits and pieces of food he didn't even taste; then, finally, she held a small piece of meat between her bared teeth.

Dante came to her, his mouth on hers. He bit the food from her teeth and chewed, then embraced her, moved with her toward the bed.

"Let me take off your pajamas. God, but you are beautiful."

Then he undressed her and for the first time saw, actually saw, Lucia-Bianca's perfect body. It was better than he had dreamed it: smooth and strong, with lush pubic hair, firm breasts, flat stomach, rounded hips. His hands moved lightly, then began to grasp, and she matched his passion.

She had always matched his passion; she lost herself in his kiss. She seemed to devour him, to suck his being into herself, as her hands pulled and worked through the back of his head, his neck, his shoulders. Finally, this time, there would be no holding back, no leaving into the cold empty night with the sickness of desire.

He spread her legs and started to enter her, but Lucia-Bianca suddenly stiffened.

"What? It's okay. I'll be careful. I won't hurt you."

He heard a deep sob, almost a cry. He looked down at his wife's distorted face. She looked terrified.

"Not that way," she said. "There are other ways."

"Baby, it's okay. We're married now. I promise you to be careful. I understand . . ."

She slid herself from under him. Her face was frozen. Her voice was harsh.

"No, you *don't* understand. How could you *ever* understand? There are *other* ways. I will do things for you . . . to you . . . but you mustn't do *that*."

"Lucia-Bianca, what the hell is this, what are you talking about?"

She held her arms across her body, and her eyes burned with tears. She suddenly seemed like a total stranger.

"Dante, my God, do you want to kill me."

He turned to Megan Magee. Of all the people he knew— friends, family, colleagues—it was instinctive for Dante to turn to Megan. Not only did he love and trust her, but amazingly now she was completing her psychiatric residency at Bellevue.

He had told Megan about Lucia-Bianca almost from their first date: how different this girl was, how special his feelings for her, how ready he felt for those feelings, how he felt they were reciprocated. If he saw

the sudden stab of pain, of disappointment and loss, he never acknowledged it. Probably never realized it. Megan kept a poker face at times;
she could experience her feelings later, in private.

She had had to admit, grudgingly, at their engagement party, that
Dante and Lucia-Bianca were well matched, not just physically—both
were tall and slender, graceful, with black hair and dark eyes—but
intellectually. What more could she wish for her best friend than such
a perfect match. Even if the woman's name was Lucia-Bianca Santini
and not Megan Magee.

"Dante, I'm not sure of the ethics. I mean, we're friends. I could
recommend a colleague. Right now I'm specializing in damaged kids,
traumatized by whatever event brought them here."

"Well, wouldn't you say Lucia-Bianca was, in effect, a damaged
child? My God, her mother murdered her baby brother, then killed
herself, and Lucia found them. In a way, she deserted her daughter
when she was barely three years old. Doesn't that qualify her as a
'damaged child'? Even though she's an adult?"

They sat in a small coffee shop around the corner from Bellevue. The
constant noise—conversations, clattering dishes, waiters yelling out
orders to disgruntled countermen who yelled back—screened their
voices from prying ears. Megan hunched across the table, took Dante's
hand, prevented him from lighting a cigarette. He already had one
burning in the ashtray.

"Danny, explain something to me. Her father said that Lucia believes
her mother died of a heart attack after the death of her newborn twins.
That she has no memory or knowledge of what really happened."

He shook his head. "No memory, but she's heard—through the
years, she's heard talk. From aunts, cousins. She knows some of the
truth, but it isn't really clear, the exact sequence of events."

"Her father never discussed with her what happened? She never
directly confronted him, never asked?"

"Her father forbade the mention of her mother's name. Every picture
of her mother was destroyed. He would only tell her, 'Your mother
died when you were three years old. It was very sad and hurts me to talk
about it, so we will not.' The old man went deathly pale when he told
me the true story. And you never saw such hatred on a person's face."
He stared at his hands a moment. "What the hell, the woman killed his
only remaining son, and deserted her daughter and husband."

"Hasn't Lucia realized the hate her father felt toward her mother? I
mean, my God, making up a story about a heart attack is one thing, but
forbidding any mention of her name—that *must* have been confusing."

"What she grew up with was the knowledge that her mother—some how or other—was responsible for the deaths of her twin brothers. Her father's *sons*. And that her mother deserted her. What she's gathered from her 'well-meaning' aunts is that the birth of the babies somehow made her mother go crazy. Crazy enough to kill them and desert her. So she feels . . . I guess . . . hell, I don't know."

"She feels that if she has a child, she might, to use a very technical term . . . go nuts. Hurt the baby, kill herself, or desert the baby in some way."

"Megan, I want you to understand this. Lucia-Bianca is a brilliant woman. She *knows* the way she feels is illogical. She *understands* that. But . . ."

"But intellect and emotion are two different things, Danny."

"There's something else. She says she *feels* that something else happened that day. The day, she was told, she found her mother and the baby. Not that she remembers, she just feels. Hell, how could she *remember*? She was only three years old."

"She remembers. Not consciously, but it's recorded, Danny. And Lucia-Bianca is smart enough to know that. Is she tough enough to find out? To face that day, now, as an adult?"

"Megan, if we don't straighten this out, I don't know what we'll do. We can't go on like this. It's been crazy."

She reached out and stopped him from lighting a cigarette. "Will you please stop doing that? Since I stopped smoking, I can't stand the smell of cigarettes. Besides, I have an almost overwhelming impulse to reach over and grab a butt for myself." She squeezed his hand hard, took a deep breath. "Okay, Danny. Let's set it up. But remember one thing—and this goes, or we don't do it. This will be between Lucia-Bianca and me. Patient and doctor. You don't ask *me* anything. She can tell you whatever she wants, but you don't ask *me*. And . . . no guarantees. Deal?"

He returned the pressure on her hand. "Oh, God, Megan. Thanks."

She finished her coffee and tried hard not to reach out for him again.

Gee, Megan, thanks for trying to save my marriage. You jerk. You damn jerk.

Why didn't you wait for me?

They met five times in Megan's small consulting room. It was a bare white room with municipal furniture except for a beat-up leather couch she had bought secondhand, two fairly new comfortable chairs her father had given her as a gift, and a desk lamp on the metal desk.

At first, Lucia-Bianca had rejected the couch. "Too movie-ish," she said, smiling.

But finally, by the third session, she lay down, staring at the ceiling. Finally she began to express the deep underlying anger she felt toward her mother.

"How could she desert me like that? How the hell could she have just *deserted* me? Abandoned me. God, what I remember of her, she was a soft and loving woman. My father, he was . . . he *is* . . . a cold man. An unforgiving man. How could she have left me alone with him like that? He never remarried. You know why? Because he could never trust another woman. God, sometimes he used to look at me in such a strange way. As if he were looking at her. Because, I've been told, I resemble her. But, on the other hand . . . he's always been loving to me. In his way."

"You've told me he made sure you were surrounded by love. Your aunts and cousins were there for you."

"But, God, how he hated her. We were never allowed to mention her name. I asked him once, could I see a picture of her. Was I like her at all? God, his face went rigid. 'Never, ever ask such a question as that. You are *nothing* like her. We will never discuss this again.'"

"Is that what you're afraid of? That you *are* like her? That you would kill a child? Or maybe yourself, desert your child, as she did?"

Lucia-Bianca sobbed; her breath caught in her throat. "I *will* be my mother. How can I help it? God, how could she *do* such a thing? How could she have killed the baby? How could she have left me?"

"Use your adult intelligence, Lucia. You've told me you studied postpartum depression. Not something too many doctors acknowledge, but it *is* a medical fact. You can understand the depression that was triggered by the death of the second baby. Approach it intellectually now, as an adult. Not as an aching child."

"Don't you think I understand? God, yes, intellectually. She was ill, heartbroken that the first baby died. But there's still something wrong with the equation. Something I can't seem to grasp."

"What? What doesn't seem to fit?"

Lucia-Bianca leaned forward, sat up, turned to face Megan. "She seemed to be coming out of it, the sadness and shock of the loss of one baby. My aunt told me that. She finally reacted to the new baby. And reached out for me again, playing with me, combing my hair, fussing with me. It was two months after she had given birth, and she was taking more and more responsibility for the baby. She held him, sang to him. God . . . I remember that, she sang to him. And to me. I was there, she sang some little Italian nursery song. I remember that . . ."

"Do you remember the day it happened? Dante tells me you were out with your nursemaid. You came home from the park and ran into your mother's room and went into the bathroom and . . ."

Lucia-Bianca lay back and shook her head. "No. I don't remember. I was told that, but I don't remember. But there was something . . . that morning. How could I possibly remember? I was a baby myself."

"Because *you were there*. Because it is somewhere inside your memory. Would you like to try, Lucia-Bianca? We could try."

"What do you mean? Try? How?"

Megan got up and pulled down the shades, then switched the lamp to its dimmest setting. "Lie back. Would you consent to a deep-relaxation technique? Would you go along with it? It must be with your total consent. It might be very painful."

Lucia-Bianca leaned back on the inclined pillow of the couch. "You mean . . . hypnosis?"

"A form of hypnosis. But you will never lose touch with reality. You'll be in total control, but there will be a conscious relaxing, you'll allow yourself to drift back. It *is* there, inside you. You'll face it now, as an adult, not as a child. Just at first, the child may return. That would be hard. Are you willing?"

She sighed. "God, nothing, nothing could be more painful than what I am doing to Dante. I owe it to him to get this worked out somehow."

"No," Megan said. "You owe it to *yourself*. To your own healthy life. You say there is something you do remember, but can't quite visualize. Let's try to get back to that moment and move on from there."

Through a series of gentle, informed relaxation techniques, calmly and quietly, Megan guided the woman back in time. To early childhood; to her fifth birthday party, all gold and silver balloons; friends, cousins, aunts, uncles, her father, bringing presents all wrapped in silver and gold paper. Children singing to her; her aunt, that night, after the party, at bedtime, quietly singing an Italian nursery song to quiet the excited child.

Softly, Lucia-Bianca sang the words: a song about a mother and a child, about moonlight and stars and a soft breeze and an angel watching over the child.

As she sang, her voice became lighter and lighter, younger and younger. The soft whisper-lisp of a small child, then of a baby, barely able to articulate the words. And then the sound became stronger. It was her mother's voice, singing.

And then a very small girl's voice: "Sing it again, Mama."

She seemed to be listening, smiling.

Softly, Megan asked, "Where are you, Lucia? In what room?"

"The baby's room. Nursery. She's singing to me, because she loves me. Baby is sleeping. Mama loves *me*, not just baby. Me too."

"Were you worried that she didn't love you because of the baby brother?"

"Yes. But Mama said, 'You will always be my darling girl. My beautiful darling girl. You will be big sister and Mama's little helper. And Papa will be so proud of you because you are such a help to Mama. We both love you so much, and little brother Aldo will love you too, so aren't you the luckiest girl?'"

"Your mother sounds very happy."

"Mama is so happy. And baby brother wakes up and Mama brings him to me from his basket. 'See how tiny he is. How much he needs us, both of us, to help him grow. Sit here, on the rocking chair, and you can hold him while I get a fresh diaper and we'll put him on the changing table. Oh, there's the phone. Stay right here, my darling, Mama will be right back.'"

Suddenly the young woman began to groan. Her body seemed to go into spasms. Her fists clenched; her arms flailed as her staring eyes looked at something in the past. She wrapped her arms around herself and began to groan.

"Oh God oh God oh God."

"It's all right, Lucia-Bianca. Talk about it. Tell me what happened. Your mama went to answer the telephone. You are on the rocking chair with your baby brother in your lap. Tell me—it will be all right, if you tell me now. What are you seeing?"

The child had wanted to be helpful, to be the big sister, to be Mama's little helper, to make her father proud. She wanted to surprise her mama, show her how good a helper she was. Instead of waiting for her mother to come back into the nursery, the small girl carried her baby brother over to the changing table, the top of which was high over her head. She would get the baby ready for his diaper change. Wouldn't Mama be pleased? She lifted the baby high over her head, to the edge of the table. She managed to reach the edge of the table, and then the baby rolled over from her hands, fell straight down, hitting his head with great force against the metal wastebasket. His neck snapped.

There wasn't even a cry. The baby's body jerked once and there was absolute silence. Her mother, smiling, entered the room.

Lucia's voice, filled with anguish, moaned the words over and over again. "Oh God, oh God, oh God. I hurt baby brother. I hurt baby brother. Mama, Mama, Mama, make it all right."

Slowly, carefully, step by step, Megan brought Lucia-Bianca back to the present. She began to breathe quickly, shallowly, gasping for air.

Quietly, Megan told her, "You will remember all that you told me. You will quietly, rationally remember the moment a tiny three-year-old girl has lived with all this time, without understanding. Now, all grown up, you will understand the accident that happened. Lucia-Bianca, it's all right. It was a long time ago."

They stayed together for hours, Megan and Lucia-Bianca, ignoring the traditional fifty-minute hour.

Quietly she told Megan, "My mama made me promise *never, never* to tell Papa or anyone else about what happened. Forget all about it. It never happened."

"And of course you did—consciously—forget. And never spoke about it. Until now."

"And always I *knew* there was something I couldn't find."

"How do you feel about what happened to that little girl? Do you feel guilty about it?"

"Yes. Of course. God, it was all *my* fault, what happened." And then, quietly, "No. Not really. Not logically. I was a baby myself. What happened was terrible, but it *was* an accident."

"Let's talk about your mother. Whom you've been raised to hate, who *abandoned* you. Why do you think she did what she did?"

Her mother had done what she did to save Lucia-Bianca's life. She had known that if her husband found out the truth, he would banish the little girl from his life. As he, in fact, banished all traces of her mother from his home.

"So what she did, the suicide, the faking of the baby's death at her hands, she did for you, Lucia. She sacrificed her life for yours. She *didn't* abandon you. She gave you the gift of a loving life; she gave you your father's love, because she couldn't bear to think of your life otherwise."

Lucia-Bianca wept hysterically. "But it was an *accident*. A small child's accident. Oh, God. She *did* love me, didn't she? All these years I believed she loved me so little that she didn't even think about me in those last moments, but it was for *me*. She knew my father so well. He would have . . . God, he is so filled with hate. He would have destroyed me. Oh, God, why did this happen? Did I secretly *want* to kill my baby brother, could that have been it?"

"It happened," Megan said, "because accidents happen. And your mother couldn't think of any other way to handle it. So, to save you, she took the responsibility. To save your life, to save it from shattering, Lucia-Bianca."

After the session, Lucia-Bianca visited Megan a few more times, then managed, after talking with Dante, to get on with her life, as a normal, loving, trusting wife.

Six months after her first session with Megan, she was pregnant with their first daughter. When the child was born, Dante sent Megan a huge bouquet of roses with a note: "To my pal, Megan. A lifetime of thanks."

Megan smiled, shrugged sadly. Hey, what the hell is a *pal* for, anyway?

CHAPTER THIRTEEN

It was strange to be seated in Frankie Magee's "unofficial office" on the first floor of his brick three-story house, right next door to the apartment house where Dante was raised. The last time he'd had this kind of meeting with Frankie was during his senior year at Columbia Law. Magee was the Man to See, and he had been instrumental in getting Dante his appointment as an assistant district attorney. After three years working for the county, Dante had been in private practice and found it unfulfilling. The money was good, but money wasn't enough.

"Thanks for seeing me, Mr. Magee."

"Frankie," he said easily. His thin Irish face had a hard quality somewhat at odds with his wide, easy grin. His dark blue eyes narrowed for better observation. He was a lean, quick-moving man, graceful, with thinning curly dark hair and the suspicious gaze of a born cop. Though he had left Ireland as a small child and had a distinct Bronx toughness in his speech, he would slide into a soft brogue at times.

"Well, then, Danny, how are you doin' in private practice? Handle criminal cases, do ya? Quite a change, taking the other side from your days as prosecutor with the DA."

Dante spoke carefully. "I learned more in my time with the DA than in my years at law school. It's been interesting, working the other side. But it isn't exactly my idea of 'serving the law'—defending the punks. It's just good practice, you might say, for seeing to it that the law does what it's supposed to do."

"And what might that be?"

"Not to sound too pompous"—Dante shrugged and grinned because, of course, he did sound pompous—"the purpose of the law is to serve the constitutional rights of the people."

Frankie tilted his head to one side. He carefully evaluated every word. He liked the way the young man met his eyes; liked the straight but relaxed way he sat in his chair; liked the look of Danny D'Angelo, whom he had observed through the years. A good neighborhood lad from a decent, hardworking Italian family.

"Well, then. It's *been* interesting, you say, and it's 'good practice.' And what is it you're getting ready for? Seems to me you're beginning to talk about one part of your career in the past tense. Now, I'm no grammarian, mind, but am I right?"

"I think I'm about ready for a professional change, yes."

The Bronx voice spoke now, the Irish easiness gone. "What kinda change didja have in mind, Dan?"

"I've been thinking along the lines of running for the state assembly. Or maybe the state senate."

"Well, then. Why'd you come to me?"

"Everyone knows if you want to do anything in New York City or New York State, you clear it with Frankie Magee. So here I am."

Magee tapped a pencil against his front teeth, his face thoughtful. Finally he said, "Well, if you're smart enough to know that, then why the hell aren't you smart enough to know that once you head for the state senate, that's where you stay? It's a dead end. You can move to a certain level, get certain leverage through the years, and period. What you had in mind, Dan, is it to be a big shot in Albany? You like the snow that much, do you?"

Dante knew he wasn't being turned down or discouraged. Something very important was happening. Frankie Magee had evaluated him and had something else in mind, something Dante hadn't dared yet to consider.

He spoke in the rich baritone voice that played so well in the courtroom. "I figured Albany would be my *next* step, not my *final* step."

"Same thing, lad." Frankie leaned back in his chair and studied the ceiling. He asked quietly, "Do you own your own home, up there on Pelham Parkway?"

"Yes. Mortgaged, of course, but it's in my name. We bought it from my father-in-law a few years ago."

"Good, good. Shows serious roots in the community. You active in local civic affairs? The church, the veterans, the neighborhood improvement societies and such? The club?"

Of course he meant the Democrats. There was no other club.

Dante reeled off the number of neighborhood activities in which he was actively involved, and Frankie nodded: good; good; good; good; good.

"Well, so they know you in the congressional district, do they?"

"They know me."

"Well, let them know you better. In the community. In the club. Especially in the club, and not just during election time. *All the time.* Be a presence. Be the guy who volunteers to do anything that gets you out and around. Start doing small favors for the neighbors; move out among the people." He dug into his top drawer, searched around, then tossed a pack of rubber-banded cards to Dante. They were filled, on both sides, with names and telephone numbers. Dante glanced at the cards, then at Frankie, who never took his eyes off him. "These are the people you talk to, to get a favor done. The son into a good law school; the daughter into a nursing school; the father into a union. These are the people who make things happen. A bell going off, is it? Are you getting some idea what we're talkin' about, Mr. Prosecutor, Mr. Defender, with the fine record?"

No games, no hedging, straight out, Dante said, "United States Congress."

"You've got the background. War hero, top man at your law school, great record with the DA, man of compassion as a defense attorney. Good family on both sides. Decent, fine, hardworking father; good honest sisters and brothers all married and raising families. Any black sheep anywhere I should know about?"

"If there were, Frankie, you'd have seen to it I'd never have gotten appointed to the DA's office three years ago."

For the first time, Frankie Magee's grin erupted into a loud, respectful laugh. A sharp, tough kid. "Damn right. Them uncles of yours over on Bathgate had me a little worried, but they're just a good buncha hardworkin' Eyetalians. Now tell me something about this father-in-law of yours. I know about his altar-wine business and the real estate.

Well fixed, is he? Ready to support you, not just with his mouth but with his wallet?"

"Yes. All the way."

"Well, good then, good, Danny. Well, son, with the 1954 congressional elections coming up, you've got a little more than a year to work with. The future is gonna belong to you young fellas. The general, well, his great smile sure helped him get elected, but he's not the same as you guys. There's a good group of you all around the country, making the first move. Congressional seat."

"*First*, congressional seat. For a couple of terms, I'd say," Dante said. "And then, in due time, the Senate. And then . . . who knows?"

Seems to me *you* know, Frankie Magee thought. They relaxed, spoke of the old days, the neighborhood kids, all grown up.

They parted with a long handshake, the pressure between them hard. Frankie Magee studied the young attorney closely and nodded with recognition.

Oh, yeah. He had it, this young Italian. He had the hunger, the determination. He was a comer, all right.

CHAPTER FOURTEEN

It took Suzy Ginzburg nearly two years to make an almost complete recovery. After she was taken from the iron lung, her body shrunken and atrophied, she worked with the courage and perserverance of a world-class athlete.

"Hey, this is me, this little bag of bones. I gotta get these arms and legs going. Maybe not to dance, but for Christ's sake, I'm gonna walk, and maybe run, on my own."

Through her years at Sarah Lawrence, where she majored in fine arts, she and Megan corresponded and, on the occasional weekend, got together in Greenwich Village. She introduced Megan to her family's way of life, to an assortment of exciting and sometimes frightening bunch of people, who, despite her being a medical student, they considered their "special Bronx baby."

By the time they were in their twenties, Megan with a beginning practice, Suzy with an emerging art gallery in the Village, Suzy undertook the renovation of Megan's private life.

"My God, you don't read novels or magazines or newspapers. You don't go to the theater or concerts, or even the movies. You haven't the vaguest idea of what is going on in the *real* world. If it ain't psychiatric, for you it doesn't exist. You are a cultural zero. So, in the interests of rescuing you from your dead-end life, you *will* come to the new show I'm having Friday night. There is a certain artist, blond and gorgeous and immensely talented and funny and bright, and I want you to meet him. I'm showing four artists, and Jeffrey Madison is the best and you are going to fall in love with him instantly and proceed to do mad, dirty, unthinkable things with him or I will never speak to you again. Except to nag you to death. You will come. I absolutely command you!"

Suzy's gallery was crowded with friends and families of the artists and with critics and serious or opportunistic collectors. Megan waved to Suzy, accepted a champagne cocktail, and wandered around to see the pictures mounted in four separate sections.

Jeffrey Madison was constantly surrounded by admiring women; but when he was introduced to Megan, he squeezed her hand and whispered, "Listen, I want to come back to you, okay? Don't leave without me." He shrugged helplessly and was lost in his own crowd.

Megan caught just a glimpse of his work: bright colors, strange shapes and forms. Christ, she didn't understand any of it. She edged away from the others, put the untouched champagne down on a table, and took a deep breath. There was one section of the gallery that was virtually deserted. She studied the card: *Work of Mike Kelly*. And then the paintings. They were larger than any of the other work on display. And darker. Megan glanced from one painting to another, and then stopped short. The painting in the middle of the group, titled *Sometimes*, was a dark, brooding representation of a canyon. On one side, the rocks of the sheer wall were blackish, with jagged edges. A thin gray river ran far below. The other side of the canyon was angry purple, nearly black, with broken ledges, strange ominous rock shapes. A terrible place, devoid of hope or light, a place of desperation. Megan was uncomfortable. She hated the painting, and yet she could not move away from it. She examined the gray waters and saw a tiny touch of light. A raft? A person? It was a nightmare. The rocks seemed to move closer together, closing in on the figure in the water: a vise, crushing and relentless.

"Well, Red, you like what you see?"

She jumped. The voice was deep and harsh. No one but her father had called her "Red" since she was ten years old. She turned to confront a tall, solid man with disheveled thick black hair and a beard.

At first Megan thought he must be some bum from the Bowery who had wandered in, but he stared knowingly at the scene before them.

"I don't think this is the kind of painting that you 'like,'" she said.

"Okay, what kind of painting is it, then, Red? You seem to know what you're looking at. Go ahead. Tell me."

She was going to walk away, but there was something challenging, daring in his voice. "Okay, big boy," she said sarcastically, "it's a *terrible* picture. It makes me feel nervous. It's like looking at a nightmare." She turned then and said quietly, "You're Mike Kelly? This is your picture?"

"I'm Mike Kelly. This is my picture. It's not a nightmare. It's a state of mind."

"I didn't mean to insult you. I mean when I said it was terrible. I don't know much about art."

"But you know what you hate."

"I don't hate this; it just makes me feel . . ."

He put his large hands on her shoulders and grinned. "Well, kiddo, you've just said the best thing you could say to an artist. My work 'makes you *feel*.' Look around at all those pretty pictures. All those bright colors. Wow, they'll be bought for whatever the hell Suzy asks. They'd look great over a fireplace or in a dining room. I bet you some people will buy one of those pictures by Jeff Madison, and have their decorator work a whole room around it. Would *you* buy *my* picture?"

"Hell, no," she said quickly. "I wouldn't want to live with that . . . that *Sometimes*. What times are you referring to?"

"As the title says, 'sometimes.'"

"But when you feel that way, you wouldn't have the energy or the need to paint it. Not if it's as terrible as that. So how far up do you have to get before you can face painting a world that looks like that?"

As she studied the painting, the artist studied her. "What the hell are you, Red, a shrink?"

"As a matter of fact, yes. And don't call me Red. My name is Megan Magee. Doctor."

When she turned to face him, he put out a large, warm hand and held hers. "Well, as you know, I am Mike Kelly. How do you do, Megan Magee, Doctor? What'll I call you?"

"Don't call me anything. I think—"

"I think you and I have a lot of things to say to each other, so I guess I better call you Megan."

                    *   *   *

He pushed buttons. He teased her just enough to both infuriate and charm her. She fell back on her tomboy toughness. Okay, buddy, you wanna play, you better watch out. I'm a match for you any day.

"I want to show you something. Another side of my work. I want your professional opinion."

"I told you. I don't know anything about art. I'm not the one who—"

"You are *exactly* 'the one who.' Come on. Maybe if you're lucky I'll buy you dinner."

She went to his one-room studio/apartment. He made a great show of keeping the door open into the hallway. He had no intention of compromising her.

What he showed her was the most beautiful collection of watercolors—a set of subtle, engaging illustrations for a children's story. The characters were charming. The faces were of children, rounded, expressive, without worldliness. They were dreamy faces, wiseguy faces, tough and soft.

"Take a look at this, kid," he said, pointing to a redhead, a small girl with a raised chin, a challenging look, an I-dare-you expression. Megan looked closer. The girl had a steel brace on her left leg.

She turned to Mike. "Wrong leg, pal."

He shrugged innocently. "What, wrong leg? She's a character in my story. *I* decide which leg. Did you look like that when you were a kid? God, Megan, I love your face."

He put his hand under her chin, bent and kissed her lips. Megan pulled back.

"There's more to me than a face. In case you hadn't noticed."

Mike Kelly leaned down, pulled her braced leg into the air, making sure that if she lost her balance, a mound of pillows would break her fall. He frowned, ran his fingers over the brace, ignored her protests. He examined the brace almost clinically.

"I don't understand why this brace is so big and heavy. Hell, I could design one a lot less disabling. And lighter." He looked up and smiled. "And prettier."

Megan shoved him away. "You think this is funny? You think I'm charmed by you, you . . . you big jerk?"

Kelly's laugh was loud and genuine. He gasped, shook his head. It was a contagious laugh, and Megan couldn't help herself. She laughed at herself, at him, at both of them.

It was their first true good moment.

He was as good as his word. He designed a neater, lighter brace and consulted with a friend who did metal sculpture. He gave it to her as his gift, and, with a few adjustments, it worked. She practiced learning to walk a different way, repositioning her weight, modifying her gait.

Eventually, to his surprise, he sold his illustrated story to a major publisher. When they went out to celebrate, Megan noticed a strange quietness about Mike.

"What's going on?" she asked him.

He shook his head. "It's a cycle in my life. It has a life and rhythm of its own."

"Is *Sometimes* beginning?"

"Yes."

She moved in with him and watched him throughout the weeks of his sliding depression. He couldn't attend the small publication party in his honor. She pleaded the flu, and went in his behalf.

When she returned to his apartment, she heard a soft moaning in the dark room. She switched on the light and found him lying in a corner, hugging a pillow against his chest, nearly breathless.

She realized talking could not help him. It had nothing to do with specific things that were bothering him. When she held a marvelous review of his book out to him, he merely closed his eyes and shook his head.

She consulted with colleagues, who suggested hospitalization, electroshock therapy, intensive talk therapy. She gave him amphetamines and they brought him lower.

Megan sought out his friends, artists he had shared studios with, guys who knew him in the service. They recruited others and took turns staying with Mike, coaxing him to move. They dragged him outside, made him run, forced him to exercise, get his adrenaline going. When finally he reemerged, he didn't want to talk about any of it. He was okay now. He knew the routine; the time had passed.

Megan researched all she could about clinical depression. Very little was known about it, other than that it came on without any precipitating factor, an unexplained chemical imbalance of the brain.

Once the depression cycle passed, he soared, becoming manic and nearly violent. Finally, with his consent, Megan had him committed to a small private psychiatric hospital in New Jersey, where he remained, during one of his worst depressive cycles, in a practically catatonic state.

Finally, in an obscure medical journal Megan found an article by an Australian psychiatrist who had been having some success with the use of lithium in the treatment of manic-depressives. She corresponded with him and, with his guidance, started Mike on a regimen of lithium which, as a natural salt, was easily obtained from any lab.

It took months of monitoring and experimentation, careful blood-level tests, and finally, almost without either of them being aware of the change, the down cycles eased, becoming milder and less frequent, without any noticeable change during his more normal cycle.

Under Megan's careful and loving guidance, Mike Kelly's life belonged to him for the first time in as long as he could remember.

After knowing each other for nearly a year, and living together for a few months, they decided to get married. Mike was working on another children's book. He enjoyed his professional life and loved the pictures he worked on. The stories flowed from the pictures, and his books attracted a great following.

But first Megan had to tell her fiancé about Tim O'Connor and her abortion. She told him about the redheaded baby girl flushed away, knowing the reality, haunted by the nightmare. He held her, comforted her, loved her. Finally, quietly, feeling his fingers gently raking her short red hair, she propped herself on an elbow and told him, "There's one thing I have to tell you, Mike. It might change your mind about the whole thing. But I've got to tell you."

Mike Kelly tensed. God, now what?

"We've got to be married in St. Simon Stock. The whole thing, white wedding gown, you in striped pants, my dad handing me over to you—the whole deal. Whadda ya say?"

He groaned. "Jeez, leave it to a Catholic-school girl."

As a successful children's author–illustrator, and in an assertion of his maturity and seriousness, Mike had shaved his beard and cut his hair. Somewhat. He realized Megan's family was prepared to hate him. After all, what father was going to look kindly on a guy who lived with his daughter without benefit of clergy?

He and Frankie Magee had a serious talk in Frankie's office. It was part of the deal; he had to ask Frankie Magee for his daughter. Frankie asked him about his wartime service. Mike had been in on the invasion of Sicily, as an infantryman in Patton's army. He had a couple of medals.

And yes, he had a decent family. His mother was a homemaker, his father an insurance man; they lived in Spring Valley, New York. His sister was married to an automobile dealer, and they had three kids and lived in Connecticut.

Yes, he could support Megan. Yes, he thought it was a great idea for her to continue her practice. No, neither of them wanted to live in the suburbs. They had their eye on a brownstone in Greenwich Village. He could have his studio; she could have her office; they could have a home. Yes, they both wanted children. After a while. And yes, by God, he loved and cherished Megan. He thought she was the funniest, toughest, brightest girl he ever met in his life.

"And," he added, "we are evenly matched."

Frankie narrowed his eyes. He liked this guy, who sure seemed to like himself as well. "Well, that remains to be seen," he said, but offered his hand and wished them luck.

Secretly, he was joyous.

Having spent a year in Los Angeles, Monsignor Eugene Sebastian O'Brien received permission from his cardinal in L. A. and, with the help of Frankie Magee, permission from New York to perform the wedding of Mike Kelly and his cousin Megan.

Her mother insisted on the works: a beautiful white dress with a long, graceful train, to be held by nieces and nephews; a ring bearer, Megan's brother's four-year-old boy. Her sister, Elizabeth, was a very pregnant matron of honor, and four cousins, looking typically unhappy in terrible bridesmaids' dresses (as the theory had it, the uglier the bridesmaids, the more beautiful the bride), matched up with Mike's friends in their rented outfits. Suzy Ginsburg couldn't serve officially—she wasn't Catholic—but she showed up drop-dead gorgeous in a designer suit of blue silk. A huge wedding feast was held at the Concourse Plaza, with a couple of hundred guests—friends, families, politicians, judges, representatives from the mayor's office, even the state's lieutenant governor. Dante D'Angelo and his pregnant wife, a beautiful girl with dark, flashing eyes; Megan's cousin Charley, a fireman, attending with Ben Herskel's sister Deborah, whom he was planning to marry. There were aunts and uncles and cousins and friends.

Megan had a private moment with her Aunt Catherine, who hugged her and whispered through tears. "Thank God, baby. I want you to be happier than anyone in the world. I've loved you better than anyone I've ever know."

Being in St. Simon Stock church, built underground beneath stone staircases, dark, mysterious, lit mostly by candles, incense mixed equally with oxygen, brought Megan back to her earliest childhood. She felt the tightening of her stomach, the catch in her throat that alerted her to the presence of the Holy Mother and God's only begotten Son.

She glanced at the confessionals at the back of the church, remembering the voices of children: . . . *and I used God's name in vain seven times and I dishonored my mother and smacked my sister and cursed and oh God my very existence an abomination, my continuing existence by the grace of a living God.* Her youth was encapsulated in this place. In her lifetime she had committed two serious sins; she had never, truly, fully confessed her part in a man's death, nor her abortion. She had used words to get around both events, had manipulated each situation; and now, in this primary church of her life, all her intellectualizations deserted her. The sad statue of the Holy Mother rebuked her. The all-forgiving, tortured figure on the Cross suffered for her sins.

But she wasn't a kid anymore, and the Church was just one compartment in her life. Even this elaborate legalization of a union to which she and Mike were already committed was only a gesture to please her family.

The church was filled with people who had known her from her earliest years, and with the important people in her father's life, and with Mike's family and with their mutual friends. In the dimness, with memories and long-denied knowledge filling her, Megan, on her father's arm, felt her leg suddenly lock. She had misstepped, or caught her foot in her train, which one of the children had dropped. However it happened, Megan Magee went sprawling facedown on the aisle between the dark, well-filled pews.

A hushed gasp of shock was followed by the stark silence of tension, as Frankie rushed to help her. Mike Kelly left his assigned place at the altar, came to her side, and lifted her in his strong, capable arms. Holding her, he turned, surveyed the stunned guests, and in words that forever endeared him to Megan's father, he said, "Megan and I are going to carry each other through the rest of our lives. It's my turn now, so I'm gonna carry my bride to the altar."

It was a good start to a good marriage.

CHAPTER FIFTEEN

Charley O'Brien did a few things that surprised his family and friends. Aside from seeking out his Jewish relatives. Aside from converting to Judaism.

He took the newly announced civil service exam for the New York City Fire Department. His father and his two brothers "on the job" figured this was all part of whatever had affected Charley's mind over there in Europe. He sure wasn't the same good-natured, easygoing Charley they had all known and loved.

His father's only request to him was that he go on one good retreat with the Vincentians, and try to get his head straight, try to catch up with himself. He was, after all, a Catholic, born and baptized and confirmed. What he was planning was a foolish thing. Even his Jewish cousins thought so, didn't they?

Charley's Jewish relatives had viewed him with suspicion and alarm—especially the older ones, the brothers and sisters of his mother. Yes, he could have names and addresses, but what, exactly, was he after?

His mother's sister Rhea—her one remaining contact with her family—had died years ago. Cancer. That and heart problems ran in the family. His mother's younger sister, Harriet, actually looked much older than his mother, and did not resemble anyone Charley knew. She was a short, heavy woman, her body encircled by a dirty white apron over a thick sweater, her head covered by a woolen scarf. Between dealing with customers in her fish store, she glanced at Charley suspiciously.

"I hardly remember her. Miriam. Miri. I was so young. So she went her own way, why should I remember her? I was a child, ten years younger, maybe. And you, why do you come here anyway, what are you looking for?"

Cousins. People his own age. Faces he could recognize, bloodlines he could feel. Who the hell knew?

His cousin, Artie Kramer, a Navy veteran, had just bought a small tract house in New Jersey. He had heard about his cousin Charley O'Brien, and was delighted to meet him.

"My God," he said, "I have a first cousin who looks like you? A Charley O'Brien, for God's sake. You look like every Irish kid who ever beat me up when we lived in Queens."

Artie was a rabbi who had been a Navy chaplain. After a kosher meal provided by a curious Ruth and shared by their three children, the two men in the small backyard sat watching each other. Searching each other.

"Yes," his cousin told him, "we lost family in the Holocaust. Uncles, aunts, cousins. Of course. Everyone lost someone. All the Jews who came here left family behind. So, Charley, tell me—what is this all about?"

It took Charley a while to talk about what he had seen and felt at the camps. He shrugged heavily.

"An overwhelming experience, I'm sure. One you will remember all of your life. But to decide to become a Jew . . ."

"My mother never converted. So I was born a Jew."

"But baptized and raised a Catholic. Charley, don't hurry into anything. Seek answers in your own religion. I'd bet you practiced your religion by rote, without any real thought or feeling. I agree with your father. Go on a retreat. Search your own religion. First decide what it is you are seeking. To find God? He exists everywhere. To try to relieve some of the horror, the guilt? All of us feel guilt—we were safe from all of that. Imagine how the survivors will feel, for the rest of their lives. So what is it you really want to do?"

"I want to become a Jew. To marry a Jewish girl and to raise my children as Jews."

Artie smiled. "First, find out a little bit what being a Jew entails. With a name like O'Brien, a policeman's face—a brother who is a shining light in the Catholic Church, Charley. You can still be a good man, remaining a Catholic. To become Jewish is not a magical thing, it—"

"In the Catholic religion, there have always been saints. People who claim to have spoken with God, to have gotten messages from God. Maybe it was all psychological, all in their heads, I don't know. I never heard God's voice, but I have had this feeling that this is what I was meant to be. Jeez, I never knew I'd get so much resistance from the Jews."

"We don't proselytize, Charley. From what you've told me, you've already studied Judaism, technically, a great deal. Take some time. If after you've been home, say, a year, and reflected, and you definitely feel committed to do this, well, it would be my pleasure to prepare you, to preside at your bar mitzvah. But not now. There is no hurry. Agreed?"

On a bright April day, Charles O'Brien, age twenty-six—was bar mitzvahed at Tempel Hillel in a small new suburban town outside of Tenafly, New Jersey.

He had done everything everyone had asked of him. He had gone on a two-week Vincentian retreat; he had discussed his religious feelings with his confessor. He prayed. He agonized. And he made his well-thought-out and irrevocable decision.

It was his cousin, Rabbi Arthur Kramer, who finally accomplished the entrance of Charley O'Brien into the world of the Reformed Jews.

His brother, Gene, wrote to him from the leper colony. He didn't try to dissuade Charley, just asked him to be very careful and very sure of his motives. If, after contemplation and soul-searching, he felt truly at peace with his decision, than Gene would pray for him and ask God's blessing on Charley for his intentions. Even though he didn't agree with him.

It was the most Gene had to give him, and Charley was grateful. He didn't expect his father to attend. They hadn't spoken much about the conversion, but Charley accepted the fact that, for the first time in maybe ten years, his police captain father had to work a Saturday morning. If that was how his dad handled it, well, okay. He knew his father was hurt and bewildered, but he hadn't tried to dissuade Charley. Just asked him, as Gene had, to be sure of what he was doing.

None of his brothers or sisters attended, or any aunts or uncles on his father's side; they considered what he was doing a mortal sin, and could not be any part of it. His cousin Megan switched her shift at Bellevue to be there. She hugged him and told him she knew he must have thought about it carefully. She told him she loved him and was proud of him.

Many of his aunts and uncles and cousins from his mother's side of the family attended, though not all; the older ones were skeptical. Not so much of Charley, but what was this "Reformed Judaism," anyway? Men and women, sitting together. English spoken during the service. It was all too American to be truly Jewish.

Dressed in a new pale blue dress with a matching felt hat, Charley's mother sat down front with the Herskels. He and his mother had left much unsaid. There never had been a great need for words in his family. His mother had always been too busy for much serious discussion: raising kids, keeping house, working split shifts as a nurse. Her life was orchestrated in set patterns, around designated responsibilities: getting the kids to school, through illness, accidents, religious rites, graduations, marriages, grandchildren. The war, the fear, the chin-up letters, packages with photographs inserted among the Rice-Krispies-squares. Even the happy, tumultuous family events, holidays that were never really hers, she made into celebrations for her family and kids: Christmas and Easter and the various saints' days.

This event was different from anything she had seen in all the years of her life, since she had married the handsome young patrolman, Tom O'Brien.

Charley had explained it to her quietly. His reasons went bone-deep. It hadn't been just the horror of the camps. It was something that had been missing in his life without his ever realizing its absence. And he was reclaiming something now that by right of birth belonged to him. It would not tear the family apart; they were all adults now. They would have to accept him on his terms. As she had accepted them on theirs.

Charley listened to the prayers in the synagogue, felt the rhythm of the words inside his very soul.

"And you who cling to the Lord your God are all alive today."

Then he was given his Hebrew name, Yechezkel, for his public entrance into the fellowship of Judaism.

His voice was a clear and bell-like tenor, his pronunciation careful and exact:

"Bor'chu es adonoy ha-m'voroch."

The congregation responded with the prescribed words and then Charley continued in Hebrew, as every Jewish boy through the ages had done: *"Boruch attoh, adonoy eloheynu, melech ho-olom, asher bochar bonu*

*mikkol ho-ammeem, v'nosan lonu es toroso. Boruch attoh, adonoy, noseyn
ha'toroh.''*

And then, "I have chosen to read from the prophet Isaiah:

> "Thy sun shall no more go down,
>   Neither shall thy moon withdraw itself;
>   For the Lord shall be thine everlasting light,
>   And the days of thy mourning shall be ended.
>   Thy people also shall be righteous
>   They shall inherit the land forever;
>   The branch of My planting, the work of My hands,
>   Wherein I glory.
>   The smallest shall become a thousand,
>   And the least a mighty nation;
>   I the Lord with hasten it in its time."

Charley closed the section he had read, took a deep breath, and
addressed the congregation, his eyes moving automatically to his
mother.

"Today I join the community of Judaism as a man returning from a
long journey. It is a true return home for me. As my mother followed
Naomi's admonition and followed her husband, as Ruth did, I now
return to the congregation. She raised her children to be good and
loving and to believe in the Lord. She always respected her husband and
her children's beliefs, and it is through my mother that I return here
today, as a man and as a Jew."

His cousin, Rabbi Arthur Kramer, pointed to the reading on the
podium, and in a clear strong voice Charley finished the ancient
ceremony.

*"Boruch attoh, adonoy eloheynu, melech ho-olom, asher nosan lonu toras
emes, v'chay-yey olom nota b'socheynu. Boruch attoh, adonoy, noseyn
ha'toroh.''*

There was a small buffet luncheon at Artie's home, and three of
his cousins, men in their forties, cornered Charley and presented him
with three fountain pens.

"Now," said Herb, the oldest, "*now* you're one of us."

Deborah Herskel embraced him, and they walked through the
celebration arm in arm. The next important event, everyone knew,
would be the wedding of these two young people.

Finally his mother approached him. She embraced him and then pulled back.

"What, Mom, what is it?"

"Charley," she said softly, her face radiant, "you are my redemption."

His decision to accept appointment to the fire department rather than to become a policeman was puzzling to those of his family who were cops, but not to those who were firemen.

Throughout his growing-up years, within both his immediate and his extended family, among all his parents' friends, neighbors, and acquaintances, most of the men were in one department or the other. The verbal rivalry and kidding between the two camps sometimes turned hard and edged on nastiness, but the men were careful to stop short, given the home setting of their conversations.

Firemen, according to the cops, were "checker-players and cooks," thieves who waited for that one big fire in a mansion or jewelry store or furrier's with maybe thirty minutes unaccounted for when they could load up whatever they could carry, and then get on with official business.

Policemen, on the other hand, were blue-suited gangsters with one hand out front, one behind, wishing they had a third to fill with graft. Fill it up, sucker, or answer for violations, real or not, that encircled every small business enterprise of any kind—any small corner grocery store, luncheonette, shoeshine parlor, not to mention the corner taverns and after-hours bars and dives; the gambling in backrooms; the faked robberies for insurance, *and don't think you're fooling us, bub*. Without even suggesting the take from department stores: *Hey, know why Murphy the cop's kids always dress in the latest Alexander's fashions? Yeah, because he got transferred out of Manhattan, and Saks Fifth gotta take care of their local boys, don't they?*

But it wasn't the roughhouse kidding, the ridicule, the barely concealed anger that occasionally got out of hand, that stayed with Charley.

What he remembered were the calm, reflective, story-telling times when these men related what their jobs really entailed. Charley had listened and remembered and thought a great deal about what the differences were between the cops and the firemen.

The cops, the guys "on the job"—as though that were the only job in the world, as though those three words defined an entire life that anyone would understand—the words spoke of violence, of fights, of riots, of beatings downstairs at the "house," where everyone had a go at the bastard, who wasn't so tough by court time the next day. Of the many culprits who "fell down the stairs." ("Jeez, sometime soon we gotta fix up them fuckin' stairs.")

Some of their stories were funny; actually, they were howlers, better than the silly stuff you heard on the radio each week. So many of them were great storytellers. They impersonated voices, stood up, moved around, played all the roles.

They talked about nooses hanging from beams that collapsed, taking part of the ceiling with them, and a poor bastard who thought he was gonna be finished ended up only half-choked and in line to be sued for damages by a furious landlord.

They told about arriving at the scene of a suicide where a young woman, whatever her problem, had jumped from the roof of a six-story building. Her divorced parents showed up and stood over the decapitated corpse—the girl hit some electric lines going down—and argued loudly. Whose fault was this? Who should have done what and now, who was going to take over? In effect, whose busted-up corpse was this, whose dead girl was this? The storyteller recalled that it was an oldtimer, Tommy Halloran, on the scene. ("Jesus, remember him? He was always a pisser.") So Tommy took all the shit he was gonna take and finally he just goes over and gives the head a shove with his foot, and then pokes the body with his foot. "Here," says Tommy. "This part's yours, Mom, that part's yours, Dad."

The men convulsed over Tommy Halloran. ("Jesus, dead these many years; won't be one like him again.")

The firemen told different kinds of stories. They weren't as determined that each recitation have a beginning, a middle, and an end. Sure, they had their share of hilarious firehouse high jinks. The taming of the newest kid, the endless attempted comeuppances of the best practical joker ever born, who always managed to top everyone anyway. But their stories lacked the meanness and small-spiritedness Charley heard in the stories of the policemen. And when they talked about the job, he heard a different sound.

They spoke of rescues, attempted rescues, failed rescues.

Someone told the story of old Uncle Matthew, who nearly killed a uniformed cop. It was at one of those damn fires started by neglected kids in the middle of Harlem. No father around, the mother off doing God knows what with God knows who, and four little kids playing in their top-floor tenement bedroom with kitchen matches. Standard toy for those little colored kids left on their own. Not a very tough fire—hell, pretty routine, until the mother showed up, counted three kids, and pointed toward the smoky, steaming building. The smallest kid had been missed in the thick black smoke. Again, not unheard of, one forgotten lost little colored kid left behind by the huge rubber-coated and booted men who hadn't a clue about how many lived where.

Uncle Matthew and a couple of other guys went up the big ladder, back into the blackness, and he, leading, found the kid under what was left of the crib. A small child, unburned, a somewhat melted rubber duck clutched in tiny hands locked over the still chest. Matthew ripped the toy away, held the little arms aside, breathed for the child. Breathe, baby. That was what mattered, not a replaceable toy. Breathe. All the way down the ladder, Matthew breathed for the child, his mouth gulping air and delivering it to the nonfunctioning lungs of the dead child. He knew, they all knew, it was useless. The kid was dead of smoke inhalation, but you did it anyway. You tried. Goddamm it, baby, breathe. Sweat, and finally tears of utter frustration, ran down Matthew's face as his breath became more and more labored. His lieutenant put a hand on Matthew's shoulder.

"All over, kid. C'mon. Let it alone."

Matthew nodded. He knew. He gently laid the small, suffocated body down on a folded edge of dropcloth, wiped his forehead with his wet sleeve, and looked squarely at the child for the first time. Two years old, maybe, light brown skin, open mouth showing pearly white little teeth, eyes unfocused but bright, glowing.

A patrolman who had been assisting with traffic control, who didn't smell of steaming wet rubber, hot smoke, or anything else, came over for a look. With the tip of his shiny black shoe, he carefully poked at the cheek of the dead child, turning the face so he could get a closer look.

"Jeez, pretty enough little kid," he said. "For a nigger, that is."

Matthew rose with a roar. It took two uniformed cops and three of his own buddies to pry him off the cop, and a few more of his mates to hustle him back to the engine. There was no question in anyone's mind that Matthew had fully intended to kill the cop. Who would never understand why.

And it wasn't that Matthew spoke or thought or felt any differently about the coloreds than anyone else. It was something that none of them articulated but all of them understood. It had to do with a one-on-one battle against death, with an inexplicable covenant with life. Your breath into the suffocated, sharing your life-force, defeating the searing, indiscriminate destroyer: Fire. It had nothing to do with race or color or sex or age. It had everything to do with the most primitive, powerful assertion of life.

Like most of the young men in his class, veterans in good physical shape, competitively bright, Charley loved the training course. He felt strong and capable and ready.

His first fire-related injury came toward the end of his first full year as a fireman. He hadn't personally saved anyone, though his crew, as a team, had saved lives, had rescued kids and old folks. It had been a kitchen fire on the top floor of a five-story building on Creston Avenue in the Bronx. A decent, middle-class building of neatly kept apartments. Panic had led a family of four to all the wrong moves: flinging open doors, creating a chimney for the fire to sweep through the flat. The crew came through the windows from the ladders, brought families from the now-burning building to safety, brought in the big hoses, had it all under control.

Charley helped to evacuate the building; everyone seemed accounted for, no one screamed, *My baby, my baby.* But instinct told him to sweep the third floor one more time. Hell, the kids might have had a pal over before supper and forgotten him in the excitement. In the smoky hallway, Charley heard what at first sounded like a cough, then became a snuffle. Low to the floor, gasping at the remaining oxygen, he crept in the blackness toward the sound within the apartment, reached under a bed, and pulled out a large, bony, shaking young dog, who collapsed in Charley's arms. Automatically he breathed into the animal's nose and mouth, his brain pounding: *Live. Live. Live.* He was so intent on what he was doing that he miscalculated the time he had left to get out safely. A wall caved in and Charley, still holding and cradling the dog, still sharing whatever air he could find, folded instinctively into the fetal position, clutching the dog to his body. He was conscious as he was lifted to the stretcher and watched as the family grabbed at the revived mutt, hugged and cried and yelled with relief.

He woke up in Fordham Hospital to be told his injury was a lucky one. Yeah, he would have a burn scar on the outside of his right arm, from elbow to wrist, but what the hell? Every fireman, sooner or later, experiences some kind of injury.

His crew visited him and regaled him with one horror story after another of seared lungs, melted faces, broken backs. What no one had prepared him for was the unspeakable pain, which he never forgot, not ever. Which he carried into every fire he ever attended, and which reinforced his normally strong determination to save any life facing that exquisite pain. An injury, he thought, made a good fireman a better fireman.

His picture was on the front page of the *Bronx Home News*, the *Mirror*, the *Daily News*, and the *Journal-American*.

There was his picture, grinning weakly in the hospital bed, and there was a picture of the rescued dog, being hugged by the family. And there his nickname was born: Snuffy O'Brien.

His life in the fire department reinforced his childhood impressions of the firemen and the cops and their "war stories." He'd had the sense that most cops didn't really love their jobs, were putting in their twenty, counting off how many years they had until retirement, while the guys who were with the fire department considered their jobs the truest part of their lives.

He never met a fireman, at any age or in any condition, disabled or lung-damaged, who wouldn't respond to that bell in a minute if he could.

There seemed to be an almost amorphous connection in Charley's mind between his commitment to fighting fires and his memory of the burnt remains of the thousands of corpses he had seen during his time at Auschwitz. He shared his powerful life-force with those he could save, in some way easing his pain for those no one had saved.

Charley O'Brien and Deborah Herskel were married at the Tremont Temple, Reformed, in the Bronx. For the first time since he had gone to Israel, Ben Herskel, at thirty-two serving as an assistant to a cabinet minister of the Israeli parliament, came home to the Bronx to attend the wedding and to introduce his wife to his family.

The two young men studied each other. Charley's smile was not as quick and easy as Ben's. There was a seriousness about him that Ben understood. They shared a memory that would forever define them. Ben seemed older than his years. He felt overwhelmed at the abundance of everything material in the Bronx—food and cars and clothing, toys for children, disposable items; in Israel everything was carefully garnered. The wartime U.S. admonition, "Use it up, wear it out, make it do, or do without," applied even in peace in his adopted country, with no change in the foreseeable future.

Ben's body had thickened, his hairline had receded. He hoisted his trouser leg to show Charley a not-bad prosthesis.

"We've got more doctors per square inch in Israel than you've got trees on the Grand Concourse. Life may be hard, but it's certainly exciting. There's a different kind of Jew being born and raised in Israel, a biblical warrior Jew. Maybe one day, now that you're one of us, you'll come and see for yourself."

Everyone was in awe of Ben's wife. A tall, well-built, beautiful, strong girl who disdained makeup, wore her honeyed hair pulled back off her face, she regarded the Bronx with mild interest and apparent distaste. Within days of her visit, she just about convinced the older Herskels that life in Israel would be just the thing for them. To be near their grandchildren. Well, only one grandchild right now, a boy too young to travel such a great distance, but there would be more children. In Israel, children were the most treasured people of all. And for older people there was no boring retirement, but an active, fruitful life.

At the wedding reception, the Herskel and O'Brien families mixed easily. After all, the bride and groom had grown up together, even if, as kids, they had ignored each other. The two mothers had had their secret Friday nights. There was good-natured joking and good food and good liquor.

Ben could not believe that Megan Magee was now Dr. Megan Magee Kelly. The little tomboy, with a hint of the impish kid she had been, was a married professional with a tall, beaming husband who wrote and illustrated children's books. Hey, they would be useful in Israel, too. Come and visit us.

He pulled up his trouser leg, compared her new lightweight brace with his own handsome artificial leg.

"God, they did a good job, Ben. You're really lucky. You don't even limp."

Ben grinned. "Come to Israel—we'll fix you up with a sexy leg to match your other one." He leered playfully, then pinched her arm, one of the guys.

Ben's wife liked Megan; women should get out in the world and accomplish whatever their intelligence allowed. And they should marry men with enough good sense to appreciate them.

Eva glanced at her husband with manifest pride. "He is a hero in Israel, you know. Imagine, a military tactitian coming from such a peaceful place as this. Ben wasn't able physically to lead the troops, but during the War of Independence, his planning—"

Her husband placed his hand over her mouth. "In Israel, we are *all* military geniuses. And politicians." He turned at the touch on his back, then embraced Dante D'Angelo.

As the two men spoke earnestly, catching up on their mutual political careers, Eva spoke quietly with Megan.

"He doesn't look as young as the rest of you. Ben has much responsibility. He will be an important man in our government." She watched Ben and Dante talking, gesturing, laughing. "As I think this Dante will be an important man in your country." Eva narrowed her eyes, making a decision. Then, she confided to Megan, "Ben has had heavy responsibility, from his days at the Nuremberg trials. He has carried inside of him much information that has been instrumental in bringing to justice—of one kind or another—many of the criminals who were 'liberated' by your government." Then, softly, she said, "I tell you this because Ben has told me about his childhood, about you and the wonderful girl you were. I am glad you shared his childhood. Especially since you went on with your own life, on your own terms. That cannot have been easy, in a world always dominated by men."

Megan shrugged. "What about you? Ben told me you were a captain in the army. And a pilot. You've no idea what that means to me. A childhood ambition . . . to fly a plane."

Eva laughed. "It is not all that dramatic. Women are used as ferry pilots. It is like anything else in life, one does what one has to do. And that beautiful black-haired woman over there by Ben and Dante—Dante's wife?"

Lucia-Bianca was aglow with her third pregnancy, tall and carrying small as she always had. For a second, Megan felt a wave of something—some unresolved feeling—gone as quickly as it had come.

"Yeah, that's Lucia-Bianca. Not only beautiful, but absolutely brilliant."

"And what does she do with her brilliance?" Eva asked pointedly.

Megan grinned and took her arm. "She keeps Dante happy!"

CHAPTER SIXTEEN

Among the many lessons Willie Paycek learned in Hollywood was how easily illusion could substitute for reality.

When he finished cutting his first legitimate movie, a very low-budget "small picture," he changed his name to Willie Peace. His company was Peace Productions, and his first theme was the transition of one small town from wartime to peace. There were many high-cost productions dealing with the same subject, with major stars agonizing through the process of return. Willie Peace's movie took the point of view of one small man, the town postmaster, wounded and held in a Japanese prison camp for three years. He returned changed in every way imaginable, and his agony increases as the townspeople, his family, the friends he went to school with, recognize no change beyond an evident physical weariness.

The hero marries his childhood sweetheart, takes out a GI loan, buys the old Johnson house they have always dreamed of, and gets on with his life. The postwar dream, the good American life, the hard-earned rewards, all seem to fall into place. The film ends on an apparently happy note, but with an extreme closeup of the returning soldier's face, and the camera seems to look right through his eyes into his deadened soul. This is a man serving time until his death.

Not too many people saw the movie. Only a few reviewers caught it, but one or two took note. This was an interesting film, not what it seemed at first glance. This was a film that worked on many levels. Remember the name: Willie Peace.

As his films grew and his financing increased, attention began to focus on Willie Peace. His movies were never what they seemed. The man had an uncanny way of seeing, through the eye of the camera, into the heart of a man or a woman. One of his most successful films was about a woman who lived a perfectly normal, ordinary life. A good daughter, a good wife, a good mother, a good neighbor. A decent woman. But in her fantasy life, she was all things: a whore, a heroine, an adventurer, a murderer, a saint, a savior, a mother of heroes, a leader of armies. Through the unwinding of the film, the woman's interior life began to spill over into her reality until the two parts of her life became indistinguishable. It was a puzzle. Was her role of good woman—daughter, wife, mother—part of her dream, just another figment of her imagination? What was reality, what was fantasy? The film did not answer the question, and some reviewers, as well as the average weekly moviegoers, were angry and felt cheated and confused. Tell a story, for God's sake, and stop playing games.

But a movie by Willie Peace—written, produced, and directed—became something special. It attracted attention, passion, anger, and admiration. Who the hell was this guy, anyway?

Willie Peace was a handsome young man in his early thirties, who, with the first real money available to him, had made significant changes in his life.

He sent his wife, Maryanne the whore, off to Mexico for a divorce. He provided her with enough money to stay away for a year, during which she obtained the divorce, married a Mexican shopkeeper, and bore a dark-skinned child with light gray eyes.

Her oldest son, Daniel William Paycek, was a handsome, bewildered child, bright and quick, who learned to speak Spanish in order to survive. His stepfather drank heavily, and the children—there were several more through the years—had to be fast on their feet. Their home was filled with chaos, violence, drunken orgies. The brighter ones somehow managed to survive. Danny was smartest of all; he kept his eyes open, storing away all that he saw and heard. He was more than just a mere survivor.

Danny Paycek was nearly twelve when his newly widowed mother took him and her four other kids back to East Los Angeles. When she tried to find Willie Paycek, it was as though he had disappeared off the face of the earth.

She knew no one named Willie Peace. She did not go to the movies, would not have made any connection if she did, and would not have recognized him if they met. He had changed many things about his life and himself.

Her former husband, however, knew every move she made, and he watched and waited. Not out of any interest in Maryanne, but out of curiosity; he wanted to see what would become of her oldest son.

Though not a particularly bright woman, Maryanne was a shrewd survivor. She made a meager living at first, charging for what she had given away free as a girl. She realized that Hollywood men wanted youth and slenderness, as well as a semblance of innocence, in their nightly encounters. They were in Hollywood; even the whores should be beautiful, magical. Maryanne didn't have too much trouble recruiting among the young, hungry, desperate would-be movie stars. She was kind and motherly and provided them with a safe haven: room, board, and spending money. Most important, she gave them a base, an address, a phone number where they could be reached when the magical call came from "the studio." She had rented a large old frame house in East Los Angeles, and she screened her clientele, as much for her own safety as for the safety of the girls. She wanted to maintain a low profile, to avoid trouble. This was a moderately priced, clean whorehouse that doubled as a boardinghouse for young actresses, for girls hoping to break into the business. A few actually did get studio employment from time to time. Those who did gave hope to all the others. In the meantime, Maryanne ran a clean, safe place.

Sometimes Danny Paycek, a tall, well-built boy of fourteen, pimped. He also screened clients; he was available, very visible, in case of difficulties. He was bright and handsome and helped his mother keep her books and made sure the profit margin made it all worthwhile. He had a good head. He was too smart, worldly, and sophisticated for high school, and because no one checked on him, while his younger brothers and sisters attended grade school, Danny dropped out of high school. He had other interests.

Maryanne had a shrewd eye and a peasant's sophistication. Occasionally she gave massages at fancy country clubs for women and, if asked, would work at their homes. She sensed in the thin, tense, artificially beautiful women a hunger born of neglect. For weeks at a time they were deserted by their successful husbands on location, at the studio, in emergency meetings, on trips to New York. They were left in their magnificent homes, furnished down to the last inch of space with whatever some decorator said was "the latest thing." They could shop, play cards and tennis, have lunch, gossip, get massages. Take lovers.

She didn't identify Danny as her son, but as a wonderful, strong, beautiful, kind young friend of hers. Eighteen or nineteen, she wasn't certain, but his wisdom and maturity had nothing to do with age.

She pimped for her son, giving Danny, at fifteen, entré into many of the most beautiful estates in Beverly Hills. Women adored him, showered him with presents—jewelry, clothing, tennis lessons—anything he wanted or they imagined he wanted, in addition to the money they slipped into his trousers pocket.

When he tired of a woman, or sensed she had tired of him, they worked their scam, Danny and his mother. They called it "the big kiss-off."

At a prearranged time, Maryanne would enter the house through the unlocked door, following her son's directions, and head directly for the bedroom. There she would find, to her horror, her fifteen-year-old son being seduced by a middle-aged woman.

The claim that she had arranged the original liaison was a complete misunderstanding: she thought her *child* had been hired to clean the pool, to tidy the tennis court, to scrub the marble floor, polish the plate-glass windows.

There was not only a special place in hell for the corrupter of childhood, but there was, Maryanne explained, a place in the penal code of the County of Los Angeles. Maybe Madame wouldn't be sent to prison, if this was her first offense, but just think of the publicity. Think of her reputation, her husband's ruined career. She'd have to go back to some small town in Tennessee, if they'd have her. My God, to think she had delivered her innocent young boy into such corrupt hands.

Danny and Maryanne took cash—no jewelry, no checks, no promises to pay. It was strictly cash, from the bedroom to the bank, cash in hand and good-bye, lady.

And by the way, should you mention this whole episode to anyone at all, let's say to your lady friends, as a warning, why, then the whole thing would be blown wide open. The exchange of money would be denied. You would be accused of handing over this poor fifteen-year-old for sexual exploitation by your rich idle, corrupting friends.

No one ever talked.

*   *   *

And her ex-husband, the former Willie Paycek, knew everything that was going on. He gathered information from a collection of would-be actors, writers, all those young people who worked as maids and baby-sitters and drivers; who taught the rich kids how to swim and dance and ride; who listened and observed and reported to Willie, who rewarded them with a day's work, a recommendation—a *chance*. He filed away data, bits and pieces, names and dates and places, in the incredible bank of his brain. He knew who and when, and how much at the end. He thought the boy a remarkable operator. He considered Maryanne no more than a clever whore who now used her son's body, since her own was unacceptable.

The most significant physical changes the new Willie Peace achieved were through the services of a good plastic surgeon, at whose office he arrived carrying an eight-by-ten glossy of Alan Ladd. The surgeon studied the photograph, and then the contours of his patient's face. There was some good bone structure, despite the uncorrected broken nose. The slightly crossed left eye could be fixed by a good eye surgeon, whom he could recommend. The lank, colorless hair could be bleached and styled so that a soft light wave would fall naturally over the newly dyed, dark eyebrows. His pale coloring could be suntanned; his lips were full, and he must stop biting them. The procedures would not be pleasant, but not overly painful either. The results would be worth the discomfort, of that he could rest assured.

And he did, in fact, emerge looking very much like his favorite movie star.

A custom shoemaker provided him with invisible lifts that added a good two inches to his five-foot-five-inch stature—Alan Ladd's exact height. Exercise and body-building trimmed and firmed and shaped him so that his custom clothes, both for dress and casual wear, showed off a good tight body with a firm torso. He learned not to slouch, to stand as tall as he could, head held high, viewing the world through handsome, expensive, tinted aviator glasses that added some mystery to his face.

And he learned when to maintain a silence. He taught himself to stop babbling nervously. When he was tense, he breathed deeply in a relaxing, cleansing manner he had been taught. *Never let the other guy know you are tense. Keep the upper hand, the cool, calm exterior.* He cultivated a slightly sinister manner. It was hard to know what Willie Peace was thinking when he disappeared into his increasingly well-known staring silences.

No one actually knew the murderous rages he experienced. He kept all anger and fury deep inside himself. He realized that the more stillness he showed, the more maneuverable others around him became. When he worked on a Peace project, regardless of the funding, there was one power, one force behind every aspect of the production, a power and force he had developed through a lifetime of neglect and rejection. It was a form of getting even with the world at large. Individual scores could be settled one at a time. Willie Peace kept quiet score.

He came into his office very early one Sunday morning, giving himself two hours before his staff arrived. He wanted to go over current production figures. His control depended on his total familiarity with every facet of the work.

Until he switched the radio on, he had forgotten it was Sunday morning. Seated at his desk, he stretched, rubbed his eyes, waited for the music, and felt irritated at the preachy voice over background organ music. He got up, went to the windowsill to snap the radio off, but stopped, his fingers on the dial, and listened.

". . . Monsignor Eugene O'Brien, just recently back from the leper colony at Gabon, will speak to us this morning. Monsignor, representing the Society for the Propagation of the Faith, will speak to us about . . ."

The introduction went on and on, filling Willie's memory with fumes of incense, recalling the smoky dimness, the candles, the darkness of the church. The next voice surprised him and he leaned on his elbows, listening.

"I went into the leper colony filled with pride. After all, I had been a very important assistant to a cardinal. I had spent five years at the Vatican, involved in the most worldly aspects of our Church, surrounded by comfort and privilege. It was for my pride that I was sent. It was in search of humility and closeness to God that I spent my days.

"I would like to take the theme of my talk this morning from a question asked of me by a child, seven years old, dying slowly of the terrible disease of leprosy. His fingers were stumps; his feet were gone; all that was left of his face were two glittering bright eyes that could no longer blink. His lips were gone so that his teeth shone in a perpetual grin—a death's-head smile. I spoke to the child for a moment. I prayed for him without really seeing him. It was too painful a sight. I felt afflicted by the damage before me. I wanted to turn away. I wanted to be somewhere—anywhere—else.

"After I prayed, I forced myself to look upon this child's wasted body, his damaged face. When he spoke, his voice was so soft, so hoarse, I had to lean forward, inhaling the terrible odor of impending death, breathe his breath, his presence, his condition, into my own being.

"'Father,'" he whispered, "'I know that God loves me, but how can I love Him better?'

"This wasted child, this destroyed little body, with all the reason in the world to despair, this blameless child *acknowledged*, accepted unquestionably, without a moment's doubt, from his bed of pain, the love of Our Lord. His concern was not for himself, not for his situation, but for the grace of his soul. *'How can I love God better?'*

"I thought of my own initial anger and resentment at being sent to this terrible place; of the loss of luxuries I had accepted as a daily right; of the prestige that had been accorded me. How easy it had been there, under those circumstances, to love God, to *say* I loved God unconditionally, as this child was able to do from his ragged bed of pain.

"This dying child was in a state of grace so rare, so incredibly beautiful, that he took my breath away. I felt humbled and devastated, not for *his* physical condition but for the deplorable condition of *my* soul."

He went on for another fifteen minutes. The thrust of the whole thing, of course, was a plea for funds. The Church's various charities must be funded. The victims of disease and poverty could be helped not just through prayer, but with medication, doctoring, bedding, sanitation, better food.

It was not what Eugene O'Brien said, though his words were powerful. It was his voice, the musicality, the pitch, the rising and falling. My God, Willie Peace thought, my God, Gene is incredible. He has a marvelous voice, a skilled actor's delivery. He remembered how handsome Gene had been as a young boy. Was he still handsome? Had he matured out of his beauty or into it?

He would have to see for himself.

Monsignor O'Brien was a very popular guest speaker at breakfasts, lunches, and dinners. He was comfortable on the dais, flanked by the rulers of the Hollywood industry. He was casual, polite, but unimpressed by the beautiful movie stars who sought his attention. He developed an easy, meaningless repartee that served him for all public occasions, and although he gained a reputation as a poised and powerful speaker, very few could recall his actual message. They gave huge amounts of money to the Church solely because of the presence of the gorgeous priest.

At the end of an LAPD Holy Name Society Breakfast, where the politicians rather than the moguls held sway, Willie Peace sat quietly at the table for ten for which he had paid. He was on good terms with working cops; he used them as extras, security, and sources of information. He had watched carefully as the guest speaker rose, comfortable with this crowd. The monsignor told them he was the son of a police captain and the nephew of a policeman. That immediately established him as "family" to the assembly. He complimented their organization, praised their work and their spiritual leader. His talk was brisk and to the point. He had a few good things to say about Senator Joe McCarthy, and warned them of the necessity to be vigilant against the Communists and their hidden conspiracies. Especially out here, in Hollywood, the leading shaper of public attitudes. Things could be slipped in so easily, influencing the innocent and the unsuspecting. It was their responsibility as Catholics to be especially watchful.

They loved him and cheered his message, which was quite different from the speeches he delivered in other settings.

So Gene was not only articulate, he was shrewd. A savvy guy, whose looks, through time, had fulfilled the promise of his youth.

He was beautiful in the way of the camera-perfect star. From almost every angle, his pale, high-cheekboned, fine-featured face seemed flawless. His hair was thick and pure white; his eyebrows were dark and well shaped; his eyes, fringed by thick, dark lashes, were strangely colorless: pure round circles of ice with pinpoint pupils that seemed to bore into the object of his gaze. His smile was easy, his white teeth were dazzling. He used his hands sparingly, but with effect.

The guy was an actor, with a voice that was deep and compelling, and he had a feel for phrasing. He was a natural.

Willie waited until the admiring crowd of policemen had had their moments, shaking hands, congratulating the monsignor, thanking him, assuring him of their commitment to Catholicism and against Communism. Willie edged along with the crowd, following close behind as the priest headed skillfully toward the door, his smile including everyone, his departure timed carefully to offend no one. Just before he reached for his expensive black coat, which was handed to him by a young priest, Willie Peace touched his shoulder. Gene turned politely, the smile ready, the coat already slipped on.

"Gene, you really know how to deliver to your audience," Willie said.

If the overfamiliarity annoyed him, the priest showed nothing but a bland smile, a slight nod, a politely mouthed, automatic "Thank you."

"I've got a check here I wanted to give you myself."

He handed over the check, which Gene automatically handed off to his young assistant, without looking at it.

"Thank you so much." He extended his hand, which gave a quick, hard, practiced shake, then he looked slightly startled when the small, neat man didn't release him.

"Don't you know me, Gene? I guess I've changed a lot more than you. Jeez, you look as young as you did on Ryer Avenue. Just as sharp, maybe a little taller, but then, to short guys like me, you O'Briens always looked like giants."

The voice seemed vaguely familiar, a voice from the past, but the articulation was different, devoid of the Bronx sound, flattened into the universal middle-American usage of most of Hollywood. He bit his lip, shook his head slightly, then stared intently.

"Willie? Not Willie Paycek? Willie, out here, in Hollywood?"

"The same, Father Gene. Only not really the same." He pulled off his glasses, lifted the chin, offered himself for inspection. "A few improvements, but it's still me. Changed the name, too. I'm Willie Peace now, Gene."

"Well, that's a good name: Peace. Willie Peace. Why is that familiar to me?"

For the first time, the kid from the Bronx emerged from behind the pleasant features. He ran a hand through his straight blond hair. The grin showed good teeth: no more gray, broken, neglected horrors.

"I'm a producer, Father Gene." He named his two latest pictures. "So far, no problems with the Legion of Decency."

"Glad to hear that. Have you a family, Willie?"

"Footloose and fancy-free. This is a different world out here. You don't have to marry your high school sweetheart and stay in *that* mess for the rest of your life. Hey, no offense, okay? It's just a different world out here. I guess we've both found that out, huh?"

They spoke vaguely of the Bronx, of family ties that, in Willie's case, had been broken long ago, but were maintained long-distance by Gene. Finally, as he carefully prepared to make his departure, Gene realized there was something specific that this new Willie wanted from him.

"I'd like to make an appointment with you, Gene. There is something I've been thinking about since I first heard you on the radio one Sunday morning. That's why I came to this breakfast. I wanted to see you in person. I'm doing some television work now. Some kids' programming that's been doing very well. And I think you are wasting your time doing these small fund-raisers day after day. How many of these lousy breakfasts and chicken dinners can you eat? I can show you a way to reach millions—literally millions—of people at one shot."

Gene O'Brien gazed thoughtfully at Willie. "Call my assistant, Father Randall, for an appointment." He gestured to the young priest, who handed Willie a card. "Good to see you, Willie." And then, smiling: "Willie Paycek, my God. Sorry, Willie *Peace*. A good name. I'll have to get used to it. And to your new look, Willie Peace."

"And I'll have to learn to call you Monsignor."

"Gene will be fine. After all, we were boys together."

"Yeah, we were." Willie nodded abruptly and was the one to walk away first, but then he stopped and turned back.

"Oh, by the way, Gene," he said casually, "the check I gave your priest here. It's my *personal* check. For your children's fund. *Ten thousand dollars*. See ya."

CHAPTER SEVENTEEN

Within the next year, there was a most astonishing, magical connection made between Eugene O'Brien and the eye of the television camera. He seemed to enter into another dimension of life as he stood for a motionless moment, letting the camera find him, and then, with an almost imperceptible nod, as though to a long-sought soul mate, he began to speak.

At first, television executives groaned. They couldn't believe it—one hour of a talking head? And a *religious* talking head, at that? Just this guy, with a chair and a lectern, without guests, without notes, spouting pious platitudes at the Catholics in the country, turning off the Midwest, the Bible Belt, the tight-assed Northeast? In prime time? Willie Peace might be a helluva good producer, with all his movies and his Saturday-morning kids' shows, but Jesus! "Monsignor Eugene O'Brien Welcomes You"?

They hadn't known what to expect. They hadn't seen Gene O'Brien. And when the rest of the country, by the second or third week—maybe because of the interesting reviews, or word of mouth, or just for the hell of it—gave him a quick look, they stayed with him.

It was as though the man had been made for the medium, the medium for the man. His image could not have been more effective; he wore simple priestly black and a clean white collar. His white hair reflected too much light and had to be just slightly sprayed down. He consented to face makeup when told that, with his fair complexion, he would be lost under the lights. But it was his eyes that mesmerized the fascinated audience. And his voice, mellifluous, forming ordinary words into beautiful sounds. He was a natural, in total control of a still-new medium. For one hour before the camera, another entity took over his beautiful presence, limited his long pale hands to careful, graceful motions. His pauses were as meaningful as his words; his timing was superb.

He spoke to a country that was in a hopeful, growing mood, that wanted to hear about possibilities and dreams. His cautionary words reminded them they did not live in a perfect world, although they had suffered through four years of war and were anxious to get on with their perfect lives in the exciting postwar time of growth and change in the good old U.S.A.

"There is a new war, or rather a continuing war, for hearts and minds. An insidious enemy that we must encounter, recognize, and expose, individually and as a nation."

He spoke of the Communist threat—how it affected every aspect of our daily lives through subtle propaganda disseminated in novels, newspaper columns, movies, and radio and television. He told his audience of new ways to listen, to read, to understand. He told them about the Washington hearings, the Hollywood Ten, the potentially devastating writers and professors who were, even as he spoke, corrupting the innocence of our youth.

That was his favorite theme: Communism.

But he always ended on a warm, joyous note. He spoke again of the small leper who asked, "How can I love God better?"

"He didn't ask for a deal with God. You know what I mean. Schoolchildren pray 'God, just let me pass this math test and I will do such-and-such for you.' Businessmen pray, 'God, just let me make this deal and I'll give x number of dollars to the church.'"

He spoke lightly, with humor, with understanding of human foibles. He implicated himself; he was a sinner, he could not stand comparison with the unblemished love of that dying child. It would forever be his measuring rod on which he would forever fall short.

"But we must try. Truly. No matter how far short we fall of that total purity of love offered by the dying child, we must *try*, to the best of our abilities, to love God."

He ended with a long, penetrating gaze directly into the hearts and souls of his unseen audience. "I will pray for you for the grace of God. I ask that you pray for me. Thank you and God bless you."

Fade out on the mysterious, beautiful face of Monsignor O'Brien.

He had commercial sponsors waiting in the wings. The price for a minute of advertising on his program matched and topped any price commanded by the most popular entertainment shows.

When he spoke of the need for contributions to maintain missionary posts, when he spoke about the need for new parochial schools and for university education for the teaching nuns, when he spoke about the necessity to convince young men to enter the priesthood and the funds needed for their recruitment, education, and preparation, the funds came in from all over the country.

He was a much-sought-after guest at the fanciest of Hollywood fund-raisers, and would consent to appear only after a guaranteed donation to the Society for the Propagation of the Faith. He was sought after also by both Jews and Protestants. This was no Father Coughlin, teaching hate and disruption. This was a thoroughly American voice, and checks were gladly given to aid his vast interests.

There was a major change in the production of his show. A new producer, Church assigned, took over.

Willie Peace, moving toward more and more experimental motion pictures, more explicit films, was proscribed by the Legion of Decency. He agreed to export his pictures to Europe, where the standards were looser.

Willie began showing up at Hollywood parties with a beautiful young Irish would-be actress, a girl named Ellen McDougal. She was eighteen, black-haired and blue-eyed, and spoke with a marvelous, musical lilt. Slender, graceful, intelligent, and deeply religious, she had left her home and family in Dublin, when she had won a talent contest sponsored by a local beer brewer. It just happened that a Hollywood company was shooting scenes in and around Dublin—a historical romance set in the eighteenth century. As a publicity stunt, the movie company added to the brewer's prize—five hundred pounds—and awarded the girl a trip to Hollywood and a guaranteed screen test as her prize.

Reluctantly, the girl's family allowed her to pursue her dream. She came to America, to the arms of a welcoming Irish-American family of distant relatives. A young aunt accompanied her across the country, and

the two young women showed up for the promised screen test. The
movie company was bankrupt, and no one was about to reimburse them
for their travel expenses.

Ellen McDougal would not return to Dublin to admit that she'd been
taken. She was not a quitter or a whiner. She remained in Hollywood
after reassuring her reluctant aunt that she would be fine, having found
a job as a receptionist-typist for a talent agency. The aunt returned to
the Bronx with misgivings, but reassured of her niece's morals.

Willie met Ellen McDougal one day when he was recruiting child
singers and dancers for his Saturday-morning show, which he continued
producing because it brought him easy money and security.

Everything was special about this girl. She was the *real thing*. A
perfect, storybook girl, bright and virginal. She was both untouched and
untouchable, and Willie carefully charmed and cultivated her. For the
first time in his life, dating became something to be treasured—pure
enjoyment.

Willie led her about the studios, let her watch the process of
filmmaking and television production. He showed her the Hollywood
tourist sights and the sights that tourists never got to see. He told her
stories, true and embellished, about legendary stars. He dazzled her and
did not even try to seduce her; she'd made it clear from the very start
that she was a good Catholic girl.

For the first time in his life, Willie was totally, overwhelmingly in
love with a girl who seemed to return his devotion. He wanted
desperately to marry her. She had abandoned all childhood dreams of
being in the movies. Willie told her about any number of professional
jobs associated with movies—safe jobs relying on ability, technical jobs,
union-protected—and then gave her a job as a production assistant in
his Saturday-morning company. She worked with the talented kids and
took to it wholeheartedly. It was what she wanted to do, for a while.
She loved kids.

And she loved Willie.

There was one obstacle. Ellen McDougal would only consider
marriage in the Church. Willie, his Mexican divorce from Maryanne
long forgotten and never mentioned, had not taken communion for
years. That marriage had to be annulled or there could be no wedding
with Ellen McDougal. It was just that simple.

Willie's feelings about the Church were ambivalent. But the answer
flashed through him quickly: find some dinky little church, get on a
Saturday-night line, give a quick version of a confession, without

getting into hard specifics, do his penance, and take Ellen to church that Sunday morning, a true penitent newly returned to his Church.

He would forget the snuff movie, the beautiful black girl, the bloody head of the blond stud. That had happened a long time ago. And after all, *he* hadn't killed them. There was no undoing any of it, no going back and changing things. In fact, he wouldn't if he could. It was the snuff movie that had made the rest of his life possible.

The simple, logical thing would be just to forget it. He had a lot of other usual shit to confess. Who the hell would know the difference, or care? Not some overworked Mexican priest down in the *barrio*.

God would know.

It wasn't exactly that Willie believed in God. It was more that he was afraid not to. He was, after all, a born-and-raised Catholic. The confessional, next to communion, was the most sacred rite. Better to avoid it altogether than to lie. You could skip quickly over a lot of the usual shit—adultery, lying, cheating, blah-blah-blah—but something like taking part in a murder? Shit.

God would know.

The Catholic boy deep within Willie would not permit him to do what he had originally planned: take communion without confession and what the hell. He just could not do it.

He picked his confessor. Someone who would understand. Someone who had been, more or less, in his situation. After all, they went back a long way. All the way back to a winter night on a cold hill in the Bronx.

When he approached Gene after a particularly wonderful show, Gene, exultant, carried by the passion and emotion of his sermon, shrugged him off.

"Willie, come on. I'm not your parish priest. I haven't heard confessions for years. Besides, it wouldn't be right somehow. We are associates. There isn't the anonymity of a good confessor."

Not friends. *Associates.*

Willie insisted. "I want to marry this girl, Gene. She is the purest, most wonderful young woman. I've never touched her; I've never felt like this before about any woman. She is a sincere, dedicated Catholic, and I want to be worthy of her."

Gene studied the supplicant. A trace of Willie Paycek still trembled beneath the handsome even features and modulated voice. There was a slight wheedling tone if you listened closely, a strong degree of manipulation. But Gene also detected an earnestness and sincerity he found difficult to refuse.

Gene relented. He dimmed the lights; gave instructions not to be disturbed. Willie had insisted: "Please, Gene, right here, right now. Don't let me waver; don't let me change my mind. I want to do the right thing, right now."

They sat on chairs, not facing each other, and went through the ancient, familiar opening litany and prayers. Both fell naturally into the assigned roles of priest and supplicant.

Many years since his last confession, followed by a litany of sins, leading closer and closer to what both men knew to be the reason for this confession.

First, though, he told about his marriage to Maryanne. Lying about a thing like that wasn't really a sin, just expedient, necessary, something to get out of the way. They had eloped, after a quick Bronx service in a small, unfamiliar rectory by an unknown priest, to Hollywood.

After Maryanne obtained a Mexican divorce, Willie had applied for an annulment through church channels. He had no doubt about the outcome, it was all in motion.

"But on what grounds, Willie?"

The marriage had never been consummated.

"But I heard you had a child."

"She was pregnant when I married her, Father. By someone else. I never asked who. I didn't even know, for sure, that she was really pregnant. I did it for money. From some people I can't mention. As a favor. And they sent us out here and helped me get set in the Teamsters' union. And I never touched her. I felt nothing for her. I did it to help out some people. And in a way, to help out the girl. She was pathetic, so I figured, what's the difference to me? I got what I wanted out of it. So we didn't really live together; she went to Mexico years ago and got a divorce and married some guy there and had some kids with him. Nothing at all to do with me, so I'm expecting my petition to be granted. Never, *never* touched her, Father."

"You used the sacred ritual of marriage for your own ends? To get to Hollywood, to get a good job?"

"I confess to that. Yes, Father. I knew it was wrong."

"But you realize you can't marry this girl Ellen until that is all cleared up. It might take a long time."

"However long it takes, we'll wait. She understands that."

After a few minutes, Gene, his hands over his eyes, intoned the familiar prod of the confessor. "Anything else, my son?"

And then Willie told him about the snuff movie. Matter-of-factly, he described how he supplied the girl, the script; how he shot the movie, recorded the actual murder. For which he was well paid.

Gene stared in horror. "Did you *know*, Willie, all along, that this was the way it was going to be? *Did you know, Willie?*"

Willie hesitated. Then, what the hell. "Yeah. I knew. That was the purpose of the whole thing. It was quality, but it was a real snuff movie."

"You took part in the murder of this young girl? And the young man?"

"Well, no, *I* didn't kill either of them. The other guy did, this Arab big shot or whoever he was, the guy who financed the whole thing. I only—"

"Willie, you are responsible, particularly for the girl's death. You *recruited* her. You knowingly set her up to be killed. You knew. You are guilty of her murder. Surely you know that."

Willie shrugged. "Yeah, well, that's why I'm here. I'm really sorry about all of it. The girl, the guy, all of it."

Eugene stood up abruptly. "What do you want from me? Absolution? For a horrible double murder? Surely you didn't think that I would—"

"Look, Father, I'm here to confess. You know 'I heartily despise my sins'? I want to do penance. I want to get right with, you know, God and the Church. I want to be able to take communion with . . . what the hell did the nuns call it, 'with a pure heart.'"

Gene stared at him. "Do you feel genuine remorse for what you did to this girl, for what was done to this young man?"

"Sure. Sure I do, Gene. That's why I'm here. To make it right with God. You know."

Gene took a deep breath, then sat down and leaned forward, speaking directly to Willie, who tried to avoid his gaze. "Willie, what you have to do is go to the authorities. To the police. Tell them what you've told me. Do you have a copy of this . . . film?"

"Yeah, sure I do. But what good would that do? I don't even know where the bodies are. I—"

"Willie, there are two things involved here. Your confession to God and your hope for redemption. And, second, your involvement in a terrible crime. It can't be 'handled' here, in this room. There is no way I can grant you absolution at this point. Surely you know that."

Willie's voice went low and harsh as his body stiffened. The Bronx kid emerged from the Hollywood-handsome face. Paycek emerged. "Why not, Gene? What the fuck, it was done for you, wasn't it?"

There was a stark silence between the two men as each remembered a battered, bleeding man lying in the icy snow. Gene met Willie's furious intensity for a moment, then looked away.

"Willie, *we* didn't kill Stachiew. Your father did. What we boys did was defend ourselves, and then we ran away. And then your father came along."

"We *boys* and your little cousin, Megan the doctor, right? You all made out pretty good, didn't ya? Danny a lawyer—now a congressman. Ben some kinda bigshot in Israel. Me, a leading talent in Hollywood, with a future wide open. You, with the Church and the country in the palm of your hand. Jeez, your brother Charley's the only one settling for being a nobody. Well, I guess one big shot in the family's enough." He stood up and glared at Gene. "The church took care of you, Gene, and I want you to take care of me. I want absolution, no strings attached. That's what they gave you. Look at you now, best-known priest in the country, maybe in the world. And *I* did that for you, kiddo. I made you "the television priest." I took you off the chickenshit suppers and soggy-pancake breakfasts and gave you the whole country to collect millions of dollars from." His voice softened, became earnest, pleading. "Gene, I have a real chance with this little girl. She's the best thing that ever happened to me. I want to marry her in the Church and get on with my life. Isn't that what the Church is all about—to give a sinner a second chance? Look, it's just you and me here, and you got God's power, He gave you the right—so, Gene, come on. Let's get on with it. Gimme a second chance."

He met the implacable stare as Gene slowly shook his head from side to side.

"Damn you, Gene. They did it for you, but you won't do it for me? Shit, how about when my old man fried? Didn't you count that as murder number two, the old man sizzling for something *we* did? Hell, they let you off the hook for that one too, right? So that you could be their pretty-boy priest. Gene, listen. You better—"

Gene said quietly, "Willie, I think you'd better go. I can't give you absolution. I think, however, somehow, there is some hope for you. Obviously, you sincerely want to return to the Church, for whatever reason. You believe enough to know you can't fake your way to a return. It is also pretty obvious to me, however, that you have no remorse, no moral regret whatsoever, for the people who were murdered with your collusion. Willie, you're not beyond redemption, but you have to start legally, and then you have to approach your confession through a true sense of spiritual remorse. There's nothing I can do for you now, Willie."

Finally, Willie stood up, paced the small dressing room, whirled around, and said, "Well, maybe there's something *I* can do to *you*, Gene. Maybe I can shake your boat. How'd you like the world to know that their wonderful Mr. Terrific TV Priest was nothing but a punk murderer, and maybe hear the reason why you personally got involved? Remember, Gene? Remember why, pretty boy? Stachiew had some body on him, didn't he? Did he teach you to give it or take it, Gene? I've always wondered."

Eugene, standing six-foot-two, towering over Willie, his face stiff, his voice controlled and soft, said, "Willie, get out of here. Right now. I don't want to hear another word from you. You do whatever you feel you have to do, but don't you threaten me. Just get the hell out of here."

Willie left. The hate burned hard. He'd get even. Not right now. He felt himself in too much jeopardy, even though he knew Gene couldn't reveal anything he'd said. It could wait. He would plan it and do it right when the time came.

Willie Paycek was a boy who knew how to wait. And how to get even.

Ellen McDougal, reconciled to the fact that she could not, ever, marry Willie Peace in a church wedding, returned home to Dublin. She had lived through her shattered dream of Hollywood stardom. Why, she could still sing and dance at the local church or pub at home, where the people could be trusted and where her family would be around her. She missed the softness of the voices of home, and the mist and dampness and the incredible green of the hills and fields and the quietness of her world. She had had enough of the sun and the tanned, thin, frantic faces and the scheming and the planning and the fakery and the broken promises.

She realized she did not have the driving ambition required to survive in Willie's world.

She had no idea how deeply he truly loved her, but she felt her own love of him turn to indifference. She was more anxious to return home than she would have believed possible.

After she left, of course, Willie was not long at a loss for female companionship.

His highly rated children's Saturday-morning live talent show, hosted by a bright, saucy, precocious twelve-year-old, led to his downfall and exile.

The child's mother, a starlet who seemed to accept that her dream of stardom would be limited to her child's achievements, moved into Willie's Beverly Hills star-home. Along with her daughter.

They were a threesome.

The mother, a slender but now tired-looking redhead, thought she had Willie's promise of a shot at the star role in his next movie, to be filmed in France. She was mistaken. Was he responsible for her misconceptions?

She went to the most vicious gossip columnist in Hollywood, a woman who lived for the big story. Willie Peace, she said, had tricked her; he had asked her to move into his mansion, had given her and her daughter an entirely separate wing. There the child could have singing, acting and dancing lessons, as well as the tutoring in school subjects mandated by law. It seemed a sensible setup; it made the child's life more contained, more normal. All her lessons in one place.

But then, the tearful woman said, the abuse began. The child didn't tell her right away; she was terrified of Willie. He was a powerful man in the industry, and he could destroy all of the child's dreams.

It wasn't until Willie turned his attentions to the mother, forced himself into her bed, that the hysterical child rushed to her mother's side, whacking at Willie with a golf club, screaming, "You raped me, but you won't rape my mommy!"

Before the story broke, Willie Peace was in Paris, arriving to work on his planned movie. He had moved as much of his wealth as he could to Europe. He was glad he'd had the foresight to open a Swiss bank account years ago. He had no intention of returning to the United States to stand trial on the accusation of rape and child abuse.

The future of Gene O'Brien's show was never at issue. His highly rated show was now produced by another well-known producer, one who had been thoroughly investigated and accepted by the Catholic Church.

The child star of the Saturday-morning kiddie revue went on to star in a series of poorly made porn movies, along with her mother. She was not twelve years old, as had been believed, but eighteen. Her mother was actually closer to forty, and together they were known in the porn trade as a hot property. Hell, these two, mother and daughter, would do anything to anyone, alone, together, whatever—as long as you paid them enough.

The case against Willie Peace was dropped. The two women had mysteriously come into an unspecified sum of money from an unspecified source.

When Willie finished producing his most artistically acclaimed film in France, he wrote to Monsignor O'Brien, expressing pleasure that the filthy case had been dropped.

Monsignor Eugene O'Brien never answered the letter.

CHAPTER EIGHTEEN

Megan was puzzled at first. The voice on the phone wasn't familiar, although the name certainly was.

"Of course, Willie. It isn't Paycek anymore, right? It's Peace?"

He was pleased. "Well, hey, I wasn't sure you'd make the connection. I've been working in Europe for a couple of years, but now I'm back home in the good old U.S. of A. You know the old saying, home is where the heart is, right?"

She tried to picture Willie Paycek, a grown man of forty. All she could visualize was a small, squinty-eyed, gray-looking kid with a shifty manner. He came right to the point of his call.

"I have this screenplay with me. That's why I'm on the East Coast, trying to raise some backing. It's different from all my other projects, and I don't want the usual Hollywood people involved. It's sort of a psychological drama, Megan, that's why I'm calling you. I'd like you to read it for me, before I take it around to the money guys. I want to make sure it's technically, psychologically correct. I do research on all my work, but I really want an informed opinion on this. So, since I'm here in New York, I thought of you. You've got quite a reputation in your field, Megan. I've read a couple of your articles; and you lecture and teach and all that, am I right?"

She was stunned. How the hell would he know any of that? She was gaining a certain reputation, but not on any greater scale than any other fairly ambitious, hard-working professional in her field.

"So, I'd like you to read it and give me your opinion."

Megan protested. She knew nothing about screenwriting. She wasn't an expert on psychological drama. Surely he knew people who did this kind of thing professionally.

"Yeah, but you see," he said, "when I pay for an opinion, I get the opinion I pay for, understand? You're the ideal person to read this for me. No ax to grind. And you'll bring a fresh approach to it—non-Hollywood, objective. Megan, I'd really appreciate it." And then, as though telling her a secret that would hold special meaning or interest for her, he added, "It's about a father and son."

Out of curiosity, she agreed to read it. In little more than a hundred pages, it told the story of a father-and-son robbery team, up against hard times and fairly new at their trade, in desperate straits for money. The son has a gun, which he promises not to use; he wants it for backup, just in case. The jewelry store is closed and deserted at midnight. No one in sight, but the theft backfires. As they exit the store, a passerby, walking his dog, confronts them suddenly. There is a brief struggle. Desperately, the father wrenches the gun from his son's grasp. A struggle ensues between the father and the stranger. A shot rings out. The passerby falls, seemingly mortally wounded, as his dog whines piteously over him. The son takes the gun from his father's bare hands, holds it in his own gloved hands, tells the father to run; go home. I'll take care of things here; meet you later.

When the father is out of sight, the son, realizing the man is still alive, leans down and fires a shot into his head, then shoots the whimpering dog. He drops the gun and leaves the scene.

Eventually the father, having been traced via an anonymous phone call to the murder scene—his fingerprints on the death weapon—is tried, convicted, and sentenced to the electric chair. He believes, completely, that he actually committed the murder. He finally admits his guilt, and spends days getting right with his Church and his God. He is prepared to meet his fate; he is reconciled to his punishment.

The night before his execution, he is visited by his son in his death cell. In a scene of terrible cruelty, the son tells the father not only that *he* killed the man, who was only stunned by the first shot, but also that he framed his father and reveled in his conviction and impending execution.

Payback for a lifetime of cruelty. And thank you, Pop, for once in your life protecting me. Not telling anyone I was with you that night. You bastard, as though you could make up to me for a lifetime of your vicious abuse.

The father, who has been stoically anticipating his impending death, loses control, screaming, striking out at his son, sobbing as the stunned guards fight to restrain him and rescue the younger man from serious injury.

The movie ended with what was called "CU on Son": the expression of a victorious, vindicated man who has seen all the scores of his life settled in one joyous last encounter with a hated father.

Megan finished reading the screenplay and shuddered. She wondered about Willie. About his father. Had anything anywhere near this scene *actually* taken place, or was this the abused child's final, fantasized revenge against a monstrous childhood? In either event, she was awed by Willie Paycek Peace and his grasp of the emotional implications of the story.

He had insisted they meet in a very expensive French restaurant in midtown. She could bring her husband if she wished; he'd like to meet the famous children's book writer and illustrator. But Megan saw nothing unusual about dining with another man on her own. This meeting was of no concern, or interest, to her husband. She and Mike led their own professional lives; so she spared her husband, and herself, the strain of a group meeting, and had Willie make a reservation for two.

He looked, as Gene had told her years ago, more like Alan Ladd than Alan Ladd. She noticed heads turn, saw people whisper, puzzled, yes or no? It was eerie. He was movie-star handsome and affected a careful, bland pattern of speech. Standing straight, he was a good two inches taller than Megan, and every inch of him was easy and self-assured. His dark suit was obviously expensive, his tie was of a heavy silk, his wristwatch a flashy gold. He smiled, showing a flash of white teeth, dazzling, unfamiliar.

"You didn't recognize me, did you? C'mon, admit it."

Megan nodded. "I admit it. I never would have known you, Willie."

"I'd have known you. Some people never really change. Same short red hair, same freckles, and of course . . ." He stopped himself, but it seemed a deliberate blunder.

"Yep. Still wearing a brace on the same old leg. It's okay, Willie, I've lived with this for a long time now."

"But you do seem different—your limp, I mean. It isn't as bad as it used to be. Has there been some improvement? Is that possible?"

Megan brushed the subject aside quickly. "New kind of brace."

The maitre d', smiling, pleasant, obviously familiar with Willie, led them to a table in the corner, where Willie directed Megan to a chair across from him.

She studied him frankly and grinned. "God, it's amazing."

"Yeah, considering they didn't have much to work with."

"No, that's not really what I meant, Willie. But, God, you do look good, really. You look . . . happy. Are you happy, Willie?"

"Hey, I got it all," he said easily. "That stupid mess, with that lying dame and her lying daughter—its all straightened out. You heard about that? It was in all the papers."

She nodded.

"And I got my own production company, so many movie prospects I can't even start to choose. How about I order for both of us? I've been here a few times, I know the kitchen."

She realized this was important to him. She thanked him, lavished praise on whatever was put in front of her, whether she liked it or not. The food didn't interest her; Willie fascinated her.

Yeah. He'd been married—twice, in fact. Not counting that first fiasco in-name-only with whats-her-name, you remember her? He had two kids by each subsequent marriage, and another kid or two, so it was claimed, by a girlfriend or two. Who knows? Everybody's got a scam. He had a nice new girlfriend; no more marriage for him. Life was lived differently in his worlds, in Europe and on the West Coast. He believed in the fast lane; get while the getting was good, because it didn't last forever, right?

Hey, the neighborhood kids had all turned out pretty good, hadn't they—the Ryer Avenue gang.

"Jeez, look at Danny D'Angelo. Quite a step up from shoemaker's son to newly elected senator from New York. What the hell, maybe Danny would be the first Italian-American President. What a background: war hero, assistant DA, successful private practice, U.S. congressman. Married to the gorgeous, bright daughter of a wealthy Italian wine merchant and real-estate bigwig. And now he has three little daughters."

Megan was amazed—and a little uneasy, without knowing why. "You sure seem to know a lot about Danny."

"I keep track," Willie said quietly, "of those people who interest me. People I grew up with, especially. After all, how many people grow up with someone who might become President? And that Ben. Benny Herskel. Another smart Ryer Avenue kid. I don't know how the hell he managed, after he got hit so bad by that bomb."

"Ben has managed quite well."

Willie knew all about Ben, it seemed—about all of them.

"Member of the Israeli parliament, right? That's a step in the right direction. I guess as long as a guy's got his brains, he doesn't need all his arms and legs. Boy, wouldn't it be something if one day Dante was President here, and Benny was Prime Minister of Israel?"

"Yeah. We've all come a long way, Willie. *You've* certainly been successful."

But he wasn't finished informing her yet. "And your cousin Gene. Back in Rome now, isn't he? Probably gonna be made a bishop any day now, and then, one day, cardinal, and who the hell knows? Maybe the first American Pope. How's that for a kid from the Bronx?" He tapped his fork for a moment on his nearly empty plate. "And you, of course, Megan. Not only a doctor, but a psychiatrist. You sure didn't follow the normal neighborhood-girl route." He paused, as though deciding whether or not to ask the question. "Do you think, Megan, you'd have gone on to medical school and all if, you know, you hadn't gotten polio? Would you have gotten married right away, right out of high school, like your old pal—Patsy, right? And just settled down to the *normal* life of all the other girls you grew up with?"

"We'll never know, will we? Things are the way they are. You've sure kept tabs on us, Willie. I was surprised you knew so much about my career. My articles—on women's rights and things—aren't really that well known."

"Oh, I read magazines, all kinds of stuff. Keeps me up to date. Funny how, of all of us, only Charley is a flat-out failure. A fireman, for Christ's sake. Not much of a move up from his father's generation."

"As a matter of fact," Megan said coldly, "Charley is a lieutenant in the fire department. And the happily married father of three great kids who adore him. And he is the happiest, most well-adjusted guy I know. How can you call that failure? You've got a funny measuring device, Willie. Doesn't happiness count?"

Willie shifted easily into a neutral tone. "I guess I'm talking in relative terms. Measured against how the rest of us Ryer Avenue kids turned out."

With an effort, Megan relaxed, offered a smile. "Well, look at you,

Willie. The janitor's kid all grown up to be a movie mogul. You've done everything but act. Ever think of that—acting?''

Willie smiled back a cold, wolfish glint of teeth. "Why, I act every day of my life, Megan. Don't we all?"

Carefully she said, "To some extent. I guess so."

"Yeah," he said softly, leading the conversation back where he wanted it. "We were quite a group, the Ryer Avenue kids." He hesitated, then leaned toward her and asked, "You ever think about that night, Megan? On Snake Hill?"

Megan took a careful sip of white wine, put the glass down, and wiped her lips, raised her brows. "What night was that, Willie?"

"Ah. So that's the way it is. Okay by me." He seemed to shift gears, relinquish the past, get to the present. "So now tell me. What did you think about my screenplay?"

As a newcomer to reading scripts, she told him, she'd had a little difficulty at first with the form; but yes, she came to a point where she could visualize what she read, and when she did, it seemed to become a movie. It was very powerful stuff. Yes, psychologically correct. Yes, she said, the action of the son toward the father was credible, a form of patricide, as old as mythology.

Willie beamed. "Great. I'm gratified, Megan; I'm very thankful. Now, here's what I'd like you to do for me, Megan. On your letterhead, I'd like you to write that down. That it is valid psychologically, that in your opinion as a psychiatrist—"

Megan interrupted him sharply. "Hold it, Willie. I said I would read it and discuss it with you. Period. It would not be professional for me, as a psychiatrist, to involve myself in this."

He snapped his fingers. "Easiest thing in the world, Megan. Just a short letter. I'd just use it to show to prospective backers, who would want to be sure it's correct, and would be impressed as hell by your credentials and—"

"Willie. No way. Hell, you could get that kind of letter from anyone out on the West Coast. Surely you know people."

For the first time his voice went low—street-kid tough and smart. "I know people all over. All kinds of sources who can give me all kinds of information. You're becoming pretty well known, Megan; don't be modest. I think one day you'll be the most important woman shrink in the country. Listen, I could get from you what I can't get from the professional yes-men on the coast. Megan, listen, I would make it well worth your while. I have contacts with God knows how many movie stars and big-shot executives who freak out when they come east because they have to leave their shrinks behind. People who will pay outrageous fees just to have someone sit and reassure them, for fifty minutes at a time, that, yes, they're still beautiful, still desirable, still talented, still wanted. You have the credentials; I can supply you with patients who can double or triple your normal fee, and they'd eat it up. These nut cases are very lavish with their presents—you wouldn't believe it. You'd be an easy street, Megan."

"Willie, you don't seem to get it. I'm not for sale. Thanks a lot for respecting my opinion. I told you what I thought of your manuscript, which is what I said I'd do. I have a pretty full schedule, with my private patients and teaching assignments, and lectures and articles and some VA work. My professional life is well in hand. So that's it, okay? Thanks a lot, but no thanks."

Willie Paycek from Ryer Avenue appeared, as if from her memory, through the handsomely crafted face; the angry, desperate boy hunched toward her, his speech patterns finally familiar, his old personality reemerging whole.

"I'm asking for a *favor*, Megan. For old time's sake. As a *friend*."

She shook her head. "We were never friends, Willie. And I've given you my answer, so knock it off."

He pulled his lips back into a bitter grimace. "You're just the same, aren't you Megan? Just what the fuck makes you think you're better than me? Your degrees? Your old man's connections? Your family? Listen, you're still the same crippled kid everyone made things easy for, that's what you are. I didn't ask much from you, but you really enjoyed turning me down, didn't ya, Megan? Well, I remember things and people, and I have ways of finding out things about all of you. I got a latch on all of your friends, your pals, your cousins and buddies from the old days. I got stuff on all of you. I gave you a chance to do something for me, not for nothing. I was willing to do you some real good. I could do plenty for you. Huh, crippled little Megan with the peg leg everyone's supposed to pretend isn't there. That how you deal with it? And your husband, how does he deal with it? Can't be very nice, having a wife who—"

Megan pulled herself to her feet. She felt suddenly awkward, angry at herself for being clumsy in front of him. In the voice of a furious, tough twelve-year-old, she surprised herself. Her words came spontaneously. "Willie, go fuck yourself!"

He watched with some satisfaction as she laboriously worked her way through the narrow aisles between the closely placed tables.

"I can also *do* plenty of things *to* you. Someday," he whispered to himself. "Someday. All of you. Same lousy bastards you always were. *Bastards.*"

Years later, when *The Dark Night* was produced in France, it became not only an instant hit, a prize-winner in every competition in which it was entered, but the prison film against which all future prison films would be measured and found wanting.

The Dark Night became a classic—Willie Paycek Peace's masterpiece.

CHAPTER NINETEEN

The last time Megan had seen Patsy Wagner was at her wedding to Randolph Fenton, nearly twenty years ago. The phone call, early in the morning, had been strange. It wasn't just the words; her voice was bright and chipper, and slightly manic.

"Boy, I wasn't sure you'd even remember me. I don't know, I've been thinking about you—us—lately, and I'm going to be in Manhattan later today and I've never even seen Greenwich Village. I can't believe you actually live there. I thought it was all a big tourist attraction—but to actually live there!" And then a long silence, and then the distress became evident not just in the voice but in the words. "Megan, could we have lunch today? Or just get together, maybe for an hour or so? Megan?"

She hadn't changed very much physically. Within minutes the thin, pretty face with the dark blue eyes and the perfect nose, the slightly tough mouth, became the Patsy of old, still slender and wiry.

Everything else about her was unknown to Megan Magee.

Patsy scanned the room, glancing at the clutter of magazines and books and paintings, at the pillows thrown around casually. It was obviously not what she was used to.

With a grin, she said, "This place looks like something in a magazine room makeover—*before*." She put her hand over her mouth, shook her head. "Oh, God, Megan, I'm sorry. I'm not at my best right now. I seem to pop out with things I should just keep my mouth shut about."

Quietly, Megan asked, "Do you like this room? Find it comfortable and flat-out a mess?"

Patsy looked around, flopped into an easy chair, hugged a huge pillow against her body. "Ummm. It's comfortable. So . . . *safe*. Informal. My God. My house is decorator perfect. Even the kids' rooms. Enough storage that everything can be scooped up at the end of the day, and there's no sign left of anyone actually living there." As though talking to herself, she added, "Even the kids' rooms. All in order."

"That's an interesting word to use—*safe*."

"Hey, c'mon, Megan don't start playing shrink with me, okay?"

"I *am* a shrink. I don't play at it. Okay, you're right. I have to remember when to turn it off." Casually, she reached over and handed Patsy one of Mike's latest books. "Do you recognize this?"

She smiled suddenly, a relaxed, warm smile. "Yes, of course. Mike Kelly. His books are wonderful. They're fun, so human. My kids were raised on Seuss and Kelly. Do you know him?" She hunched forward. "Is he a patient of yours?"

Megan grinned. "He's my husband. He has his studio on the top floor, and I have my office right here. This room. We live in the rest of the house."

Patsy looked astonished, as though Megan were talking about another world. "You're married? But . . . I found you listed in the telephone book as Dr. Megan *Magee*."

"I kept my professional name. After all, I had been building a practice before I got married. Professionally, I use Magee. Otherwise, I'm Mrs. Kelly. We have a son, Jordan. He's nearly ten." Without knowing she was going to do it, Megan reached down, patted her braced leg. "You didn't think old Pegleg Megan would ever get anyone to marry her?"

"Oh, Megan, God. I never called you anything like that. No. It's just—how can you use your maiden name? Doesn't he—Mike, your husband—object? You have your own separate life? I mean, my God, you're famous. You write all those articles and give lectures and things. How did you get so lucky?"

Megan watched her closely, picking up clues. "Mike doesn't *let* me.

It isn't for him to give me *permission*. We're two adults. He's my husband, not my keeper."

"But who takes care of things? The house, your kid, the cleaning and cooking, the planning, the entertaining, all of that?"

"We have a cleaning woman once a week." She glanced around. "She's no dynamo, but she is reliable. We take turns getting Jordan back and forth to wherever he's supposed to be. We work it out. As for cooking, I gotta tell you. I can't wait for Jordan to take his turn. He's pretty good at salads and some basics, and Mike is a *much* better cook than I am. And, my God, there are enough restaurants within walking distance, we could eat out every night for a month and never eat the same food twice. Not that they're all wonderful—God, every kook with an apron and a pot seems to try things out down here. That's the Village. Very laid back. What's wrong? You look confused."

"This is very different from my life. Oh, we all read what's-her-name, Betty Friedan—*The Feminine Mystique*. Frankly, I can't buy into most of it. But some of your articles about women—I've read them in the supermarket magazines—they're really interesting. Make you stop and think."

Megan had begun recently to write for popular magazines rather than just the professional medical journals. She wanted to reach a wider audience, not just the stuffy, critical, threatened world of her male colleagues. She went for the most readily accessible outlet—the largest-circulation women's magazines—to tell women that times were changing, that they were growing up to be adults. They had a right to be full partners, a right to a piece of the world.

"But I don't know anyone who actually lives the way you write about. Women going back to college, planning for regular careers when their kids are grown. Thinking . . . about themselves. Not in Lloyd's Neck, anyway."

"Well, I guess suburbia has its own pace and its own rules. God, looking at you, I bet you play tennis three times a week and beat everybody you play."

Patsy smiled bitterly. "I ran out of women opponents a long time ago, and I don't play men anymore—they can't take it, being beaten by a woman. It's just not the 'done thing.' I guess we have our rules, even if nobody calls them that. My normal weight is about a hundred and ten, for instance. I never go over that, at least when I'm not pregnant. We're all slim, all well groomed, wear the latest clothes, entertain to the hilt. Our kids are cookie-cutter kids, all good at everything. We get them to swimming lessons and tennis and Little League, the girls to

Brownies, the boys to Scouts. There are dance classes and art classes . . . well, I don't imagine it's all that much different in the city. You must do pretty much the same for your son."

Megan shook her head. "He's a city kid. We manage. He seems happy. He's a good student and a good athlete. He goes to a good private school, but they don't emphasize competitive sports very much."

"Ah, that's the word, kiddo—*competitive*. God, we compete about anything in my little world. If you come up with a recipe, you'd kill before you'd share it with your best friend. One woman found out her kid's IQ was one-sixty. You can't imagine how often the subject of intelligence tests pops up in her conversation.

"Mostly, we try to be subtle. Sort of casually mention our husband's new promotion, our new car, how much money the damn new cleaning woman wants.

"And I'll tell you the dirtiest secret. No matter how great your newest success is—it's only perfect if your best friend just failed at something. Nice, huh? Aren't we great? *Jesus!*"

"Which is a way of saying life's too short not to live it, at least in some respects, the way you want to. Right?"

Patsy hugged the pillow against her again. Megan studied her old childhood friend. She looked for the nearly forgotten face, remembered the high-spirited, tough, determined young girl, who took any dare, any challenge. What she saw was a desperate and defeated woman.

"Patsy, you've got a lot of things on your mind. I think you could use some help. We all do from time to time. I get the feeling you're about to explode. Have you had any therapy? It's not as hard as you think, once you get started."

"Therapy? Yeah, I had therapy. I went to this old guy, with his picture of Freud staring straight down at me from the wall. This was after my third kid was born, in less than four years. I felt tired all the time. I felt like a prisoner. Know what this sonofabitch asked me? He asked me what I wanted out of life. He told me I had everything any woman in the world would envy. A husband who worked hard to give me a beautiful home; pretty, healthy kids; nice friends. What more could a woman want? I told him I didn't know. I thought maybe I was missing out on something. Maybe I should think about going back to school, just take some night courses—you're for that, right? So, someday, when the kids were older, I could get a job. Start a little business of my own. You know what he asked me? Did I want to wear the pants in the family? Maybe my husband should stay home, wear a skirt, be a housewife? He told me to stop putting myself first, and think more about my husband and children. That was a woman's greatest role, most fulfilling place in life. He told me to put things into perspective; to count my blessings, weigh them against my discontent. Then he suggested that if I really needed time away from the household—everyone did from time to time—I should buy myself a gorgeous nightgown, get my hair done, buy some new perfume and makeup, and have my husband take me away, just the two of us, to a wonderful hotel suite in the city, or a lodge upstate, where I could be a wonderful lover to him. Maybe try something new. After all, husbands work hard, they get tired and bored. It was up to the woman; otherwise, their men might stray into other fields, look toward other women. And if I needed some time away from my daily responsibilities during the day, I should hire a baby-sitter once a week or so and do volunteer work in a hospital. Period. End of therapy."

Megan cursed softly, in words that seemed to shock Patsy. "Fucking sonofabitch. You didn't have 'therapy,' you had male-dominated brainwashing. I know some good *women* therapists, Patsy. One in particular who'd be just right for you—"

"Forget it. That's not what I need. That's not what I'm here for."

Finally, Patsy was getting to it. In a quiet, neutral tone, Megan asked, "Okay, Patsy, why are you here? What do you need?"

"I want an abortion."

"An abortion? Patsy, I couldn't help you out there. I'm not . . . I'm a psychiatrist. And anyway—"

"You're a doctor. You know doctors who—"

"For God's sake, Patsy. Abortion is illegal. Surely you know about birth control. You've had five kids already, why the hell didn't you—"

"I did. Try. But he—Randy—I know he can't rape me. He's my husband. But that's what he did. He *raped* me. He got mad about something and it carried over to the bedroom. He threw my diaphragm down the toilet, and we had a terrible fight. A physical fight. Randy is a big guy, and I'm not so tough anymore. I'm worn down. *He forced me.* It was like a stranger, doing that to me. If he was anyone else, you'd say he raped me, but he's my husband. He's done it before. So here I am. Nothing I can do about it. He was entitled. That's what he said. He was entitled, anytime he wants."

Megan said, "*He raped you.* You better believe it."

"I won't have this kid. I want an abortion. I can't go through this all over again. Not the way this happened. I don't know what else to do. I will not have this baby."

"Don't you have a doctor you trust, who you can talk to?"

"My regular doctor is one of my girlfriends' husbands. You know what a pal he is? He gives us all amphetamines a few months after we give birth, and the baby is on the bottle, so we can 'get our energy and our figures back.' We're all a bunch of speeders, Megan; sometimes I don't know if I'm coming or going. So that's my life. That's it. I'm waiting and I don't know what for. Nothing will ever change. My life is what it has been and will be, and it's worth nothing at all."

Megan went to her desk, fingered her Rolodex, then looked at Patsy thoughtfully. "Patsy, tell me something. It's always bothered me. When we were fourteen, when I got back from the rehab, why did you just *abandon* me? It was when I needed a friend most of all in my life. I needed *you,* and you just dumped me."

Patsy shrugged. "Megan, c'mon. I was fifteen. I got into a group of girls and the word was, 'Hey, what boys are going to come around if they see . . . a crippled girl hanging around with us?' I guess all kids are cruel at that age." She covered her face with the pillow for a moment, then emerged. "Don't you think I've realized by now I threw away the best friendship I ever had? We were always so *honest* with each other. No bullshit—for better or worse, we never had to pretend with each other. I've never had that kind of relationship with anyone again. Megan, *I've thrown my life away.* It's nothing. You, look what you've done. Me, I'm a ghost. Nothing."

And then, suddenly, Patsy smiled. Her grin was warm and familiar and she laughed and tossed the pillow at Megan, stood up, and spread out her arms as though imitating an airplane, the way a kid would do.

"God, Megan. I almost forgot. The one thing I *did* do. The one dream I *did* fulfill."

Megan held her finger on a card in the Rolodex surprised to see the change in Patsy.

"What? My God, Patsy, what?"

Patsy flopped back onto the couch and put her feet up on the heavy, cluttered coffee table.

"I took *flying lessons.* I used to sneak out, God, after my fourth kid was born. *He,* Randy, thought I was learning Chinese cooking, for God's sake. Only one of my friends knew. She'd go to cooking class, then give me the recipes, and we'd prepare a joint dinner. To fool Randy. Megan, I actually soloed."

"What was it like?"

Patsy's face glowed; her expression was that of an ecstatic twelve-year-old. "It was like liberation. To get into that plane and look straight ahead, to be in complete control, complete charge, to rise up off the ground, to go into the air. On my own, so . . . so alone, but not lonely. To look down, to be above it all, to . . . Oh, God, Megan, it was like being a kid again, only a competent kid, a grown-up kid. It was dream time."

"What happened? Did you get your pilot's license?"

"Randy found out. He went nuts. Told me how crazy I had been. What if . . . you know, all the what-ifs. I put my life in jeopardy; what would have happened to my children, to him, to our home, to our life? How could I be so irresponsible, so selfish, so unthinking?" She shrugged. "Never did get my pilot's license. I came close, though."

Megan latched on to this. "How close? How many more . . . solos, lessons, would it take?"

"Oh, it would all come back. I've never forgotten one single thing about it. I could get into a plane now, right now, and take off. And fly. God, the feeling."

Megan said, "Then hold on to that. Keep that for yourself. Get back to it. Let that be yours, Patsy. It *is* yours. Wow, Peerless Patsy takes to the sky."

Patsy smiled. "Oh, boy. Remember that? 'Peerless Patsy' and 'Magnificent Megan.' Well, you *are* magnificent, Megan. Your whole life is. You are."

"Oh, I have my very less-than-magnificent moments, believe me. We all do." She jotted down the name of a doctor, said, "Okay, look. I'll give this guy a call tonight, you call him tomorrow morning. Oh, how many weeks pregnant are you?"

"Not weeks, kiddo. Months. Almost . . . more than five months. I've always been irregular, so at first I wasn't sure. But I *do* know. For sure. I never even show until the sixth month. But it's been that long."

Megan crumpled the piece of paper in her hand. "For God's sake, Patsy, it's too late. Why the hell didn't you come earlier? There's no way, now, at this late date—"

"There has to be a way."

"Patsy, there's a real, live, well-formed baby there. An abortion now . . . no doctor I know would—"

Patsy stood up, the toughness seemed to come back over her. "Thanks, Megan. For nothing. Oh, well, what the hell."

"Patsy, your life doesn't have to be the way it is now. After you've had the baby, call me. I promise—you can get help, honestly. My God, you're barely forty years old, you've got the whole future to get on with. You *can* have a better life, I promise."

Patsy looked around the room, then back at Megan. "*You* were the tough one, kiddo. You really took charge of your life. Well, we can't all be Megan Magee. Bum leg and all, you really did it." Abruptly, she reached out and hugged Megan. "I *did* love you, Megan. I loved us. All those dreams we had, we were so innocent. But we were *girls.* Wrong plumbing, that's what they used to say. 'Those tomboys got everything but the right plumbing.' Well, it was good to see you, Megan."

Patsy pulled back and stared at Megan, as though memorizing her face. Megan felt a cold, helpless fear, which Patsy caught.

She grinned. "Listen. I always have an easy birth. This one will be quick and easy—not to worry. And then, after a while, God, I will get back to flying. I'll make you a promise, Megan. I'll get my license and take you up there with me. Just the two of us. We'll be twelve years old again, how about it?"

For a split second she saw the young Patsy; the two of them together, funny, brave, silly, crazy with their own sense of life and determination.

"That is one promise I'm gonna make sure you keep, kiddo."

After Patsy left, promising to call, to keep in touch, Megan gathered her notes for her evening lecture at NYU. Maybe it *was* because she had had polio, and was out of the race, didn't have to get on with the same prescribed life as all the other girls she grew up with. Maybe her braced leg had given her the freedom to make special demands on herself. Maybe the steel brace and the limp had kept her from becoming Patsy.

Megan shook her head. She couldn't go back to being twelve years old, not for more than a few reminiscing moments at a time. But she wished she could, she and Patsy, even for just a minute—just long enough to make life plans.

Megan would not have changed anything at all about her own life. She wondered how many people would be able to say the same.

A little after six o'clock, between the classes she taught at NYU, Megan stopped off at her small office for some coffee. There was a message on her spike to call her father. Jesus, did she forget her mother's birthday? Again?

Her father's voice was low and calm. "They called me because someone recognized your name on the note and remembered you were my daughter."

Patsy Wagner Fenton had left Megan's brownstone in Greenwich

Village, taken a cab to the Empire State Building, got on an elevator to the seventy-fourth floor. She'd tucked a note, addressed to Dr. Megan Magee, into one of her carefully placed shoes, next to her neatly folded jacket and coat and her pocketbook.

Then she'd opened the window at the end of the hall and jumped. She'd hit the side of the building on the sixty-eighth floor, bounced hard against a window, then ricocheted out into space. She'd landed on Thirty-fourth Street, a few feet from Fifth Avenue, where she'd nearly hit two tourists from Iowa who were deciding whether to visit the Empire State Building now, or first thing in the morning.

The note, addressed to Megan said, "Peerless Patsy decided to solo without you. Hello, Amelia. Goodbye, Magnificent Megan."

Mike held his wife in his arms and let her talk.

"God, I shouldn't have just let her walk out. I *wanted* to believe that she'd make it. That she'd come back and ask for a therapist, after the baby was born. It wasn't realistic of me. It was just the easy way out."

"Megan, you can't blame yourself for Patsy's whole adult life."

"But she reached out to me and—"

"For an instant fix. A miracle that only she could accomplish, and with a hell of a lot of hard work. I shouldn't have to tell you this; you're the doctor."

"But it hurts so much."

"That's why I'm here, Red. To try to make it hurt a little less."

"That was some note she left, wasn't it? You know, it's been a running gag with some of my friends and me. I think it was Suzy who complained that my generation of women had no role models outside of Eleanor Roosevelt, and God, who could be Eleanor Roosevelt?"

"You'd sort of need an FDR, I guess."

"With or without him, that was one hell of a woman. My God, in all the movies, the only way a woman succeeded was to land the guy. If she was an ambitious businesswoman, at the end she had to capitulate, choose between the whole world and some stupid guy. You know, when we were kids, Patsy and I, we loved Amelia Earhart. You know the joke Suzy and I had? We loved Amelia Earhart, and look what happened to her. She disappeared!"

"*You're* here. Suzy's doing what she wants. Other women are out there, babe. They're beginning to reach out. You're at the very beginning of something very important."

"But it was too late for Patsy."

"Think about it, Megan. She didn't really expect any concrete help from you. She just wanted to touch base with the kid she was a long time ago. She wanted to go out with that kind of bravado. Instead of sleeping pills, I guess. There was nothing you could have done for her but what you did. Spend an hour or so talking, listening. Remembering."

Megan turned around in his arms, distraught. "But I should have caught it. I should have . . ."

Mike put his finger on her lips. "Shoulda, woulda, coulda. Redhead, your little pal Patsy died a long time ago. A ground-down, middle-aged stranger came to see you to catch some memory. Not reality. She lived her own reality for a long time, none of it to do with you."

"So why do I feel the loss so strongly? Why do I feel like I'd almost found Patsy again, and then lost her, twice? Why should I believe you?"

"Because I've had a very damn good teacher for a long time, Red. And because I'm the 'story man' and I like to spend my life making everything come out all right. That's my job, kid. So you let me at it, okay?"

Mike held her.

CHAPTER TWENTY

After a short stay at the Vatican, where Eugene learned he still had both friends and enemies, he was assigned to the Archdiocese of New York to work as an assistant to "the boss," the cardinal who ruled New York politics from the gothic residence next to St. Patrick's Cathedral. It was known as the Powerhouse for good reason: the Boss had enjoyed unprecedented national influence for decades.

In Rome, Gene was informed of his elevation to bishop. He met privately with the aging, unlikely Pope, John XXIII. They spoke in comfortably colloquial Italian, and Gene was immediately aware of the intelligence and sharpness beneath the grandfatherly image. The press of the world relished the public sweetness of the man; the hard, shrewd residents of the Vatican had underestimated him completely on the same account. They had thought he wouldn't live for more than a year or so following his election, at age seventy-seven. His very election was, in fact, a tactic intended to give the various factions more time for deliberation before selecting a Pope they really wanted.

Gene was surprised that the Pontiff knew so much about him. He had read transcripts of Gene's television and radio talks. He studied Gene carefully and spoke knowledgeably about his past. He asked, quietly, where Gene had been happiest during his priesthood.

Without hesitation, Gene responded. "At the Gabon colony, with the lepers and the sisters and the doctors. It was where I felt my vocation most strongly."

The Pope smiled. He was pleased with the answer. "Yes," he told Gene, "to be among God's own people. To be part of their daily lives. My own happiest days were as a parish priest." He looked around the vast office, at the sumptuous surroundings, and shrugged. It was a peasant's gesture, honest, instinctive. "And look where we are now, we two. God's will. We cannot question it, can we, my son? Although"— he smiled the reconciled smile of an old man—"we have our memories. But we must serve where we serve God best."

Gene felt a chill. It was the Pontiff's way of preparing him for his next assignment. It was a warning that Gene must serve in a capacity best suited for the needs of the Church. As an individual, he did not matter.

After his meeting with the Pope, Gene was escorted to the office of Cardinal Capanari, who had long watched over Gene's career with pleasure and a sense of pride. He had known Gene from his early days at the Vatican, followed his sojourn in Africa, and watched, amazed, his success as a fund-raiser and television star in Los Angeles.

"In New York you will be close to your family. Surely that should please you, Gene. A bishop, at your age."

Gene stiffened. "My family is one part of my life. They will always be close to me, regardless of where I serve. But, Eminence, you and I both know that I cannot successfully serve the Eminent Cardinal of New York, who sees himself as the American Pope."

It was safe to speak this way to Cardinal Capanari. Under both Pius XII and Paul VI, he had quietly but firmly made known his opposition to the New York cardinal.

"Eugene, my son, there are reasons. The most basic is the one I have already discussed with you. He is, after all, the head of the Society for the Propagation of the Faith. You are not the only one who has complained about the misuse of Society monies for personal pleasure. You will be right there. You will be, so to speak, the keeper of the books. You could hardly effect such close guard from Los Angeles."

"You think I'll have anything to say about the distribution of the monies?"

"I think you will be in a position to oversee things. But, Gene, there is a more important reason. We, who love and respect you, want you in place. After all, the cardinal, though he believes himself indestructible, will not live forever. And you know that he fell out of favor with Paul over the Vietnam War. Good heavens, Communist, Communist, Communist. You Americans are obsessed with the very word; we, here in Italy, manage to live side by side with our Communist children. But more than that—the cardinal has been steadily losing his power. He is no longer the political force he once was. He controlled the Church in America for so long. He once shaped the political life of New York City, sometimes by a single telephone call. But now, well, he is slipping away, isn't he? You know how the Pontiff feels; for all his great compassion and forgiveness, he doesn't really forget the past. Your New York cardinal called him, out loud, in many places, 'a mere peasant.' He has ridiculed and demeaned the Pontiff. He is no longer welcome here, where once he had such power. His followers at the Vatican, politicians all, have pulled back. When power begins to slip away, wise men fade and change sides."

"But his probable successor is already in place, Eminence. I have no ambition in that direction."

"His heir apparent is a fine man. An ambitious man and a very different man from His Eminence. But what is not generally known is that he is also an ill man. It will be a matter of time, Eugene. Years, yes, but what are years when measured in terms of the life of the Church? Your cardinal will be succeeded by his chosen man, who will serve for a few years, as his health permits. And *he* will need a protégé, who knows all there is to know about the needs of the New York Archdiocese. Gene, one day it will be given to you."

Gene O'Brien felt a chill throughout his body. For a moment he heard a soft whisking sound, a suspension of time. He hadn't experienced anything like it since his childhood. A warning, a premonition of a grand-mal seizure. The cardinal was alarmed at the sudden stiffening and pallor that came over his protégé.

"Eugene, what is it? Shall I send for a physician?"

Without waiting for an answer, the cardinal picked up the phone, and within minutes a Vatican physician was at Gene's side. Very carefully the doctor asked the cardinal to wait outside.

"So," the physician said, carefully monitoring his patient. "And when was the last time you had the grand mal?"

Gene shook his head. "Years ago, when I was a child of ten or eleven. It isn't going to happen, Doctor, it was just . . . sometimes, very rarely, I feel just on the verge. It has never progressed beyond a momentary dizziness, vertigo, nausea. It is under control now, I assure you."

"Yes. I believe you, Bishop O'Brien. I shall prescribe something to help you sleep. You are, I think, exhausted. It is stressful, all this traveling and the tensions here at the Vatican. I understand you have seen the Holy Father. He is a lovely man, isn't he?"

"Yes. A lovely man. Doctor, no sleep medication, please. And . . . what you and I have discussed . . . the grand mal . . ."

"Is between the doctor and his patient, as between myself and my confessor. I have been at the Vatican a long time, Bishop. A very long time."

He told the cardinal that the bishop needed a light supper and a quiet time to sleep. He was suffering from exhaustion. Period.

Gene lay motionless on the hard, narrow bed in the cell-like room he had requested. The only furnishings were bare essentials. He stared at the plain crucifix on one wall, below which was a prie-dieu. He could not distract himself with anything: he had to confront the truth.

When he had spoken with the Pontiff, he had seen beyond the soft, pleasant folds of a rather undisciplined man. The friendly eyes, which had spent a lifetime searching for the way to serve the Mother Church and God, were shrewd and clever beyond their innocence and kindness. Upon election, the man had become the Pontiff, the direct descendant of Saint Peter, chosen by God through the medium of the College of Cardinals. He was not like any other man, nor was he like the man he had been until then. And he was wise enough to realize it.

What Gene had seen, but could only now admit, when looking across the ancient, magnificent desk of the Pontiff, was a testament to possibilities. Here was what had been an ordinary man, serving in unexceptional capacities until, without notice, he had been elevated. But first, he had had to serve an apprenticeship.

No Pope ever elected had declined. Most Popes, while possibly overwhelmed, had grown into the assignment, though some grew more easily than others. This unlikely Pope had slid right into his vestments with an effortlessness that suggested his election had been not a fluke, but predestined.

Had Pope John XXIII dreamed, ever in his long life, that this would be his destiny? Had he known, that no matter what anyone else might think, however ridiculous the possibility might have seemed, it was inevitable?

As Eugene considered his own life, he felt suddenly confident that he knew his destiny. Ultimately, he had to admit to himself, and would have to admit to his confessor, his overwhelming pride and arrogance: he *knew* his destiny was to rise within his Church. He would become a cardinal. The reasons for his lifelong strangeness, his being regarded by others as "special," different, were clear now; and he had to admit his joy, his sense of excitement, but, far deeper than that, his sense of validation. His guilt itself revolved around the unspeakable joy he felt at acknowledging that he was ready and eager to accept his destiny.

He would serve the New York cardinal as best he could, with forbearance, lack of confrontation, pleasant conciliation. He would not rise to the petulance of the old man, not accept his challenges. He would ignore his insults, his barbs, his known cruelties to those he considered his enemies. He would wait and he would serve.

And put in this time.

And eventually prevail.

To God alone knew what final role.

CHAPTER TWENTY-ONE

It didn't take longer than ten minutes for Eugene to realize fully that he had been assigned to the camp of a bitter enemy.

The cardinal extended his pudgy hand and Gene bent his head and his knee, pressed his lips lightly on the ring, and stood up. He was a good head taller than the cardinal, whose round pink face, snub nose, and high forehead were just as he remembered. A few times they had met informally, at the Vatican. They had been diametrically opposed in their viewpoints and their politics.

The cardinal sat behind his magnificent desk and folded his hands on his lap. It was difficult to see his eyes behind the glint of his rimless glasses. He waited, motionless, for a full sixty seconds before gesturing the bishop into one of the uncomfortable but beautifully carved and upholstered chairs before the desk.

The cardinal touched the nose piece of his glasses, leaned forward slightly and said in his light voice, "Well, that's a remarkable family you come from, then."

The New England twang mixed slightly with a strange Irish lilt that must have been genetic. The cardinal had never spent any significant time in Ireland, from which he was two generations removed.

When Eugene didn't answer him, the cardinal's voice went just slightly higher.

"Whatever possessed your brother Charley to renounce the Holy Mother Church and become of all things, God help us, a Jew?"

Eugene raised his chin just slightly, but it was his eyes that gave away his fury. Pale and still, they settled on the Cardinal with the impact of two ice daggers.

"My brother had his reasons."

"Saw those death camps, eh? Well, so did plenty of others, but they didn't renounce their faith."

"But my brother did."

"You talk to him about it, did you, Bishop O'Brien?"

"My brother examined his conscience and spoke with his confessor. He made his own decision, Your Eminence."

"And is risking his immortal soul. Or don't you believe that?"

"I believe that."

"And who was this . . . this *rabbi* that brought your brother into the fold of the Chosen People, may I ask?"

As if he didn't know. As if he was asking information for the sake of his own enlightenment.

"Our cousin, Eminence. An ordained Reformed rabbi. My brother's conversion was, I gather, carefully considered by him and not undertaken lightly. How *I* feel about it is another matter."

"Ah," the cardinal said softly, "and you are not your brother's keeper, is that it?"

When the handsome face betrayed nothing, not the slightest flicker, the cardinal shook his head slightly.

"And all through your priestly years, you never could get *your own mother* to join the Church, could you? Not too persuasive, are you, Bishop O'Brien? Ironic, isn't it, you being such a passionate fund-raiser for the Society for the Propagation of the Faith? A strange thing, won't you admit?"

Eugene said nothing.

"Ah, well, to me it is a mystery. Why in the world would she choose to remain a Jew, when there was the enlightenment of her own six children to show the way?"

Gene's voice was soft and deliberate. The cardinal leaned forward slightly to catch his words.

"The mother of our Savior was a Jewish woman. His earthly father was a Jew. And He Himself was raised in the Jewish religion."

"Don't you *dare* try to educate me, Bishop O'Brien!" And then, after a moment's reflection, he leaned forward and smiled. "Ah, is that it, then? See yourself as the son of a Jewess, even as Our Lord was? Putting in your time until the day, is that it?"

When no response came, the meanness and stupidity of the remark agitated the smooth-cheeked cardinal. He cleared his throat.

"Well," he said by way of dismissal, "get yourself settled in for a day or so. I'll give you the advice my own dear father, may he rest in peace, gave me through all my lifetime." He smiled, trying to set a more welcoming mood. "'Always stay close to those smarter and better than yourself,' he'd say. 'It's the only way to learn.' And then he'd add, with a grin, 'That shouldn't be too hard for *you* to do.'"

He laughed bitterly and waited for the expected, usual protest: *But, Your Eminence, who could be smarter or better than you?* It was his familiar setup line. He waited, but the man before him gave no indication that he was aware of what was required of him.

Angrily, with a clumsy lurch, the cardinal stood up and held out his hand. He watched as the tall, slender, handsome priest came alongside him, bent his knee, lightly touched his lips to the ring.

The Cardinal dismissed him with a curt gesture.

The pretty-boy little bastard would *really* learn to bend if he wanted to survive.

For nearly two years, Bishop O'Brien worked out of the Powerhouse, which for many decades had been the true center of political, religious, and governmentally approved philosophical life in New York City. He witnessed the loss of the cardinal's power as the young mayor, John V. Lindsay, rode into City Hall on his still-white horse.

Though he was still consulted about public issues, the cardinal's advice was largely ignored. His accustomed influence in civil service matters diminished. He could no longer block or supervise the appointment of judges, commissioners, or political investigative groups.

Eugene dined at the cardinal's table when he was summoned. He behaved quietly and inoffensively, but his very lack of reaction, his quietude and complacency, irritated the cardinal.

The other fortunates, chosen for their various talents to work for His Eminence, watched the bishop carefully. He did his assigned work without complaint, with diligence, and with success. He avoided any discussion of politics—local, state, or national. He had the appearance and attitude of a man quietly waiting. And watching.

Because of his elegant presence and his almost seductively persuasive voice, the bishop was a sought-after guest at fund-raisers, political dinners, Holy Name breakfasts. His academic background was impressive, including a doctorate in political science in addition to his religious degrees and a degree in business administration. He was offered appointments to scores of major Catholic universities, not only in the United States but throughout the world.

Occasionally the cardinal permitted him to conduct a semester-long course at Catholic University, at Notre Dame, at Loyola. But when reports of his effectiveness and his impact—and especially, his popularity among the young seminarians, who one day would become Church leaders—reached the cardinal, he would order the bishop back to his tasks in New York.

There were many needs closer to home base. Eugene was sent to lobby the rich, the beautiful, and the powerful on a variety of assignments. He raised vast sums of money to be used for parochial schools, which were forever in financial difficulty. He studied and prepared for the cardinal a rational assault on the defined separation of church and state. Surely there were constitutional ways around the stringent rules and laws that systematically deprived Catholic parents of desperately needed state financial assistance for their institutions. Surely Catholic-school children were entitled to free academic textbooks, school lunches, and bus and subway passes. Surely the state could be persuaded to help pay for nonreligious school projects, for sports, for team expenses, for after-school recreational use of parish houses by the entire community. Things the cardinal had been accustomed to taking care of with a phone call, a friendly chat, a nicely served dinner could no longer be so easily handled. The bishop approached problems academically, rationally, in a businesslike manner more appropriate to the modern world.

When the cardinal and the bishop appeared together at society functions, Gene never noticeably deferred. If he attracted the lion's share of the attention, the adulation of a television star, that was just the way things were. The power, such as it now was, was the cardinal's. He was at liberty to use and take credit for any or all of the bishop's ideas, plans, and connections. When they succeeded, and they usually did, the credit went to the cardinal. When they failed, the cardinal turned on the bishop with the wrath of a schoolmaster toward a much-despised pupil.

As one of his responsibilities, Eugene kept careful watch over the monies collected and the monies spent within the archidiocese. It had long been a policy of New York City's power elite, regardless of their religious affiliations, to respond generously to any Catholic fund appeals. What Gene discovered was that there were too many luxuries, diverted funds, expensive dinners, and extra limos provided for these important "friends." Too many out-and-out political contributions were made with money he had brought into the Society's fund for the use of the school system, for training programs for the disabled, for special education needed by handicapped and retarded children. He had his records; he quietly kept score.

The cardinal's health waned as steadily as his authority. He watched what had mattered most in his life, his role as ultimate consultant to the most powerful people in the country, steadily erode; by the time he died in 1967, it was as though he had already been dead for several years.

Gene watched as the cardinal's recognized protégé was elevated. He accepted, with resignation and patience, the important role offered him—to remain at St. Patrick's, to serve the new cardinal.

It was just a matter of time.

Only months later, Eugene found himself co-hosting with the new cardinal an informal dinner for newly ordained priests. It was one of his responsibilities to put the young men at ease, and he was good at this. He understood their discomfort, their actual terror, and he regaled them with stories of his days as a television star, always putting the joke on himself. He had them relaxed, laughing in relief and admiration, as the new cardinal, himself not truly at ease with his new role, watched gratefully.

A slender young seminarian who was helping serve the dinner quietly whispered into the bishop's ear as all around him chortled at some off-color remark he had just casually thrown at them. The more perceptive among the guests might have seen the bishop's body stiffen, the color drain from his already pale face, the slight shaking of his hand as he placed his wineglass on the table.

He rose quickly and said, in the sudden silence, "Gentlemen, you must excuse me. It is a family matter. My mother is ill."

His mother was in a private room at Beth Israel Hospital in Manhattan. Gene hugged his eldest sister, with whose family his mother had lived since the death of their father more than a year before. It was their mother's second heart attack in less than eight months.

"It's very bad this time, Gene. She insisted we bring her from Jersey to New York. Megan made some phone calls and got her the private room. Megan was here a while ago, talking with the doctors. Looks like . . . you know."

The family, gathered outside the hospital room, conferred briefly with the specialist who had been called to treat their mother. They were able to keep her comfortable; she was in and out of coma. It would not be long.

The collection of family members, all more or less cordial, polite strangers who came together less and less frequently, talked quietly among themselves. They brought each other up to date: children graduating from college, getting married, giving them grandchildren. Each family unit seemed closed around itself, the joyous, wide-open family celebrations of childhood now only vague memories.

As they sat quietly in the waiting room, there was a growing relaxation; their voices became less hushed as they showed each other snapshots, exclaimed over the growth, beauty, and excellence of the new generation. They all told their success stories, avoided their disappointments. No one spoke about Vietnam, about sons who had gone into the service or sons and daughters incomprehensibly involved in protests. They didn't talk about drugs or new lifestyles, but only the good things, the picture-pretty children, the ideal offspring perfected in their dreams.

When Eugene arrived, in his simple black suit and white collar, the family surged around him—the brother who had become a priest, a television star, and now a bishop. He had always been the brightest and most beautiful of them all—always, from childhood on, set apart. He was the family observer and, their instinct had told them, the family judge.

When Charley came, Eugene seemed to relax.

The brothers had always been close; and yet in almost every way they presented a study in contrasts. Eugene had matured into a stronger, more masculine and polished beauty. His face was not touched by the cares and difficulties of raising a family, the nights spent worrying, the days arguing, trying to understand this new generation. He was still lean and graceful; he held steady and firm, looking directly, with total concentration, at whomever he addressed. It was hard sometimes to know whether his mannerisms, so controlled and careful, were natural or calculated for effect.

Charley, on the other hand, was the most natural, feeling, and open-hearted among them. His face and body showed signs of the battle of the years. His dirty blond hair had receded alarmingly, the fringe now mostly gray and unruly. His large brown eyes blinked behind bifocals he constantly adjusted back onto the bridge of his nose. He had put on a few pounds, and his pants were beginning to ride below his waistline. He had a slightly rumpled look; even a brand-new suit turned into used goods as soon as Charley put it on. He lived in Forest Hills, Queens, where he was an active member of the local Reform synagogue. His two sons had been bar mitzvahed; his daughter, mysteriously, had opted for studying exotic Oriental religions while a law student at Columbia. He worried about her—indeed, about all his kids. He worried about drugs and radical politics, and he didn't understand some of the passions and arguments of his children, but he respected, loved, and trusted them. And hoped for the best, that they would outgrow some of this stuff. He loved his wife, who taught at the local junior high school. He had recently retired, as a lieutenant, from the New York City Fire Department, and worked at odd jobs that took up most of his time. He was a good roofer, an excellent housepainter, a fair plumber, and a capable, though unlicensed, electrician, who was very much in demand in his neighborhood. People trusted Charley; he was an honest and decent man. His sons seemed to feel slightly ashamed: Why hadn't he pursued higher education? Why hadn't he ever risen higher in his department? They failed to perceive at this stage in their lives, that Charley lived that rare life—that of a happy man.

He was glad to see all his older brothers and sisters and their families, despite the circumstances. Their parents' deaths, after all, were natural. It was the way the cycle of life was supposed to be. There were other degrees of sadness and grieving and devastation that Charley and his wife, Deborah, knew about.

Years ago they had made a trip to Israel to attend a memorial service for Ben Herskel's wife and two of his four sons. They had been blown up by bombs placed in the school where one of his sons was a student, one a teacher, and his wife the principal. That was true tragedy, those young lives cut short. They had visited Israel several more times in recent years; once Charley went alone for a short visit. His sons talked about migration; Charley hoped they wouldn't. It was too far away and it was too dangerous. Again, he hoped it was just a stage.

Ben hadn't given in to his tragedy. He and his remaining sons renewed their resolve to serve their small nation with whatever skills and strengths they had. One son was a physicist, the other, as Ben had been, an intelligence officer and a pilot in the Israeli air corps.

And Ben—large, burly, tough, blunt-talking Ben Herskel—had moved through the ranks of the Israeli parliament, getting elected, defeated, reelected, and now, nearly fifty, becoming the newly appointed Israeli delegate to the United Nations.

Charley updated Eugene; he introduced him to their cousin, Rabbi Arthur Kramer, who had officiated at Charley's bar mitzvah. The two clergymen shook hands cordially. They had met casually, once or twice before, at Charley's house.

"And those others?" Gene nodded toward a group of young men who seemed to be present for a specific purpose.

"My sons," the rabbi said, "those two over there, twins. The others are our nephews, cousins. They are related to you, too, Bishop O'Brien."

Awkwardly, the younger men were introduced to their Catholic relative, a bishop of the Church. Gene counted them, then asked his rabbi cousin, "Ten altogether, including you and Charley. A *minyan*. Is my mother that close?"

Charley squeezed his brother's arm and nodded. The doctor came and asked that the family visit the dying woman one at a time, briefly. She was conscious and fairly alert, would be aware of them, at least momentarily.

"She especially wants to see you, Gene. She told me that once. 'At the end, I must see Gene.'"

"Charley, are you sure? I somehow think I tend to upset her."

Charley pushed his brother gently and indicated the closed door. "Go ahead, Gene. Mom really wants to see you."

Gene entered the room and, with the merest glance, dismissed the nurse in attendance. She left immediately; after all, this was Bishop O'Brien.

He went to his mother's side and stared down. The small, gray face was that of a stranger. It seemed to have collapsed; the cheeks were sunken, the lips, thin and stretched over glinting teeth, were unfamiliar, almost frightening. This had been a strong-jawed, tough-mouthed, powerful woman who had borne and raised six children successfully; had guided them through a religion that ruled their very lives without ever embracing it herself.

Sensing a presence, Miri opened her eyes, blinked, focused. For a split second there was a look on her face of terror, panic, fear. She gasped, shook her head from side to side, and moaned, "Oh. No."

He took her hand and leaned close and spoke softly. "Mother, it's Gene. I've come to see you. Mother?"

"Gene?" She sounded surprised, confused. As though she had just seen someone else. "Ah. Yes. Gene, my son."

He was surprised and shaken by the tears that now streamed down her cheeks.

"Who did you think I was, Mom? When you first looked at me?"

She shook her head and then decided. She took a deep breath. "My father. I thought it was my father. You have his eyes."

"Do I, Mother?"

"Strange eyes. The moment I held you, I saw . . . my father's eyes." She shuddered; her whole frail body trembled, but her grip on his hand tightened. She whispered something and Gene leaned closer. The tightening thin fingers bit into his hand, pulling him closer as he started to back away, afraid he was upsetting her.

"No," she said. "I must tell you. Oh, Gene. My dear son Eugene. Will you forgive me?"

He was startled by both her words and her desperate tone. "Forgive you, mother? For what? I love you. I—"

She shook her head to silence him, and he realized it was important to let her speak.

"My father died, you see, when I carried you. I carried his curse. And when I saw you, that first moment, when I saw your eyes, *his eyes*—Gene, do you know the word *dybbuk*?" She whispered it, her breaking voice giving the word terrible, unbearable power.

"Dybbuk?" he repeated softly. "Yes. A sort of devil, the spirit of a dead person that inhabits a living one."

"He put a curse on me, Eugene, when I married your father. On me and on my children. With all the others, each time, I looked for signs, but they were all healthy, normal. Then, when I first saw you, and he had died during my pregnancy with you, and I saw your eyes, so strange, so powerful, so like his—it was terrible of me, cruel of me, to believe such an awful thing, that he inhabited you somehow, that you were his dybbuk. I was afraid of you, of him, of the devil. Oh, it was so cruel of me, so terrible. Can you forgive me, please, Eugene? Now. At the end. Can you forgive me?"

He wanted to explain: there was nothing to forgive. He understood superstition and curses and devils better than any of them, the power of these ancient stories to overwhelm any common sense, any rational thinking. He knew. But what she wanted from him was not an explanation. She wanted—needed—his forgiveness. He kissed her forehead.

"Yes, Mother. I forgive you. Now you must forgive me, too."

"Nothing to forgive *you* for, Eugene. You were my perfect child, my bright, shining child, who I was . . . afraid to love. Afraid!"

"Forgive me, Mother, for trying to change you. For trying to convert you. I had no right. Through the years, all those times, *I was wrong*. You had a right to come to God in your own way. You were more wonderful than any woman I ever knew. You not only allowed us our own religion, you never interfered. You listened to our lessons and our prayers, you made special occasions of all our celebrations. You've been so good . . ."

She studied his face intently. If anyone had the answer, this son, with his closeness to God, would surely have it. "Gene, do you think that . . . He who is too powerful to name . . . do you think he will forgive me for marrying out of the Jewish faith?"

He wanted to lift her in his arms, to bless her, to tell her she was one of the special people, pure and unselfish. To tell her he was so sorry her life had been lived under the curse of an ignorant man. But he knew that the curse and her belief in it were valid on their own terms. The mysteries of religion—the good and the harm it brought. He gave her the answer she sought, and she accepted it, gratefully, from him.

"He forgives you, Mother. I am sure of it."

"And you, Eugene, the wrongs I've done you?"

Again, there was no point in protesting. He told her what she needed to hear, however irrational her self-accusation. "Yes, Mother. I forgive you. *And I love you, Mom.*"

He held her hand, aware that the tight grip was weakening. He turned as Charley entered the room. They both looked down at her, watched as she drew in one loud, sibilant, shuddering breath, and released it with a deep and final sigh.

Gene stepped back as Charley leaned forward, kissed his mother's face, and, with a large and trembling hand, closed her unseeing eyes. He glanced up quickly to see his brother step back away from the bed, turn discreetly, make the sign of the Cross, and silently, lips moving, offer a pray for his dead mother.

"Did you make peace with her, Gene? Whatever it was about between the two of you?"

"Yes. I did. *We did.*"

Charley was surprised to see the stream of tears. He had never seen his older brother cry. Never, not once in his life. Charley went to the door and signaled for his cousin and the younger men who entered the room and formed a circle around his mother's bed.

Softly, Charley's voice began the prayer for his mother.

"Yis-gad-dal v'yis-kad-dash sh'meh rab'bo b'ol-mo . . ."

He looked up, startled at the sound of a strong, familiar, beautiful voice. His brother, the bishop, joined Charley in saying Kaddish for their mother.

The others prayed with the mourners, and then the two brothers alone, in quiet unison, said the ancient words for their mother. Eugene's Hebrew was precise and strong, and he carried Charley when his brother, grieving, faltered.

And then the brothers stayed alone in the room with the body for a few moments.

"Gene, I didn't know you knew the Kaddish."

"I'm a scholar of religions, Charley. I reread it a few nights ago. Just in case."

"We're burying her in the morning, after services in my synagogue in Forest Hills. Out on Long Island. In the Herskel family plot. Where Deborah and I will be . . . one day."

Gene nodded. He would be there for the burial.

"And we'll be sitting *shiva* in my house. Starting the day after tomorrow."

The word jumped out at both of them; back came the memories, happier times, silly, boyish, nonsensical times. Gene said it first, but Charley thought of it too.

"Gonna sit and *shiver*, are ya, Charley?"

"Oh, God, yes, Gene. We're gonna sit and shiver. Remember?"

They looked into each other's eyes and started to laugh; they forgot they were in the presence of their dead mother, of the sorrowing relatives who had entered the room. They laughed and embraced, gasping and sputtering, and were unable to explain their demented behavior. But they knew their mother would understand, and laugh with them.

CHAPTER TWENTY-TWO

After more than twenty-five years of marriage to Aldo Santini's daughter, Dante D'Angelo was still slightly in awe of the man. Santini's appearance was substantially the same as when they'd first met. He had aged well. His black hair was still thick, though laced with gray. He had gotten neither fatter nor leaner. Everything about him spoke of moderation.

Even in his own home, there was still power in his manner, which was careful, controlled, deliberate, and expectant. While he accepted subservience from most people, he seemed pleased with the courtesy between equals extended to him by his son-in-law.

Santini went through his elaborate ritual of selection before presenting a wine to Dante. An exceptional vintage, hardly the altar wine with which he had made his handsome living all these years. He had sold his altar wine business to two nephews several years ago, but was still active in his real-estate company. He handled expensive properties, and he had been pleased years ago when his daughter and son-in-law carefully selected a beautiful, larger house for themselves and their two daughters in nearby Bronxville. Aldo Santini still lived in his house in Pelham Bay; it was convenient for his business needs.

He extended the gleaming crystal to Dante, who closed his eyes and inhaled. He nodded and exchanged toasts with his father-in-law and swallowed the remarkably fine wine.

"I gave a case of this—nearly my last—to the cardinal last year, to celebrate his anniversary. He doesn't set a very lavish table, this cardinal, but at least his wine is the best."

They indulged in small talk, the polite exchange that preceded the real reason Dante had been asked, alone, to dinner.

"I hear you sold your father's house to your sister and her family. Will they be happy upstate in the Catskills?"

"They bought it as a second home. For weekends, for summer vacations."

"Ah, yes. Second homes." He shrugged slightly. "Your father could never have imagined such a thing. He was happy there?"

Dante had bought the modest property for his father's retirement years. It was in a colony of houses owned mostly by Italians, an old-world place. Dante knew his sister had bought it as a speculation. She wouldn't be caught dead in that setup.

"It was a good life for him there."

"Your father was a good man."

Dante had always been deeply moved by the unexpected relationship between the two men.

"You were a blessing to your father, Dante. I'm not sure he could ever adequately express his pride in you. The immigrant's son, a member of the United States Senate. A wonderful accomplishment."

"I knew of his pride. He didn't need the words."

"Yes. Between a father and a son, there is a special bond." His eyes glowed and he sipped the wine, then said, "A tragedy for both of us, Dante, that we had no sons. I'm not too pleased that my brother's sons have taken over my business, but they are family at any rate. And you with two girls—not that they aren't wonderful. College girls, so bright."

The older man put the glass of wine down, rubbed his eyes, then gazed thoughtfully at his son-in-law. Speaking very carefully, as though with great effort, he said, "You, Dante, through the years. You have become my son. In every way. You have been a wonderful husband to my daughter, a wonderful father to my grandchildren." He hesitated. "And a wonderful son to me. For this I thank you."

He shook off Dante's reply. He had needed to say this and it had been said. Now he continued, in a different tone of voice.

"I have been hearing some interesting things, Dante. Some very exciting things about your future plans."

"Nothing is definite yet, Don Santini."

Dante had been spending the last year testing the national political scene. Elected to his second senatorial term by the widest margin of any candidate in the state's history, he had become known as a temperate but liberal man of high ideals and values. He was the American son of an immigrant with strong blue-collar ties. A war hero, who had worked his way, with help from the GI Bill, through college and law school. He spoke exactly the same way—thoughtfully and honestly—regardless of his audience. He was able to represent all the far-flung and disparate interests of his constituency in such a way that each particular group felt that he was *their* man. Dante loved public life, yet had never been pompous about the privileges of his position. His daughters had attended public high school. His wife had returned to her job as a translator for the United Nations and could converse not only with his constituents but with his colleagues, on any level.

When their first daughter was born, Lucia-Bianca became tense and moody. The first thing she had said to him was, "Forgive me, Dante. I know you wanted a boy." When their second daughter was born three years later, she told him in no uncertain terms, "I will never, ever consent to have another child. I will do anything else you want to please you, in bed and out. I will be your wife and your hostess and a good mother to the girls, but I will not become pregnant again, and there are no words in this world you can use to change my mind."

Those were her terms. She did not bar him from her bed, she did not deny him her body. But there could be no further pregnancy. While it was not said between them, it was implied: Live your life any way you find necessary, but be discreet. It was hardly the only marriage conducted on those terms, and he had successfully abided by their unspoken agreement.

Lucia-Bianca conducted her own life fully and happily. She was a wonderful mother. Their daughters, Roseanna and Josephine, were beautiful, dark-haired, black-eyed girls who took top honors all through their parochial school days; each insisted on attending the local high school and choosing her own college.

The shrewd Don Santini knew enough not to ask any pertinent questions. He had warned Dante; he had had his own experiences with

Lucia-Bianca's mother. He wished he had been as intelligent with his wife as Dante seemed to be with his daughter.

There were always prices to be paid, and he was pleased that his daughter and son-in-law had led such circumspect and apparently contented lives. Their daughters were proof of a good home, and the younger daughter, Josephine, even seemed to enjoy the challenge of political life.

Dante D'Angelo was not afraid to embrace public issues that others avoided. When he spoke, everyone hearing him knew one thing: whether you agreed with him or not, Senator D'Angelo always spoke exactly what he felt. He told the truth, and, agree with him or not, you had to respect him.

All during the Vietnam War, he never changed his position. He felt it was a bad war, one the United States never should have undertaken. He spoke out boldly for impeachment almost as soon as the first reports about Watergate began to emerge. Nixon, the man who had been elected President by the greatest plurality in American history, resigned and a friendly, warm, inept Gerald Ford would probably stand for election in 1976.

Quietly, polls had been taken, surveys prepared, data gathered. Of all the Democratic possibilities, Dante D'Angelo stood head and shoulders above the rest.

Prior to his first election to the Senate, Dante was one of the most investigated candidates ever. Italian-American—did that include Mafia connections somewhere along the line? Everyone knew that every Italian had a cousin somewhere in the mob.

For a long time, Dante had been concerned about his mother's relatives, the Ruccis. In his characteristically direct way, he held a meeting with his resentful family.

"We're tough guys, Dante, sure, but mob? My God, if anybody but you dared say such a thing, he'd be in big trouble."

"With the wise guys?" Dante joked. He ducked as one of his uncles aimed an index finger at him. "You understand, I'm sure, that these things will be asked about all of us. Going in, I have to be sure that my being in public life will not in any way hurt or jeopardize any member of my family, so if there's anything anyone wants to say, please, for all our sakes, say it now."

His uncles told him the truth he already knew; they were tough-guy immigrants who had fought their way through every obstacle in order to establish their fresh fruit and vegetable business, from which they had branched out into the meat industry, and had later seen some of their sons go into construction.

"Dante, you know yourself," a cousin told him, "I'm gonna do business with the building industry, I'm gonna be sure I don't have labor problems from the union, ya know? I pay a few guys, I got peace. In any kinda business this goes on, you know it and I know it."

"As long as none of *you* are the guys who *get* the money, okay? Yes, I know what goes on in any business. I couldn't have been a DA and a defense attorney for all those years without learning a coupla things. I just gotta be sure no one in our family gets hurt in any way."

His male cousins were veterans. On both sides of his family, without exception, they were all hard-working men with families. Some had joined together and formed companies in the various trades: construction, manufacturing, a taxicab business. A few had gone on to college. There were two lawyers, one doctor, and a teacher—and he, this last, was low man on the family list. What kinda man wants to be a teacher? A girl's job. The fact that he was a professor of English at Fordham University didn't change the older family members' opinion.

Their manner, tense at first, resentful at being asked to explain themselves, mellowed as Dante reassured them. His voice soft and friendly, he recalled old family jokes, his modesty evident: *Me, Danny, the shoemaker's kid, running for the U.S. Senate, hey, who's kiddin' who here?* By the time the evening ended, they had saluted each other with good red wine, stuffed themselves with the heavy, robust meal prepared by the women in the family. Dante left his relatives a relaxed group, amused, but also a little awestruck. Our little Danny, a senator, *marone.*

His oldest uncle, Joe Rucci, walked him to his car, parked outside the line of attached houses still owned, if not occupied, by the suburbia-bound younger Ruccis.

His uncle embraced him hard, pulled back, and, under the streetlight, studied his face.

"Your mother would be so proud, Dante. Maybe a little hurt you came tonight to ask us these things. Your father, I think, maybe he always thought we was bad guys."

"Not really, Uncle Joe. You know Pop. He never felt any of you considered him good enough for Mom, that was all."

"Hey, Danny," his uncle began tentatively, seemed uncomfortable, "there's something I wanna ask you."

Dante held his breath: God, what?

"About your father-in-law. The Don."

Dante smiled, puzzled. "My father-in-law?"

"Hey, he's a rich man, from the old country he came here and he's all set up. He didn't have to get his hands dirty, like most of us. So maybe, Dante, you might just take a look there, huh? If all of us is gonna be under some kinda spotlight, we better make sure we're all clean. How they make so much money, the Santinis, they got real estate and that wine business and olive oil and everything. You think maybe, somewhere along the line . . . maybe somebody *there* is connected?"

Dante stared at his uncle. He really couldn't vouch for his father-in-law. He simply didn't know.

It wasn't that he hadn't thought, at one time or another, about the great power his father-in-law seemed to wield. He had always assumed the arrogance of wealth was something that came with the rich man's territory.

"Jesus, Uncle, I gotta tell you I really don't know."

His uncle, a short, muscular man, punched Dante on the side of his arm, and said, "Well, kid, you better find out, right?"

He asked Aldo Santini. It wasn't as difficult as he had feared. Through the years, Dante had learned how to talk to all kinds of people. He knew when to be street-smart and when to be diplomatic. He knew how to get to the heart of things, particularly when his own future might be in jeopardy.

"You know, as an Italian-American I will be under particular scrutiny, Don Santini. There are plenty of people who will immediately cry 'Mafia.' I've checked with my family, the Ruccis. Now I must ask you. Is there any reason at all that you would ask me not to pursue this course? Is there any possibility that my running for public office would in any way injure or embarrass you or any other member of your family?"

Aldo Santini considered his son-in-law for a moment. A good-looking young man, dark hair, bright black eyes, a sincere manner, a nice voice. He was a good man and a respectful man.

"Dante, you are a born diplomat. You will be a good senator. There is no way in which any investigation into any aspect of my life or that of my family will put any of us at risk. I assure you." And then, with a knowing smile, he asked, "But what about your family? I always wondered about the Ruccis."

Dante grinned. "Don Santini, if there had ever been anything suspect about them, you would never have consented to my marriage to your daughter."

"And was it the Ruccis who told you to look carefully into my family background?"

"Ah, Don Santini, how can you say that?"

Both men laughed out loud and shared wine.

When he was elected to the U.S. Senate, first the Ruccis and then the Santinis held great family parties. They were in different locations, but the feeling of love and family was present.

Aldo Santini had never asked Dante for anything: neither advice nor assistance nor information. Dante had no idea what this meeting this evening was about, but he knew the timing was up to the older man. He was more curious than disturbed.

For the first time since he had known him, Santini seemed uneasy. He seemed to be searching for a way to begin. Finally, Dante set him at ease.

"Don Santini, you have always been so wonderful to my wife and daughters and to me personally. You've made everything I've ever achieved possible with your support, financial and otherwise. How can I, in some way, serve you? I am forever in your debt, so what can I do for you now?"

It was a courtly speech, carefully phrased to put the aristocratic man at ease. Dante knew it did not come easy for this man to request anything at all, from anyone at all.

"Dante. When I came to this country, I was most fortunate. My father came from a family with great resources. He had been sent here to establish a branch of the family wine business. He was able to provide my sisters and me with a wonderful life. We went to the best schools, we traveled. And of course, he taught us to take care of members of the family who were not as blessed as we.

"One particular memory of a day spent with my father—may he rest in God's own peace—has been with me always. It was a spring day, warm and sunny, and I knew whatever treat my father had planned for me—as the only son, he gave me many responsibilities, but also many privileges—would be special. He took me that day by car—with his driver, a privilege I took for granted—down to Manhattan, to Saint Patrick's Cathedral. There was a special ceremony he had been invited to attend. Not to *participate* in, you see, but *to witness.*

"It was the installation of those chosen to be members of the Knights of the Holy Sepulchre. I was a small child, maybe six or seven years old, and impatient with these things I did not understand. It was a long and amazing ceremony and my lasting impression was of giants in magnificent white robes, coming down the aisle of the cathedral. The air filled with singing voices, with chants and prayers, with incense and a feeling of holiness that even I, as an ignorant child, understood.

"After the ceremony, my father took me for a long walk. We went up to Central Park, and finally we sat on a bench. When my father began to speak, there was a mixture of awe and sadness in his voice. I didn't really understand, at the time, what he was saying, but through the years I have come to appreciate that mixture.

"The sadness, I learned, came because *he* never was chosen. He had served the Church all his life, with his altar wines, his contributions, through whatever methods he could be of service; yet he was never selected to become a Knight. What he told me that day was of his sadness, but also of his understanding of the circumstances.

"Being good and helpful and conscientious, serving our Church in every possible way, is excellent and only as it should be. The honors of the Church, however, are granted to very few people. The difference, he told me, is a thing called *power*. *Powerful friends*, who can call attention to your commitment and to your service. The friends, the power, the honor—was never to be for my father."

For the first time Dante realized that his father-in-law had grown to be an old man. He seemed drained by his reminiscence, by the confrontation with his own physical weakness. His face seemed not only sad, but weakened, with the deep lines of age and disappointments Dante knew nothing about.

"You, Dante, my son, have such powerful friends. That could make the difference."

Dante nodded, but didn't speak. He was thinking.

"I remember a conversation we had, you and I, a long time ago, when we exchanged, each of us, a deep and significant secret. Neither of us has ever referred to those things again. Through the years, I have seen you keep up your friendships with the friends of your childhood, and that is a wonderful and special thing. The friends of my childhood have disappeared, through the years and through different circumstances, from my life. It is only from such friends, I believe, that we have the right to request special favors."

He leaned forward, lifted his crystal goblet, and took a deep drink of wine. The years suddenly slipped away. The image of the dark prince once again confronted Dante. The man who knew all secrets but who still had asked for confirmation.

"Bishop Eugene O'Brien was one of your close childhood friends, was he not?"

Dante said nothing. He waited.

"He was one of the youngsters on the hill with you that night you told me about. So you and he have special ties that go far deeper than the usual boyhood memories. Can you call upon this special friendship now? For me? For this honor I have dreamed of all my life, for my father's sake as well as mine and my grandchildren's?"

Dante took a deep breath. In all these years, nothing further had been said by either of them about that night; and yet, as he had known, Don Santini had stored the memory away against the moment. And this was the moment.

"I think, Don Santini, that the request could be made."

"Yes. Dante. Thank you. You do not have any idea what this would mean to me."

Dante came to the old man's side and embraced him.

"Yes. I think I do," he said softly. How old the man had become.

CHAPTER TWENTY-THREE

Dante had scheduled a seven-o'clock meeting with Megan Magee Kelly. He maintained a small efficiency apartment on the upper East Side for times when it was inconvenient for him to commute from Westchester to Manhattan. It was where he relaxed, studied, entertained on a very small scale, and held discreet meetings with lobbyists out of the glare of Washington, D.C. It was also where he went to be alone and to be left alone, to pull back from the demands of the Capitol and the sometimes overwhelming burdens of his senatorial duties.

In preparation for their meeting, he sorted through his position papers and through the various papers Megan had prepared for him. Her psychiatric practice was mostly with women, and she had been concentrating on a disturbing trend among many of her most educated, intelligent, and ambitious clients—women who came to her because of her activism in women's rights.

Among other things, Megan's research was beginning to reveal that many women were becoming emotionally crippled as a result of violations of their most basic civil rights. Megan cited, in her report to

Dante, the case of a young policewoman who, a few years ago, had been given a headline promotion, in the glare of publicity following an outstanding act of valor. Some time later, the young married detective took maternity leave. When she returned to her job, she was told that she had been "redesignated" to the rank of policewoman, a loss not only of prestige and authority, but of pay. After all, she was told, she had a husband to support her. The gold shield went to a man with more responsibilities, if less public validation. None of her arguments of entitlement made a dent. Not even the PBA would take up her cause. Even worse, emotionally, the young woman found no support among other women on the job, who had been brainwashed so totally that they supported her demotion.

Finally, reluctantly, the officer accepted Megan's offer of political intervention. Surely not the psychiatrically proper procedure, Megan knew, but an expedient one. Through Frankie Magee's intervention, the gold shield was given back to the young woman almost without delay. In her report, Megan discussed the woman's intense resentment and humiliation. She had felt degraded and devalued. She was a prisoner of a time when it was mandated by law that a woman could not even take the sergeant's exam—the first step up the NYPD ladder—for the simple reason that she was a woman.

Megan maintained in her position papers that it should not be necessary for women to have to approach every violation of their civil rights on a case-by-case basis.

Megan arrived exactly on time, tapped a code—two-two-one-two-three—that harkened back to their childhood days. When Dante opened the door, they both grinned in recognition of the longtime signal.

Nearly fifty, Megan still had the high energy, the quick movements, all the enthusiasm of her earlier years. She also looked pretty terrific. Her two-piece bright blue knit outfit set off her pale, redhead complexion. She had taken to wearing eye makeup that brightened her honey-colored eyes. Her hair, as red and springy as ever, fell carelessly over her freckled forehead; in a characteristic gesture, Megan ran her fingers through it, without much effect. That his old friend the middle-aged psychiatrist should still have smooth skin and a mischievous grin gave him a real kick.

Megan looked around, impressed. "So this is your pad. I wonder what deeds have been done here, away from prying eyes."

"All kinds of nefarious intrigues, believe me. You drinking these days?" He gestured to a tray set up with an assortment of liquors, wines, soft drinks.

"Oh, yeah. You know me. A strong seltzer with lime, if you have it."

Dante shook his head, smiling. "*Perrier*, Megan. Can't you get with it, kid? *Seltzer*—jeez, once a Bronx girl . . ."

Megan settled into a chair sideways and swung her good leg back and forth. "God, did I ever tell you about Patsy and me and the seltzer caper? We were about ten, eleven. Remember how the seltzer man used to come around every Wednesday with those wooden crates? He'd hit about eight families in the apartment building across from my house. Patsy and I used to wait till he was gone; then we'd creep around with paper cups and squirt some from every bottle in a crate, drink it, then go to the next door with a crate in front of it. We'd get so bloated. Hell, we didn't even like the stuff. Then we'd worry—did we take the same amount from each bottle, so they would look even? So nobody'd notice any was missing? I think the worrying was half the fun."

Dante handed her a tall glass of Perrier and lime. "Like cutting a hedge, a little more and a little more, to even it out."

"Worse than that. One day we just kept squirting and measuring and drinking and squirting until, oh, God, there was about four inches left in every bottle in the crate in front of Mrs. Steinberg's door. Remember her—nice old lady whose three sons all became dentists? She was home all the time, but we didn't know it, so we thought we were getting away with it. But we were nervous. We'd never gone that far before. We almost died when she opened the door and caught us redhanded. Gulping her seltzer and squirting more to even up the bottles."

"You were never cut out to be a second-story man, Megan."

"Well, Mrs. Steinberg shook her head at us. She asked us to carry the heavy box in and put it on her kitchen table. She took the bottles out, one by one and held them up. Then she went to her cupboard, took out fruit-jar glasses, went from bottle to bottle, filled them up, and gave them to us. "Drink, darlings," she said. "You want seltzer so bad, you should just ring my bell and ask. That's all."

Dante laughed. "Beautiful. Old Mrs. Steinberg."

"Of course, we both started to cry and pleaded with her not to tell. 'Tell what?' she said. 'That two young girls were so foolish? No, I will just tell you both this: Don't do things like this. *It isn't nice.*'"

"Talk about being a natural-born psychologist."

"It ended our career of crime."

They smiled with the warm memory of simpler times. Megan

glanced at Dante. He had kept himself in good shape, carefully groomed, and had a good head of thick, just slightly graying black hair. He needed a shave, but that only made him more attractive somehow. He looked tired; that made him seem more relaxed, less "on" than when he was in public. More like Danny. Less like the senator.

"So, kiddo, let's get to it. I read through all of your papers. I have no argument with any of it—just the timing, Megan. Everything in Washington is timing. Once we get my new bill through Congress, it will open doors to all kinds of other rights and entitlements."

"Push it through now, Danny, while you've got the momentum. I'm talking about women of every age, educational level, skilled or unskilled. I'm talking about—"

Dante held his hand up. "Oh, jeez, Megan, not from you. Okay? It's just you and me here, no audience, just us guys from Ryer Avenue. I agree with you. Totally, completely. It's just in the timing. You have to leave that up to me."

Danny stood up, poured some Perrier into his glass of white wine. "They call this a 'spritzer.' Very classy. My father-in-law would have a stroke if he saw me desecrate wine like this." He walked to the window, looked out for a moment, turned, and seemed to be thinking of a way to continue.

Megan, trained to read body language, leaned forward. "Danny, you've got something on your mind, right?"

"Boy, try to fool a shrink."

"You and Lucia-Bianca okay?"

He smiled. "Fine. Nothing like that. As a matter of fact, I do have something on my mind. That you might be able to help me with. Are you in close touch with Eugene? Now that he's in New York?"

"Well, I wouldn't say 'in *close* touch,' but you know Gene. He's remote, but available if you need him. Yeah, I'd say I could talk to him, if it was important." She put her glass of soda water down and watched Dante closely. "We talking here about some kind of a deal, Danny? You and me? You know, the old quid pro quo?"

He grimaced. "God, I've created a monster." He sat down opposite Megan. "Not really. Not exactly. Let's just say yes, I suppose I *could* introduce a bill to include women's rights, specifically, as part of my new civil rights package. I can't promise anything; I'm still not convinced this is the time. But I could try to get as much support as possible, going in. And no, it would *not* be contingent on what I'm going to ask you. So, it really isn't a quid-pro-quo situation."

"But sort of."

Danny grinned and shrugged. "But sort of."

He told her of his father-in-law's lifelong dream of becoming a Knight of the Holy Sepulchre. He knew that Gene could effect it. A dream is only overwhelming and unobtainable when you haven't anyone to help you.

"I'd like you to set up a meeting for me with Gene. I want to do it on the quiet." He glanced around the room. "Just Gene and me, here, one evening."

"I'll talk to him. I can't promise anything either, but I'll try. To get Gene here, anyway. Brief him, then let the two of you talk."

"Great, Megan. I don't think it would be wise for me to call him directly. Since this is definitely not a political favor. Just between friends for a member of my family. God, it would mean so much to the old man."

"Just like I want to keep this addition to the civil rights program between friends. You turn it into politics, Danny. That's your part of it." She looked around the room. "Hey, this is a nice place. Real class. You have a decorator here, or did Lucia-Bianca take a hand, or what? It really is lovely."

Dante took her arm. "C'mon. I'll show you around, take you on the grand tour, all two rooms and hidden kitchenette."

He told her the history of the building. Built in the early twenties by a group of multimillionaires for their home away from their real home, up in Westchester, the building had contained ten apartments, each consisting of fourteen rooms. After the Depression, the apartments had been broken up into as many as four small rental units each. They were the New York base for famous actors in from Hollywood for stage or television work, for artists, for dancers. And, in this case, for a politician.

"I bought the furniture as it stood. Not bad. And I got it cheap. From guess who? Our little old movie-producer chum, Willie Paycek."

"You're kidding. This was Willie's place?"

"Yep. I met him at a fund-raiser of mine a couple of years ago. He contributed quite handsomely. He told me he was relocating more or less permanently in Europe, between France and Italy, he said. Felt he had more 'artistic freedom'—maybe it was more freedom for his particular lifestyle—over there. He'd kept this apartment for a few years, and was planning on dumping it. He gave me a great price on the furniture, and I took over the lease; the rent is very good, particularly in today's market. So here I am, with the breath of Willie all around me. Not bad, huh?"

"It's great. I hear he's knocking them dead in Europe. Winning all kinds of awards for his films. Not bad for the neighborhood shrimp."

"Hell, his whole life is pretty amazing." He took Megan's hand. "I guess you could say that about us, too, right?"

"We learned about hard work early, Danny. We earned everything we got."

He held her by the arms and studied her. "Hey, did I ever get around to telling you how terrific I think you are? Running your practice, getting involved in all these public issues. Like your father always said, you'd be running the country if you'd been a boy."

Megan's face went serious. "Wrong plumbing. That's what my father always said."

There was a growing sense of something very serious happening between them. Dante's eyes went to her lips, full, smiling slightly in the corners, tempting. He leaned down and whispered, "Hey, remember when I gave you your first kiss?"

Her hands went to his face. He leaned down and kissed her gently. Then, as she returned his pressure, the kiss went deeper. When she pulled back, they were both stunned by the intensity between them. They had actually never been alone like this before.

Megan reached for him this time, and they embraced and moved together, the sudden electricity stunning both of them.

Finally they pulled back, breathless, and Dante put an arm around her and carefully led her to the next room—the bedroom.

"Not exactly my taste, but here it is." He turned to her, cupped her chin carefully, kissed her lightly. "Up to you, Megan. What do you want to do?"

Suddenly, Megan began to laugh. Dante looked at her, momentarily stunned, then, catching the glint in her eyes, he laughed with her. They fell on the bed together, laughing. Tears ran down Megan's cheeks and she snuffled, then supported her face with her hand, her elbow digging into Dante's shoulder.

"Oh, God, Danny, if you only knew how many times, through the years, that I . . ."

Danny pulled himself up and looked down at her, grinning. "Me too. And you want to know something?" He gestured broadly. "Every time I fantasized about you, about making love to you, it started out perfect, and then, goddamn it, you would burst out laughing and I'd get mad at first, and then laugh too. Just like now. So what does that tell us?"

Megan playfully pinched his cheek. "It tells us what we both have always known, buddy. You and I are *friends*, and I'd sure hate to spoil that with a quick roll in . . ." She stopped speaking, thumped the bed, and began to sputter with laughter. "With a quick roll in Willie Paycek's bed, for God's sake!"

CHAPTER TWENTY-FOUR

Despite her family's lifelong warnings that Aunt Catherine would be left destitute upon the demise of Albert William Harlow, "the old man," she was left with a handsome house in Hollywood, Florida, and the considerable furnishings of the Riverside Drive apartment.

Wisely, Catherine invited Harlow's sons and their families to take whatever they wanted from among his collection of paintings, silverware, antiques, and clothing. Though she was totally protected by the terms of his will, she wanted as little trouble from anyone as possible, and the distribution of the estate went smoothly.

Megan agreed to help her aunt pack up her own belongings in preparation for her move to the South.

"I've always loved it down there, and Pop knew it. I have made a nice group of friends, sweetie, through the years. Both women and men, families and single people. It will be a lovely retirement."

Aunt Catherine, in her seventies, despite a cigarette-hacking cough, remained vital and interested in everything around her, determined to live her own life with or without the approval of anyone in her family.

She kidded Megan. "Looks like your boyfriend from Ryer Avenue is getting to be a real political dynamo, kiddo. Think he'll invite you over to the White House one day, for old times' sake?"

"We're good friends, Aunt Catherine, you know that. I don't think Danny's decided yet. When he does, I'll let you know personally."

"Good. I'll drum up the elderly vote down in Florida. Most of my friends—well, a few, anyway—try to keep as active as I do. C'mon, let's knock off the packing and take a break for a nice cuppa. I still have some of that strong loose Irish tea you've always loved."

Despite the weight her aunt had put on over the years, her face was still lean, and her dark blue eyes bore an amazing resemblance to Megan's father's. In their later years, Catherine and Frankie looked more and more like twins.

As they sat over the steaming cups of tea and slices of coffee cake, Catherine seemed dreamy. She had spent most of their time together talking about her move to Florida, the disposal of all the remaining things in the apartment, insisting Megan take some antiques the sons didn't want. But now, relaxed, she began to talk of other things, as though this might be the last time the two of them would be alone like this.

"You know, Megan, last night I dreamed of Papa—my father, your grandfather. Isn't that the strangest thing? I guess the death of Pop here sent my mind back in time, but, oh, it was so real, this dream. That's your department, isn't it, dreams? I never have talked to you about Papa. He was so handsome. None of us kids looked like him. Well, my brother Timmy did. But Timmy died when he was just a kid. You never knew him. Timmy was a hotshot. Just like Papa."

Megan had heard, vaguely, of a Tim Magee who had died long ago. Her aunt's voice became stronger; her eyes glowed with memory. She seemed stronger, more alive than was possible.

"Mama gave poor Timmy a hard time. 'Just like your father, look like him, act like him. A bum.' He couldn't help it, poor Tim, he was only a little kid when Papa died."

Softly, Megan asked, "How old were you, Aunt Catherine?"

The eyes went vague, then blinked. "Three years old. A baby. But I *remember* him. I remember running down the block—we lived on the West Side in those days, on Forty-third Street. All Irish then. I think it still is Irish. Who's left anyway? And Papa was a dock walloper. You know what that is? A longshoreman. He was so big and so strong and so handsome, black hair and blue eyes—'black Irish' my Mama said.

With the moods, you know. Gloomy, so sad, God knows. That's why he drank. That and the bullet in his head they could never get out."

"Bullet in his head?" This was news to Megan.

"From the war, you know. The Spanish-American War. He went down there, to Cuba, with the Fighting Sixty-ninth. With Father Duffy as their pastor. He baptized us, you know, Father Duffy. That statue across the street from Macy's? That was him. When Papa came home with the bullet, they said it was better to let it alone than try to get it out. He got such bad headaches. And so he drank. To get away from the pain. Mama said he was just a no-good drunk, period. And one day he just walked off a dock and drowned. Right in the middle of a morning's job, just walked off and drowned. I was almost four. I remember. Oh, yes, I remember."

Megan had been told her father's father had died of a heart attack in his mid-thirties. Had been buried out in Pinelawn, because he'd been a veteran. She'd never heard of a bullet wound or a drinking problem or a drowning.

"It didn't take Mama long to get married again. Another longshoreman who knew Papa. Oh, he was a bad one, that Johnny. Call me Pop, he'd say, your father would want you to. Like hell he would, Frankie said, like hell. Oh, he and the new one had a terrible time of it. And Timmy, he just up and left home. He was maybe fourteen—ten years older than I. He just up and left home and no more than a year later, there he was, killed in a barroom brawl. Poor Tim, wanted to be just like Papa, and I guess he was."

She squeezed her niece's hand. "That's why your dad and I never touch the booze. God, we were afraid to. After Mama . . . well, she started drinking because of troubles with Johnny. After three more kids . . ."

"You have half-brothers and sisters? I didn't know that. Dad never told—"

"Oh, they weren't part of our lives. They went off to the Protectorate. Same as I did, when I was nine. Your dad was old enough to take care of himself, I guess—fourteen, fifteen, when Mama died. Just under forty, and here I am, an old woman in my seventies, still here. How do you explain that?"

"Maybe because you didn't drink? I always wondered about that, you and Dad, not even a taste at Christmas."

"Oh, we signed the pledge. Remember? All Catholic-school kids did, promised not to drink until twenty-one years of age. Oh, boy, do I remember parties, schoolmates hoisting a beer and saying, 'Well, here's to the pledge—I'll drink to that.' It was a big joke in those days, but to Frankie and me, it was no joke."

"When did you get out of the Protectorate, Aunt Catherine?"

"Well, I was thirteen. Your daddy and mommy got married then, and he took me out, to live with them. Oh, your mom wasn't too happy about that, with a new baby on the way and them struggling to make ends meet. But it was a promise your dad made, and he kept it. I was supposed to help your mom, but boy, I guess I was a pistol—playing the hook, running around with all the freedom in the world. No one was *ever* gonna tell *me* what to do again. Not me! A real terror. Now, I can feel for your poor ma. God, she was just a teenager herself. But your dad, bless him, he tried to keep peace, he worked so hard, three jobs at one time, and he always knew the ropes. Hung around the Democratic Club, had some uncles who knew the score, could always get himself a job. Your dad never forgot the hard days, that's why he's always so good to the underdog. Frankie, boy, he put up with a lot from me, I'll tell you!"

"How did you come to live with 'the old man'? I've always wondered about that. Why didn't you get married? God, you'd have made a great mother. I always felt closer to you than to—"

"No, don't say a thing about your mom. She had a full plate, with your dad involved in union politics and coming home with a busted head in the early days, before he got himself connected with the right side of things. And the babies. Frank junior, the first, who died on the day he was born, God love him, and your oldest sister, Maureen, not ten months after, and James and Edward and then, that time . . . when Eddie was only four months old and her pregnant again, poor thing."

Megan leaned forward. There had been no child for four years after Edward. Then Frank junior, the second child with that name, then Megan, then the last, her younger sister, Elizabeth.

"But she wasn't pregnant again for four years. . . . was she?"

Her aunt smiled. "Oh, darling, you think all you younger women in this modern day and age know everything—how not to get pregnant, what to do if you get caught."

"Do you mean my *mother* had an abortion? I don't believe it. Aunt Catherine!"

Her aunt shrugged. "Believe it. She wasn't the only one. Young Catholic women, Jewish women. Plenty of them got things 'taken care of.' They all had so many kids in those days. Yes. My God, there've been abortions since there've been pregnant women. And there I was, not helping her out one bit, skipping high school, skipping the secretarial school they scraped and scrimped to send me to, and your dad, getting me a decent job in an insurance office as an office girl. God, I hated it."

Megan said, "I remember when Mom told me I had to take shorthand and typing so I could get a good office job, and I had a fit—*not me, not me*—and she said, 'you are a brat, just like your Aunt Catherine.' I was so proud."

"Ah, darling, she had so much to deal with. You don't really know your mom. She and I had our moments, but when *I* needed *her*, she was there."

My God. What?

"There I was, Miss Smarty-ass, working when she felt like it in this office, running off and doing what I pleased with whatever boy I fancied. You see, Catherine would never get caught, but I did, baby, at seventeen. I couldn't even say which boy it was. I was so stupid; it couldn't happen to me. Ha. If your dad ever found out, he'd have killed me. And probably about four or five boys. I tried to handle it on my own. God. Went to some back-alley butcher."

Megan clenched her teeth. "What happened?"

"Oh, a back-alley botched job is what happened. And your mom rushed me to the hospital in the middle of the night, bleeding like to die, and they did what they had to do. Hysterectomy at seventeen. Imagine. That's why, when you were born, with that red hair, that chin, that Megan-Catherine attitude, God, I felt reborn. I loved you so much."

"But surely you and Mom had to tell Daddy what happened? How did he handle it?"

"Oh, sweetie, remember, I told you a long time ago—men have convenient minds, don't they? Your mother told him it was something that somehow went wrong with girls sometimes, and he never asked another question. What he didn't know, he didn't have to deal with, did he? But I'll tell you, Megan, to your dad, you were his Catherine from the start. What he wished for in me, he *saw* in you. Not that he didn't love you for yourself, because he did, but also for the me that he saw in you. The baby I'd never have."

"But how did you ever get to live with the old man?"

"Funny, everyone always called him that—'the old man.' Well, I went back to the typing and shorthand and I landed a job in his company. I was a crackerjack, once I made up my mind to it, fast and smart and not afraid to let anyone know it. The old man's company had these contracts with the government, they made uniforms, and boy, when the war broke out—the First Big One—sweetheart, the company quadrupled in size. We employed, God, so many people, and I was moved along pretty fast and was secretary to one of the big shots, one of the top assistants. And one day the old man's secretary came down with influenza and he needed some letters sent off real fast, and there I was, and there it was. I was faster and brighter and, I guess, cuter—little Irish kid with a big mouth and a mess of red curls." She batted her eyes and held her head coquettishly. "And, oh, those eyes—there was a song about that, 'Them There Eyes,' and sometimes we'd get into a thing—I mean I'd just open up my mouth and tell the old man if I thought there was something wrong in the letter he'd just dictated, or in the presentation he was getting ready to make—and he'd get sore, or pretend to, and then he'd shake his head and start to whistle that song and I'd get madder, because I thought he wasn't taking me seriously. He was just teasing, having me on, because he *did* listen, at least sometimes, and he gave me a lot of responsibility, and I made a good salary.

"And then, after the war, the old man had a stroke. It damn near killed him, but he was a tough guy, a real fighter, and he didn't even consider turning the company over to his sons. Three big dummies, those guys, for all their Harvard-Yale educations. And they'd send a car for me, right from the Bronx, up to his estate in Westchester. His wife was the nicest lady; she was the one suggested it'd be better, maybe, for me to move in with them. Do my work right there, with a driver—a real limo, kiddo—to take me to the office, or to bring the work back and forth. It was an unbelievable place. My room was beautiful. And they had a real honest-to-God library, books from floor to ceiling, and I could read anything I wanted to. You got that from me, Megan, your love of books. And then the missus died and I just stayed on and worked for him. And took care of him—he was all alone, the boys had moved out, had their own homes and lives. When he retired, why, I just stayed on with him. We traveled all over the world, and he bought his home down in Florida and the one in Providence and of course this place, here on the Drive. His wife never wanted to leave Westchester, and she thought he couldn't travel, but we did. Oh, boy, did we ever."

"But why didn't you ever get married, Aunt Catherine? It doesn't seem fair."

Her aunt tapped her hand playfully. "Why, darling, he was an upright Episcopalian, a good church member, an elder, heaven help us. And here was I, this Irish Catholic girl with red hair no less, and not even a high school diploma to my name, against his fancy Harvard education. It didn't matter, dear, not to me or to him."

"Well, I'm glad he took care of you. It could have turned out badly. His sons could have protested the will and made trouble for you."

"Oh, he took care of all that. With a lawyer and statements for them to sign, don't you worry. And, oh, Megan, what a life I had with him."

"Were you lovers, Aunt Catherine?"

"Oh. In a manner of speaking. But then, there are some things I'll keep to myself, some specific things, if you don't mind, kiddo."

"Well, you always *did* seem happy to me. And I always thought the family—you know, they always had something to say about it, but I thought they should just mind their own business. Hell, you lived your life the way you wanted."

Catherine poured more strong, dark tea for both of them, studied the surface of her cup, then looked up at Megan, her eyes glowing.

"Let me tell you this one secret, Megan, just for the two of us, something you'll never repeat, all right?"

"God, Aunt Catherine, of course."

Her aunt's face was radiant almost girlish. "We loved each other dearly. He was the *only man* in my life I ever loved or wanted to love. So much for all those 'missed opportunities' the family filled my head with through the years. So don't you ever feel I missed out on anything in life, or that I was somehow gypped by not being his wife. I had the very best of it with Albert William Harlow. After his wife died, and until the day he died, I had his love and he had mine."

Megan nodded. What more could anyone want, to live with the person you love, and who loves you?

"And I'm not grieving for his loss, either. He was a good bit older than me, and he had a full life and I had a large portion of it. I made him a promise—and I'm like you in that, Megan, a promise is a sacred vow. I promised him that I would get on with the rest of my life, however long I had left. Let's face it, baby, I'm no spring chicken, but I've got some more living to do myself. There's still some things to see, some people to love, some things to care about. So I'll do what I promised him and myself. I'll get things organized, get myself down to Florida and get on with my life. Oh, you'll visit me down there, won't you, darling? You and your darling Mike. Maybe he could do a book set down in Florida; the colors are so lush, the water so blue-green. And even Jordan, if he ever gets around to taking some time off from his graduate school. But you, Megan, you'll come, right?"

Megan nodded and grinned. "You better believe it."

And she meant it as much as her Aunt Catherine meant the invitation—another promise between them to be kept.

PART THREE

CHAPTER ONE

Willie rubbed his stomach. The pain was terrible at times, bearable at best. He swallowed three or four pills with a mouthful of orange juice, but he had been drugging the pain for so long they were hardly effective. He didn't even get groggy anymore, which was good. He needed to be very clear-headed for however long he had left.

What a bitch, Willie thought, *stomach cancer at fifty-three.*

Until last year he had looked damned good. He had the right kind of skin for the lifts, and a hell of a good surgeon who did just a bit here and there to make him look healthy, relaxed, and, damn it, ten years younger. He'd kept himself in good shape: slim but strong, hair more blond than gray. Alan Ladd.

When his illness was diagnosed, he had refused the chemotherapy right off the bat. He knew, the way you just *know,* it wasn't worth it. He didn't want to speed into that awful cancer-look. He didn't want to lose his hair. Hell, he'd go as far as he could with the damn thing and then he'd bail out on his own terms. One powerful injection.

Willie wondered what effect his death would have on his brother, Mischa. Through the years he had supported his misshapen, retarded brother. Various housekeepers—some good, some not so good, it was all the same to Mischa—saw to it that he bathed and changed his clothing regularly, ate on some sort of schedule. The three-room apartment in the Bronx was Mischa's home until he had a massive heart attack in his early forties.

Willie had been in New York "doing a deal," and he took one look at the small body with its large head, the feeble but happy sign of recognition in Mischa's usually blank eyes, and he had his brother transferred from a ward in Fordham Hospital to a private room in the Harkness Pavilion at Columbia Presbyterian, New York's best hospital.

Mischa was the only one in his life who offered Willie total, uncomplicated, undemanding love and admiration. It was both comfortable and comforting to have Mischa live with him at his villa, some fifty miles south of Rome. He never asked for anything, was delighted by the smallest glance or gesture. Like a pet dog, little Mischa.

As he thought about the deformed body topped by its mop of graying blond curls, Willie wondered, was Mischa his penance? Against all the things in his life, would this final kindness to his brother count?

Damn Catholic reasoning. It wouldn't count if that was how you considered it—part of a deal. All the rules he'd broken, sins committed, confessions made with conscious calculation. Hell, what did it all add up to, anyway? Some kind of games played by priests. He didn't *really* believe in any of it.

Well, it wouldn't be long before he found out. And that thought, in itself, was an admission of belief.

Or was it?

This last year, despite the pain and sickness, had been extraordinary. He spent his time speaking softly from his deepest memory, into his tape recorder. Willie hadn't forgotten—or forgiven—one single moment of his life. Not one lousy bitch-nun, not one single punch in the head, not one terrifying screaming fight that paralyzed his childhood. The telling came with a sense of relief—and, of course, it was for a specific purpose.

He talked about people and events from his earliest memory, at three or four years old, through his latest production, a small, graceful, low-budget film about a woman's coming of age, which had won a prize at Cannes. Added to his other awards. But this had been his own favorite film, and the most surprising one to the critics, who always decried the violence and sexism they claimed permeated his films. Well, Willie knew what he knew. His critics might not like his vision, but every one of his films made money. In this business, that was the fucking bottom line, wasn't it?

Willie knew things no one in the world would ever imagine he knew. He knew, through the years, what *they* had all been up to: who they'd met, influenced, corrupted, screwed. How they'd lived their lives in public and in secret. There was an army of invisible investigators out there, drones willing to spend their lives going through endless dusty records, gathering names and places and times and dates. As long as you had the money to pay them, you could hire the very best.

Now Willie was telling it all. Not just about himself, his marriages, his seven or eight legitimate and illegitimate children, his own crimes and misdemeanors, secrets and mysteries. He had painstakingly traced the lives of those who were at the very center of his boyhood. He knew now how they had all turned out, what they had done and achieved. What they would want to keep hidden. He knew the public and the private facts. Some unsubstantiated, some inferred, and some actually fabricated. It would be just as difficult to refute fiction as to disprove truth. And the reader, realizing Willie had told the most godawful things about himself, wouldn't doubt what he told about the others.

Willie savored the irony—in due time, *he* would be the one in control of the rest of *their* lives.

Payback time. Even though he wouldn't be around when it all blew up, it was enough that he would die knowing he had done it: little dispensable Willie. That fact gave him the courage and strength to go on against the pain. A lifetime's achievement. A completed circle.

Yet his satisfaction was mixed with a finally-admitted sadness and frustration. At the pit of his life was a great sense of loss and emptiness. It might have been so different.

He had known by the age of fourteen who and what he was. The hated, hateful outsider. The punching bag, the kid who didn't matter.

If they had only acted differently, at that precise moment when that single shared event transformed all of their lives—if they had included him, acknowledged him—none of this would now be about to happen to them.

After they had beaten Walter Stachiew to death, Dante had rounded them all up. He took care of Megan first: *She hadn't been with them that night.* Her cousins, the O'Brien brothers, looking out for each other, and the Jew Herskel and Dante, all together and safe in their lifelong friendship, had discounted him. No one had said, *Willie, you're one of us. We did this thing together, and it binds us all more tightly than brothers or cousins or best friends. You are in; you are one of us now and for all time.*

That was what he had needed.

But Dante had just told him to go home and keep his mouth shut, and that was what he had done. No one had come to him later, when his father was arrested. It wasn't that they trusted his silence. It was that whether or not he spoke didn't matter. His old man had confessed and been arrested, and no one, not even Dante, the would-be President who told people he felt their pain and suffering, had come to him.

Willie had hoped, for one fleeting moment, that everything in his fourteen years of life would be changed. His two worst tormentors, his father and Walter Stachiew, were out of his life. He was part of something immense and important. But nothing had really changed. It was as though he hadn't been with them that night.

But he *had* been with them.

Although he had lived an amazingly successful life, on his own terms, Willie had never lost the feeling of terrible injustice and immeasurable loss. Couldn't they have seen how much he needed what they so casually gave to each other: friendship, a shared pride and pleasure in all his accomplishments?

Willie knew that in Dante's mind, he *had* taken care of Willie: gotten him the driver's job with his uncles, then gotten him out to Hollywood. But none of that was for Willie. All for the good of Dante.

When he had produced Gene O'Brien's television show, Gene was cool and crisp and professional. He could never be led to talk about the old days. Gene's life had always been remote, even from his own family. But he'd acted as though there had never been that cold December night on Snake Hill.

Willie had watched Gene carefully. He was damned good at what he did, a natural. And so fucking beautiful. He remembered the encounter in the storeroom, Gene not only terrified of Walter, but sexually excited by him. That was a long time ago, and Gene had been an inexperienced boy. By the time he did the TV show, he had had a lifetime of situations and opportunities.

Hell, it was a known secret: priests either grabbed the altar boys or waylaid the little schoolgirls or comforted the frustrated housewives. Willie had a feeling about Gene.

But he was wrong.

Willie had tried to set Gene up with a homosexual stagehand, but it had backfired. Gene was not interested, except in the welfare of the very shaken young man. As quickly as he could, Willie had had him transferred to the East Coast with some extra cash in his pocket.

Willie got the facts about Gene's days at the Vatican. Successful money-raiser, darling of the wealthy widows and wives whose husbands stayed home to earn more money, he had led a life of luxury:

tailor-made clothes, cars, expensive restaurants, vacations in the villas of the rich and famous. Willie had amassed names, dates, locations, and the amounts of money expended on Father O'Brien, who was soon to be a monsignor, and surely soon a bishop. It wasn't a great stretch of the imagination to assume that Gene gave these women favors other than his mere presence. That was the beauty of allegations. You put someone in the position of having to deny one incident after another; explain; justify; testify; swear; deny. The more defensive the accused became, the more harm was done.

When Gene was the television bishop in Hollywood, he was always in demand by the movers and shakers, Catholics and non-Catholics alike. Gene would have been a real killer on the big screen. He had star quality, but he had made his choice a long time ago.

Now it was well known that Gene was awaiting the demise of the pleasant, sweet-faced cardinal who relied on Gene more and more as a slow death interfered with even the simplest of his commitments. And after a few years as the most glamorous cardinal in the church, how did Gene see himself? First American Pope, Gene?

Then there were Ben Herskel and Charley O'Brien—always a team in Willie's mind. They had taken equal part in Walter's death, one coming to the aid of the other, each smashing at the huge drunkard with hard and deadly accuracy. It was amazing, the way they met in Germany. Especially since Herskel was a captain and Charley, always the loser, was only a corporal. But they were a team. It was nice how they did it, the murdering of the SS officers. Ben had taken care of the first alone, but Charley had helped with the second. Willie was surprised, in a way. He hadn't thought they had the balls for what they accomplished.

Charley had been a fireman: brave and daring "Snuffy" O'Brien, for God's sake. He was the only real dud among them; he had been promoted to lieutenant before his retirement, big fucking deal. And turning Jew—that was a real puzzle to Willie at first, even though Charley's mother was an unconverted Jew. But one of the leads on Charley paid off—it explained it all.

For nearly twenty years, Charley O'Brien had been an intermediary in Israel's illicit arms trade. Innocent, wide-eyed Charley, with his sweet tenor voice and pleasant personality, was one of the biggest underground movers of money for arms in the world. His trips to Israel "to visit his in-laws" were supposedly nice family get-togethers, but were in fact missions undertaken to conclude illegal deals.

They were quite a team, Ben and Charley. What they also were was big-time illegal: that would be heavy federal time. Well, what the hell. They'd had a good long run. Time to pay up. It wouldn't look too good politically for Ben Herskel, would-be Prime Minister of Israel, to be implicated in a world-wide criminal conspiracy. Along with his ex-fireman of a brother-in-law.

Payback time, guys.

Megan Magee Kelly. The damn little cripple who thought she was better than anybody. They also protected her, the little girl hanging around the boys. Well, Willie knew about Megan, the would-be boy.

She and that friend of hers, Patsy Wagner, were queer for each other for years, but Patsy got away. Got married early and had a lot of kids and never saw Megan again (as far as Willie could find out) until the last day of her life. The way he figured it, Patsy must have been sick of her damn suburban life, her husband, all those kids, whatever. She'd probably read something in the paper about Megan; she was a name in the damn women's movement. Willie pictured the scenario, the way he'd have set it up. Patsy looking at her former "friend," now living in Greenwich Village, married to a successful writer of kids' books. Surrounded by exotic people, doing whatever the hell she wanted to do and getting rich and famous for it.

In Willie's movie of the end of Patsy's life, he could see unhappy Patsy envying Megan. Maybe saying, Hell, let's get back to where we were. Let's . . . you know. Who'd ever know? And Megan laughing. Too late, baby. But lotsa luck. It was good drama, what happened next. Patsy—whatever her married name was, Willie couldn't remember— had gone from Megan's office to the Empire State Building and jumped. Great timing.

Why the hell would Megan want her back? She'd had her lover, that Suzy Ginzberg, that lesbo she'd met down in Warm Springs who probably showed her things Megan could never even imagine. She was the one, Suzy, who'd introduced Megan to Mike Kelly.

Mike Kelly, world-renowned children's author and *drug addict*. Megan Magee Kelly, psychiatrist, had her husband hooked on drugs from the first year they were married. Wouldn't his publishers, not to mention the parents of all his little readers, like to know the guy was a head?

Willie wondered if Megan had ever told her husband about her role in the murder of Walter Stachiew. Oh, that's right. *Megan wasn't there.* The gang protected her. But, of course, she *was* there and she sure as hell did her part.

The fact that Megan and Mike Kelly had a son didn't mean shit.

Megan was still queer. The kid was probably just to make things look normal. Willie knew about things like that.

Megan, Megan. Willie'd offered her the most incredible opportunity to become rich beyond her imagination, with a stable of famous nut cases. She could have been right smack in the middle of all the glamour and excitement Willie lived in. He had offered it to her and she had turned it down as though he'd insulted her.

He knew, too, about her aunt Catherine: rich man's whore and baby-killer. The latter he assumed from some information handed to him: while she was in medical school, Megan was pregnant. But guess what? No baby. That aunt of hers would have been the one to see to it that was taken care of, right? A rich old lady now, living in Florida with her ill-gotten gains.

Megan's old man, Frank Magee—it was no secret that he carried the cash to the Bronx bosses, the money to buy judgeships and commissioner's appointments. You want a city job, qualified or not; you're trying for a city contract, low bidder or not; see Frankie Magee. He was the man. Clear it with Frankie.

Willie had the goods on her old man.

Megan, Megan, it could have all been so different.

Willie was amazed sometimes at all the information he had on all of them. Did people really think that what they did in the dark of night or behind closed doors would remain there? If two or more people knew something, it was always possible to find out, if not the whole true story, at least enough facts or details to ruin a reputation.

Then there was Dante D'Angelo, United States senator from New York, with his Italian eye on the White House. Dante, with the crazy sister and a mother-in-law he'd never met because she'd died murdering her newborn son. Drowned him in his mother's blood, the whole thing covered up because Don Aldo Santini, his wife's father, was an important man. The power of the Church extended even to the Church's wine merchant.

Dante, who'd delivered a couple of death blows of his own on Walter Stachiew's skull, had then told them all to forget about it. It had never happened.

Dante, with the Rucci uncles who didn't have to be "connected." They were a law unto themselves, those Ruccis.

Dante D'Angelo, who made a baby with Maryanne Radsinski and shrugged: Who, me? Never heard of her.

That son would be his father's ruin and Willie's finest retaliation.

*   *   *

Willie waited in nervous anticipation for the kid to arrive at
the villa. He hadn't seen him in five, maybe six years. He wasn't a kid
anymore, not in any sense of the word. He was close to thirty, and he
had made a great success of his life. Changed his birthname—Daniel
William Paycek—to Danny Williams, and without even a high school
education he had achieved his own growing fame as a columnist.

Willie always kept an eye on Danny. When he was twenty, Willie
got him into the stagehands' union, where he looked after him to a
limited extent. Danny Williams would be important to Willie for his
own reasons.

He was glad Danny was an independent, bright guy who worked his
own game, and kept his eyes open and his mouth shut. It was funny
how in some ways Danny reminded Willie of himself—not physically,
but in the clever way he took control of his own life.

At first he moonlighted as a source of information to a couple of
movie columnists. It was amazing, the kind of things any bright
craftsman on a set could pick up. He held back a lot of stuff, though,
saving it for another day. By the time he was twenty-six, Danny was a
successful, well-established (if not particularly well-respected) syndi-
cated columnist with his own small organization of gofers and private
sources.

It could be helpful or harmful to get your name in Danny Williams's
column. Everyone wanted to get on his good side, and often the easiest
way to do that was to give away—to sacrifice—others. He didn't deal
so much anymore with show biz. God knew, it was getting harder to
shock people when everyone, all over the world, was doing anything
and everything with anyone, anyplace. What Danny learned early
on—in his teens he had a hundred years of raw experience—was that it
was the politicians, the makers and upholders of public morality, who
made the best copy. You had to be high up to fall hard.

Danny did some sensational interviews with public figures for
reputable magazines. Advisers told the interviewees, *What the hell, this
kid has a reputation; he gets read; just make sure he spells your name right.
That's all anyone remembers, that your name was in his column, when they go
to pull the lever or make that contribution or buy your latest book.*

People smarter than he, more successful, more important had it all
figured out. They could use Williams. They would come away from a
couple of hours with Danny a little dazed—some easy time, some
laughs, some serious, gut-wrenching, unanticipated stuff. It went okay.

It would be all right. But in the dead of night, unable to sleep, the interviewee would sit up in bed and say, Oh, my God, did I tell that rotten little bastard that? I couldn't have. Oh, shit, I couldn't have.

But they did. One after another, his targets agreed to Danny Williams's interviews. You'd have to be stupid to let this little nobody get the best of you, right?

Willie, sitting by his pool in the hot Mediterranean sun, was surprised at his uneasiness. The transatlantic phone call had had a hollow, mechanical sound. Yeah, Danny had gotten Willie's letter, he just hadn't had a chance to reply, but he *had* thought it over. Yes, he would come over to see Willie. He'd never been to Europe, and when would he get a chance for an all-expenses-paid vacation again?

Willie leaned back and closed his eyes. He could hear little Mischa, tapping away in the coolness of the marble-floored entrance hall. What the hell, the poor thing still thought he'd win contests, make movies, become a dancing star. He had no idea that all he did was bang his feet back and forth, that the clicking steel plates attached to the heels and toes of his dancing shoes gave off no rhythmic beat, nothing but an annoying banging clatter.

Willie thought about his family for the first time in years. When his blond, blue-eyed, pretty brothers and sisters had grown up and contacted him in Hollywood, he'd refused to see them. Let them get themselves a couple of tourist maps, hunt for the homes of the living stars and the graves of the dead. They were no more a part of his life than his mother, who had married one drunk after another and spent her life getting beaten senseless once a month. One sister had come out to the studio in the sixties with an overweight, uncomfortable truck-driver of a husband and two white-haired little girls in tow. She'd thought maybe Willie could make the girls into movie stars or something. Yeah. *Something.* He'd studied his sister's hungry face, remembered her the day before their father's execution. She had had a nun's face, had poked and glared and corrected the manners of the other kids, had looked with undisguised disgust at their mother and right through Willie as though he were invisible.

He told his relatives bluntly what he could do for the little nieces. Just give them a few years and they'd be of age, but keep them young-looking. That went over better. It was the last time he ever saw any of his family. With the exception of little Mischa.

And now he was awaiting Danny Williams, whose birth certificate bore Willie Paycek's name as father and Maryanne Radsinski's as mother.

Willie's children were scattered throughout the world. Four of them had been by three of his wives. Two girls, two boys, and none of them promising in any way. He had, in addition, maybe four or five illegitimate children, and every year some hopeful starlet tried to add to the number with a paternity suit. Sometimes, for a short period, he'd pay some support, sometimes not. It was all the same to Willie. They'd either make it on their own or not. Hey, it was tough world.

Danny Williams arrived exhausted from his long trip and jet lag. Willie sent a limo to drive him from the airport to the villa, and met him very briefly to make sure he was comfortable in the large, airy bedroom overlooking the pool. He sent him some supper on a tray; late the next morning they met for breakfast on the terrace overlooking the Mediterranean.

Willie studied him with a director's eye. He would be a natural for the street-wise, tough-but-tender, mysterious, slightly menacing, and sexy working-class hero. He was just under six feet, well dressed in a lightweight dark suit, a good white shirt, and a silk tie. There was a certain cockiness in the way he moved and held himself. With a slight shrugging of his shoulders, as though settling his jacket, he seemed to be releasing tension. Nice move; Willie missed nothing. His black hair and eyes were in startling contrast to his fair complexion. His nose, obviously broken, gave his face a rugged look at odds with his sensuous mouth. He had a strong jawline, and though he had just shaved—he smelled of lemon after-shave lotion—there was a dark, shadowy edge to his face that women would find attractive.

He had a nice style, cool and impressive. A civilized punk with something dangerous and exciting beneath the well-groomed surface. Danny shook a cigarette directly from the pack into his mouth, then lit it with a sleek gold lighter. He had the timing and awareness of a movie star; for a fleeting moment, forgetting the hard and terrible history of the young man's life, Willie wished *he* could be Danny Williams.

Willie indicated the plates of fresh fruit and pastries, the steaming black coffee, the pitcher of cream. Danny sipped the coffee black, then regarded Willie with open curiosity. He had a mocking tone, a pleasureless grin.

"Well, Papa Willie. You look like the end of the line. Why am I here?"

Willie swallowed, then choked on a piece of peach, the juice running lushly down his chin. He dabbed at himself with a linen napkin, then hunched forward slightly.

"You're here in pursuit of truth—of a sort, Danny. I got a lotta things I wanna tell you."

For nearly six months, Danny listened to Willie's taped life story, discussed parts of it with Willie. When he came to the story of his own conception, Danny jotted down a few questions.

"Did Dante D'Angelo ever know I was born?"

"He shoulda. It was why they sent Maryanne to the Coast, with me as her blushing groom." And then, catching something, a tightening of the young man's mouth, a hardening of his eyes, Willie asked, "What did your mother ever tell you about . . . ya know, about Dante. And her and me."

Softly, Danny said, "My mother told me lots of things. Oh, by the way, Willie, I'm having my youngest sister, Dolores, come over to type the manuscript."

"Why? I thought you—"

"Hey, I'm not a typist, Willie. Don't look so worried. Dolores has worked with me on a lot of my columns and articles. I trust her completely. She's just turned twenty, and I know I don't have to warn you in any way . . ."

Willie shrugged. "A coupla years ago, you'd have to warn me. Now . . ." the feeble shrug spoke for him.

But he could still take pleasure in the sight of the girl. She was tall and slender, with a healthy, graceful body. Oh, how Willie regretted his dying. He studied Danny's half sister, her Mexican heritage evident in her tawny skin, dark hair, and bright eyes. She was one of Maryanne Radsinski's four Mexican-adventure children. He could hear the hum and click of the electric typewriter and visualize the lovely girl concentrating on her work.

Willie wondered what Danny Williams would say about the fact that he knew how he and his mother had survived during Danny's teen years, the blackmailing of rich women. But he never said anything.

When it was all finally on paper, Danny flew with his sister to Paris, where she was to study fashion at a famous house. She wanted to be a designer. Willie read the manuscript. It was all there, his indictment of the Ryer Avenue kids.

By the time Danny returned, he could tell by the uneasy, worried smile on Mischa's thin lips that Willie was slipping away. Even though he had watched Willie slowly grow thinner and grayer, watched him huddle in sweaters and woolen blankets against the heat of the sun, which could not warm his interior coldness, Danny was shocked by the rapid deterioration Willie had undergone in just a few days.

Willie had had a meeting with his attorney, and put some of his affairs in order. He was leaving the villa to Mischa, with Danny as his guardian. At his death, the villa would be Danny's.

"He won't live much longer than me," Willie said. "He'll blink out like a star." He started to laugh, gagged, held a thin hand on his throat. "Mischa, the little star. I want you to know, Danny, I've signed over all the rights to my autobiography to you. All legal. You two are my only heirs named in my will. The rest of my estate will be up for grabs."

The thought of the worldwide chaos among his international survivors amused Willie—his legacy to his large number of uncaring and uncared-for offspring.

"Obviously," he instructed Danny, "you don't hit the big legit publishers. You go to the sleaze press. Or you make a deal with one of the gossip rags. Whatever they print will be picked up by everybody. All over the world. No matter who brings it out, that old gang of mine will have to spend the rest of their lives answering charges."

"How much of it is true?"

Willie grimaced and clenched his teeth against pain. "Enough of it. Danny, you look puzzled."

"I can't figure the *why* of it, Willie. *Why?*"

In a whisper from his aching throat, Willie said, "I got my reasons. Listen, I want you to take Mischa out tonight. Take him to a restaurant, to a park, a movie, somewhere. I don't want him to be here when I . . ."

Danny shook his head. "No. You're not taking that magic shot tonight."

Willie squinted and tried to see the expression that went with the odd tone of voice. "Hey, kid, that was the plan all along. I finished what I had to do. So now it's time. Don't feel bad, Danny."

Danny Williams stood up, turned his back on Willie for a moment, then sat down and faced the dying man.

"Willie, I don't feel bad. But *I* need a few hours of your time. Then you do what you gotta do."

"I don't get it. What—"

"I listened to you for all these months and worked on the manuscript. Now, Willie, it's my turn."

"What do you mean, your turn?"

A shudder as strong as a convulsion shook Willie Paycek as he squinted at the tough strong face and tried to read the meaning of the tight smile. The implied threat.

"*I* got some things to tell *you*, Willie. And then, when I'm finished, you can take your shot."

He pulled a chair close to the lounge where Willie was huddled, stiffly facing the sea but trying to read the meaning of the words. Knowing something terrible was about to happen.

"You know the scene you describe about when you faced your old man the night before his execution and told him what *really* happened that night on the hill? How you told him so that he'd fall apart? Jesus, you even did it in your prison movie, it was so dramatic. Your payback for the rotten life he gave you. Well, Willie, everybody oughta get a chance at that."

A few hours later, when Danny Williams finished speaking and Willie had stopped listening, it was obvious that the fatal injection was no longer needed.

Willie sat slumped, wrapped in blankets that could no longer warm him, as the early evening breeze ruffled his thin, grayish-blond hair.

Danny studied him for a moment, then walked into the magnificent villa, caught the arm of one of Willie's servants, and told him to call a priest and an undertaker.

Then he went to Mischa, helped him wash his face and hands and change his clothes, and took him to a nice quiet little restaurant where nobody would stare at him.

CHAPTER TWO

Dante was exhausted. It had been a typical day, a hell of a day. First a labor-and-management breakfast meeting with the State Civil Service Workers. Then a brief speech dedicating a new yeshiva in Brooklyn. Then back to his Manhattan office, calls to and from Albany, to and from Washington, D.C.

Petitioners, assistants needing his okay, his suggestions. A quick political get-together with some party boys. A short speech at a NOW unity meeting at the World Trade Center as a favor to Megan, who was conducting some family-violence seminars.

He checked through his correspondence, rapidly tossing letters into one of three baskets labeled Personal Reply, Standard Reply, and Fuhgedaboutit! He read his calendar. This evening, a black-tie dinner at the Waldorf welcoming UN delegates to the city. Note: Call Ben Herskel at the Carlisle; arrange a quick drink with him after the dinner.

Eight A.M. shuttle to Washington tomorrow morning for hearings on—God, whatever and whatever and whatever.

He really wasn't up to this interview, but he was told he should do it. This Danny Williams was a kid, but he had a good track record. He had switched gears from Hollywood gossip to serious political columnist. And his stuff appeared in fairly heavy national magazines.

Be careful, Dante, this kid is very very sharp. Oh, for Christ's sake, if he didn't know by now how to handle a savvy young writer, he should pack it in. But he *was* tired. He needed a nap. Well, he'd either fit it in before dinner or not.

His chief assistant and confidant, a small, round, bald man named Jerry Maldonato, tapped three times on the door and leaned in, so that he was visible from the waist up. He jerked his thumb over his shoulder and said, from the side of his mouth, "He's here, boss. Don't look so bad-ass to me." And then a wink. "But what the hell, better safe than sorry, right?"

Dante peered at him over the top of his half-glasses. Pretty soon he'd have to start wearing those damned bifocals. "Give me five minutes. I'm just touching up this talk for the thing tonight at the Waldorf. That's definitely, *absolutely* black tie?"

"Unless you wanna feel awfully outta place, boss. Up to you. I got the suit in your closet already, case you don't get to the apartment."

"I will definitely go to the apartment when I finish with this guy. I need a long, very hot shower. Make sure the suit comes with me."

"You got it, boss."

A long time ago, Frankie Magee had told him, "Get yourself one special good man you can trust with your life. And tell him everything you need him to know. Almost. He's gotta be a guy who'd kill for you or die for you. Most important, he's gotta be a guy with no personal ambitions; his life should be in the shadow of yours. That was J.F.K.'s old trick, and a good one." Dante's man was Jerry Maldonato. He was no more than five years older than Dante, but some time ago he had taken on the supportive-father role. He would probably lie for Dante, or kill for him, or die for him. Jerry was not only loyal, but smart and knowledgeable in ways that St. John's never taught him. He'd been an amateur boxer, a bartender, a CPA, and even, for a short time, a Secret Service agent. They had known each other when Dante first came to Washington as a congressman. Not too many Italian-Americans around the big town in those days. They had hit it off immediately, and Jerry had done a few favors for Dante, mostly information gathering. Through the years, Jerry had developed an us-against-them mentality, and the main man in the *us* was Dante D'Angelo.

Dante added a few words to his speech notes with his old Waterman pen, the thick one with the dark blue and black stripes his father had given him when he graduated from Columbia Law School. It was the by-the-book, standard after-dinner speech. No promises, nothing offensive, just a courtesy. They just wanted his presence. In black tie.

Three quick taps, and Jerry entered his office followed by a well-dressed young man. Jerry placed a tray on the coffee table, jerked his chin: *Anything else?* Dante shook his head. Jerry glanced once more at the journalist, then left.

Dante took off his glasses and offered a handshake to Danny Williams. He reacted with surprise at the young man's hard grasp and at the way he prolonged the contact. They were just about eye-to-eye, and there was an intensity, contained but evident, coming from the younger man. With a nod, he released Dante's hand.

Dante gestured toward the leather couch and chairs. "Some coffee, Mr. Williams?"

The journalist declined, while Dante took a cup and drank down the energizing caffeine. He glanced at his watch, rubbed his eyes briskly. "I don't mean to be rude, but we have to wrap this up by six at the latest."

Danny Williams sat very still. He glanced slowly at his own watch and then said softly, "Oh, I think you can spare me more time than that, Senator."

There was a bantering tone, a slight smile, as though the young man were amused. Dante became alert for whatever the hell *this* was all about. He had no time or inclination for games. This guy could just cut the Hollywood theatrical crap right now.

"Look, let's get on with this, okay?" He rubbed his fingertips over his chin. He'd have to shave again; the damn five-o'clock shadow was a real pain in the ass. The journalist sat watching him with unnerving intensity and a slight smile at the corners of his mouth.

"Look, Mr. Williams, are you having a problem with something? Because I really don't have time for this. You want an interview or what?"

"*I'm* not having a problem, I think *you* are, Senator. Or are about to have one. A problem."

Dante rose abruptly and pointed to the door. "Look, sonny, that's it. I don't know how you usually operate, but as of right now, this is concluded. There's the door, Mr. Williams."

The journalist leaned back in his chair. "That's not my true name, you know. I had it changed for professional reasons."

Holy Christ, Dante thought. I'm in a room with a total looney tune, never mind his reputation for excellence. What was he, on something? Dante started for the desk phone. He'd have Jerry get this guy the hell out of here. Right now.

But the kid moved quickly. He had anticipated Dante, and got between him and the desk. Dante took a sharp breath and stepped back. He became tightly controlled. You don't provoke a crazy, but you don't show fear, either.

"Okay, pal. What's your story?"

Danny Williams grinned. "*My* story is *your* story, Dante."

Because he wasn't wearing his glasses, Dante couldn't see the journalist's face clearly, but he felt the physical closeness. Where the hell was Jerry? He'd seemed to sense something not right; why wasn't he checking in? Christ, was he about to have a fight with some weirdo right here in his senatorial office?

"Don't be upset, Senator. Not yet. Take a good long look at me. Hey, we're exactly the same height—five-eleven—but if we stretch it, we can just make six, right? Do I look familiar to you? Do I remind you of anyone?"

You handle a crazy gently for as long as you can. Humor him, keep things calm. Dante shrugged.

"I think you'd better have Mr. Maldonato cancel your appearance tonight at the Waldorf. You and I have a great deal to discuss."

"Look, pal—"

"No. We're not *pals*. To start with, the name on my birth certificate is *Daniel William Paycek*."

Dante went blank. Okay. Relax. *Paycek*. Willie.

"Your old man's Willie Paycek?"

"That's what it says on my birth certificate. Registered in Los Angeles. Hollywood division. Glamour capitol of the world."

A stillness settled on the younger man. His dark eyes registered intelligence, his mouth amusement, his whole attitude an almost patronizing superiority.

"I've been told, by my mother, that I favor my father."

"What are you talking about? Willie's a short, thin blond and—" Dante took a step back and leaned against his desk.

"Yeah, Willie *was* a shrimp all right. Past tense. He died a week ago. Willie was a hell of a talent in movie land, but he never *was* much of a father. Not even to his *biological* kids." He smiled at Dante. "I have something for you." He saw the sudden alarm on Dante's face, and lightly touched his arm. "Hey, nothing lethal. Although, in a way, I guess it might be considered lethal."

Dante watched him retrieve his briefcase from the sofa, dig into it, and come out with a thick, neatly bound, book-sized manuscript.

"Willie's legacy to me. And a couple of mementos of my own." He slipped his hand inside the front cover of the book and retrieved a photograph, which he offered to Dante.

"Surely you remember my mother, Maryanne Radsinski? The little kid in her arms, that's me. Here's my birth certificate, with Willie's name and Maryanne's name, all legal and documented. That was part of the deal, wasn't it?"

Dante held on to the picture and the birth certificate without looking at them. He sat down and stared at the manuscript on his desk. His head began to throb. Without having given one single thought to it through all the years, without having asked or been told, having left it all in the hands of his uncles, as though it had nothing to do with him, *he knew.* Deep inside him, it had been there all the time, all his life, and now he was confronted by the secret he had willed himself to forget.

He looked up as Danny Williams spoke quietly. "That's Willie's autobiography. We've been collaborating on it. My God, Willie was a real monster. He's never forgotten one single thing that ever happened to him in his life. I think he's been keeping notes since he was a kid. He had boxes full of note-books and diaries and documents." He paused and studied Dante thoughtfully.

"And?"

"*And* he knew every single thing about all five of you, starting with that night on Snake Hill, right up to the present."

"What the fuck are you talking about?"

"You *know* what I'm talking about, Dante. What I had trouble understanding was his total obsession with all of you. It was a lifelong thing, like a sickness. Almost his reason for living, to keep score, to find out all your secrets. Against the day. Well, Senator D'Angelo, this is the day. And if you're at all interested, Willie tells the story of *my* life, too. Things I didn't realize he knew. Pretty grim stuff. I'll just have some of this coffee while you read. It starts on a cold winter night, December 28, 1935, and goes on from there."

Dante buzzed and Jerry Maldonato came quickly into the room. In a tight, don't-fuck-with-me voice, Dante said, "Give my excuses for tonight. I've got a fever of a hundred and two and laryngitis, *capice*?"

Jerry stared at Dante, glanced at the journalist, then back at Dante.

"And don't disturb me. In fact, go home, Jerry."

Jerry locked eyes with Dante, whom he had known for so many years. He did not say one single word, but nodded abruptly and, leaving the office, headed to the banquet to say what he'd been told to say, and then he would go home.

Dante glanced at the first few pages, stopped, rubbed his eyes, then dug into his top drawer for his scratchy old reading glasses. He scanned quickly, then took his glasses off, reached into his bottom drawer, extracted a bottle of old, expensive Scotch, poured some into a crystal tumbler, and drank it down quickly.

He studied Danny Williams, who was relaxed and comfortable on the leather couch.

"What is it you want, Danny?"

"I want all of you to read the manuscript. I have a copy for everyone. Nice that you're all in New York right now."

Dante rubbed his chin hard with the side of his fist. He looked up quickly when the journalist laughed.

"Jesus, I do that all the time when I'm uptight. Do you think it could be genetic?"

CHAPTER THREE

Megan leaned back, her legs propped on a hassock Dante had pulled over for her. Ben and Charley sat side by side on a couch, and Eugene sat rigidly on a straight, hard chair. Dante's apartment hadn't changed much through the years. He and his wife used it occasionally when they went to the theater or a casual dinner. His daughters and their husbands stayed for a day or two of Manhattan museums or art exhibits, to break the boredom of suburbia.

"How much of Willie's book is true?" Megan asked.

"What the hell difference does it make?" Ben snapped at her.

"Well, I know what's true about myself and what he made up."

"That really isn't the point, Megan," Dante said. "If this book gets published, we'll all be called upon to answer every single allegation."

"We'd spend the rest of our lives answering allegations. I haven't got time for that." Ben Herskel stood up, walked to the small bar, and added vodka to his glass. "I'll tell you right now, everything he said about Charley and me"—he glanced at Charley O'Brien, who just shrugged—"is true. I killed one SS man at the camps, and Charley helped me kill another one. Big deal. That would be well received in my country. I've also provided classified information to Israeli intelligence units about the whereabouts of the "essential Germans" who managed to slip through the government-approved nets. The Israelis have managed to take care of a few, with my help."

"What about the arms deals?" Dante asked, his voice curt, clear, and crisp.

"What about them?" Ben looked at each of them. "Okay. Here, in this room, among the five of us. Yes. *Absolutely.* Charley has been my number-one go-between. What we've been doing for the last twenty years is absolutely illegal." As he spoke, his face darkened with anger. "It's the only goddamn way we've *ever* been able to arm ourselves adequately. A small nation does what it has to do to survive."

Charley cleared his throat. He had the sweet, bland, round face that Megan cherished from childhood. Even now, as he spoke hard words, his essential decency came through.

"We did what we had to do, Dante. There's a vast secret network of arms dealers operating below the surface, and I can tell you, our government and other governments not only know about it, but are the ones who permit it and even encourage it. That way, they let countries like Israel be armed and ready without having to take a public stand."

Ben interrupted. "You know that better than anyone, Dante. You're part of the government, for God's sake."

Without responding to the implications, Dante said, "For a minute, let's go back to the killing of the SS men. That was all documented by Army Intelligence at the time, right?"

"Two suicides," Ben said. "A couple of commanding officers were transferred for incompetence. End of investigation." Ben shrugged. "And he accuses all of us of killing Stachiew. That is all officially recorded too. His old man was tried and executed for that crime. So?"

Dante held his hand up. "Let's get to that later."

Megan spoke up. "Except me. I wasn't there, remember?"

"According to Willie you were there, sweetheart, swinging hot and heavy," Ben said.

Megan raised her eyebrows and her voice was very soft, almost childish. "Who? Me?"

"Let's get on with it, all right?"

Eugene cleared his throat and took a deep breath. "Let me address his charges against me. During all my years at the Vatican, I was very popular with women who made substantial donations to various building funds. And it pleased them to give me valuable gifts, which I turned over to the different curators. The tailor-made suits they provided, *mea culpa*. It made me a more compatible dinner guest. Generally, these were very decent women, some of them quite troubled in their personal lives. Whether any of them ever suggested any kind of sexual liaison with me, I will not say. I *will* say, however, that at no time did I ever become sexually involved with any of them. Not ever, so Willie's allegations, based on whatever information he came up with, are totally false."

Megan raised her hand. "My turn." She realized they had all read the various allegations about her, the lies and half-truths. "Since he went back to my childhood, so will I. My friendship with Patsy Wagner was just that—a friendship. If there were any sexual connotations—and there probably were; we were, after all, awakening adolescents—they were never acted on. We both hated being girls, because it all seemed so unfair. Any ambitions we had, any adventures we dreamed of, were unavailable to us for the simple reason that we were girls. Patsy married early and had a lot of kids. I met Suzy Ginzburg down at Warm Springs when we were both recovering from polio. When she came home, to Greenwich Village, yes, we were good friends. The first thing she told me was that she would never, in any way, corrupt me or compromise me. Yes, Suzy was a lesbian, and I wasn't even certain what that meant. She introduced me to a whole new world of artists and actors and writers and free spirits and radicals. She made it clear to them who and what I was: a straight little Irish Catholic redheaded girl from the Bronx with a brace on her leg, who was studying to be a doctor. She was a loving, caring, faithful friend who was responsible for me meeting Mike Kelly. Suzy delighted in our love for each other and the fact that she had played matchmaker."

Dante put a hand on her shoulder; she seemed very agitated. "Megan, you don't have to defend yourself to us."

"Hell, I know that. You all know me. But I might have to defend not only myself but my family. I can handle whatever he said about me. No problem. But he attacked my husband, my father, and an aunt I adore."

Charley said, "C'mon, champ. We all know what a lying little piece of crap Willie was."

"I know that, Charley. Let me tell you about Mike, because I've never talked about this with any of you. And you guys are my family, right? Mike is manic-depressive. He suffered terribly from a deficient brain chemistry. I won't go into any of the things I tried, the colleagues I consulted, the studies I researched, the programs Mike went into. I was in touch with a psychiatrist in Australia who had done a paper on a substance called lithium. He had done some experiments on its use in the kind of illness that Mike had. Lithium is a natural salt, a very common substance. A couple of other psychiatrists and I began an experimental program with Mike and about ten other people suffering from this syndrome. We had to determine the amount of lithium, the timing, the possible dangers of too much, too little. It didn't work for all those in the trial. Thank God, it worked for Mike."

Quietly, Dante asked her, "Would that in any way justify Willie's description of Mike as drug-dependent."

"Sure, if you'll concede that a diabetic is drug-dependent because he needs insulin to stay alive."

"What I don't understand," Charley said, "is not only how, but *why?* Why did Willie keep all these records on us, then make all these charges? Megan?"

She shook her head. "He was some piece of business, our Willie. Let's just say it was *his* mental illness, caused by the kind of life he had as a child. Charley, it is very complicated. Why didn't he just put it all behind him, enjoy his many successes? Other people do. But Willie was Willie, and he was obsessed with us all his life."

"I just don't get it," Charley said.

"It doesn't matter whether you get it or not. Willie was always a head case," Ben said, as though that settled all there was to be said about Willie Paycek Peace.

"A very *vicious* head case," Megan said. "I can't look at all of this clinically. He called my father a bag man and my aunt Catherine a whore and . . ."

Charley came to her side, took Megan's hand, leaned forward, and kissed her gently on the forehead. "C'mon, Meggie. Anyone who knows your dad and your aunt—"

Ben said, "Yeah, but that's the point. Other people will know only what they read."

Gene asked, "Can this book be published? Dante, I would think there would be all kinds of legal entanglements that we would all—"

"Of course there will be legal entanglements—and the more sordid, the more free publicity for the book. Look, we'd all be smeared across newspapers and magazines all over the world. The media would have a field day. Willie would ruin all of us from his grave."

There was a silence as they all let Dante's words sink in. No matter what was true or false, it would all be the same.

Finally, Ben asked Dante, "How about what he said about you, Dante?"

"You all know my sister had a breakdown when she was a kid and my mother died. It would be very painful for her to have this dragged out in public. As far as my wife's mother . . ."

He turned to Megan, who said, "Lucia-Bianca's mother had a serious bout of depression when one of her twin sons died at birth. No one can say what went on in her mind, or how she and the second child died. Whatever story the family put out to protect themselves did not change the tragedy they experienced. Willie's informant was a filthy liar. Period."

Dante nodded at her. Thank you, Megan.

"And now, about me being the father of Danny Williams. Born Daniel William Paycek." Dante pulled over a chair and sat facing all of them. He yanked his tie away from his collar, opened the top buttons of his shirt, rubbed his mouth hard, then swiped his fist across the new stubble on his chin.

"Possibly."

There was a momentary silence as they all absorbed this.

"It was a difficult time for me," Dante said. "Lucia-Bianca and I were engaged, and"—he shrugged—"it was a given. A good Italian girl—no premarital sex. So I strayed. Yes, I went to my uncles, the Ruccis. They told me they would take care of it. I should . . . forget about it."

"Jesus, Danny. Just like that? Forget about it, they would take care of it? What did you think they meant?" Benny stared at Dante, waiting for an answer.

"Not the way it sounds, for God's sake. My family wasn't 'connected,' not mob. Just . . . tough guys who took care of their own. Yes, they got together with Willie and offered him a deal. They gave them a wedding, Willie and Maryanne. And sent them to the West Coast, where there was a good job for Willie."

"And then Willie abandoned her. And her baby," Eugene said quietly.

"Yes, and I believe all the terrible things Willie found out about how Maryanne and her son Danny Williams survived. Just as I believe what he said about his own involvement in the snuff movie."

Dante studied his shoes for a moment, then looked up, anguished, not meeting anyone's eyes. "Yes, there is a strong possibility that Danny Williams is my son. Maryanne told my uncles she hadn't been near a man for six months before . . . before me. That she wanted to be 'pure,' she said, for me."

There it was, out in the open at last.

After a full minute of silence, Eugene spoke quietly but firmly. "That wasn't the truth. She was lying about that. Not having relations with other men for that period of time."

Megan became sharply alert. Ben looked puzzled. Was the priest going to break his vow and reveal a confession. Charley waited, his eyes on his brother.

"What do you mean, Gene?" Dante asked.

Eugene's smooth, handsome face tightened. "It was a terrible time for me. I had just come home from Rome. I was heading for a leper colony. I wasn't sure about anything in my life."

He remembered something and turned to Megan.

Yes, she nodded. She remembered he had come to her.

"I was having coffee one night, Benny, in your parents' luncheon-ette. Maryanne came over to my table and asked if she could sit with me. I was wearing civvies, but of course she knew who I was. We didn't talk. Not at all. It was a very peculiar moment. We left together and went to her parents' apartment. My God. They were at the Loew's Paradise. It was Screeno night." He blinked a few times and shrugged. "It was all over in a matter of minutes. It had the quality of a dream."

"When was this?" Dante asked anxiously.

It was during the time Maryanne had claimed to have been "pure" for Dante.

Ben Herskel's voice was raspy, and they all turned to him. "That was when I was going to Columbia for law courses, to get ready for the assignment at the Nuremburg trials. Maryanne Radsinski." He shook his head. "I bet I was the only one who paid her. Hey, come on. Maryanne was a pro, among other things. *Me*, she charged."

"Me too," Charley said. "Once or twice. I had just come home and . . . for whatever reason, she approached me and it just happened. Twice."

Dante looked from one to the other. "None of this was in Willie's book."

"Either he didn't know, or he wanted to get you, Dante. Tell me . . ." Ben hesitated for a moment. "What does he look like, this Danny Williams?"

"Well, you'll see for yourself. He'll be here in less than an hour."

"Why, Dante? Why does he want to see us?"

"I don't know, Benny. He said it was important that he see us all together."

"Okay," Megan said. "Let's get to the killing of Stachiew. He named all of us as his murderers." Then, in an almost childish boast, Megan said, "I've never spoken about that night. In my whole life. To anyone."

"Attagirl, Megan. She kept her promise," Dante said.

"For all the good that does," Ben said. "That little bastard put it all down in his book."

"Let's talk about it, okay?" Megan looked at each of them. "I really want to know something. Each of you, how do you feel about what happened that night? Benny, do you feel you took part in the murder of Stachiew?"

Without hesitation, he said, "Damn right I do. We left him dead."

Eugene shook his head. "No. He was alive. Willie's father came along and killed him. Ben, do you honestly think I could have continued at the seminary if I truly believed that I—"

Ben's face darkened and his voice was low and mean. "Yeah, I honestly believe that, Eugene. Hell, I've seen SS Catholics lined up for confession at the camps, and the next morning take communion. All forgiven. Back in the fold. All straight with God."

They had seen Eugene's anger before, as a kid, but not the fury with which he stood, lean and rigid in his plain black suit, the stiff white collar digging into his throat.

"Are you equating *me* with the murderers of Auschwitz? Is that what you just said, *it's all the same*? That my confessor would say, 'Okay, as long as you admit to murder, get on with your life'?"

Ben stood and confronted Eugene. "Yeah, that's what I'm saying, Bishop O'Brien. Not that what we did was anything like the camps, but you guys got a nice little gimmick going for you. Confess, and God'll say, 'Hey, okay, welcome home.'"

Eugene swung his fist, but Charley intervened smoothly and grabbed his brother's arm.

"Knock it off—we can't afford this." He wrapped an arm around Gene's shoulder. "What we're talking about is whether or not we killed—or *think* we killed—Stachiew. Megan, how about you?"

"Well, frankly, yes. I think we did. My God, we knocked him into a bloody mess. I think Willie's old man was beating a dead man when the squad car came by and the cops saw him. He was drunk. He said whatever the hell he said and stuck with it. And it got him the electric chair."

"So you think we were responsible for two deaths?" Gene asked.

"I don't know, Gene. I really don't know. But Charley asked me and I answered. Yeah, I think we did it. Then again, *maybe* we didn't. But I'm not positive, one way or the other."

To lighten the terrible mood in the room, Dante said, "Megan, how the hell would you know what happened that night? You weren't even there."

"That's absolutely right, Dante. And *I'm* pretty sure I'm not Danny Williams's father, either."

"Now *that* wasn't funny, Megan."

"You know me, Dante. I always go too far."

They sat, each trying to assess what the damage would be. Each thought of lives lived, honors earned; of families, careers, hopes; and of ruin.

It was Ben who articulated what they were all thinking. "Well, we can't just let this happen, can we? What does he want, this Danny Williams? Is he setting us up for blackmail, or what?"

"I don't know, but we'll find out in a few minutes."

"Dante, listen." Ben's face was hard, almost ugly with what he had to say. "All my life I've had to deal with violence. And my father before me—that's another matter. I don't know how many men I've killed, in the U.S. Army and in the service of Israel. I just know that there are ways for things to be handled. Quiet, secret ways. People disappear all the time, and are never heard of again. And other lives go on. None of you needs to know anything about any of this . . ."

Megan said, "Are you talking about *murdering* this young man?"

"I'm talking about saving our lives, that's what I'm talking about. And you don't have to know any more than that. None of you."

Megan looked around the room. No one said anything. They all seemed, for the moment, to accept what Ben Herskel had just said.

"Ben, you don't mean that, do you?"

"Look, Megan, you keep out of this, okay?"

"Keep out of this, *little girl*? That what you're saying? Because this little girl *was* part of that night on Snake Hill, and my family and I *are* included in this rotten book, so don't tell me this has nothing to do with me. This has as much to do with me as with any of you."

"Benny, we're talking about a young man who might be *my son*. Or Gene's. Or Charley's. *Or yours*."

In a deadly, hollow voice, Ben said, "Two of my sons are dead, and the other two put their lives on the line for their country and their beliefs every day of the year. *I have no other son*."

There was a soft chiming sound: the downstairs bell. The silence was intense as they waited, heard the elevator stop in the hall, the door slide open. And then the soft knock on the door.

Unnecessarily, Dante said, "Well, here he is."

CHAPTER FOUR

He walked directly to Megan and, with a self-deprecating grin, said the most obvious thing. "Of course, you're Megan."

He used her first name easily. After all, he had put together a manuscript that dealt with all of her secrets—some real and some not. He had a trick of totally focused eye contact that created an immediate intimacy. Megan thought he must be really hot stuff with the ladies; but for all his directness, he gave himself away, at least to Megan's analytic eye. There was a quick tongue-flick to one corner of his mouth, a shrugging of his shoulders, and a nervous flutter of his thick eyelashes as he turned to confront the men in the room.

Megan watched all of them closely. They each seemed to be searching for some clue, some point of recognition. He did favor Dante in height, hair, and eye color. But then, they were all close to or over six feet tall. Danny was slender, as they had all been at his age. The dark eyes seemed to rule out Gene, but his brother Charley had dark brown eyes. And Danny had a very light complexion. Megan tried to picture him with light hair. He might resemble Eugene.

His smile and easy manner, his handshake and friendliness, did nothing to relieve the tension in the room. They stared at him as someone come unexpectedly into their lives to bring destruction upon them. Yet, he was a son.

Megan offered him a drink, gesturing toward the collection of bottles and glasses; he nodded and helped himself. The men seemed mesmerized. Ben's scowl was softened, perhaps, by the question, Could this be a son of mine? Brother to my living and dead sons?

Eugene's lips were slightly parted; Megan couldn't begin to guess at his thoughts. Charley seemed unable to do more than glance a few times at this stranger. Or was he a stranger? Was he a continuation of Charley's line?

And Dante, a father of daughters, who had desired, through all his young manhood, a son. What did he see as he studied this handsome, self-assured young man?

Finally, after swallowing some Scotch, it was Danny Williams who totally dominated the room. With a generous wave of his arm, as though he were the host and not the unwelcome guest at this strange, tense gathering, he said, "I wish you'd all relax. I'm here for a special reason. I wanted to talk to all of you at the same time, since we are all connected." Quickly, with a grin, he added, "Through Willie and his autobiography."

It was Benny Herskel, guerrilla fighter, intelligence general, negotiator, who responded in a sharp, don't-try-to-kid-me tone. "Okay, kid. We're here. You're here. What do you want from us?"

Danny held his hand up in a reassuring, calming gesture. "I want to tell you about my last talk with Willie Paycek—Willie Peace—just before he died."

"Skip that. *What do you want from us?*"

Megan broke in. "What do you want to tell us, Danny?"

"First, I think I'd better tell you about my relationship with my mother. It is relevant to what I want to say. What you've read in Willie's manuscript—yeah, most of it is true about us. My mom and the kids." His voice filled with warmth and affection. "But what Willie missed was that my mother never once, in her entire life, *ever* let one of her kids go hungry or homeless or unloved. I was the oldest and the only kid, until she had the five kids from her Mexican marriage. I was, I guess you could say, her confidant. And her collaborator, when necessary."

"What Willie wrote was true? Your mother set you up with those wealthy women and—"

"Yes, Charley. That was true, all right. And you know what? We never *harmed* anybody. The rich ladies paid for their pleasure. And my *family* survived. My mom even took care of the girls who came to live with us. She protected them. But that's another story."

"What did your mother tell you about your father?" Megan asked directly.

"My mother told me what Willie never knew or even suspected. Oh, yes, I *know*. Any one of you could be my father."

"She told you *that*?" Megan, who knew so much about the human condition and relationships, was still surprised at what she did not know.

"When I was a little kid, we'd see you on television, Bishop O'Brien. My mother would put her hands on my shoulders and say, 'Listen carefully to what he says. He is a good man. A holy man. Someday he might be Pope.'" Danny paused for a moment, then said, "And she told me there was a possibility that you were my father."

They watched him closely as he spoke to each one.

"Dante, when you were elected to Congress and then to the Senate, my mother said you might one day be President. And that *you* might be my father."

Megan interrupted. "And how did that make you feel?" She burst into laughter. "Wow, a real shrink-question. Sorry."

Danny Williams looked at Megan with genuine affection, as though she were the only other person in the room. The men never changed expression; they were frozen into their own concerns.

"It made me feel very strange, Megan. And special, I guess. When Ben was in Israel leading missions—when one of your capers was made into a TV movie, my mother and I watched and she predicted you would be a very important man. Maybe Prime Minister. And—" he shrugged—"she said *you* might be my father."

"You knew all that, growing up?"

"Yes, Dr. Magee, I knew that all my life. And Charley, my mother cut out pictures of you from the newspapers every time you rescued someone from a fire. 'Snuffy O'Brien,' she'd say. 'A very brave man . . . who knows?'"

There it was, all out in the open, and no one knew what to say. Danny swallowed some Scotch, put the glass down, and leaned against a table, his arms folded over his chest.

"I'd like to tell you now about my last conversation with Willie." He paused, measured them, and watched for the impact. *"Willie Paycek, my father."*

"You mean Willie and your mother . . ."

Danny shook his head. "No, Ben. *Never.* Willie was my *legal* father. His name was on my birth certificate. But my mother told me it was impossible, and she never lied to me. What I did, in the last few months, was to accept Willie Paycek as my true father."

"Did I miss something here?" Ben demanded.

"Danny, what? What is it you want to tell us?"

"Willie Paycek was the only one who *knew of my existence.* It was because of me that he had his chance in life. Got to Hollywood. Was in place to do what he wanted with his life. Yet he abandoned us without a second look. Until it suited his purpose to keep tabs on us. On me."

Dante said, "Danny. I should have known. I should have—"

"Okay, maybe. But Willie *did* know. Let me tell you about my last conversation with Willie. When he was dying. Willie, with all the things he knew about all of us, or made up, really didn't know about any of you others. That each of you might be my biological father." Danny stopped speaking, then added softly, *"So I told him."*

"But why? What was the point?" Ben wanted to know.

"Danny, what else did you tell Willie as he was dying?" Megan asked.

Danny Williams grinned. "If I tell you that I closed a final circle, will you know what I mean?"

Carefully, thoughtfully, Megan said, "Maybe."

"You lost me, kiddo," Ben said.

"Then listen. I told Willie two things before he was to take his fatal injection to ease himself into death. First, that each of you could be my father—so he missed a good bet. Think what he could have done with *that* information. He asked me if I would add that to his autobiography."

Danny paused, staring straight ahead, not seeing anyone in the room with him. He saw only Willie and his death-face.

"I asked him, 'What autobiography are we talking about, Willie?'"

"What do you mean, Danny?"

"Dante, what you read in his manuscript about *his* last meeting with *his* father, the conversation that was Willie's payoff to his abusive old man—well, that was my payoff to Willie. I told him his autobiography would never be published. In fact"—he gestured around the room—"you have the only copies. And I've got the tapes in my briefcase, for you to do whatever you want with. I told Willie that as a writer, I was working on his biography right alongside the work I was doing for him on his *auto*biography. And as his biographer, it was up to me to decide what to include, what to exclude. I told him that the night on Snake

Hill never happened. Not with any kids involved, anyway. Just his old man and Stachiew. The only mention of all of you was by way of suggesting that maybe Ryer Avenue was some unique kind of background for a bunch of kids. A great neighborhood: turned out a future Senator, maybe even a President; an Israeli general and rep to the UN who might become Prime Minister; a priest who might one day be the first American Pope. And his brother, who was so affected by what he saw in the concentration camps that he converted to his mother's religion and spent his life saving lives as the hero of his city. Finally, a very special girl who grew up against the times and became not only a psychiatrist and a teacher, a wife and mother, but a *spokesperson*—is that the right word?—for women."

For a moment they could not absorb what he had just told them. It didn't compute. It didn't connect with the turmoil they had been feeling since receiving Willie's manuscript.

Ben, the strongest, toughest realist, asked him, "What do you want from us, Danny?"

Very quietly, looking from one of them to another, Danny Williams said, "Absolutely nothing. I don't want *anything* from any of you."

"You don't even want to know who's your father?" Megan asked.

Danny smiled. "*Willie* was. And I left him the same deathbed gift he gave his father. And that was the end of it for me. In no other way can I ever identify with him. I learned certain things from him, and from all of you. Yes, I wonder which one of you is my father. Of course I do. But you see, it doesn't matter. I can't deal with it anymore. I want to be free of Willie and all of you. So I gave him, as my father, exactly what he gave his father before me." He stared directly at Megan, who saw the tears shimmering in his dark eyes. "Circle closed."

Megan nodded, but then asked him, "Why did you want all of us to know about this? You gave us the manuscript, Danny. You didn't have to do that. You could have kept it between you and Willie."

Finally there was a flash of anger. "I'm not your patient, Megan, and I'm not into deep soul-searching. Let's just say I wanted all of you to know certain things about me. Maybe about yourselves and each other."

There was a diminishing uneasiness in the room. No one looked at anyone, as though each were having his or her private thoughts.

"One more thing," Danny said. "About my mother. Whatever else she was—and none of that is anyone's business—she was and is a terrific mother. Right now she's settling in at Willie's villa with a couple of her grandkids and little Mischa, who will finally get a taste of mothering that he's never had in his life. Willie was wrong about Mischa. He's gonna live a long and happy life."

Ben Herskel laughed. "Jesus, did you tell Willie about *that*?"

"I wish I had, but I didn't think of it until after he was dead."

"It's a little spooky, isn't it?" Megan said. "This apartment was once Willie's, and now his home will be your mother's."

"Life is spooky," Danny said. He turned toward his briefcase and dug out the tapes, which he tossed on Dante's desk. Then he reached into it once more, and took out a fairly thick manuscript. "I only have one extra copy, so, Dante, if you want to read it and then pass it on to the others . . ."

Dante opened it and read the title page. The Biography of My Father, Willie Peace, by Danny William Paycek.

Dante turned the next page and read the dedication. His mouth dropped open and he handed it back to Danny. "You read it, Danny."

Danny Williams nodded, then read, "To the Ryer Avenue Gang, with my admiration at how far they all have traveled. From their spiritual son, Danny Williams."

Finally they all left, except Megan and Dante. She collected the glasses, and he dumped the leftover snacks into a wastebasket.

"So. What do you think?" Dante asked her.

"I don't know. I guess life can really be as strange as all the case histories I've studied and all the stories I've listened to." She shook her head and whistled, then said, "Wow, Dante. Whadda ya think about the kid?"

"Wouldn't it be something, Megan? I mean, he *does* look like me, right? Whoever's son he is, he seems to be a real piece of work, doesn't he?"

"How could he miss? He's got Ryer Avenue in his gene pool."

"You know, Megan, I've been doing so much thinking these last few days. About when we were kids. Do you realize, if it hadn't snowed that night, during Christmas vacation, and if we hadn't all been on Snake Hill, maybe Willie would have turned out differently? Maybe he wouldn't have been obsessed with all of us; maybe he would have concentrated on his own life, getting himself straightened out without all that hatred and vindictiveness. Maybe, if he'd used his energies better . . . maybe . . ."

Megan interrupted quietly. "Maybe it would have been different for him if we'd all been able to *love* Willie."

But it *had* snowed that night.

And they *hadn't* been able to love Willie.

And he'd died hearing a son's vengeance burning into his brain. As had his father before him.

E P I L O G U E

On Saturday, December 28, 1935, at approximately 10:25 P.M., Walter Stachiew raised his right hand to his bloodied head. He felt the cold, thick wetness and squinted as he brought the hand before his eyes.

Them little rotten bastards, what the hell did they hit him with, anyway? He moved his legs, and his feet slipped on the snow. He knew them, all of them, he'd fix them good. They really think they could do this to him and then just leave him there and run away? Well, they was wrong, because he knew all of them.

He pulled himself into a sitting position, his knees up, his hands on either side of his head. They musta whacked him with a steel bar or something. A shovel, yeah, they hit him with his shovel, whatta bunch a' little bastards. He didn't need no shovel to fix them. He just had to catch his breath. Maybe get another drink.

Yeah. His pal, Stanley, would help him with the price. Yeah. Stan was mad at him about something or other, but they was always mad about something or other.

Stan was still inside, probably, still drinking inside, so that's what he'd do, go find Stan, and Stan would buy him a whiskey or two. That was what he really needed.

He pulled himself up to his knees, but he felt terrible with the cold and the headache, so he decided to just sit down and wait there for a minute. He reached out. There was his shovel. Yeah. He could make maybe a coupla bucks, shovel some snow for somebody, and then *he* would buy *Stan* a drink or two. Maybe. Maybe not.

He looked up. "Whadda ya think, Stan, ya wanna treat me first, then I pay, you pay, huh?"

Stanley Paycek stood over him. He seemed to be swaying. Ah, fuck it. Walter realized he musta used up all his money for himself, to get himself drunk. There'd be no money left to buy a drink for *him*. Some friend.

"Why you no treat me, Stan, you sumavabitch, you?"

Stanley Paycek remembered what he had come to do. He reached down and picked up the shovel and stood over Walter.

He knew he was mad at Walter. He knew he'd said he'd clobber him with his own shovel. He just couldn't remember why, but what the hell.

"You no good bastard, Walter, ya know? I'm gonna kill you, ya know?"

Walter lunged for his friend's feet, but fell flat. He tried to grab Paycek's legs, but Stan moved back slightly. He looked up right into Stanley's face and cursed.

Stan was saying something. Something. Some curse words. He remembered the handle of the shovel jammed against his throat.

Stan lifted the heavy shovel high over his head and brought it crashing down right on Walter's face. Walter felt his body fall back, then forward as he tried to rise. He lifted a hand behind him and tried to tell Stanley something, but he didn't know what. He felt the next blow, a numbing cold crack on the back of his skull.

He never felt any of the other blows that killed him.